THE BEST OF ALL POSSIBLE WORLDS

'A rewarding, touching and often funny exploration of the forms and functions of human culture. Plus, it has flying monks – a universally improving ingredient!'

SFX

'The author is clearly a class apart, and doubly so in terms of her prose. Astonishing'

TOR.COM

'Lord proves she can write as well with pace and verve as she can with reflection and empathy . . . . One of the ones to recommend. Delightful'

CONCATENATION

'The imagination behind her galaxy and its variation of the human race cannot be faulted'

SCIFINOW

'A fantastic read with very unique, memorable characters'

BIBLIOSANCTUM

'The kind of novel that truly illustrates what science fiction is capable of doing. Lush and yet not overwhelming, it is a love story firmly rooted in a story of humanity'

BEST FANTASY STORIES

REDEMPTION IN INDIGO

'*Redemption* extends the Caribbean Island storyteller's art into the 21st century and hopefully, beyond'
SEATTLE TIMES

'Wise, funny, and very promising'
LOCUS

'A fairy tale for the new generation, filled with spirits, magic and touches of African and Caribbean folklore'
VOICE NEWSPAPER

'Lord is doing something different and that's to be applauded'
INDEPENDENT ON SUNDAY

'A wonderfully told rather magical story'
SAVIDGE READS

'Balances traditional roots with a contemporary take on the folktale form . . . enormous fun to read; heartily recommended'
DAVID H BLOG

'Karen Lord is one of the hot writers of the day . . . a beautiful work of fiction'
STAFFER'S BOOK REVIEW

'Progressive. Intelligent. Entertaining. It is clearly a modern tale, but at the same time timeless'
GLEN.MEHN.NET

'Her words flow smoothly and unobtrusively, quietly sucking you into the story and characters. Lord is a master storyteller'
BIBLIOSANCTUM

Also by Karen Lord

Redemption in Indigo
The Best of All Possible Worlds

KAREN LORD

Jo Fletcher
BOOKS

First published in Great Britain in 2014 by Jo Fletcher Books
This edition published in Great Britain in 2016 by

Jo Fletcher Books
an imprint of
Quercus Publishing Ltd
Carmelite House
50 Victoria Embankment
London EC4Y 0DZ

An Hachette UK company

A CIP catalogue record for this book is available
from the British Library

ISBN 978 1 78429 042 9 (PB)
ISBN 978 1 78087 691 7 (EBOOK)

10 9 8 7 6 5 4 3 2 1

Typeset by Jouve (UK), Milton Keynes

Printed and bound in Great Britain by
Clays Ltd, St Ives plc

For Alicia, Fatima and Adrian, with many thanks for keeping me sane and happy.

PROLOGUE

The only cure for a sleepless night was to lie in bed and watch the constellations projected on his ceiling. He knew them by heart, had known them since his boy-days on Cygnus Beta when he would climb the homestead water tower to stargaze (and escape his father). Then, they were a distant dream, an ancient tale that he could only trust was true. Now they were the dirt on his boots, the dust in his lungs and a constant pang of care and concern that he carried in his heart. He was homesick for everywhere, for scattered friends and family and colleagues, each with a claim on his attention.

He whispered names in soothing ritual. The First Four, crafted worlds found already seeded with life – Ntshune, Sadira, Zhinu and Terra. Then there were the colonies, bioformed planets shaped and settled by emigrants – Punartam, Ain, Tolimán and more. The Terran system was nearest to his Cygnian heritage, but the Punartam system was closest in travel time and galactic rank. Its sole habitable planet, a first-wave colony almost as prominent as the First Four, was reputed to be the first fully bioformed world, a point still debated by the Academes. Was Cygnus Beta a crafted world that had failed and been restored by human or non-human effort, or a bioforming experiment unrecorded in human history? Punartam could prove its origins; Cygnus Beta could not. Punartam was, of course, the Cygnian name (from a Terran language, like so many other Cygnian names). In Terran stellar nomenclature it was *β Geminorum*, and Galactic Standard offered a collection of syllables that told the full story of the star's location, age, luminosity and life-bearing potential. The name they used for themselves was in Simplified Ntshune and it meant the same thing as in Galactic Standard – behold! we are here, we have been here long, see how brightly we shine, we are *we*.

The founders of Punartam traced their origin to the system called the Mother of humanity. Cygnian name: Ntshune (also from a Terran language). Terran name: *α Piscis Austrini*. True name: a delicate and yearning melodic phrase in Traditional Ntshune. But there was another claim to Eldest – Sadira. Terran name: *ε Eridani*. Sadiri name: something unpronounceable (the Sadiri language, even in the simplified standard form, was still a challenge for him to speak). Former leader of the galaxy . . . or at least policeman and judge and occasional executioner. Not much liked though rarely hated, and now occasionally pitied. Sadira was dead, or almost dead, its biosphere locked in toxic regeneration for centuries to come. The seat of government had moved to New Sadira, formerly known to Cygnians as Tolimán. Survivors had settled throughout the colonies, mainly Punartam and Cygnus Beta, but not Ain. Certainly not Ain.

Next in rank. Cygnian name: Zhinu. Terran name: *α Lyrae*. Most Zhinuvians used the Galactic Standard name, but there were variations of that. In spite of several layers of modern tech and some extreme bioforming, the origin planet of the system had begun as a crafted world. Then there was Terra, Earth. Source of most of the settlers on Cygnus Beta (Terran stellar nomenclature: the unmelodious *16 Cygni B*). Youngest of the First Four and most in need of protection. Zhinu, an example of long-term, well-intentioned meddling from both Ntshune and Sadira, was now playing the role of delinquent middle child while the two elder siblings tried to shield Terra from outside influences.

With eyes still fixed on the stars, he reached towards a bowl of datacharms on his bedside table and brushed a familiar piece with the tip of a finger. A woman's voice filled the room and he sank back onto his pillows with a sigh of comfort.

'In the beginning, God created human beings, which is to say God put the ingredients together, embedded the instructions for building on the template and put it all into four separate eggs marked "Some Assembly Required".

'One egg was thrown down to Sadira. There humanity grew to revere and develop the powers of the mind. Another egg was sent to Ntshune, and the humans who arose there became adept at dealing with matters of the heart. A third egg arrived at Zhinu, and there the focus was on the body, both natural and man-made. The last egg came to Terra, and these humans were unmatched in spirit. Strong in belief, they developed minds to speculate and debate, hearts to deplore and adore, and bodies to craft and adapt. Such were their minds, hearts and bodies that they soon began to rival their elder siblings.

'When the Caretakers saw the Terrans and their many ways of being human, they were both impressed and appalled. Some declared, "See how they combine the four aspects of humanness!

Through Terra, all will be transformed – Sadira, Ntshune and Zhinu – into one harmonious whole." Others predicted, "How can any group survive such fragmentation? They will kill each other, and the rest of humanity will remain forever incomplete."

'After some discussion, the Caretakers decided to seal off Terra from the rest of the galaxy until Terran civilisation reached full maturity. They also decided to periodically save them from themselves by placing endangered Terrans on Cygnus Beta, where they could flourish and begin to mix with other humans.'

The voice chuckled and concluded, 'And that, my dear, is five creation myths for the price of one.'

He smiled. 'Love you,' he murmured to the recording. He would see the owner of the voice soon enough. Reaching out once more, he stirred inside the bowl with a finger . . . and frowned. The weight, the chime and the texture of the contents – something was off. He immediately sat up and turned on the lights. Grabbing the bowl, he sifted through the charms with one hand and glared at every trinket and token that rose to the surface. Finally, he turned the bowl upside down, dumping everything into his lap. He scanned the spread of charms on the bed-sheets, counting and cataloguing, although he already knew what was missing.

He looked up, furious. There was only one person who could have taken them, and only one place they could be.

Terminal 5 was a suborbital city strung between the icy surface of Ntshune and the icy, pitted armour of a single arc of the geosynchronous station. The core of the Terminal was old, a nostalgic remnant of another era of expansion, but the station was entirely new and under constant construction, forming a fragmented ring of bends and bows that girdled ancient Ntshune with a scanty, homely touch of modernity. It represented a humble proclamation of galactic ambition and a dogged focus on one thing – control of the main hub of galactic communications and transportation.

More lived and moved in the space station and its terminals than on the surface of Ntshune, but it was a population in constant flow to and from transports and through transits. The only residents who could claim any permanence beyond the staff were the databrokers, credit wranglers and small-goods sellers. They came from all over the galaxy – entrepreneurial, nomadic and at once heroic and pathetic. A glance would not distinguish between the adventurer and the refugee; both exuded the adrenalin of chasing and being chased by fate, and translated that urgency into a directness bordering on discourtesy. The market sector of Terminal 5 buzzed with loud voices and high emotions. Only the unprepared and the unlucky came to do business, and they learned quickly not to expect gentle handling.

'No. Not that, not here.' The broker's palm slapped his desk in emphatic negation. 'Waste of time.'

The young traveller froze with one hand suspended in the air, dangling the delicate bracelet with its many charms. 'But you know what it is?'

'Too well,' the broker replied. 'Datachip, Cygnian; datacharm, ditto. Assorted Punarthai audioplugs, one Sadiri vault and one Sadiri card, Ntshune—' He stopped himself with a gape, leaned forward and gave the charm a few seconds of close attention.

'Ntshune filigree,' he admitted with nod of grudging appreciation. 'Beautifully made. A timeless piece.' He leaned back. 'I can work with that or the Sadiri vault. No guarantees with the audioplugs. Some of the channels are no longer on-air and plugs won't play without their channel linkup. The card is another antique, likely biolocked. The Cygnian matter – trash. Too much trouble.'

'I have credit—' the traveller began.

'Credit is not the issue. Do you have five Standard years?'

The face stayed neutral but the hand drooped, and there was something regretful in the curl of the fingers as they slowly gathered up the loop of motley charms. The broker briefly yielded to the suggestion of softening, like a shy tug at his heart, but he soon braced himself sternly against it.

'Stop that,' he cautioned. 'We are Sadiri still; we don't have to stoop to Zhinuvian tricks. If you do not have five years, then go to Cygnus Beta, Tlaxce Province, the library city of Timbuktu-kvar. They specialise in data extraction from the most ridiculous and obsolete tech.'

The young face tried to continue its neutrality, but to another Sadiri every microexpression was a shout. The broker blinked and guessed. 'You are a Cygnian Sadiri?'

Head bowed, mind shielded but alert, the traveller quietly replied, 'Yes. I was born there.'

The broker was not perfect. He saw and sensed the obvious, and misread. 'There is no need to be ashamed. Whether you are taSadiri or half-Sadiri, we all share the same ancestors, mourn the blackened skies of Old Sadira and curse the Ainya for their failed attempt at genocide.'

He stopped, gave the traveller a swift but thorough glance that assessed and appreciated from head to toe, misread further and decided to be vulnerable.

'I thought I was fortunate. So many women died, we Sadiri men became so many wifeless husbands and motherless sons. But I had a wife still living. New Sadira took her from me not too long after. We were assured it would be temporary, so at first I was patient. I should have gone to Cygnus Beta with the rest of the young rejects, but I assumed I had status and protection – a place in the new world order. Now I am a lonely and ageing databroker working in the corners of space stations and transit terminals. Sometimes I hope that my wife found happiness, but from the tales I have heard and the emptiness in my heart . . . I know she is dead. It has been many years since then . . .'

Mind no longer closed, the young Sadiri tried to cringe away in polite but clear retreat, but the broker had gathered steam and courage and was no longer looking for the usual mental cues and courtesies. It was time for a coarser message. He tugged desperately at the neck of his plain black jacket, letting the hidden fastenings fall open to reveal a bare, smooth chest etched with silver tracings of the best Ntshune make. The broker stuttered to a stop, trying to navigate through several layers of faux pas to formulate some kind of coherent verbal or mental response to the traveller's demonstrated unavailability for short-term flirtation or long-term engagement.

'May your period of kin contract be long and mutually advantageous. And yet . . . you are full Sadiri? Born in the settlement on Cygnus Beta?'

The traveller did not reply, did not need to. The broker's lazy mind was at last communicating at the appropriate level and his questions were rhetorical, a verbal trick for emphasis.

7

'But I did not think they permitted men to be born there.'

'We are not New Sadira,' the traveller reproached him. He reproached him not only for the insult to his people, but also for the broker's vague, unvoiced support for that policy. He did not always encounter the caricature of the desperate, marriage-hungry Sadiri, nor did he embody it, but when it appeared it made him feel personally injured, as if conscious of a great fall in which he was complicit though not culpable.

The broker raised his hand, opened it in surrender and let it fall, a gesture of apology that went beyond what was required towards one so much younger. His very pores exhaled embarrassment, regret and resentment. The traveller felt such pity; if he had not been convinced of his own mental strength, he would have suspected the broker of influencing his emotions.

'I would be grateful if you could do whatever is possible with the vault, the filigree and the audioplugs,' he said.

The broker's ego steadied and grew stronger, anchored by the familiar process of business. 'What formats do you wish for the final compilation?'

'Ntshune-filigree compatible.'

'That can be done.' The broker held out a hand for the charms; the tiny lights on his desk blinked and beckoned, ready for transfer.

The traveller hesitated. 'How long?' he asked.

'The filigree, less than a day. A week for the vault, perhaps, and I really cannot say for the audioplugs. I may have to have them sent for testing.'

'Send each one as soon as you finish extraction,' the traveller told him, extending his treasure.

A hand intervened, tweaking the bracelet of charms from the traveller's fingers. The hand was almost prettier than the bracelet. Silvery new lines overlaid the faint, pale scars of long-removed filigree, like embroidery over damask, fingers to forearm. The traveller's heart seized with fear and disappointment as he looked into dark, opaque eyes and an unreadable face. The databroker assessed the situation with a glance, and folded his desk and vanished before he could become either accessory or witness.

'You could have asked me, Narua.'

The words were quiet, unthreatening and devoid of reproach, but they still stung. 'I *did* ask, Patron.'

'Then you should have been more patient.' The Patron tucked the charms into an inner fold of his jacket. 'Come with me.'

Narua followed his Patron along corridors and through private doors to a small dock. The shuttle linked to the entry port hummed quietly, its engines run-ready. Narua hesitated for a moment before boarding, but sighed and let the habit of trust take his feet obediently into the Patron's domain. He stayed standing and kept himself from fidgeting while the Patron seated himself at the main console and spoke the commands to seal the entry and begin their departure clearance from the Terminal. When the necessaries were concluded, the Patron gestured to the chair beside him. Narua sat and tried to look away, but eventually he raised his head and endured the Patron's steady, and almost painfully caring gaze.

'I'm hurt. We're practically family.'

'I know.' Narua motioned impatiently towards his still-exposed chest and the tracings there that matched those on the Patron's arms. 'A lesser branch of the Haneki dynasty, a collection of the unregistered, the foreign and the irregular, all kin but few blood. I know what I am, what *we* are.'

Reproach came at last in the form of a hard stare and a rare sternness. 'And the Haneki markings lend you great privilege, lesser branch or no, or you would be answering directly to Terminal Security instead of me. But' – the Patron waved a hand, dismissing the tense moment – 'we were family before that. Do you honestly believe I'm keeping information from you? Or are you hoping to gain some hold over me? My past is relatively boring. No scandal and a very little crime, long since pardoned. It would be so hard to blackmail me.'

Narua smiled, unable to help himself. The Patron always had that effect on people, persuading them that he was never a threat, and somehow, in spite of all the evidence, it worked every time.

The Patron's voice became heavy with regret. 'Or do you think I don't want you to find her?'

Narua winced but could not lie. 'They say that her decision put you on a path you might not have chosen for yourself.'

A gentle frown appeared briefly on the Patron's face, showing perplexity rather than anger. 'Is that what they say?' he said drily. 'In the absence of other witnesses, the missing conveniently take on our sins. Let me tell you directly – I bear her no ill will, quite the opposite. I want her found, for my aunt's sake as much as my own.'

'She is only one missing person among many who concern you. I understand that.'

'I am glad that you understand my responsibilities, but you still fail to comprehend my heart.'

Narua fell silent, chastised.

'Let us go. As I said, Narua, you only had to ask. I'll unlock the charms for you and you can see what secrets are dangling on this chain.'

Because he was the Patron and thus a busy man, and also because only his time and his timing mattered, they did not, as Narua had hoped, go straight from landing at Port of Janojya to a viewing at one of the port's extensive conference facilities. Nor did they, on return to Janojya proper and re-entry to the Haneki domains, immediately settle down to a private meeting in the Patron's workroom or living quarters. Narua found himself gently dismissed, left alone for days to consider and worry and finally fret, and then at last he was summoned.

The Patron sat alone at the edge of a sunken holo projector pit in the centre of his workroom floor. He sat so still that Narua thought for a moment that he was meditating. Narua crossed the threshold, courteously quiet but sensibly announcing his entry with an inaudible beat of presence that could be discerned by any but the most primitive Terran. The Patron's eyelids flickered, lowered rather than closed, and Narua saw that his focus was on something held in the upturned palm on his lap.

'Narua . . . or may I say Kirat?'

Narua smiled. 'You may say Siha, but childhood names don't matter any more. Not for me.'

'Then let me start again. Narua, I wish you well in your search. This role I fill comes with many opportunities and many restrictions, and if I cannot help, I will at least not hinder. Here.'

The Patron waved him to a cushion beside him. Narua looked before he sat and picked up a single charm, shaped like a watchtower, from the dip in the soft fabric.

'A full copy of everything you tried to steal,' said the Patron, both chiding and amused. 'Use it wisely and don't embarrass me.'

Narua nodded, too pleased to speak, and quickly put it into a pocket. The Patron's gaze returned to the object in his own hand.

'For this,' he said, holding it up to clear view, 'I had to make a request, and then I had to wait.'

Narua stared. It was an old Cygnian datacharm of a design that slightly pre-dated the one the Patron kept on the chain, and the style was familiar. He began to speak, then bit his lip.

'I think you have one like it,' the Patron said. 'This belongs to my aunt. I only found out about it when it came up during our recent chat on your latest shenanigans. She said we should watch it together, before you go through all the other journals and chronicles.'

It was the moment to ask, but Narua stayed silent. He could already guess who was on it and more questions seemed superfluous. The Patron nodded his approval and gently threw the charm into the depths of the holo interface. The first image was sudden and large, and they both jumped back reflexively at the brightness radiating from the semicircle before them. There was the face and form Narua knew so well, which belonged to a woman he had never met – his mother. She was sitting in an office. The wall behind her right shoulder had shelves of books, discs and unfamiliar artefacts, and a tall window at her left shoulder opened out into greenery and birdsong. A breeze played intermittently at the draperies.

'Commander Nasiha,' she said, looking straight into the vid recorder with a slightly distant, almost distracted gaze. 'Formerly of the Interplanetary Science Council, presently on leave from the

New Sadira Science Council, cultural consultant of Sadira-on-Cygnus in Tlaxce Province on Cygnus Beta—'

A brief, staccato cough cut off the lengthy introduction and another voice spoke softly. 'This isn't a research report, Nasiha. There's no need for formality.'

Nasiha blinked and her eyes focused and grew warm. 'I asked you to prompt me, not interrupt me,' she admonished the unseen speaker, but it was said gently enough to be teasing as well.

'I *am* prompting you. Try to relax. Tell it like a tale.'

Nasiha frowned. 'Perhaps reports would be better. Anything can change, and what I say now will have little utility.' She moved as if to get up.

The off-screen voice sighed. 'And I say again, it's not a report.'

'Nor is it a memorial,' Nasiha replied harshly.

Sorrowful, almost hurt, the voice countered, 'That's not why I suggested this.'

The vid's view changed in a blur, resettling at a higher point to show the whole room and the second occupant, her hand just pulling back from flinging the vid recorder to its new perch. She reclined in a chair on the other side of Nasiha's desk, her fingers laced tightly over her belt in a way that should have been casual but instead demonstrated an inner tension held close and quiet. Grace Delarua, godmother of Narua and aunt of the Patron, had never been good at hiding her feelings. The new angle also provided some temporal context for the vid. Narua noted with fond reverence that his mother was heavily pregnant and that he had been, in fact if not in full awareness, present at the time of recording.

'It's a memory,' Grace Delarua said, 'not a memorial. It's a way for you to talk to the family you'll never see. Once we kept letters, journals and flat, monochrome photographs. Now we have data keepsakes and trinkets. It's as significant or insignificant as you want it to be. Say hi. Recite a poem or a blessing. Tell a dirty joke.'

As Grace spoke, Nasiha gradually unstiffened, slowly leaned back and absently clasped her hands in similar fashion over her belly. She fought not to smile, but by the last sentence, she smiled. Narua glanced at the Patron and noticed with not a little ruefulness that he too had fallen into the same posture as the Patron – legs crossed, hands loosely held in lap, body leaning slightly forward. The Patron looked at him sideways and gave him a quick wink.

'I will have to think of one,' Nasiha said drily. 'We're not as amused by sex as Terrans and Zhinuvians.'

'Sadiri are far too grown up for that,' Grace agreed cheerfully.

Nasiha's face became shadowed again. 'Or we find less humour in things, or the wrong kind of humour. New Sadira is a joke, but no one is laughing.'

Grace also sobered. 'But how much of what we are hearing is true?'

Nasiha unclasped her hands and began to tap out a tally on her fingertips. 'First, our pilot brethren. They are very loyal to all things Sadiri, but they are also expert at objective observation. I would assign their reports a high level of veracity. Second, the attention our consultancy has been getting from the Academes of Punartam, not only in increased requests for collaboration on projects concerning the Sadiri culture, but also in the number of times our papers and reports have been quoted and referenced by other academics and consultants. This goes beyond the first wave of stranded Sadiri after our biosphere disaster. They are dealing with a second wave of refugees from New Sadiri, many of them traumatised by new, unexpected crises.'

'Your Consul . . .' Grace began slowly, as if already doubting the words she was about to say.

'The Consul of New Sadira is in an unenviable position. Cygnus Beta is too distant from the galactic centre for his office to be fully cognisant of the situation on New Sadira, and the community he is tasked to represent has become too independent to pay him much attention. It is no wonder he clings to any semblance of authority.'

'Like ordering you back to the Science Council,' Grace said.

Nasiha clasped her hands again and shook her head slightly. 'Well, my leave is coming to an end. We knew this would happen – but,' she continued, her eyes narrowing with something like anger, 'the galaxy was a different place then.'

'What does Tarik say?' Grace asked, still with that gentle voice.

'He is concerned. I know he does not want me to go, but he is leaving the decision to me.' Nasiha smiled suddenly. 'He tries his best to assure me in every way that he will be an exceptional parent. That was never in doubt.'

They fell silent for a while, then Grace spoke. 'Do you know, when we first started hearing the rumours, I was convinced it was something the Zhinuvian cartels were doing. I imagined them sweeping up every lost and undocumented Sadiri female they could find and selling them on to the highest bidders.'

Nasiha laughed bitterly. 'The cartels have too many other opportunities now that galactic security is so lax, but I am sure there are some enterprising small groups and individuals who are filling the void. Sadiri women are now the galaxy's rarest and most valuable commodity. Ironically, this fact has put severe limitations on their safety and security.'

Grace sighed. 'I almost wish that Ain wasn't cut off from the rest of the galaxy. If the government of New Sadira had more genetic options, they might not be so desperate.'

'Taking Ainya genetic material as reparations for attempted genocide? Would that mean taking Ainya women as wives, or breeding stock? Unimaginable. Perhaps Ain is better off in isolation. It removes the temptation to other atrocities.'

'Go to the Academes,' Grace pleaded. 'If they've taken over the Interplanetary Science Council, why should you go to New Sadira? It's too far. We'll never see you again.'

'A seven-year posting is not for ever, Grace,' Nasiha chided absently.

'They will make it for ever. You know that,' Grace muttered. 'And you . . . you're keeping secrets from me.'

Unexpectedly, Nasiha laughed. There was so much fondness and joy in her laughter that Grace responded with a huge grin, immediately disarmed. 'Of course I am keeping secrets from you,' she said, 'but I thought you knew why.'

Grace shrugged. 'I know you love me, but I also know you don't take me seriously where some matters are concerned.'

Nasiha dipped her head and gave Grace a stern and censuring look from under frowning brows. 'Nonsense. I am doing you a favour. I do not think that you would not keep my secrets, but it may be that you *could* not. And I do not wish to put your husband in an awkward position. He must maintain a good relationship with New Sadira in general and the Consul in particular. If I must plot disobedience, I will not involve you two.'

'You should give us the choice,' Grace grumbled.

'We are all of us caught between duty and choice. They tell me that my children are the future of my people and I have a duty. But how can I ransom the freedoms of the unborn to an unknowable future?'

'You say that now because of Cygnian influence. When you first arrived, all of you, your sole duty was to the survival of Sadira. Now you allow Terran and Ntshune riff-raff like me into your community and you don't even flinch at the prospect of a diluted bloodline. That's quite a change.'

'New Sadira has changed, too, but in the opposite direction. There lies my dilemma.'

'I wish you would let us do more.'

'I *do* want you to do more. Would you save only me when so many others are in danger? Do your research, collaborate with the Academes, and as for your husband . . .' Nasiha looked down, drew a breath and exhaled. 'I know that Dllenahkh will strive to keep the name of Sadira from dishonour. I believe he has some challenges ahead of him. You must keep him stable and save him from despair.'

'These sound like goodbyes,' Grace said, her voice wavering.

Nasiha nodded. 'One way or another, I will be leaving Cygnus Beta, and I believe it will be soon. I hope it will be in a way that I choose.'

She looked pensively at the window view as Grace quickly wiped her eyes and cleared her throat.

'I've got some reports to finish. Call me if you need anything, and . . . finish recording that message, okay?'

Nasiha nodded as Grace stretched up to the recorder on the shelf, her hand filling the view as she reached towards it . . . then darkness and silence indicated that the glimpse into the past was at an end.

The Patron cleared his throat in a little staccato rhythm that made him sound far too much like his aunt. 'That's it. I take it you have the datacharm Commander Nasiha recorded for you?'

'Yes,' Narua said, or tried to say, but his voice was below a whisper, dry and tearless. He tried again with more force and spit. 'Yes.'

'What did she put on it?'

'An old Sadiri lullaby. The melody is very pretty but the lyrics are a bit grim. Something about how getting married and having a hundred descendants is preferable to dying alone and forgotten and useless.'

'Ah. I suppose things haven't really changed that much in the Sadiri mindset.'

'But she said . . . she said family can be a matter of choice, not birth.'

'That's a very Ntshune sentiment.' The Patron sounded pleased.

'And if your family is as large as a dynasty, your priorities change,' Narua acknowledged.

The Patron shook his head and stared earnestly at the young Sadiri. 'They don't change, Narua. They deepen, they expand, but they don't change as much as you think.'

He stood up briskly, bent and picked the charm out of the holo pit. 'Keep looking for her. I will give you what help I can when I can. I only ask that you answer my call if I need you. Now, if you will, I have appointments elsewhere. Feel free to use my workroom and quarters while you go through the rest of the charms. All the tech is secure and surveillance-free.'

18

'Thank you, Patron,' Narua said, his voice almost breaking with surprise and emotion at the unexpected generosity.

He waited for the Patron to exit before tossing the bracelet of charms into the pit before him. Then he stretched out on the cushions and began to listen and watch.

PART ONE

Cygnus Beta

CHAPTER ONE

It was that hour of the game when sweat and blood began to rub together, skin sliding on skin, smudging the marks of allegiance and territory and leaving only the grav-band colours to identify the two teams. The audience was global and the cacophony shocking. Every drop and pull and sink was cursed and celebrated. A mosaic composed of myriad images of frenzied supporters enveloped the Wall in a hemisphere of seething colour. Players would occasionally look outwards into that mad, tilted sky and add their voices in shouts of triumph or fury, but for the most part they saved their breath for speed.

Adrenalin spiked high in players and spectators alike, pushed by the high risk and higher stakes. This was the best part. It was ruined by unfriendly white light flooding the room and washing out the rich, broad holo projection of seventeen carefully coordinated school slates. Cries of dismay rose up and as quickly died down again at the sight of the schoolmaster standing in the doorway with a tired expression on his face.

'Boys, you are loud. Go to sleep. You will find out the score in the morning. Caps on, Riley, Kim and Dee. Caps straight, Pareti

23

and Sajanettan. Put away those slates. Let all be in proper order before I leave this place. You – Abowen, Abyowan, however your name's pronounced – aren't you the new Saturday boy?'

The master's voice was a marvel. It started at a resentful mutter, swelled to stern command and concluded with a sharp, querying snarl directed a student who was standing casually at the edge of the room. The boy looked as if he had been hoping – no – expecting to be overlooked. The sudden question startled him badly.

'Yes, but . . . it's Friday.' Now he looked bewildered.

'Not any more – it's midnight. You know who I am, don't you? My sister teaches you Telecoms and Transfers.'

'Of course I know,' the boy replied, oddly offended. 'I'm not that new.'

The master's expression turned suspiciously mild. 'Barely a year, big school, high staff turnover with some teachers you know of but never see face to face – it wouldn't be surprising if you didn't know the connection. My office, east wing, nine tomorrow morning.'

The room had settled down. Leaving the Saturday boy to worry whether the appointment was for work or punishment, the master scanned the dormitory and, finding it relatively neat and its denizens subdued, gave a brief, approving nod.

'Lights out,' he said, closed the door and set off without a backward look. The slow fade would give them all plenty of time to get into bed.

He jogged down the corridor with as much haste and dignity as could be managed on too many sedentary years and a creaky ankle. 'Loud,' he grumbled to himself. 'Pestilential interference is the problem. A seventeen-slate array! Selfish, unthinking poppets!'

The lift tower at the corner of east and south was illuminated solely by the starlight from its long, narrow windows, but he stepped onto the lift pad with the sixth sense of familiarity and gave it a solid stamp. It carried him up to the second level as he muttered, this time with a touch of admiration, 'Enterprising little *moujins*. Galia will be proud.'

Their lodgings were at the opposite end of the wing from his office. He had insisted. Life was too complicated without maintaining a few artificial boundaries. Galia did not have an office; she did not need one. She stayed in their small set of rooms, keeping mainly to the large study. *He* called it a study. Most visitors simply called it . . . strange. The walls were full of fixed shelves, the upper air dangled leashes from a couple of floating shelves, and nothing touched the wooden floor but Galia's own feet and her old-fashioned walking stick. She stood leaning on it, considering a slate propped on a shelf opposite her. It was silently broadcasting a small flat-view of that same match he had shut down in the north wing first-level-boys' dormitory.

'In, Silyan,' she told him as he hesitated in the doorway. The brief exchange said everything about which sibling was elder and dominant.

The floor of the study had a pleasing give, a slight bounce. He enjoyed it. It was how his feet knew he was home. Galia turned away from the slate and the movement of her considerable mass sent a familiar pulse through the floor: the sharp vibration of walking stick and the low-amplitude surge of the shifting from left foot to right.

'Image improved. Well done. How many?'

'Seventeen.'

She acknowledged the feat with a nod and a minor show of her dimples. 'Sometimes they pay attention.'

She tapped her cane. Two other slates switched on from their stations on the walls, there was a momentary blur and the full holo coalesced in the centre of the room, almost filling it to the ceiling. Her brother's eyes went wide from the sheer impact of the holo's size and fine-grained detail. He silently watched both the game and Galia's concentration. He would have been making notes, looking up strategies, anything to keep a proper sense of what was going on rather than superficially enjoying the speed and skill of the players, but she was far above him and only her mouth moved as she whispered numbers and formulae to herself.

A sadness as sudden and deep as a Punartam double-sunset fell over his spirit. 'Are you so sure? Are they so sure?'

Galia was untouched by any doubt. 'What else is there to do?'

They balanced each other, moments bound by a shared pivot point – blood, ability and a common prison. The more information they received, the more certain she became; the greater the potential for success, the more his terror grew that they would fail. Hope for a distant dream was sweeter, gentler and easier to bear than hope on the blade-edge of freedom or utter disaster. At different times they kept each other from despair. She looked at him with a small smile that teased him for his cold feet and sparked enough of the old sibling rivalry to fire up his courage again.

'I have not moved or fought,' she said, 'but standing still is not surrender. Look at the players. It's about timing. It is always about timing. You must move when the circumstances are right or you will fall. Look at the strategists. They stand still and hold the reins. Sometimes we are players and sometimes we are strategists.'

Silyan looked. Anyone could understand the game with a

glance. Players ran and climbed and slid from the base of the Wall to the top. They obstructed their opponents and carried their mates. They moved together as closely as possible; a scattered team lost weight and leverage in more ways than one. They tried to tilt the Wall in their favour, making it easy for even the weakest to reach the goal. That was the game at first glance and many supporters needed no more to enjoy their wins and mourn their losses. For those who knew, there was more, much more. For example, how a certain concentration and configuration of players could tilt the Wall against the other team, or how the sudden shifts of gravity might cause not merely a fall but even, in the case of a slow or unskilled player, a dangerous shear that could rip limb from body. Most of all, the true aficionados knew that the key to the game was in the hands of the strategists, a pair of players who never ran or climbed but stood before the Wall, working at low-slanted grids on easels and orchestrating the moves of their team with pre-programmed manoeuvres coordinated through the push and pull of grav-bands on their wrists. One commentator described it as holding the reins for an entire derby of horses while trying to keep them from trampling each other, running off the track or colliding with the rails.

Silyan had never ridden a horse, but he had kept order in a dormitory of fifty boys of varying parapsychological and physical abilities. The reins were long enough and strong enough that he could, as Galia said, stand still and manipulate them with knowledge and timing alone.

There was hazard, too. A player on the Wall might run the risk of shear or a tumble to the base with no hope of medical assistance until the traditional whistle for game-over, but a strategist captain and his deputy were the only ones who faced consequences after the final whistle, consequences that could be as trivial as a brief loss of credit or as permanent as dismissal and dishonour.

Silyan and Galia had no credit to lose, and dismissal, whether under cloud or glory, would have been a gift. So they stayed, he anxious, she calm, both awaiting a shift of forces that could tilt the Wall in their favour.

In the end, he was the one who almost forgot the morning appointment with the Saturday boy. It had been a late night, watching and pondering the game, and he had not slept well, watching and pondering his dreams. It was fifteen minutes before nine when he came to his office, not for the appointment but to reread some recent articles from Punartam. He was not fully the schoolmaster, still rumpled and too-comfortable in an old tunic and a frayed but warm mantle to shield him from the chill of the building's thick, ancient stone. The knock on the door startled him upright from his recliner, disorientating him from a reality of formats and formulae until he remembered who and where he was and shouted permission for the boy to enter.

The door opened.

'Master,' the boy greeted him. There was deference in the lowered head, but his eyes were cautious and his jaw tense as if, though no longer a novice, he still did not know what to expect.

'Sit.' He made the command friendly but his eyes kept a close watch on the boy as he sat on a chair beside a table with breakable things like confiscated games, old-model slates and half-full pesto jars, and in the middle of it all an intricate game strategy board wedged between two slates and a stack of old books.

'Rafi Abowen Delarua. You've spent a full year at the Lyceum now. How are you faring?'

The reply was pleasingly blunt, if typical. 'It's boring. I could cover twice the work in half the time on the homestead.'

'I know,' murmured Silyan. 'It's almost as if we wanted to keep you here for as long as possible.' He met Rafi's suddenly horrified stare with an amused gaze.

'Your mother and sister have moved to Tlaxce City,' he continued. 'Your grandmother is away most weekends – sailing season on Tlaxce Lake, I understand. These are not, however, the only reasons you are now a Saturday boy.

'You've been with us for a while and . . . well . . . we can't quite figure you out, Abowen. You're not helping. You don't speak to the school therapists, you're friends with no one but friendly to everyone, and you're ordinary. You overdo ordinariness. You wouldn't be here if you were ordinary, Abowen. What are you keeping from us?'

The boy blinked at him and said nothing. Anger, fear, uncertainty . . . what was the origin of that tension that kept his face so still? It was impossible to tell.

Silyan sighed. 'We will have to cap you.'

'No,' Abowen replied instantly. 'I won't accept it.'

'Ah, there's the problem. We do need your permission. You haven't done anything wrong, after all. Boy, where do you think you are?'

Silent confusion.

The master pressed on. 'A school? A prison? A hospital?'

'Is there a choice?' Abowen retorted.

'There is,' Silyan said gravely, 'and I encourage you to choose wisely. The Lyceum has one mandate: to bring together all the rogue and random psi gifted of Cygnus Beta and teach them ethics, restraint and community. In that we are supported by Central

Government and some of the oldest Ntshune families on the planet. If you need help, let us help you. Prove you're not dangerous and show us what you can do. If you want to learn, you can learn from us.'

Abowen studied the mess on the table and began fidgeting with the strategy board. Silyan did not stop him. He suspected there were tears on the boy's averted face.

'You like the game?'

Abowen nodded and cleared his throat before saying in a steady voice, 'We call it snakes and ladders.' He smiled. 'No one else calls it that.'

'Messenger, Wallrunning, Cliffchase,' Silyan listed. 'Of course, the original name in Traditional Ntshune is unpronounceable unless you're very musical, but it roughly translates as "messenger".'

'"Those who go before",' Abowen corrected quietly. '"Vanguard", perhaps? Or "herald"?'

Silyan watched as he flicked the flags and pins into a common formation and then quickly disassembled the grouping with a tap to the corner of the grid. 'Forerunner,' he said, and added, 'Do you play?'

'Never in real life,' Abowen said, looking up at him with clear eyes and a calm expression.

'Would you like to?'

His eyes widened. 'With the Dailies? I'm not that good.'

'They won't mind someone stumbling around during training drills. It'll keep them alert, at least.'

'They'll never accept someone with a cap.'

'Wear it after hours and don't tell them.'

Abowen looked at the strategy board again, his gaze distant and dreaming. He glanced, frowning, at the walls of the room, then met Silyan's eyes. 'I'll take the bribe and the cap. But what does the cap do?'

'That depends on you, boy. That entirely depends on you. Go and get your cap and come back at two – no, make that three. I'll find some work for you to do.'

The door to the schoolmaster's office opened and closed and there was my dear and callow friend Rafi, also known as Moo, unscathed by all appearances, but very strange-faced, as if he had a lot of excitement he didn't know what to do with. Then he saw me and went all-angry with no doubts.

'Tinman, what in all blasted Earth are you doing in halls on a Saturday?' he said, shouting with his hands, whispering with his mouth.

'Making sure the master doesn't disappear you. It's happened before, you know.'

Moo hustled me 'round the corner with his fist wrapped up in my sleeve. 'They'll disappear *you*.'

'Calm down, you're all aflitter. Come to the back gate. I flew. No nav, no trace.'

He opened his mouth, he shut his mouth. He tried again. 'You what?'

'Flew. Padr got me an aerolight to celebrate my ageday. Two-seater. Scared? It's higher than an elephant's eye.'

He thumped my shoulder. 'Never scared! But I can't. I've just agreed to be capped.'

'Pest and perdition, no!' I gasped.

He nodded. 'Going to pick it up now.'

'You should be crying. Why not?'

31

'Compensation is I get to play with the Dailies.'

'Poxy liar, no!' I shouted.

'Shh. Truth. Now fly back home and I'll see you Monday.'

He left me gaping and flapping in the corridor as if *I* were the *moujin* and not him. He's three years younger and acts superior. I should hate him, but he took me elephant riding last break, so I owe him, even if he doesn't want to be owed. But capped! That's for the crazies, the criminals and the ones who'd set themselves on fire by accident if they weren't watched. How could he be so calm about that?

I didn't come all that distance to fly alone. I went and banged on the window of the next best thing. She was deep in study, slate in hand, and she dropped it and almost fell out of her chair when I rattled the metalwork and glass.

She opened the window fully and gave me a bad-look. 'You're so uncouth.'

'You're not in the convent any more. Adjust. Come flying with me.'

'I'm busy,' she snapped and turned away. Halfway away. I stopped her.

'Moo is going to be capped.'

She froze a moment and turned back. 'What?' she whispered. She sounded truly upset. 'Why would they cap Rafi?'

'I have no idea. Fly with me and let's discuss it.'

She gave me more bad-looks, but she came. She sat on the sill, swung her feet daintily over and jumped down onto the pebble path, ignoring my outstretched helping hand. As we walked, I tried small talk to soften her up. 'So, you've been here a few months now. What is your opinion of this fine establishment?'

'Sad,' she said brutally. 'By all sacred waters, I am grateful I never came here as a child.'

'Don't judge it by me, sweet Serendipity,' I told her. 'I am an indifferent student, a less than stellar example, the despair of my illustrious tutors. On the other hand, your home is truly a blessed place for the bright-minded. I cannot blame you for your high standards. Here we learn how not to disturb the common man; there you learn to sing and soar with the highest.'

We were walking shoulder-to-shoulder, close enough to touch hands. I touched her hand. She shook me off absently, like brushing away a fly. I was too cheerful to feel hurt. My gift and freedom was before us: smooth lines, cool mint-green trim, graceful wings.

'My lady's wingèd chariot,' I proclaimed, offering her again the hand she'd scorned. She scorned it a second time and scrambled in. I tumbled in myself and sealed up the canopy. 'We'll have to trundle for a bit,' I explained apologetically as I keyed it awake with a short code. 'Too many trees in the vicinity.'

I kept quiet as we taxied silently to open space. I knew she was thinking. I didn't know what she was thinking. She always hated it when I tried to look. I merely recognised the expression, the mild worry that reminded me she was concerned about greater matters than the latest game score or the career her padr had picked for her.

'I don't think you need fret. Rafi won't tell, and neither will I.' I spoke seriously, partly because I was serious and partly because I was starting my preparation for take-off, something that always makes me stop skylarking.

She bit her lip, looking irritated. 'There's little to tell, and soon there will be nothing to tell. The day of secrets is over. I just don't trust those caps.'

'He's tried too hard to seem harmless. They probably want to check that he's not harbouring murderous urges.'

She kindly waited until I had taken off and levelled out the aircraft before glaring at me.

I smiled back half-heartedly. 'That's why we're here. What can you do? What are you going to do with it? Are you safe? Work with us. Are you useful? Work for us. Are you a mess? We'll work on you.'

'Blue, Yellow, Red,' she noted, naming our school teams. 'The safe, the useful and the dangerous.'

'And Green for the day students, from which happy cadre I do hail. We've already been raised right, or we're too weak to be much trouble. I suppose you're a resident Green, given your origins.' I almost bit my lip. Her secrets remained strong.

'Rafi's in Blue,' she said.

'For now,' I replied.

She liked Rafi. She worried about Rafi, she thought about Rafi, she watched Rafi. She did all that quietly enough that whenever I opened my mouth to ask, 'So, are you in love with Rafi,' I found myself shutting my mouth in foolish silence. I could admit jealousy to myself, but I didn't want her to accuse me of being an idiot.

'You fly really well, Ntenman.' It sounded like a concession, a patronising, pitying compliment to break the unusual pause in my babble. Serendipity the kind-hearted. She would snap my fingers off if I got too close but pat my head when I looked beaten. Ridiculous. Why didn't she just ignore me?

'Thank you. We should go back now. I have to get home before sundown.'

In one sense, 'serendipity' was a word that covered many desires and expectations for the future, but for Serendipity of distant Tirtha, it was a simplified translation of a name that the students of the Tlaxce National Lyceum would find unfamiliar. Many remote and self-sufficient communities managed to evade bureaucracy, coasting on the natural Cygnian tendency to live and let live barring outright war or exploitation. It was different in the urban belt. The greater the infrastructure, the greater the scrutiny. Comforts must be paid for – the intercontinental rail, the orbital stations, the produce of the biodomes and the monitoring of the biosphere. With respect to the latter, Sadira's fate had not increased knowledge but it had increased paranoia, so that field was flourishing with an influx of public and private funding and a bounty of fresh, keen minds.

Some things were suspiciously free, like the services of the Ministry of Family Planning and Maintenance, the Health Service (people would never forget the clone scandal, and that involved only ten specimens) and the Cygnian Military Service (conscription was rare but legal, and that fact alone still provoked healthy debate).

Even in this day and age, a community that lived simply and peaceably according to its own healing lore and bonding rituals need not be troubled by the presence of the Civil Service. Such was the village Tirtha in the forest uplands of Oleha Province.

Things change.

One thing did not change: the deep discontent that defined

and narrowed Serendipity's life. That was the only constraint. There were no barriers to leaving home. The elder monks and nuns encouraged travel at the age of majority, knowing too well that many would choose to stay and of those who left, most would return, dissatisfied with the shallow communion offered by the outside world.

Some remained in nearby villages among those whose minds could manage some small speech. There too resided those who had been born with solitary minds or faint and faltering thought-projection. The elders observed the population, the small flows in and out, monitoring the genetic heritage for improvement and decline. The arrival of a Sadiri representative from a new community of waking minds had been an unexpected gift.

Serendipity marked that day as the beginning of her discontent.

Along with the simple and humble life their community cultivated, there was also an unacknowledged but inherent belief that this life, this stability, this depth of communion and intimacy could not be found anywhere else. Leaving permanently for the outside world was for minds without speech and hearts without warmth. She had not even considered another possibility until the outside world came to her and overturned her old assumptions. She saw a man taught to speak in less than a day and saw him communicate in turn with a woman she would have viewed as an ordinary Cygnian, until something unimaginable happened between them, some connection beyond everything she had learned and experienced. She had been so thrown off balance that a day or two later, when given the opportunity to speak to the woman, she could only manage a few shy words before withdrawing in an embarrassed daze.

The reason for her diffidence was complicated. The rational part of her was intrigued by their communication, but the emotional part of her was fascinated by their intimacy – fascinated, jealous and even obsessed. They left within days, but the shock to the community and to herself lingered. Formal links were forged with the new Sadiri settlement and a slow, quiet revealing began. She could have gone with the first group of women to visit the settlement. She did not. She knew how to maintain her mind's privacy, but she was ashamed of the fantasies that played in its secret corners and afraid to face the two people who inspired them in case they showed some other unexpected talent and read her passions like a banner spread out for public view. She kept her wild dreams and her dark discontent hidden and brooded over them.

Several months later, Rafi and Ntenman arrived. Rafi was the smaller and younger of the two students of the famous Lyceum. The community was abuzz once more, all intrigued by the concept of a school devoted to parapsychology, but at first she was unmoved. His mind's voice was untutored, barely a child's whisper, and she only became interested in him when she found out he was the nephew of *that* woman. She watched him closely and was rewarded when in an unguarded moment he laughed, and whatever restraints he had placed on himself unknotted and let slip a great wave of warmth and vibrant otherness that was and was not like the strange fizzing connection she had witnessed between his aunt and her companion.

To her shame and dismay, her attachment transferred smoothly from the middle-aged couple to the teenage boy.

This time, when a group of her peers were given the chance to visit the Lyceum, she went out of sheer contrariness, angry with herself and her secret, uncontrollable obsession. It was only fitting that her punishment should be Ntenman's intense crush and Rafi's complete obliviousness.

She stood before the closed door of the master's office, hesitated and then knocked.

'Enter, Serendipity.'

She stepped in quietly and shut the door behind her but came no further. Silyan did not raise his head from his work. He waited, a faint smile on his face, but the silence dragged too long and he succumbed. He glanced up with a sly expression.

'It's been hours since Abowen left this office. I'm surprised it took you so long to come to me.'

'You are discourteous.' She conveyed so much scorn without raising her voice that he was impressed.

'I do not read your mind, Serendipity, not when your motives are so clear and open. How did you learn to lock your mind so securely but leave all else for thieves like me to pick through?' He watched her face go from angry to sullen, like a child reminded of her childishness. 'What can I do for you?'

'Tell me why you're putting the cap on Rafi.'

Silyan's humour faded. 'We need to know what he's capable of. If you knew, you could tell us and there'd be no need for a cap, would there?'

She exhaled a breath sharply through clenched teeth, a noise that was part bitterness and part disbelief.

'It's a pity that the Lyceum has not lived up to your expectations, nor the world for that matter, but no matter how you feel about it, we are doing this for Abowen's own good. But you, your term with us will soon be over. Where will you go after you leave us? You are a very restless person, Serendipity. I'm afraid you will always be disappointed.'

Her cool expression cracked for a moment and it was fear, not anger, that showed through. It almost made him feel sorry for her, but before the moment could produce any mellowing in either of them, a knock on the door startled her. She half-turned and instinctively set her hand on the door.

'My three o'clock appointment,' said Silyan, his voice steady though he too had flinched. 'We can talk some other time . . . if you wish to talk, that is.'

He settled back comfortably in his chair and watched intently as she whipped open the door with anger now unveiled and waited with perverse pleasure for her reaction. Abowen stood there, one hand raised and about to rap again, the other gripping the new cap that was the source of so much debate. She almost ran into him. The boy fended her off gently with the cap-free hand and smiled shyly, spontaneously, at her, as if he could not help himself. For a moment he looked much younger than his fourteen years.

'Hello, Serendipity,' he said. 'What are you doing here?'

She bit her lip, regarding him with an odd kind of regret. Silyan leaned forward, put his elbows on his desk, propped his chin on his hands and observed them. Serendipity glared briefly at him over her shoulder.

'Nothing,' she said. 'I'll see you later, in the refectory.'

Abowen watched her walk away, and Silyan, continuing to observe, sighed dramatically. Abowen heard the sigh, recognised the sarcasm and quickly brought his attention front and centre. The schoolmaster straightened and spoke seriously.

'That thing's no good in your hand. You might as well get used to it. Cap on.'

Galia kept an antigrav pallet for occasional sleeping in the study. In spite of the pallet's comfort and stability, she had one foot hanging over the edge and touching the floor as a reassurance and reminder. The study was quieter in a way that only large, high-ceilinged rooms could be quiet. The shelves baffled the echoes and furthered the illusion of cosy immensity. Silyan had tried it himself once or twice, but his habit was to work at his desk and nod off in his chair until some numbness of limb or creak of joint recalled him to the sensible joys of a proper bed. He usually went to his bed before Galia, so it was with a shock that he woke, still at his desk, to find her staring down at him in disgruntlement, a hand stretched out towards his desk lamp.

'It's reflecting into the study,' she explained, pushing the shade to point in another direction. 'Why are you still here?'

Silyan yawned, frowned and tried to remember. 'Abowen's cap. I'm looking at the initial diagnostics.' He fumbled with the handheld before him and revived the statistical data that had so quickly put him to sleep.

She grimaced. 'Leave that to the experts. You mustn't get too attached.'

'Hmm,' Silyan replied, a meaningless noise.

'What is he?'

'Pardon?'

'Is he dangerous?' she clarified. 'Is he viciously dangerous, unconsciously dangerous, ignorantly and carelessly dangerous?'

Silyan huffed humourlessly. 'I'll let the experts say. For now, all I can see is that he's an utter sloth during his waking hours, almost anti-psi if such a thing can be imagined. But when he dreams . . . that's when it gets interesting.'

'Do schoolboys dream of anything else but sex?' Galia said, still grumpy from being disturbed.

Silyan took the question seriously. 'According to these indicators, there is indeed some sex, overshadowed by a remarkable amount of psi activity and a truly astonishing amount of fear.'

She yawned, unimpressed. 'Sounds like rape fantasies.'

Silyan flashed her a look of censure. While he recognised that she could be right, he did not appreciate the flippant tone. 'If they are, he's not enjoying them. He doesn't sleep afterwards, and there are little spikes of psi activity, as if he's trying and failing to control himself. We want to assess him, not cause a breakdown.'

'Breakdown may lead to breakthrough,' she stated pragmatically.

Again he bristled at her apparent lack of empathy. 'I'm going to bed,' he said abruptly, 'and I suggest you do the same. I'll turn off the lights.'

CHAPTER TWO

'You might as well get used to it,' I said, pushing the bands over his hands. 'You're a booby.'

Rafi was upset, so upset he didn't even ask what a booby was, which was too bad because I was about to enlighten him.

'You're the team's *moujin*. They need to practise what happens when a teammate falls wrong or an opponent puts himself in the way of a strategy. Your bumbling around is just what they need to learn to be sharp.'

'I don't see *you* playing,' he sniped.

I showed him my teeth, both humour and bite. 'Regional standard, Moo. I don't play school teams because I'm too good to play in a team of boobies. Fortunately for you, I *am* good and I can coach you not to injure yourself or someone else. Listen and grow wise and you too may one day be able to train your own booby.'

'Stop saying "booby".'

'Booby. Booby. Boobyboobybooby . . .' He should have known me better than that. I got in fifteen *boobies* before he tried to hit me, and that, my friends, is a bad thing to do with semi-functional grav-bands on. I laughed as he overbalanced and almost fell. He got me in a headlock and I let him choke me for a bit, just to relieve his feelings, before I threw him off and pinned him down. That should have cheered him up, but he still looked fretful.

'You're in a bad mood. What's got you?' I said, letting him sit up.

'Nightmares. I didn't really sleep last night. Nor the night before.'

I frowned. We didn't talk about the cap, but the cap was there, like a terminal disease or a convicted criminal in the family, the cause of occasional bouts of vague sympathy but never, ever the topic of any discussion.

Rafi shifted restlessly. He was trying to find a way to laugh it off and I knew it wasn't going happen. I went serious for a moment. 'Moo, don't let them use you like a specimen in a lab. If you can't bear it, you refuse the cap, simple.'

He curled over in a defeated ball, knees to chest and forehead on knees. 'But if I refuse . . . I don't . . . I don't know what they've done to my father.'

I exhaled a long, slow breath. Disease and convict, all in one conversation. This was hard. 'You could ask?' I suggested.

'I'm afraid to ask.'

He was afraid to ask. I would be afraid to believe their answer. The Lyceum is all kindness and prestige to the established families like mine with generations of culture and training around psi ability; but the rogue ones, the unexpected sports, they were trouble and they were treated like trouble. Poor Rafi. I thought about patting his shoulder, decided this was too grim a matter and went for distraction instead.

'If you get really *really* tired playing Messenger, maybe you'll sleep too soundly for nightmares.'

He raised his face from his knees. 'Finally you're being helpful.'

I took that in the spirit in which it was intended, which is to say I sat on him until he howled *pax*, and then I let him breathe and curse me to his heart's content.

'Come,' I told him when he ran out of steam. 'Let me introduce you to the coach.'

We walked across the north field to the Wall. He was nervous, so I tried to reassure him. 'Good thing for you that I'm known to the Dailies. No offence to Master Silyan, but sticking in a new player at this time of the season makes *no* sense. I wonder what hold he has over the coach. Anyway, I think I can persuade them not to murder you.'

'Tinman, you're pure nonsense,' said Rafi, his nervousness forgotten under the burden of my exaggerations. I smiled at a job well done.

'Well, I can at least make you a little more welcome, how's that?'

'That sounds possible,' he admitted.

Don't mistake me. I like Rafi. He's a quiet little schemer. For someone who grew up in the backwoods he has an uncanny grasp of social networks. I've never seen him waste time cultivating anyone who couldn't do something for him – a bit cold now that I mention it, but he does it for survival, pure and simple, nothing more. He doesn't get into the more elaborate games, but he's subtle in a way that only an Ntshune could appreciate. Inviting me to trek with him was kind *and* calculated. It increased his credit immensely and presented me with both gift and debt. Gift because the trip cost me nothing, but debt because he did *me* a favour before he ever asked me for anything. And then afterwards, he never asked. Never once did he ask me for anything. So I remained in his debt and this was my way to pay it and maintain my own credit.

We stood in front of the Wall and watched the plays for a while until the coach called halt. Some of the players waved to me and I gave a slight nod – they knew my name and face, of course, but I couldn't remember which ones I'd actually met. The coach noticed and looked over his shoulder at us. Even though he eyed us with a question, I waited until he'd taken a drink with his team before approaching him – Rafi trailing behind me trying to look at ease in my second-hand grav-bands and new loincloth with full shear protection. I stood before the coach, glanced at his feet and back up at his face and waited for him to speak.

He almost smiled but turned it into a slight twitch at the right corner of his mouth. 'You bring a message?'

'I *am* a message,' I responded.

'From whom and to whom?' he queried.

'From death to life to death,' I said.

'The old must die,' he mused.

'The young may die,' I declared with a grin. These were only preliminary statements, but he would never have gone so far in front of Rafi if he meant to reject him.

He looked at Rafi then. 'Who's your apprentice?'

I sighed. 'Not really my apprentice. More like my booby.'

Rafi glared at me.

'But I think you can keep him busy,' I continued brightly. 'He might even learn something along the way. I think he could be a strategist when he gets older, but that's for wiser heads than mine to say.'

46

'This is Master Silyan's student,' the coach said, finally making the connection.

'Yes, and also my friend,' I stressed.

Rafi looked between us uncertainly, as if wondering when he would be allowed to speak about himself.

'Do you know the game, Abowen?' asked the coach. Got the name right. Good sign.

'I've watched it, read about it. Tried some amateur games on the homestead, but I've never been on a proper grav-equipped Wall,' Rafi told him.

The coach looked worried and I couldn't blame him. I caught his eye and tried to convey with something less than a nod and a wink that I would help Rafi through the time of baby steps so that he would not be burdened with that duty.

'Why not try a few runs with your friend? I can see what your skill is like.'

Rafi swallowed. It wasn't obvious, but yes, he swallowed. 'Yes, Coach.'

We walked to the Wall.

'Don't you need grav-bands?' Rafi asked.

'Not for this. It'll keep me at your speed.' I stopped to shuck off my mantle and tunic and unstrap my sandals. 'Don't worry, Moo. He's not really looking for skill. He's looking for potential. Do what you can.'

I ran up the Wall to the first level, testing its responsiveness with an exaggerated bounce of my toes. 'Come on, Moo! Don't be timid!'

He leapt up, using his banded hands to pull himself into the first level. He stood there for a while, perpendicular to the horizon, and raised his hands tentatively, feeling the varying drag of the new gravity.

'Level two!' I urged him.

I turned and dived over and upwards to the next level, landing in a practised roll. He tried to follow but balked instinctively and fell hard on his neck and shoulders. He and I spent a few seconds cursing and laughing, respectively.

I stopped laughing. 'Level three.' I kicked out, twisted sideways and landed in a careful crouch. Rafi gave me a pained look.

'Think of it as spinning through a ninety-arc,' I encouraged him.

He tried and fell. Scrabbling for level two on his way down meant that he fell again, upwards, and smacked his nose and chin painfully.

'Moo, if you're falling, let yourself fall. Trying to hook on to another level at this stage will only bring pain. You let the body-catcher take you, sit out your penalty behind the Wall and start again.'

He rubbed his face, nodded and looked to level three with determination. This time he managed it, though his landing was beyond clumsy.

'Level four is a one-eighty. Pay no attention to the horizon. Simply dive.' I showed him. He took it with fair ease and I smiled, hoping the coach had seen that if nothing else.

'Five is a two-seventy. If you try to do it as a ninety, you're guaranteed a fall. Watch closely.' Wallrunning means knowing which approaches will work and which ones will dump you in the body-catcher. It's not just surfaces and angles.

Rafi did it, but it was a struggle. Was he tired already? 'Only two more levels. You could do them later.'

'No,' he panted. 'Might as well try to finish.'

The last two were another two-seventy and a tricky one that could be a ninety or a two-seventy, depending on your orientation. Rafi fell trying to reach the last level, which I thought was a very good effort. I told him so as he writhed feebly in the grip of the bodycatcher below. He was too worn out to curse me, which I appreciated, especially since the coach was walking towards the Wall again and might have heard it.

'Not bad,' said he, offering a hand to pull Rafi vertical.

I bounced down the Wall, graceful as a mountain goat, in the time it took the coach to get Rafi's limbs untangled and his brain to understand which way was up.

'When do you want him ready?' I asked.

'No more than a day or two. Make sure he can handle each level, then turn him over to us.' His grin went wicked. 'I can use a booby. These boys are getting complacent.'

Weekdays were exhausting, with the full crush of resident and daily students passing through the corridors. Serendipity did not join them. Most of the older children came to the Lyceum already registered in a standard curriculum administered via slate or handheld. Students learned as they pleased, at their own pace and in their own environment. The Lyceum staff did not have classes; some teachers sent their lessons directly to slates, others occasionally held demonstrations for the finer points of practical work, and for the subjects which required hands-on experience they took apprentices and assigned them to their workshops.

Serendipity went to a few of the demonstrations. She would often slip in quietly after the start of the session, take a seat at the back and avoid contact that way. Fortunately, the others from her country were better at mingling, which meant that her antisocial leanings were taken as a personal quirk rather than typical Uplander behaviour.

In spite of her irregular schedule, Ntenman always knew where to find her.

'I need your help,' he said, sitting beside her.

She glanced nervously at the lecturer, afraid that he could hear them. 'Shh, Ntenman. Not now.'

'Come, you don't need this subject and I need you to help me now,' he insisted.

The complete absence of his usual slight deference towards her made her pay attention. She took up her slate and followed him quietly out. 'What is it?' she asked, pausing in the corridor near a window.

'I need your clearance. Ageday number eighteen is only good for certain kinds of information. I want to find out about Moo's father.' He extended his handheld to her, much to her surprise. She rested her own slate on the broad brick windowsill and took it carefully.

'I'm nineteen. My clearance can't be much better than yours,' she admitted.

'Yes, and no. You're not registered as a student and a minor, so you have a few more freedoms.'

She entered her ID on his handheld, but instead of giving it back to him, she held on as he tried to take it. 'What next?'

He tugged hopefully, but she kept her grip firm. His face became distressed. 'You don't want to see this.'

'I do. Is this how you get into the Lyceum staff records? Have you used that to your benefit?'

'I look. I don't tamper.'

'Then we'll look together,' she declared, positioning the hand-held at a good viewing angle for both of them.

He surrendered quickly. The corridor would soon become busy again. 'Abowen, that's a patronymic. His father's name is most likely Owen or Owain, and his homestead is in Montserrat. The nearest Central Court would have been at Ophir.'

He spoke the names in, nudged a few commands with his finger and shook his head. 'Let me try something else.'

She let him mutter and poke around with the shreds of names and family history Rafi had told him. At one point he gave her a sly smile. 'Marvellous access you've got – not only an adult, but a taxpayer!'

'My time here is paid research on behalf of my community,' she explained, mildly surprised that he had not known. His fingers suddenly tensed on the handheld. 'What is it?'

'A minute,' he mumbled. His eyes scanned rapidly and his thumb tapped past a few pages too quickly for her to read them.

'This is it,' he said at last, very sombre in tone and expression.

Ioan Adafydd ex-Montserrat

That was the name. There were some other words in the charge sheet, serious words.

Coercion. Kidnap. Rape. Illegal influence.

The final word was also striking.

Terminated.

'They executed him?' She knew enough to know that these were not capital crimes, not unless his influence had been such that they felt he could not be controlled.

'No, that means the ID has been terminated,' Ntenman clarified, much to her relief. 'Wherever he is now, they've given him a new ID. He's untraceable, unless you want to submit a formal request.'

'Me? You were the one who wanted to search.' She tapped her access closed with nervy but useless speed – if they kept track of who accessed the records, her ID had been logged long before she started reading.

Ntenman was too lost in his own thoughts to care when she shut down the handheld. 'So that's our little Rafi's father. What a charming brute. No wonder they've given him the cap. I remember a boy in my second year . . . lovely, shy person till they capped him. Then he started setting his bed-sheets on fire.'

'With his mind?'

'Of course. His uncle had been a pyromaniac . . .'

She was listening and believing, but a tremor at the corner of his mouth brought the charade to an end. He laughed as she hit his arm in exasperation.

'Your fault for shutting me out of your mind so completely,' he told her. 'But, in seriousness' – and once more he accomplished that abrupt change of character from folly to sobriety – 'Moo said the cap's giving him nightmares. He won't talk to me about it, but he might talk to you.'

She stared at him. 'If his nightmares are about rape and kidnapping, I don't think I *want* him to talk to me.'

He tilted his head and looked at her pleadingly. She had seen him do that so many times before, but this was the first time he was doing it to ask a favour for someone else.

'Of course. If he talks, I'll listen,' she agreed.

The first practice session with the team was unnerving. The coach meant what he said. The other players were given a strategy to execute, but Rafi's job was to blunder through it and force them to make adjustments. In spite of Ntenman's drills, that meant he did a lot of falling, and strictly speaking, three falls meant a four-minute period off the Wall. It took five falls before the coach took pity on his shaking limbs and dazed expression and whistled him off for a short rest.

He tottered away to the usual penalty area . . . but someone was already there, a woman sitting in the shade behind the Wall. It was the worst place for viewing the players, but the best for seeing the movement of the grav-bands in two-dimensional trails of shimmering colour cast on the backscreen. He could not tell if that was what she had been doing, because now, instead of looking at the screen, she was glaring at him. He felt he should apologise for the ugly play she had witnessed, but before he could open his mouth she stood up and beckoned to him.

He blinked, looked around to see if anyone else was watching and then approached her. She was strangely tall, even to a half-grown adolescent like himself. Most of her curly brown hair was carelessly tied back with a length of red cord into a short puff at the back of her head and the remaining flyaway ends were kept flat against her head with metal clips. As he came closer, he realised that the glare was not for him but for the borrowed grav-bands on his wrists. She took his hands and made a click of dissatisfaction.

'I—' Apologies for his substandard gear, his poor form and his utter newness at anything like real game practice all crowded together and made his tongue stumble into silence.

She ignored his noises and let fall one of his hands long enough to pull a clip from her hair. Using its flat end as a lever, she prised open the grav-band connector and adjusted the fit closer to his sweating skin. He felt a slight buzz. She shook her head, frowned and jabbed the clip in with greater force. The buzz increased and he had a moment to feel scared, but then it faded to a subtler vibration that barely crossed the threshold of sensation. The other grav-band was given a similar treatment. He raised his hands and studied them.

'Thanks—'

He got no further. She shushed him, sealing his mouth with three fingers placed emphatically over his still-moving lips. His blood beat hot in the tips of his ears, but she was looking elsewhere, gauging the movement of the shadows on the screen and listening to the sounds of the game. Her hand slowly fell from his mouth as she concentrated. He kept obediently quiet and watched her.

It was easy to see now that his eyes had grown accustomed to the relative dimness. She was not Terran, not close, not even a bit. Her limbs were long for her body, her eyes large and dark; her hair was like fluff near her temples and ears . . . no, not like his sister's hair, strongly springy and every-which-way, but light, downy and stirring in the breeze like the plumage of a half-fledged chick. There was a hint of speckling in the brown, bird-like again, as was the tilt of her head as she focused. Pale lines etched a faint, swirl-ing pattern over the dark brown of her cheek, continuing under her ear and straight down the side of her neck, right to the edge of her tunic's collar and likely beyond. He wondered if it was art or more. He suspected more. After all, she was Ntshune, full Ntshune, a rarity in the urban belt and a near-impossibility outside it.

'How—'

The sharp note of the whistle cut him off and his muscles tensed in instant reaction, ready to return to the game. She gave him a nod and a quick glance to his grav-bands. He nodded in turn, now unsure if she spoke Standard and far too shy to attempt his Simplified Ntshune, and pelted off back to the Wall.

His short rest and the better fit of the grav-bands brought some improvement, but not enough to save him from himself. He ran three levels: one a basic run, one turning and one falling. On the fourth level, his foot faltered and he lost first his balance and then his grip to land once more in the bodycatcher below. He had lasted three minutes. It was humiliating. He lingered for a while, flat on his back staring up at the other players carrying out their training drills, and knew for a certainty that he would never, never be able to play with enough skill to deserve decent gear and time on a professionally equipped Wall. The boys who made the Dailies had been running proper Walls from the time they were old enough to play and mimic their older relatives and listen to their coaching.

He rolled out of the bodycatcher and slouched despondently behind the screen again without waiting for the whistle. She was still there, sitting in the shadows, intent on the game and only sparing him a brief sympathetic look. She now held a bowl of small, hard-shelled spheres. She cracked them with the pressure of finger and thumb, occasionally prised the more stubborn ones apart with the edge of a single shell, and bit into the tough, wrinkled brown core with slow enjoyment. She took time to open them, more time to savour them. He stared at her hands and mouth, forgetting to be polite or shy.

'Are those perrenuts?'

The movement of her jaw stopped as she considered, then she swallowed and smiled. The smile had some mischief in it, but no unkindness. She split a fresh shell and held out the centre. When he reached for it, she pulled back from his hand with a small frown and brought it near his lips instead with a commanding little flourish. He obediently opened his mouth and let her place it on his tongue. He had heard tales, but . . .

'Perrenuts are quite an experience.'

Her voice was low in pitch and volume but with such a mellow resonance that she could have stood in the centre of the Lyceum's largest auditorium and reached the farthest seats with a murmur.

'There's the initial rush of stimulant, which produces a sensation of euphoria, but pay attention to what happens after.'

Rafi understood halfway through her sentence. Eating the nut was enjoyable, but immediately he found himself glancing at the remainder in the bowl and yearning for another taste.

'The true bliss is not in the flavour but in the anticipation and the wait.' She fed him another nut, which he accepted eagerly. It was true. The taste of the second perrenut actually flattened the rising exhilaration, but the memory of the taste and the likelihood of getting a third made his mouth water.

'Some people use perrenuts to test their willpower.' She held out another and looked intently at him. He closed his mouth tightly and waited, straining so hard not to blink under her stare that his eyes began to tear-up. She appeared to count to an arbitrary number, and then smiled and looked away. Picking two more perrenuts out of the bowl, she pressed all three into his hand. 'Take them home. Three in a row gives a good thrill.'

He closed his fist over the small gift and answered drily, 'Thanks. I'll share them with my friends.'

She smiled at that, but anything that might have been said was lost when the coach blew his whistle. Rafi automatically started running to the Wall before he realised he had forgotten to say goodbye, but when he looked back her eyes were already fixed once more on the swirling patterns of the screen.

Master Silyan limped briskly towards the sound of breaking furniture and yelling boys. It was far too early in the morning for such energy, but not entirely surprising as the weekend had almost arrived. Two bodies were on the ground in a grim lock that pointed their limbs in painful and unexpected directions and a cheering audience surrounded them. He banged the door hard with one of Galia's heavy canes, brought specially for the purpose, and was gratified to see the elements of the audience scatter to their beds and the antagonistic human knot unwind itself with reluctant obedience and shuffle back to corners.

'What's going on here?' He knew he would get no satisfactory answer, so he proceeded immediately into a lecture on the earliness of the hour, their complete lack of consideration and the punishment for fighting outside of the bounds of the gymnasia. When he closed the door at last, feeling greatly relieved, he almost ran into Abowen. The boy nervously dodged sideways and nearly dropped his bag.

'Master Silyan! Good morning.'

'Abowen, you're up very early on a Friday – and dressed for town, too. What are you planning to do?'

'It's the weekend, sir. I'm going to visit my mother?' He said the last with a curious, questioning emphasis.

'You're going to visit your mother in Tlaxce City,' Silyan stated calmly. 'Of course. Carry on. You don't want to miss the train.'

*   *   *

Five hours passed before Master Silyan remembered that Rafi had not been wearing his cap. By the following morning he finally recalled that Rafi had been assigned as his Saturday boy. It was Sunday before he acknowledged to himself that something might be wrong. By Monday, it was too late.

CHAPTER THREE

'We love having you visit, but really, don't you think this is a little short notice?'

Delarua looked at her nephew for an explanation. She had responded immediately, coming directly from the city to meet him at the outermost commuter station. He had been happy to see her but curiously laconic, and now he only shrugged and stared out of the window.

'I called as soon as I reached a public comm,' he said.

'I don't mind. It's just that I need to catch up on some work appointments in the city. You'll have to spend most of today with your mother and your sister,' Delarua said.

Rafi was quiet for a moment. 'Is Gran visiting, too, by any chance?'

Delarua eyed him. The train would reach Tlaxce City Centre shortly, but one of the stops was the Lakeside station, near her mother's place. 'No. You want to go see her? I'm not sure that she's in.'

He shrugged wordlessly, the repeated, meaningless gesture guaranteed to irritate, but she persisted.

'Tell me now so I can signal the stop,' she warned him.

'It's fine. So it'll be just us three.'

She examined his expression with genuine anxiety. Never would she forget that she had failed him when he had needed her most. 'Will that be a problem?'

'No,' he replied, then spoiled it with a sigh.

'Your mother misses you,' she offered quietly.

He kept silent. The view through the train window flashed green wooded parks and neatly organised suburbia, but over all was the ghost of the boy's faint reflection, pensive and pondering and sad.

'Rafi,' she said. It was a question and a plea. It was a lost call begging for a response.

He leaned against her, too tall now to rest his head on her shoulder, but his cheek settled against her temple. 'It's fine.'

Whether he was fine or not, she had people to see and work to do. On arrival, she took him straight to her old apartment – now her sister's – and assessed the meeting of mother and son with a critical eye. Maria hugged him warmly, Rafi relaxed and returned the hug before pulling away, and there was nothing in the timing that could not be put down to the natural inclination of young men to resist being treated like babies. Little Gracie – much bigger now – was a much easier encounter. She screamed happily and ran to her big brother with unreserved glee. He laughed, picked her up and spun her around. Delarua exhaled her worry. They were fine. It really was fine. A few hours would be no problem at all.

By noon she was facing an irate Maria in the living room. Gracie was on the other side of a closed bedroom door (with her ear stuck to the door, if Delarua was any judge), and Rafi was downstairs in the foyer, sitting and nursing a bruised forehead in sullen silence.

'Maria, stop pacing, stop flinging your hands about and please tell me what happened!'

Maria immediately flung her right hand towards Gracie's closed bedroom door in a dramatic fashion. 'He was *tickling* her! Making her laugh!'

Delarua shook her head slowly, dazed at the mundane revelation. 'What? Oh. You mean . . .'

'Yes! *He wasn't using his fingers!*'

Delarua opened her mouth and found herself stuck. She closed her mouth, rubbed her face with both hands, gripped her hair tightly in both fists, then tried again. 'You know, I've seen him do that before. It's harmless.' It *was* harmless. It was a simple trick, a little mental brush against the nerve endings under the skin. And yet . . . not really simple, to be honest. Done wrong it felt like the itching of a thousand angry ants, but Rafi clearly had his skill under sufficient control.

Maria pressed her hands to her face in a perfect picture of horror. Tears filled her eyes. 'Grace, you did not say that. How could you . . . you know everything that's happened. How can you call any of this *harmless*?'

'But Maria, was it really so bad that you had to hit him? With a spatula?'

Maria let the tears spill then, and Delarua felt guilty for two fleeting seconds before her following words erased all sympathy. 'You're as bad as he is, married to that . . . to . . .'

'If you *want* to say "alien",' Delarua said wearily, 'go ahead. Even though he's been here for nearly four years now.'

'You let him into your mind! How do I even know I'm talking to my sister?'

'Pause. Stop. Halt. You did not just accuse my husband of body-snatching me.'

She shook her head vigorously. 'I can't deal with this. If you can, you take him. I don't need this in my life. We don't need this.'

'Maria, ease off the drama. Please. Rafi and I are going to have a nice little break for a week or two and then we'll come back and see how you and Gracie are doing.'

Delarua collected Rafi's belongings without further excitement and went down to the foyer. It hurt to meet her nephew's eyes and see the betrayal and self-loathing there, but meet them she did. She unashamedly poured warmth and light towards him until he managed a tiny smile and stood up.

'Home?' he queried. The word was heartbreaking.

'Home,' she replied, 'but I have one more appointment this afternoon at the Sadiri Consulate. I hope you can stay out of trouble until then. Do you want to stay in the city until I'm ready, or should I pack you into a car pre-programmed for Sadira-on-Cygnus?'

He shrugged again, but this time it was less obnoxious. 'I can wait and travel with you. I promise I'll be good. I have some research to do.'

She laughed at him. 'Research, young man? Impressive! I'll set up a libraries and museums list for your comm.'

'And ministries,' he said quickly. 'Big project,' he added in reply to her look of curiosity.

'Fine, ministries, too. In fact, let me put you in touch with Gilda, my old workmate. She's expert at city tours.'

His expression turned apprehensive. 'Is that the woman Gran told me to stay away from?'

Delarua chuckled. Gilda *could* be a bit much. 'I'll tell her to keep it child-friendly.'

They took an autocab towards the bureaucratic quarter and parted ways at the main entrance of the tower that housed the Sadiri Consulate. Delarua started up the steps briskly, paused and looked over her shoulder, watching as Rafi chose a pedestrian path with only a touch of the homesteader's hesitation in the city. He carried his weekend pack over his shoulder like a new, raw collegian and glanced often at his comm, but there was something to his posture and stride, an air of purposefulness that made it unlikely anyone would take advantage of him. He was distant from her now – her own fault – and she was worried about him. Nevertheless, there were other distractions that would not wait for a convenient time. She faced the doors of the Consulate once more, drew together what courage she could manage and went in.

It was no longer a friendly place. Naraldi was no longer the Consul, and the Government of New Sadira had sent a replacement who was, to put it mildly, *tolerated*. He had been obvious in his dislike of the creeping Cygnianisation of his staff, and brusque in his dealings with the settlement's Councillors and was thoroughly hated by all female Sadiri for his inappropriate attentions. However, he was efficient, dedicated and the sole link with New Sadira. Tolerance was the only option. She tried to remember that when she entered his office and faced the man seated behind the desk.

'Grace Delarua?'

When he greeted her, his nod not quite dismissive though never respectful, she was reminded that tolerance worked both ways.

'Consul Vranhil,' she replied, offering an empty answer to his useless question.

'You are not the person I was expecting.'

'I know. Those whom you were expecting believed it appropriate to send me to convey their apologies.' She had honed her diplomacy dancing in the half-shadows of Dllenahkh's mind, a quintessentially Sadiri mind if ever there was one.

'I can accept the apology for the denied request – I understand that Dllenahkh has many demands on his time – but an order disobeyed? That requires more than mere apology. Where is Commander Nasiha?'

Delarua bowed her head for a moment. In that moment, Consul Vranhil affected to remember his manners and gestured to a chair. She sat, took a second moment and spoke. 'My colleague has a number of demands on her time as well. Surely you have received her formal request for deferral of posting?'

Vranhil shifted, frowned and spoke with a harsher tone. 'That is indeed the correct procedure, but I question whether it is appropriate given the lengthy duration of communications between Cygnus Beta and New Sadira.'

Delarua decided to be reckless. She leaned forward. 'We will be guided by you, Consul. Commander Nasiha only wishes to do her duty to her people and to the next generation of her people.' There. Nasiha had to have some status as the mother of a pure-blooded Sadiri child. What could the Consul say to that?

'Lieutenant Tarik, is he well?'

Delarua resisted the urge to bite her tongue and smiled instead. 'Busy. As you know, he is, like his wife, one of the foremost in research on Cygnian communities of taSadiri. As a result, he is much sought after as an intercultural liaison.'

'So are you, Ms Delarua,' said the Consul.

Delarua acknowledged the compliment with a nod and hid her suspicion at the flattery.

'Perhaps you can manage with Lieutenant Tarik as your main partner in the consultancy and allow Commander Nasiha to return to New Sadira as ordered.'

'Allow?' Delarua said softly, nonplussed.

Consul Vranhil clasped his hands together, set his elbows on the desk and became stern. 'You have shown me a very impressive blend of Ntshune and Sadiri diplomacy and speech, but the situation remains the same. New Sadira is awaiting the arrival of Commander Nasiha. Further delay will lead to unpleasant consequences beyond my control. Arrangements have been made for the Commander's passage to New Sadira via Punartam. Please make it clear to her that acceptance is the most appropriate action.'

'Passage . . . for the Commander only? Not for her son, nor her husband?' Delarua had to ask. Every negotiation had its fallback position, and she knew that if Nasiha had to leave, she would not want to go alone.

'New Sadira has a surplus of males, Ms Delarua. It would be foolish to waste resources bringing in more.' Consul Vranhil met her eyes with a fleeting expression of mild shame, but then he quickly straightened and briskly spoke. 'I have other matters to attend to today and I must not fall behind on my schedule. Farewell, Ms Delarua.'

She said her goodbyes in one last show of near-Sadiri diplomacy, maintaining as much poise and calm as possible. Then, as soon as the doors of the Consulate had closed behind her, she kicked the wall and silently cursed the men of New Sadiri and their *inappropriate* desire for every single pureblooded Sadiri female left in the galaxy.

A certain amount of quiet conversation took place during the latter part of the journey to the homestead. Worrying over the stalemate with the Consul preoccupied Delarua for a while, but Rafi's casual stoicism gradually reminded her that here was a problem she had a better chance of solving. There had been a time when silence or humour was the easier option, but Delarua had learned to be brave since then.

'She *does* love you. But . . . but . . . she's stopped trusting her feelings. That's going to take some time to come back. You understand what I'm telling you. If you don't keep at it, if you back off because she makes it too difficult, she'll convince herself that you never cared about her or Gracie.'

Rafi said nothing, and Delarua waited anxiously, biting back the urge to overtalk the issue.

'You make it sound like so much hard work,' he said at last.

'I'm sorry, Rafi, but the truth is you're much stronger than she is right now, and you have to be the mature one. I'll try my best from my side, but all I'm asking of you is that you don't give up on your mother.'

'You're more my mother—'

'Stop that. That's not a compliment, not now. Promise me, Rafi.'

He sighed, but promised. 'I will not give up on my mother and my sister.'

Delarua smiled at last. 'Thank you.'

After a late arrival and an even later dinner, Rafi felt himself relaxing immediately. There was a comfortableness about the main house of the homestead. The design was somewhere between communal and individual, and the result was kind to guests. Open rooms enclosed a small indoor garden in a configuration that was familiar in several Terran cultures: herbs, flowering shrubs and a small tree exuding a subtle, calming perfume. Stairs at the far end of the garden led up to the roof; broad, glassless windows throughout let in the starlight and the night breezes but kept out the insects and other, larger night prowlers. There were no closed doors within, no blind corners and no questionable shadows to make a stranger feel lost or uneasy.

Most of the familiar faces were present in the dining room. Nasiha had quickly finished her meal and excused herself to return to Tarik, who was in their rooms watching over their sleeping child. While he enjoyed the last of his dessert, Freyda told him that Lanuri was at a committee meeting for the development of Grand Bay and Joral was working at the Sadiri Sub-Consulate for the heritage communities of Vaya Province. The Sadiri settlement was another world with a buzz and activity that made the Lyceum feel artificial and trivial. Rafi especially admired Dllenahkh, his aunt's husband and a former Councillor, who appeared to have an informal advisory role in everything from the new strain of sweetgrass in the greenhouses to the social fabric of the settlement itself.

'Some of the men are asking to become co-husbands,' Dllenahkh remarked casually.

'What?' Aunt Grace sounded wary and uncertain rather than shocked.

'It *is* one of the options offered by the Ministry of Family Planning. It would reduce the number of single men and increase community bonds,' Dllenahkh explained and drank his water peacefully.

There was a small silence, then, 'Do *you* think I should take a second husband?'

Dllenahkh started. It had clearly not crossed his mind. 'No . . . no. I do not think that would be appropriate.'

Aunt Grace looked down at her plate with a small smile. Dllenahkh blinked at the remaining water in his glass.

'Don't you hate,' murmured Freyda to Rafi, 'how they pretend to ignore each other when they're communicating without words?' She spoke with humour and no bitterness whatsoever, but he felt a trace of wistfulness leaking through.

'Do *you* want another husband?' he asked her.

She smacked the side of his head lightly. 'You're too young for me,' she teased him.

'Aie! I didn't mean *me!*'

She almost laughed, but her face sobered suddenly. 'I want to go to Punartam, but Lanuri won't . . .' The unfinished sentence made Rafi itch. Won't let me? Won't come with me? 'There's a lot happening on Punartam, like research and debates on the future of the galaxy. Delarua doesn't realise. She listens to Nasiha and Dllenahkh and their sources, and I doubt New Sadira is putting out objective reports on the state of galactic affairs.'

'You're a biotech specialist?' Rafi asked, puzzled but taking care to match her light, conversational tone. *Tell me your secrets.*

'Yes, and I talk to colleagues in other fields. They're keen to talk to me. Everyone wants to know what the Cygnian Sadiri are doing and saying.' She mumbled the next words, words he was sure he was not meant to hear. 'Delarua is too busy living her dream life.' She caught the edge of Rafi's sudden tension, saw the way he bit his lip on a retort and became defensive. 'It's a beautiful place. A lovely community.' That wistfulness again, trailing her final words into a fading fall. 'We don't all share the same happy-ever-after. Even if it existed.' She paused. 'But life is good.'

Good, Rafi thought. *Good is better than a shared happy-ever-after.* He didn't trust those.

'Well,' said Aunt Grace abruptly, 'I need to talk to Freyda and Nasiha about a few things. Dllenahkh, take Rafi for a walk and show him what's changed since he was last here.'

Rafi blinked at the sudden dismissal and realised there was a very slight strangeness in the atmosphere, the kind of cautious air that comes from having a group of people talking around one person unaware of their greatest secret.

Dllenahkh took Rafi to the meditation hall, guessing correctly that he would be most interested in and distracted by their new microgravity Wall – not at all the standard for proper Wallrunning drills, but still useful training for those who wanted to keep their sense of three-dimensional space while planetside. It was especially popular with their growing community of pilots. Rafi gladly tried it out while Dllenahkh monitored the controls via handheld and pondered the discussion that was taking place back at the main house.

He was still very much absorbed when Rafi dropped down to the floor and suddenly demanded, 'I want you to push me.'

Dllenahkh set the handheld back in its slot and gave the youngster a puzzled look.

'You're powerful. You stopped my father. *Push* me,' Rafi insisted.

Still puzzled, Dllenahkh walked over to Rafi, set his hand under his sternum and shoved him so forcefully that he flew backwards, bounced off the wall and fell onto the floor. Rafi curled up slowly, holding his stomach and squinting hard as his eyes watered.

'That's . . . not what I meant,' he gasped.

Dllenahkh crouched beside him but did not move to touch him or help him up. 'No? But that was power, too, was it not?'

'Your mind . . . I meant with your mind.'

'Ah. I see.'

He sat on the floor, back to the wall, and waited. Eventually, Rafi's breath evened out and his body uncurled slightly, though his eyes remained closed as he struggled with the slow ebb of the nerve pain.

Dllenahkh continued the casual tone of the conversation. 'May I ask *why* you want to be pushed?'

He did not expect an answer and no answer was given. He sighed.

'There are several possible reasons for such a request. I hope that fear of what I could do to your aunt is not included among them.'

'No,' Rafi whispered. 'I don't think you'd hurt her. Not ever.'

Dllenahkh grimaced. '*Ever* is too great an accomplishment for any mortal, as you well know. If you do not fear for your aunt, then perhaps you fear for yourself, that I might . . . *stop* you as I once stopped your father?'

Rafi's breathing had been growing smoother and slower, but at that it hitched and quickened.

'Or you fear that no one will be powerful enough to stop you if you need to be stopped,' Dllenahkh concluded. He examined the wooden beams of the ceiling so that his nephew could take a moment to shed a few tears privately.

'I cannot stop you. I can help you stop yourself. That is all I can do for anyone.'

The boy raised his head at last, no longer caring about hiding his wet face. 'Do that for me. I can't stand the nightmares any more.'

This was news to Dllenahkh. 'How long have you been having nightmares?'

Rafi bit his lip hard. 'Since they gave me the cap,' he whispered.

'Cap?' Dllenahkh said, confused. 'Please explain?'

Rafi told him about the cap and his brief research on the use of caps for diagnosis or punishment. He stuttered for a moment, and then slowly described his nightmares. Dllenahkh absorbed the information in a silence that was deeply ominous, not least for the sensation of growing tension like the silent, rapid build of a thunderhead.

'Thank you for telling me this,' he said at last. 'May I discuss it with your aunt? It might be better for us to jointly assess whether the treatment you are enduring is in your best interests.'

Rafi exhaled loudly, a sound of utter relief. 'Yes. Yes, please.'

Dllenahkh patted his shoulder reassuringly and got to his feet. 'Concerning power, bear in mind that if you fear the strong, you should also fear the gentle. They slip under your guard so easily, and it takes only the smallest push to overwhelm an unsteady base.'

'Like my aunt did to you?' Rafi grinned at Dllenahkh.

He smiled and allowed the boy a few seconds of apparent triumph before replying. 'There are times when taking a fall is the right strategy.'

They went back to the main house. Freyda and Nasiha were sitting on the edge of their chairs, leaning over a low table with scattered documents and three handhelds. Aunt Grace was perched on a stool beside the bar, empty-handed and frowning as she hugged one knee to her chest and looked at her friends. They had finished their discussion, but they quickly gave Rafi a small share of their secrets as he introduced his own dilemma.

'Nasiha and the New Sadira government. You and the Cygnian government. That's two of you I have to worry about now,' his aunt fretted.

'But I thought Nasiha was expected to return to service?' Rafi asked in bewilderment, watching as Dllenahkh sat beside Nasiha and picked up one of the handhelds with a heavy sigh.

Aunt Grace looked at him without expression. 'New Sadira is not the best place to be right now. That's none of your concern, however. Let's talk about how we're going to get you out of that school without you getting brain-tagged for the rest of your life.'

'You've never asked me . . .' He hesitated, as if all too aware that his words could smash the last unfractured security of his childhood. 'You don't ask what I can do. Is that . . . is that you or me?'

Aunt Grace gave him a puzzled, sympathetic look. 'You don't know?'

She reached out and took hold of his hand, pulled him close. She was now small enough to tuck under his shoulder, a new thing that made the once-familiar warmth strange. He awkwardly pressed against the side of her updrawn knee and the edge of the stool and hugged her.

'It's both. You and me. You're a lot like me, but much stronger. You can charm, and you can . . .' She stopped, seeking the right word. 'Quieten. *Lull*. I never wanted you to be worried or scared of what you are, and you didn't want me to worry either, so you persuaded me and I persuaded you. We mutually pacified our curiosity. Not the wisest thing I've done, I admit, but . . .'

She fell silent, but he imagined he knew her thoughts. They were both wondering how much should be allowed for the sake of wanting your loved ones to be happy.

He pulled away gently and sat on the stool next to hers. 'You know, I'll be fifteen soon.'

Aunt Grace smiled. 'Counting down the days?'

'Three weeks, five days,' he replied with a laugh. 'Then I'm a homesteader grown and no one's responsibility.'

Her smile vanished immediately. 'No. No you don't.'

'You're not my guardian,' he reminded her, keeping his voice low, reasonable and not in the least accusing. 'I'm still registered as a homesteader, otherwise you could have kept me till seventeen.'

'You can't do this to Maria,' she whispered angrily. The whisper was useless for privacy. Rafi saw at the edge of his vision when Dllenahkh raised his head and looked at them, perplexed, then returned his gaze to his handheld with a reluctance that hinted at divided attention. He continued to protest quietly. 'I'm not trying to do anything to anyone. I'm trying to get control over my life.'

'You'll get *some* control and you'll lose *a lot* of protection. There's no easy solution to this, Rafi. Let's think things over carefully before we make any grand gestures.'

Rafi opened his mouth, paused, then rushed on before fear or common sense could make him hold his tongue. 'It's already in process. I . . . I went to the Registration Bureau in the City.'

'Your so-called research – you idiot! No, *I'm* the idiot, trusting you not to get into trouble in one afternoon!'

Her voice grew too loud to be ignored. Rafi looked anxiously at the faces now turned in their direction. 'It's not as bad as it sounds,' he insisted to the room at large. 'It's perfectly legal.'

Nasiha glanced very quickly at Aunt Grace, her eyes flickering over for a split second before coming back to give him a pensive look, and in that moment Rafi felt intensely guilty, as if her problem were being weighed in the balance with his. He was an unexpected, unwanted distraction, a family embarrassment derailing a serious matter of interplanetary importance.

'It won't be finalised until my birthday,' he said, seeking a graceful retreat. 'We can deal with it later.'

It was easy when you knew what to watch for. Dllenahkh gave his wife a look that was somehow both stern and pleading. She bit her lip, her eyes anguished as she answered her husband's silent communication, then blinked and smoothed her features leaving only a slight tension in her jaw as she spoke her words softly through clenched teeth.

'Go to bed, Rafi, straight to bed. Don't do anything – don't even *think* about doing anything until we discuss this again.'

Feeling thoroughly shamed, Rafi got up and walked quickly out of the house, running an uncomfortable gauntlet of guarded, sympathetic, querying and worried looks. At first he kept his head down as he took the short path to the living quarters, but the night breeze was so cool and comforting that he gradually lifted his heated face to the sky and slowed his pace. Stars shone intermittently through patches of drifting cloud, serene and timeless beyond the changeable atmosphere. He glanced back at the lit windows of the main house, suddenly wishing he were an adult in truth and fact, someone who could be told secrets and asked opinions, someone who could help give protection rather than always needing it.

If he had remained on the homestead, he could have used his majority to take up work at another homesteading with no need for permission or blessing. If he had remained there and the past two years had not happened and there was no cap with his name attached to it. If he had remained there and never had a father – only a mother, a sister and a normal household with the ordinary struggle of selfishness and love.

But he had a family that was not normal and a brain that was not normal and the government was too interested in both. When he stopped to think about it, he could not for the life of him see how officially becoming an adult was going to make that situation any better.

CHAPTER FOUR

Rafi had forgotten what it was like to sleep easily without nightmares or student pranks to disturb him. He should have been awake and stressed about when he would be missed at the Lyceum, but instead the next day came at sunrise instead of midnight. He stretched blissfully, cuddled his pillow and listened a while to the morning birdsong before drifting off into a few more hours of slumber.

A tugging on his ankle finally woke him. 'Get up and eat before breakfast becomes lunch,' his uncle told him.

He uncurled slowly. 'Aunt Grace?' he mumbled. She would never have let him sleep so late as to miss breakfast.

'She's attending to a business matter with a colleague.'

Rafi sat up straight and alert. 'What—'

'It has nothing to do with you,' Dllenahkh interrupted.

He fell back with a dramatic thud. Part of him wanted to wake up and find his problem solved and another part was scared of what kind of solution his aunt might put together.

His uncle chuckled quietly. 'Life looks easier after a meal. Come.'

Rafi got up and followed Dllenahkh into the main house where he allowed himself to be fed familiar fruit, unfamiliar curds, soft and bland, which might have been dairy or vegetable in origin, and a strongly seasoned broth which burned away the last traces of his fatigue and set his ears tingling. Dllenahkh joined him at the table but only drank tea and scanned his handheld idly.

Rafi looked around with more attention. 'Where *is* everybody?'

'Out on business,' Dllenahkh replied absently, still intent on his reading material.

Rafi stared at him until he stiffened, raised his head and stared back apologetically. 'It is better for me not to know details. I'm very bad at lying and I am the first one they would ask. I have tried to maintain a neutral position in all this.'

'How is that even possible?' Rafi demanded. 'Can't they make you order her to leave?'

Dllenahkh winced at his bluntness. 'It is a strange but not uncommon situation. By Cygnian homesteading law, I do indeed have that authority over the Commander. However, according to Sadiri spacefaring regulations, the Commander most certainly outranks me. I could order her to leave the homestead, but I could not order her to leave the homesteading, nor the planet. Few remain in the Science Council who outrank the Commander, and most of those are occupied with research on Punartam. Her behaviour may be described as negligent, but the structure no longer exists for it to be called illegal.'

Rafi took a momentary guilty pleasure in the complications of someone else's life – very momentary.

'So, as I am not in a position to help Commander Nasiha, Grace has asked me to talk to you about your situation. I understand that you will not be missed for a little while yet?'

'I don't know,' Rafi mumbled into his second cup of broth. 'Lots of people go away for the weekend, but I'm not sure how long Master Silyan will forget I'm supposed to be there.'

'Hm. Your mother has barred you from her Tlaxce residence. Your grandmother travels frequently and I'm sure you would agree that it would be irresponsible to involve her in this kind of trouble at her age. I *do* have the authority to make you leave this homestead, and you can't . . . *persuade* me to allow you to stay.'

He listened in horror as Dllenahkh implacably reeled off his list of dead-end options. 'I thought you were supposed to be helping me.'

'Pretend for a moment that I will not help you. What will you do?'

Panic, Rafi thought immediately, but he bit his lip and controlled his breathing. 'What I've already done. I can apply for adult status and go to another homesteading.'

'You are sure that Central Government will leave you alone?'

'I'll go to a *remote* homesteading,' Rafi said stubbornly.

'You could have done that a year or two ago but not now, not when the government is starting to ask questions about you and those questions are not yet answered.'

'Go back to the Lyceum? No!' Rafi's voice shook very slightly on the last word. He swallowed and breathed deeply again. It was actually very clever of his aunt to delegate this discussion to her husband. There was something about Dllenahkh that made him want to match the elder's calmness and maturity. He wanted Dllenahkh to take him seriously – which he was clearly doing, uncomfortable though it was.

'Grace and I have discussed this and we do not believe that returning to the Lyceum is the right thing for you to do.'

At first Rafi was comforted, but then he felt suddenly and deeply suspicious. 'Is she listening in on your thoughts right now?'

Dllenahkh shook his head with a smile. 'We have become very good at keeping secrets from each other. It began as a game, but it has proven useful on other occasions. She too prefers not to dissemble, and she cannot tell what she does not know.'

Rafi thought he heard a slight, sibilant stutter on the *dissemble* which then rendered it *disassemble* to his ear and sent him on a mental digression with images of government interrogators picking his aunt's mind to pieces and curiously turning the smooth fragments over in their hands like tourists examining pebbles on the beach. The brain was a bit-piece sculpture of specialised and adaptable segments, and the mind a nebulous entity of chemistry, energy and mystical *je ne sais quoi* that still baffled Cygnian scientists. How would his aunt pretend to not know? Don't turn over that rock, don't look at the words boldly written on the surface underneath. The question felt familiar in ways that were both exciting and disturbing.

'You influence each other,' he accused.

Dllenahkh dipped his head briefly in apologetic acknowledgement. 'Not quite *influence* but . . . something. Openly, in full awareness and with full agreement.'

'She must really trust you.'

'And I her. The things she could do to me if she wished . . . but we are wandering away from the subject at hand. You. What is to become of you? Where will you go? We may be concerned for your well-being and honoured by your confidences, but is it wise for us – your aunt and I – to hold such information when we work so hard to convince the government of our compliance with Cygnian law?' It was hard to read Dllenahkh's face. His eyes rested steadily on Rafi, conveying a sense of stability and reassurance that did not mesh well with his words of cold self-interest. 'We are not in a position to take risks, but fortunately we know someone who is.'

He got up from the table as if that was the end of the conversation. Rafi looked up at him in complete confusion. Dllenahkh started to walk away, then paused and said casually, 'You should rest for the remainder of the day. It may make you wakeful during the night but . . . well . . . we shall be able to find something for you to do.'

Dllenahkh stepped out of the dining room, crossed the garden and left through the front doors before Rafi could move his lips to frame a sensible question.

If nothing else, the way he was completely left to himself indicated how much there was going on beneath the surface at the homestead. His aunt put her head around his bedroom door around mid-afternoon, her eyes tired and her face uncharacteristically glum. She saw that he had a snack and a spare handheld, nodded as if to reassure herself that he was not being neglected and weakly returned his 'it's okay' smile. His smile did not lie; it *was* okay. Sleep and trust and love combined was the panacea, a day of idleness perfected the recipe, and if – *if* – there was something else to his peace, some air that breathed in and through each human mind, it did not surprise him that even during a time of uncertainty the Dllenahkh homestead had a more wholesome savour than the secretive, competitive Lyceum. And yet he did not know how he knew this. The Lyceum taught ancient civilisations, ethics, philosophy and sociology. It taught structure, organisation, rules and duties. It did not teach root causes and reasons, nor anything beyond the boundaries of its narrow remit of socialising the dangerously gifted.

That was going to change. Dllenahkh had given him a hand-held . . . not the student slate open to all the teachers' eyes, nor yet a junior handheld with restricted access, but a guest handheld with wide-open access answerable only to the settlement's author-ities. In addition to that, he still had an old but serviceable datacharm – a gift from Aunt Grace years and years ago, when she used to send trinkets and letters by post. It had been a useful eccentricity which got past his father's notice in a way that could not have been managed by calling or sending messages via the family comm. The charm was similarly eccentric and useful, resembling a tiny padlock made of dark wood and brass (and whether it was truly wood and metal, he had no idea). He had quietly left it at his grandmother's condo before attending the Lyceum, then just as quietly moved it to his mother's place in the City.

Tucked in a lazy nest of sheets and pillows, he industriously copied every article, report and manual that looked vaguely help-ful, even the ones that were too technical for him to understand. Then he began collecting what looked interesting. Anything authored or co-authored by his aunt and her friends automat-ically made it in, which left him with an eclectic selection from biodome waste treatment to the history of interplanetary liaisons on Cygnus Beta. He went from skimming summaries to reading and fell asleep so suddenly that when he woke up and found the room dark he panicked, thinking bizarrely that he had slept away the weekend and it was time to leave the homestead.

At last he remembered where he was, checked the time on

the handheld and saw it was barely two hours past sunset. He carefully shook the datacharm out of the bed-sheets and into his hand. The original wristband had disintegrated long ago, so he unhooked the lanyard from the handheld and fiddled until he had a double-loop high on his arm and the charm securely attached to it, resting between his inner arm and side ribs. He prayed that it was waterproof. He had done a lot of nervous sweating over the past few weeks and he doubted that would improve.

Dllenahkh looked in on him very soon after. 'Get ready. It will be wet and windy, so dress appropriately.'

'What about you?' Rafi asked, eyeing his uncle's light tunic, short trousers and sandals.

'I won't be going with you,' Dllenahkh replied. 'Commander Nasiha will meet you at the front gate in half an hour. Do not be late.'

His excitement turned to nerves. Commander Nasiha was scary at the best of times, and with the distractions of her new trouble she appeared even colder. He got himself ready with the swiftness of a Military Services recruit and half-ran to the dining room to snatch some portable food from the cupboard. If he thought this extra piece of preparedness would earn him points from the Commander, he was wrong. When he came hurrying to the gate to meet her, she began to sniff the air as he approached and pre-empted his stammered greeting with, 'What is that?'

He stared at the bundle in his hand for inspiration, almost forgetting what he had grabbed. 'Cold meat paste and pickled vegetables in flatbread.'

'It stinks,' she declared.

'Ah . . . that's probably the fermented hot sauce,' he mumbled.

She took it out of his hand and whipped it briskly into the

hedge near the gate – not with anger, but with enough determined force to make sure it settled firmly behind the spiky twigs
and broad foliage. 'Dangerous. You can eat when we return, but
that is the worst possible choice for this trip.'

'But I don't even know where we're going!' he wailed, his anxiety about the larger adventure overcoming his shyness with
Commander Nasiha.

She was taken aback. 'You do not? What did Dllenahkh tell
you?'

'He told me to sleep and to meet you, nothing more!'

She pursed her lips, considering, but soon the line of her mouth
softened and she allowed a small smile to show, tacitly approving
the secrecy. 'Then follow me,' she commanded.

He followed. She went through the gate and turned down the
road that led away from the main highway. First it was a quick
walk, later she gradually increased the pace to a jog, and then,
before he could protest or even ask why, they were almost running along the dirt track, crunching old leaves and gravel under
their feet. The road's footlights came awake on sensing motion
and painted the way ahead in a faint red haze that matched their
pace. However, as they left the gates behind, the lighting gradually thinned then ended, leaving only starlight partly obscured
by the trees marking the boundary of the homestead.

Wallrunning practice had made Rafi fitter, but Commander
Nasiha was still slightly taller, with a longer stride and the certainty of knowing her destination. She waited on him when he
stopped, once to catch his breath, a second time to retch un-
productively at the side of the road, and a third time when he
tangled his feet with a stray vine and was brought down roughly.

She pulled him upright and spoke with an attempt at kindliness. 'It is not much farther. We can go slowly now.'

She ran ahead of him, keeping within sight so that he saw when she stopped just where the rise of the road reached its crest. He staggered the last few steps to stand beside her, looked out over the landscape and had a moment of complete disorientation. Stars were in the sky, but there were also unfamiliar constellations below the horizon, twinkling . . . no, not twinkling, *dancing*. He dropped to one knee and breathed deeply to steady his head. Sense gradually returned; he was looking down at Grand Bay: the moving lights were boats and buoys on the waves; a fixed sprinkle of stardust showed the line of the coast; and a handful of bright fingers fanning out was a grouping of piers of varying lengths. It was very pretty, but nothing worth running for.

Commander Nasiha led the way downhill, talking as if she had been strolling all the way. 'This is where the pilots stay when they come to Cygnus Beta. Of course, there are staff lodgings at the Tlaxce City terminal, but it is not too strange that Sadiri pilots would wish to visit their settlement. Sometimes they bring their ships. Why not? More and more young ships and dwarf ships are being pressed into service after the fleet losses. They transport important communications and key personnel, and they are small enough to manage planetfall into Cygnian oceans.'

She turned to Rafi for a moment. Her face was unreadable in the dark but her voice held a hint of dry humour. 'Few planets have the resources to patrol and police the depth and breadth of their oceans.'

Later, Rafi realised she had been attempting to prepare him for what he was about to see, and if he had been paying more attention to what at first appeared to be small talk, he might have been less confused. It would *not* have lessened the shock. His eyes widened, his steps slowed and at last he stood on the sand a few metres away from the main pier, staring and staring at the massive silhouettes that reared from the water and blotted out the stars. At first he imagined them to be closer and smaller, but when his brain finally took in the entire scene, including the length of the pier and the regular spacing of its lights, he understood at last and let out a squeak that was both excitement and fear.

Commander Nasiha looked at him worriedly. 'Do you feel unwell? Perhaps you would like to vomit again? It would be best to continue this night on an empty stomach.'

He flashed her an indignant glare. 'I'm fine. I would better if you hadn't tried to kill me with all the running, but I'm fine.'

She gave an approving nod at his show of determination. 'Come.'

The main pier was busy and *long*. Several boats were moored along its lower level, but the upper level was a place of recreational talking and walking. Rafi recognised the pilots with their long hair and slightly odd gait that spoke of recent unfamiliarity with Cygnian gravity, but there were a few Sadiri settlers present, immediately identifiable by their ease with both the gravity and the environs. Then there were one or two others, most likely Cygnian though he could not guarantee it, very ordinary in appearance apart from some quirks of regional dress but bearing the same expression of wonder, confusion and excitement. They were, like him, probably seeing the place for the first time. And yet no one challenged them, no one asked where they were going and what business they had there. If there was any secret to the nocturnal activities of Grand Bay, it was hiding in plain sight – his favourite tactic.

The Commander stopped suddenly, her attention caught by a man walking along in conversation with three pilots. It was hard to place him: if he was a pilot, his hair was too short and his stride too comfortable, but then again, his clothes were too strange for a local and his demeanour too relaxed for a newcomer. She put out a hand and touched his arm before he could pass, and he jumped, more in delight than surprise.

'Commander!' He waved the strolling pilots on with a smile and a nod, then he spoke to her in Sadiri, which Rafi knew far too little of, but his lips were slightly smiling and his eyes flitted over to Rafi once or twice in a manner that felt deliberately sly.

'You are Grace Delarua's nephew,' he said warmly, addressing Rafi at last.

Rafi smiled and felt a little calmer. In the settlement, at least, Grace Delarua's nephew was a good thing to be.

'I am Naraldi. Dllenahkh has told me a little about you, but not very much. Commander Nasiha has told me a little about your father, but again, not very much. Tell me, can you swim?'

Rafi gaped, unable to find a coherent response. He had heard of Naraldi – the former Sadiri Consul, semi-retired pilot and political activist – and that was reason enough to stutter, but his paralysis had more to do with the mention of his father. Nasiha nudged him and broke the spell. 'Yes. A bit, I mean. I've never swum in an ocean, only lakes and pools.'

'Well, enough not to panic, at least,' Naraldi remarked. 'Let's go out a little farther.'

Rafi followed Naraldi's loping paces. He longed for the courage to demand of Commander Nasiha why she was discussing his father with other Sadiri, but he only managed one reproachful look which she might have noticed but did not deign to acknowledge. He did not have long to brood over it. They soon reached a part of the pier that swayed with the currents, its structure tethered by cables to a distant ocean floor. A warm, moist blast of air blew across their path with the briskness of a sneeze and a loud slap made him jump sideways and cry out. *Something* had hit the waves with a swift, flat stroke, but the spray felt like more than salt water. He dabbed his wet cheek warily and sniffed his hand, prepared to be disgusted, but the strange liquid was at least no more viscous than tears. The smell, though . . . it was tart and slightly metallic, like acid with a hint of zinc.

Naraldi rested a hand on his shoulder, but he looked out over the sea as he spoke. 'I am going to introduce you to a ship. There is no need to be afraid. Take your shoes off.'

'Are we going into the water?' Rafi hopped around in excitement, struggling to remove his left shoe.

'Yes, of course,' said Naraldi, calmly taking off shoes, tunic and trousers and putting the clothes into Commander Nasiha's hands.

'Should I take off my clothes, too?' Rafi asked nervously. Was this really Dllenahkh's idea of an appropriate midnight adventure, sending him to go skinny-dipping with his elders?

'Whatever makes you comfortable,' Naraldi said without concern. 'It's warm enough that a little dampness should not trouble you on your way home.'

Rafi wavered, then took off his tunic and dropped it on his shoes. 'I'm ready,' he said.

The Commander gave him a glance that was part amusement, part pity and not a bit comforting. Rafi turned away, dipped under and over the ropes that edged the pier and stood wavering on the overhang. Naraldi joined him and immediately seized him by the elbow. Rafi tried not to flinch at the strength of his fingers. 'Breathe,' Naraldi commanded. 'It's courteous to oxygenate yourself as much as possible.'

'What—' Rafi began, and then he was falling off the pier. Naraldi kept him in a firm grip so that when they hit the water feet first he was more or less vertical. The water was mild but still a shock as it invaded his ears and nose in a painful rush. He struggled free of Naraldi and thrashed upwards to the surface where he blew like a whale, shook water from his head and wept the salt from his eyes. When he could see at last, he turned and scanned the water around him anxiously. Naraldi was a dark blur a few metres away. He was holding on to the lower deck with one hand and watching Rafi closely. Rafi tilted his chin up and up until he could see the edge of the upper deck, and there was Commander Nasiha leaning cautiously over the pier, trying to see everything without accidentally dropping Naraldi's clothes.

'What—' He tried to finish the question he had started before the jump, but his eye was distracted by a cloudy luminescence slowly brightening the water.

'You are in no danger,' Naraldi shouted to him. 'Stay calm.'

That was an impossibility. He could hear the slight change in ambient noise; all the background conversations and movement of other people going about their business shifted towards his side of the pier. Other curious faces joined the Commander's and peered down at him, and the nearby lower deck became suddenly and worryingly full of people coming off their boats and running in from either end of the pier to stare at him treading water. No one looked scared, but everyone looked terribly *interested.* He tried to swim towards Naraldi and was stopped by a soft, painless tug.

'You are in no danger!' Naraldi reiterated in a louder voice. 'Try to relax!'

Rafi cried out quietly – not quite a whimper and nowhere close to a scream, but it was still a cry of distress. The eerie light in the water surrounded him; when he dared look he saw tiny, myriad filaments wafting in the swell of the tide, curling gently around him and fastening onto his skin. Sensation drained away: the caress of water moving against his body became a muted vibration . . . and then there was nothing. He was floating, isolated, numb. The faces along the dock blurred and receded, and the din in his ears grew louder, as if someone had put a tin pot over his head and was marking time with a wooden spoon. The last thing he saw was a vast darkness surrounding him and at the middle of it all a glimpse of his ten toes glowing briefly in the eerie light before they too were swallowed up in the descending oblivion.

He was never able to remember the exact moment when he lost consciousness, which was not particularly unusual. He had been knocked out before during the old homestead days, falling out of a tree when he was barely ten, and he knew that a little amnesia was common. What was unusual was that he could not remember when he regained consciousness. He first became aware that someone was speaking, he heard another voice answering and gradually acknowledged it was his own, and then realised he was staring a collection of shapes, colours and textures that coalesced in a moment of slow recognition under the identity 'Naraldi'. Someone had put a blanket around his shoulders and he was clutching the edges with cold fingers. His face felt tense; he put up a hand to touch his forehead and discovered he was frowning.

' . . . will take some time before we have enough data to reach useful conclusions. Of course we knew from the start that you probably wouldn't be successful, but given your other talents, we were curious to see what would happen when Savvi got a taste of you.'

'Savvi . . . ?' Rafi said. He looked around, collecting himself. They were indoors, sitting at a table. Beside him was a window that looked towards a dark, motionless rise. That was land. And that was a bowl in front of him, steaming and smelling of good broth. There was Commander Nasiha, unexpectedly damp and frowning to herself over another steaming bowl, and beyond her the few occupants of the commissary showed politely curious faces as they glanced over, perhaps to assess his rate of recovery. Naraldi . . . he was fully dressed again and his wet hair was tied up in spiky disarray. Rafi glanced under his blanket to check his own status. Not dressed. But – he wiggled his toes – yes, there were shoes on his feet. He reached out a hand for the bowl and gratefully tipped the warming liquid down his gullet.

Naraldi cleared his throat in a manner that hinted at embarrassment. 'Yes, Savvi. Not the usual mode of naming, I know, but it's barely a year old and the taSadiri who were playing with it became rather attached . . . and so, a name.'

'Are there any taSadiri pilots?' Rafi heard himself ask. It was strange. Part of his brain had been sufficiently awake to begin this conversation, and it appeared as if the rest of him was now alert enough to join in.

Naraldi laughed at the naïveté of the question. 'No, no, these things take time! Generations in some cases. But to be an active passenger, a conscious traveller, with no need for the artificial coma and stasis chamber . . . even that is something.'

'But I'm not Sadiri, not even taSadiri,' Rafi said.

'Yes,' Naraldi agreed, serious again. 'There is some genetic element that we have not yet identified. I am sorry.'

'Why should you be sorry?' Rafi asked. 'I'm sure you have lots of taSadiri volunteers.'

Naraldi bent his head and was silent for so long that Rafi thought he had decided to ignore the question, but then he looked up, shared a swift glance with the Commander and met Rafi's eyes once more. 'It would have been advantageous for you to find a way to leave Cygnus Beta without the knowledge of Central Government, and for that we are sorry.'

In spite of the blanket and the broth, Rafi began to feel cold again.

Commander Nasiha, never one for many words, began to speak. He remembered her demeanour and tone from previous visits to the homestead; she had an abrupt, sometimes harsh manner that could be taken for arrogance and rudeness, but he had gleaned from his aunt's comments that she was a direct thinker, economical with words and very decisive when ready to take action. Now her voice sounded slow, heavy and resentful. 'We attempted to extend the studies on new forms of psi ability that we began with your aunt about two years ago. Normally the research networks are very forthcoming with shared data, and initially that was the case. Over time, we have seen that access withdrawn without explanation.'

Data was being withheld, conclusions could not be drawn, action was risky or had been thwarted outright. No wonder she looked so depressed, unable to trust either home or host authorities.

'We can only speculate why this is so,' she continued, 'but one thing is certain. People have disappeared.'

Another image derailed his train of thought. Many times he had pictured his vanished father with a new identity leading a quiet and utterly ordinary life in a mid-sized town on the fringes, working at some harmless occupation where his charm could not cause trouble for anyone, least of all himself. Now he thought of a room with no windows and thick walls, observers posted at the screens of hidden cameras, visitors made faceless by masks, eye-shades and caps – and the permanent resident and test subject seated within, isolated and bereft of companionship and hope.

His stomach soured and the taste of bile mixed with the broth. He could not believe in the uncanny clarity of that vision; he only knew that it had first appeared in his nightmares when he was made to wear the cap.

'I don't know what to do,' he admitted.

Naraldi leaned closer and so did the Commander. 'We have a suggestion,' said the old pilot.

After a return journey that was far more leisurely, Rafi and Commander Nasiha found the main house lit up as brightly as if it were past midday rather than past midnight. Dllenahkh came to the door to meet them. He put a hand on the Commander's shoulder with a brief look of concern and a nod. Her face relaxed just a bit and she nodded in reply, touching his hand with what could have been either reassurance or gratitude or both. She continued on to the dining room but Rafi did not go with her. He stood in front of his uncle and glared.

'You could have told me I was going to get eaten by a mindship.'

Dllenahkh's eyes went wide and his eyebrows rose up. 'Is that what happened?' He chuckled at Rafi's indignation. 'Don't tell me the details. I am not meant to know, at least not yet. But I knew you'd be safe with Naraldi.'

There was so much more Dllenahkh could have said, so much that Rafi could have asked him, but all queries choked and died as Rafi's mind chased the possibilities. Did Dllenahkh know about the psi studies? Was this another area of calculated ignorance to protect the homestead and the settlement from undue scrutiny? The worst of it was that he honestly could not tell whether Dllenahkh was joking or not, but he bit his lip to stop further argument and chose instead to follow the smell of food that was coming from the dining room and trust only in the promise of a hearty meal.

CHAPTER FIVE

'*Varicella?*' said Master Silyan. He was utterly confused, and he felt that he could ascribe only part of that confusion to the boy's atrocious accent. He knew Ntenman as a gifted linguist and a clever manipulator of the ordinary, non-psi kind, which made this singing speech accompanied by a too-earnest look of sheer sincerity ring all kinds of alerts in Silyan's brain. 'Who gets varicella in this day and age?'

'Well,' Ntenman declared happily, as if Silyan had finally seen the point, 'homesteaders . . . preserving old ways . . . old diseases . . . who knows?'

Silyan looked to the other occupant of his office for clues. Serendipity sat quietly, displaying nothing more than a small, worried frown and giving Ntenman an occasional opaque glance. There was no illumination to be found there. Silyan dropped his gaze to the handheld on the desk before him and the request for three weeks' medical leave showing on the screen. The request had apparently come from Rafi's slate, and that slate was now untraceable, its location function malfunctioning or disabled – a moot point, given that the public transit ticketing records showed Rafi's clear and direct progression to Tlaxce City. It was more than irregular; it was making his Master's instincts scream.

'I shall have to call his mother,' he said unwillingly. It was almost a lie. On Monday, when the fog of a strangely tiring and unproductive weekend had somewhat lifted from his brain, he had tried to contact first the grandmother, then the aunt. Both were unavailable: the former was likely on a boat somewhere in the middle of Tlaxce Lake; the latter ... well, her comm cheerfully invited him to leave a message, but none of his messages had been answered.

The mother, Maria Delarua (formerly Adafydd) o-Montserrat i-Tlaxce, had never been in the habit of replying to messages, hence her position as third on Rafi's emergency contact list.

Ntenman winced, and that ridiculous aura of pure honesty became dimmed with an awkwardness that was far more trust-worthy. 'His mother doesn't really like us Lyceum types, does she?'

Silyan gave him a hard look. 'No,' he said slowly. 'She doesn't.' Varicella indeed! No doubt after the three-week period was up there would be some other excuse, or else complete silence. It was hardly the first time a relative had tried to take a student out of the Lyceum without going through the proper channels. The psi-normal ones were particular offenders in their suspicion and dislike for the school. He would have to submit a report to the Lyceum Board and let their surveyors deal with the recalcitrant family.

He tapped the screen on his handheld clear and straightened in his seat. 'That will be all.'

Ntenman got up and was already at the door until the realisa-tion that Serendipity had not moved from her chair slowed his haste. He gave her a look of puzzled concern; she responded with a brief, reassuring nod which he accepted with some reluctance. Continuing to glance over his shoulder, he stepped out of the office and closed the door behind him.

Silyan frowned slightly. 'How can I help you?'

'Today I submitted my withdrawal from the Lyceum, but it felt rude not to say something to someone in person,' she explained.

He smiled. 'You have always been a guest, Serendipity, not a student. I am only sorry that you will not stay until the end of term.'

She lowered her eyes. 'Some of the others are enjoying their time here. I believe there will always be a connection between the Lyceum and my community.'

He waved off her embarrassment and her stiff attempt at diplomacy. 'Quite understandable. We Sadiri tend to keep to ourselves. The Lyceum is Terran of a very specific era, and what isn't Terran is as much concentrated Ntshune as you could hope to find on Cygnus Beta. They like their communities, too, but they don't mind pulling Terrans in. Once they can keep up, of course.'

She stared at him. 'Are you taSadiri, Master Silyan? I didn't know that.'

'Yes, and no. Most Sadiri pilots live up to their reputation of being totally attached to their ships. A few act more like the Terran sailor stereotype, with a lover in every port. It only becomes unfortunate when psi-gifted offspring are born into a society that isn't really equipped for them. You at least have developed and maintained a culture that supports telepathy. Galia and I have lacked such advantages, and we need the Lyceum far more than you do.'

He truly could not read her mind, nor did he need to when he could see the changes in her face. She appeared to be encountering the sensation of empathy and finding it a new but not unlikeable experience. The moment inspired an unexpected thought that passed unchecked into speech. 'Maybe you should come to visit us.'

He was ridiculously surprised and pleased at the spontaneous invitation. 'I should say yes,' he replied sadly. 'I should say yes and thank you and how soon will you be able to receive us ... but Galia and I have a special kind of tenure at the Lyceum, a tenure that does not permit us to travel beyond its gates.'

It was her turn to show surprise and even more sympathy. It was strange how different she became when she was looking out at others rather than focused in on herself, and sad how rare that difference was. Why did people imagine that telepathy always led to closeness? He could see how her seemingly idyllic community had produced an example of such extreme self-absorption and introversion, victim of a runaway survival mechanism.

After a final formality of courteous farewells, she stood up to leave but took only a few steps towards the door before she hesitated. Before he could ask her what was the matter, she turned and spoke. 'We have a tradition in Tirtha, something they say we kept from the days when we first came to Cygnus Beta. Whenever we travel, we take with us a piece of home to make sure we return.'

She approached his desk, put her hand into the side pocket of her tunic and drew out a small grey stone, slightly spheroid and river-smoothed. 'Here is a stone from the monastery's pool. When you and Mistress Galia visit the monastery, you must put the stone back into the pool.'

He stretched out his hand to take the little gift. He rubbed his thumb over its cool surface and tried to find words. There were none to be found, so instead he gave her a grateful nod and, when he could manage it, a small smile that was neither sad nor faltering. She smiled in return, a crooked, self-conscious smile, and left his office for good.

Serendipity took so long I feared the old boy had taken her captive or something. Not that he looked the type, but . . . pretty little thing like her, schoolmaster who never gets out, it's a crisis begging to happen, isn't it? But she came out just as I was working myself up to barge back in, passing me like a queen as she walked quickly down the corridor. No use. I saw her face: calm, yes, but with sorrow-struck eyes.

'Sad, Serendipity? Why? I thought you would celebrate to leave this place.'

She threw me an exasperated noise, something between a cough and a snarl, and continued walking. I kept up. I always do.

'It's a long way home and you're not expected till term-end. Want to come travelling with me?'

That got me a full look, a look that told me where I could stick my presumption.

'Tlaxce City, maybe even Sadira-on-Cygnus. We could do a mini-tour.' I was waving my hands like a street thespian, blocking my own sight, so I ran into her when she stopped suddenly.

'Do you know where he is?' she whispered angrily. Why was she always angry with me?

'I'm going to find out,' I told her with sudden and complete seriousness.

She started moving again, her walk slow and thoughtful rather than peeved and imperious. 'I'll come with you.'

As if she would have chosen differently! 'Pack light,' I warned her, almost skipping in unashamed glee. 'We're flying.'

*　　*　　*

I planned my stops and journey times to make sure it was mid-morning when we reached the capital. Day-trippers take over the early-morning hours and I don't like heavy traffic, ground or air. Not much private commuter air traffic is allowed within city limits, for obvious reasons, but Tlaxce does have the best floating runway in Cygnus Beta, and it's all for aerolight play. I nearly cried the first time I landed there. The lake inlet was narrow, the buildings looked sharp and greedy and the wind felt far too high – but once you've actually done it, it's easier than a squat in the desert, let me tell you. I expected Serendipity to be a little nervous, but if she was she didn't want me to have the satisfaction of seeing it. Cruel Serendipity. Never any fun for me, or for herself.

I had satisfaction enough, having her with me as we made our way to the address for Rafi's sole legally registered parent. Yes, I *liked* Serendipity, but beyond that I knew everyone could see she had . . . poise? Dignity? Some indefinable quality which made it less likely that Abowen's mother would call the police when she saw us? We entered the building easily with our IDs, found the right door and set our feet on the welcome mat. I smiled at the cameras and sensors with all the bright, beaming innocence I could muster as our information went swiftly to the occupants within. The door did not open, but a chime invited us to explain our presence further.

I pitched my voice smooth, cool and neutral. 'Good day. We are here to see Rafi Abowen Delarua. Is he available?'

The welcome mat hummed lightly under our feet as invisible eyes and ears considered us. Time passed. I nudged Serendipity to say something.

'It is of utmost importance that we speak to your son.' Her voice was firm – too firm. The mat emitted a lower, less welcoming chime, a warning to step off.

'No, wait! We're not government. We're his friends.'

Her words had little effect. The warning chime paused for the space of two calm heartbeats then returned with increasing volume. I skipped quickly to the side, but Serendipity stood for a while glaring at the door. I pulled her away before we accidentally summoned the residence security.

'Appeal to authority has failed; appeal to emotion has failed. I am open to your suggestions,' I told her.

She was still glaring, all paralysed with puzzlement, so baffled at being denied. 'She didn't even open the door to face us,' she muttered.

I thought to myself that if I had spent years of my life living with an inveterate and unrepentant mind-controller, I wouldn't be too quick to open doors either. 'She doesn't know us, Serendipity. What do you expect?'

Serendipity turned quickly to look at me, suddenly smiling. 'Of course. Let us go and ask someone who *does* know me.'

There was no reason for me to feel worried, no reason at all, but her sharp swerve into enthusiasm was unnerving. In fact, so enthusiastic was she that no further wait would be tolerated. We had to leave for Sadira-on-Cygnus before sunset. She had a cousin, or maybe it was a friend's cousin, quite close, shared quarters on a three-week trek and didn't fall out once, and this person, this friendly relative or relative's friend, was now living a newly-wed life in Sadira-on-Cygnus very near to the Dllenahkh homestead.

I wasn't sure where Serendipity's new energy was coming from, but I was glad to hear she knew a neighbour we could question.

Even before we left the Lyceum, I had been sending out multiple comm messages to Rafi's aunt, messages which remained unanswered. *That* was a good reason to worry. Grace Delarua did not strike me as a woman who hid behind closed doors until inconvenient visitors went away.

Of course, we couldn't leave immediately. I had to draft a new flight plan and submit it to the Tlaxce Airspace Authority, so I coaxed Serendipity into being seen with me in a booth at a traveller's restaurant where she could eat and relax (or rather, fret) and I could access the tech I needed. It took me a bit longer than I expected, which meant it took a lot longer than her patience could stretch. She ate quickly, ordered several pots of fresh, hot tea to replace the cups I sipped then neglected and began to hover at my back trying to get inside the privacy cone of the monitor. As if she could understand the least little bit of what I was doing! For the first time in our acquaintance I grew genuinely irritated at her.

'Do you *want* to help?' I asked her. Ignoring the bad-look she gave me in answer, I continued, 'Find out from that cousin of yours how long airspace over Sadira-on-Cygnus has been restricted.'

Curiosity erased her anger in a flash as I pushed my handheld over to her. She wrote for a longish while and finally sent off a message. I'd given up on the flight plan and started researching the cost of hangar space and a groundcar instead. I wasn't pleased. I was even less pleased when I learned that city regulations required me to have five years of groundcar experience and full taxpayer status, neither of which I had, and which was completely ridiculous since the nav and autopilot do better than most human drivers and city groundcars are almost impossible to steal.

'Unless you're as handy with cars as you are with elephants, our choices are getting meagre. We could use the slow, utterly legal and far too traceable public transport, or we might be able to beg or bribe the driver of a private car going in the right direction. Perhaps if we find a driver who likes the way you smile. You *do* smile sometimes, don't you, Serendipity?'

Her face twisted with a combination of worry, distaste and that special grimace she saved for my wit.

'Might need some practice on that,' I teased her, but it was a weak effort. The monitor pulled away my attention – no, not the monitor, the flight plan I couldn't use. I stared at it for a long minute, slowly drew nearer, and slowly began to input new data. The results were slightly – very, very slightly – encouraging.

'Would your cousin be willing to meet us halfway?' I asked. 'Can she handle a draughtcar?'

'I should think so. She lives on a farming homestead.'

I began to smile. 'Ask her to reserve one, my credit to cover the cost. I'll send her the information if she agrees.'

So, you see, there was actually a good reason why we drove into the Dllenahkh homestead in a heavy-duty hauler holding my aerolight disassembled and tucked in tight. There was actually a good reason why we were so damn late.

Two days after the clandestine night swim with a baby mindship, and two days before the unexpected visit of Ntenman and Serendipity to Sadira-on-Cygnus, Rafi found himself once more in Tlaxce City. Hours of driving from the homestead, twenty minutes of travel through the city, ten minutes of waiting for the Consul to acknowledge their presence, seven minutes of sitting outside the Consul's office with Aunt Grace while Nasiha, Tarik and Dllenahkh tried whatever last-minute persuasion they could find in the depths of their uncomplicated, non-duplicitous Sadiri souls, and there was still no way to stop his hands from sweating. He crumpled the hem of his tunic in his fingers for the tenth time, shifted in his chair and tried not to look furtive.

'Are you all right, dear?' Aunt Grace asked him, her tone and expression all solicitude. 'You look like you've eaten something indigestible.'

'No, I'm— I—' He stuttered into silence, already empty of excuses, and tried diversion instead. 'It's . . . well, it's sad, isn't it? Don't you feel sad?'

Grace Delarua, eternal optimist and warrior against grim realities, looked bleak. 'Yes, it is, and I do. Not that we didn't expect this would happen, but . . . everything is so uncertain now. It feels like a sentence, not a posting.' She belatedly bit her lip after the last, hushed words.

'What is Uncle Dllen—?'

'Shh. Not the time or the place.' She looked past him. There was a small balcony at the end of the corridor, scant standing room for a few people beyond a prettily etched glass door. She stood and went to it, slid the door open and looked back at Rafi.

He joined her. The rail of the balcony was sun-warm under his hands but the breeze was cool and so was the view – several metres of green garden between the Consulate and the nearest road and a broad stripe of lake blue at the horizon. There was urban noise, but it was not much louder than the breeze and he did not have to strain to hear his aunt's voice.

'Never mind about Dllenahkh,' she said. 'Let's talk about you. You haven't really told me what you're doing. You do know your mother hasn't cooled off yet?'

'Mmhm . . . yes . . .' he admitted unwillingly.

'And I am *not* letting you wander around the City by yourself. You're not a Tlaxce collegian, not yet.' She shuddered slightly at *collegian*, as if glimpsing a terrible fate.

'Um, no—'

'So what am I to tell the Lyceum when they finally notice you're missing?'

'All I need is time. Can't we dodge them for a few more weeks? Then I'll have the freedom to go where I want.'

His aunt stared silently at the dual-blue horizon for a long moment before answering. 'After today I don't know if I'll ever see Nasiha again. Freyda wants to go to Punartam no matter what Lanuri says, and though she hasn't told me, I know she's been discussing the possibilities with people at Qeturah's research institute. Tarik's been talking about going to one of the taSadiri communities of Masuf Lagoon . . . that's in Vaya where Joral is, near Piedra. I don't know what to do. Everyone is scattering. Everyone's trying to find a place where they can do as they want and go as they please. Remember when we said we'd travel the world together?'

He felt helplessly sad after her depressing summary. 'Whatever I do, wherever I'm going, I'll write,' he said weakly.

She eyed him, clearly vexed, but at the situation rather than at him. 'I'll hold you to that. I know there's no good news being spoken in the Consul's office, so please God may your words be more than an empty promise.'

She exhaled a long breath, straightening her back and relaxing her shoulders as if shrugging off a burden. 'Very well. Go and become an adult. Make some choices, make some mistakes, but survive as best you can. If you need help and I can't come to you, I'll send help.' She gave him a look of fond pride, but it was quickly taken over by a frown of slow-dawning understanding and con-cern as he scrubbed his palms dry on his tunic yet again. 'You're scared. We all are. I'm sorry.'

He gave a bitter laugh. 'I want to blame *somebody*, but it'll never be you.'

The Consul's door opened, gliding silently on well-lubricated tracks. He saw the motion from the edge of his vision, heard the footfalls on the corridor's tiled floor and noted how the tension returned to Aunt Grace's shoulders. She nudged him, urging him back indoors, and slid the balcony door shut behind them.

For a while no one moved or said anything. If Aunt Grace was tense, the three Sadiri standing in the corridor were almost brit-tle with masked emotion. One touch and Tarik would snap, one word and Nasiha would crumble, and judging by his aunt's deep and careful breathing, Dllenahkh was on the verge of flying into a fury. When Dllenahkh's voice broke the silence at last, it was deep and slow, with a vibration that was not the least calming. It frayed the nerve endings like the sizzle of incipient lightning.

'Let us be on our way. The Consul has very kindly provided a driver to escort Commander Nasiha to the spaceport, and we shall go with her to say our farewells.'

The transit to the spaceport was too long for silence and staring at the back of the driver's head and too short for getting scattered thoughts in a sensible row. Rafi sweated. He sweated and he wor-ried and he tried to catch his aunt's attention, but she was staring at her feet with wide, glazed eyes. Tarik and Nasiha sat in the very back, hands and heads touching, occasionally whispering to each other in voices that held no trace of tears. How long had they pre-pared for this day? Was it easier to have warning of one's leaving, or to go without anticipation or anxiety like the irrevocable shift of sudden death?

He had never been inside the spaceport before. He wished for a wrist comm that could be compass and map in the bewildering twist and sprawl of buildings, channels and walkways that coiled around the sky-stabbing spire, a spire so tall it dominated both the Tlaxce skyline and the littoral so that whether you looked at it from amid buildings or over water, it similarly met the viewer's scrutiny with an immediate sense of falling and fear. It did provide a kind of falling, falling *upwards*, past cloud and hazy sunshine to the invisible presence of the orbital quarantine station, casually known as Stage One.

They disembarked from the car at a terminal entrance from which no pedestrian egress would be allowed and watched as the Consulate driver departed. Then, with one obligatory neck-craning glance at the terminal's tip, they went into a high-ceilinged hall.

To Rafi's homesteader eyes, all was confusion. There was a wealth and variety of technology he had never used nor even seen used, and people walking with busy purpose from one place to another. As he stared, he felt a hand settle on his shoulder. When he looked up, half-expecting it to be Aunt Grace, it was Commander Nasiha. She gave him one questioning look; he replied with a slow, hesitant nod. He felt his heartbeat pounding in his throat.

She bent to his ear. 'Stay close by me,' was all she said, but it calmed the painful beat from a gallop to a canter. Resolve strengthened, he nodded again and followed in silence.

The crowd grew more densely packed farther into the hall. Small groups in the throes of goodbye stood at the margins while the larger mass ambled patiently in line along a broad causeway running under an arch. The raised floor flashed with coloured lights; travellers checked their wrist comms to find a match and dutifully selected their allotted route out of several that branched off into the passenger hall beyond the grand arch. Many were destined for the other side of Cygnus Beta on sub-orbital flights, some for a period of work or recreation on an orbital installation, and the remainder for Stage One, gateway to Punartam, the nearest galactic travel hub.

'Aunt Grace,' he said. 'I'm going to leave now with the Commander. I'm going to another province. Maybe Vaya, since Joral's there.'

She breathed in, sudden and sharp, and gave him a look of pain and shock. Of course – after bracing herself for her friend's departure she had no reserves for this fresh bond-breaking, a possibility discussed barely an hour before. 'Now?' she whispered, the word faltering under the weight of emotion.

He nodded, unable to trust his own voice.

Dllenahkh drew closer to his wife and placed a comforting hand on her back. 'You have credit?' he asked his nephew.

Rafi nodded again. 'A little . . . my student allowance.'

'Don't use it. That can be easily traced,' he explained. 'We can pay your fare out of the homestead's Cygnian credit account. We always have people travelling in and out; they deposit galactic credit into our account and we make purchases on their behalf with the equivalent credit in Cygnian. It will not be noticed.'

Rafi nodded for the third time, using it as an excuse to dip his head lower and lower in the hope that his wet eyes would not be noticed. He took the small credit chip Dllenahkh extended to him and folded it safely in his fist. He endured his aunt's quick, fierce hug without breaking down.

'I'll write,' he promised, and turned away slightly to blink the salt water out of his vision.

The Commander, who had far better control of herself, embraced her husband and spoke a few quiet words to her friends. When Rafi could look directly at them once more, he saw a row of faces as calm as masks – but Dllenahkh's eyes were worried, Tarik's anguished and Grace (the hardest to bear), her eyes kept that hurt bewilderment caused by his impulsive words.

'Time to go,' said the Commander, again with the gentle touch to his shoulder, steering and strengthening him.

Rafi gave one final nod in a weak attempt to reassure, then turned and walked away with the Commander, feeling mildly annoyed by the inadequate moment of farewell. He knew it was a turning point in his life – why did it feel so flat and mundane? His emotions were confused, but somehow dampened rather than heightened, as if he was afraid to feel. He wondered if he would revisit the memory in later years and find it more moving – weighty with significance and poignant with nostalgia.

In later years, Rafi remembered the embarrassing moisture on his newly purchased travel token when Commander Nasiha took it from his sweating hand. He recalled that his nerves were so shot she had to fasten her comm to his wrist herself when his shaking fingers took too long. He tried hardest to remember her words. 'I am going with the pilots. I will send word when I can. May your aunt forgive me.'

He did not remember having the slightest inkling that he

would be the last of the Dllenahkh homestead to see Commander Nasiha alive.

The drive to the Dllenahkh homestead was long enough for Ntenman to learn that Cousin Ivali of Tirtha, now Goodwife Ivaliheni of Sadira-on-Cygnus, was far more handy with a draughtcar than he was and much more cheerful and relaxed than Serendipity. The drive from the front gate to the main complex of the homestead was long enough to discover that she was as baffled by the situation as Ntenman and Serendipity put together.

The residents of the Dllenahkh homestead gave them a courteous welcome, but some very important people were missing, leaving proxies and relatives in their place. A man exercising in a field with a small group of young men introduced himself as Dllenahkh's associate coach at the training hall, now seeing to the students in his elder's absence. A woman walking slowly along the main entry road with a toddler proved to be a hired childminder, a new but temporary addition to the homestead, there only for the purpose of caring for the offspring of Lieutenant Tarik and Commander Nasiha.

'I've never seen it like this,' Ivaliheni said quietly to her cousin. 'It's half-dead here, and no one is giving us answers.'

It was true. Both sides were cautious with each other, neither telling the full tale of events on either side. At last, after participating in the somewhat bonding experience of unlinking Ntenman's aerolight from the draughtcar and squeezing it into a half-cleared artisans' workshop, the associate coach finally revealed to them where Dllenahkh and Grace Delarua could be found.

He did not mention Rafi's name at all, but then again, neither did Ntenman and Serendipity.

Ivaliheni drove them to nearby Newbridge, the de facto political capital of Sadira-on-Cygnus and the location of the Council Hall, the Garden of Memory and buildings that housed various Civil Service ministries and affiliated organisations.

When they passed the Council Hall, Ntenman yelped out a garbled, '*Stop!*' There was Grace Delarua, sitting on a bench outside the big double doors of the Hall, looking across the road at the small trees in the Garden of Memory with an expression that said everything and nothing and none of it good.

Ivaliheni veered onto the verge with an expert and stylish sideswerve. She looked at Serendipity. *I want to know what's happening*, she told her in a firm, swift and silent mind-to-mind connection.

I'll try, I will, Serendipity replied in like manner. Then she continued aloud, 'Thanks for the ride. I'll call you later.'

Delarua's attention had been caught by the sudden divert-and-stop of the heavy vehicle on the road, so she was already staring when Ntenman and Serendipity got out of the draughtcar and crossed the road. As they approached she continued to stare, fascinated and bemused, trying to place them. They were dressed in civilian clothing, not student uniform, but the faces were familiar. The boy . . . yes, she was sure she had seen the boy at the Lyceum. Tinman, Rafi called him. The girl . . . she was a lot less sure about the girl. Not the Lyceum, but somewhere . . .

She came to a conclusion and reacted accordingly. 'You're late,' she said in a dry, flat tone, skipping all pleasantry and greeting. 'He's gone.'

Serendipity gasped. 'Gone?' she said in a voice so tragic that Delarua wondered if she thought Rafi was dead.

Delarua pointed her chin to the sky with an abrupt, truculent jerk of her head. 'He's in the orbital quarantine station.'

'Ho. Ha.' Ntenman exhaled, kept exhaling and dropped down beside her on the bench, his eyes wide with shock. 'Wha?'

She gave the young man a look that was almost sympathetic. 'You're taking it well.'

Ntenman was too stunned to notice whether or not that was meant for sarcasm. 'You let him go to—'

Before he could get any more words out, she flung up her hands to her head and let go a wail of frustration and fury. 'Let? I did not *let* him!'

They blinked at her in utter helplessness while she struggled and seethed with emotion. Ntenman eventually reached out a hand to pat her shoulder in an attempt at calming. Serendipity stood with her hand to her mouth, frozen and speechless with dismay. Her poise had evaporated, blown away, a thin wisp taken by the wind.

'The trouble with folk like us,' said Grace Delarua, speaking slowly, deliberately and with desperate control, 'is that we think we communicate so well when we aren't communicating at all. And now here I am talking to relative strangers about matters that may not concern them. Why are you here? Why didn't you stop Rafi from leaving the Lyceum in the first place?'

Ntenman flapped and fizzled, both indignant and off guard.

Serendipity saved the moment. 'We didn't know,' she protested.

Delarua's eyes narrowed. 'Wait. I know you. You're an Uplander from the monastery. That girl. Sorry, I've forgotten your name.'

Serendipity nodded, pleased beyond common sense with that slight, non-specific recognition. 'I'm Serendipity. Tell us what happened to Rafi, please?'

Delarua looked away and went silent. Her expression was unreadable, but both of them could feel the rapid current of her thoughts and emotions in their own way, and they recognised when that current slowed and reached resolution a second or two before she turned to face them again.

'No more need for secrecy as far as I can see,' she said. 'We were at the spaceport. He was supposed to take a flight to Vaya. He was supposed to keep out of the Lyceum's way until he turns fifteen. I don't know how he ended up on Stage One.'

She did not know, truly, but she could guess and it made her furious.

'Stage One is as out-of-the-way as you can get,' Ntenman offered. 'Even government can't halt the quarantine process once it's started. Maybe he did the right thing.'

Delarua's thoughts were a murky swell but her words were crisp and careful. 'I don't know. He may have done something to annoy *two* planetary governments. I don't call that keeping out of the way.'

A wave of turmoil, both felt and heard, came through the Hall's closed doors, making Ntenman flinch. Delarua watched him. 'I had to get out,' she said. 'It was making my head hurt – and my stomach, too.'

'What's happening in there?' Serendipity asked.

Delarua leaned forward and spoke quietly, but with an air of sadness rather than conspiracy. 'Insurrection, I hope.' She addressed Serendipity. 'There are stairs just inside that go up to the public gallery. You should go and listen. Your people are very much involved.'

Serendipity felt confused and apprehensive but Delarua's steady gaze was insistent rather than reassuring, and so the young woman succumbed to the pressure and pulled open the door. Behind it was a high-ceilinged foyer embraced by the twin arms of two flights of stairs in fine architectural balance and symmetry. The far wall held another set of double doors, closed and stoically guarded by two young Sadiri. The air was solid with cacophony; bursts of rumbling and blaring dissent in male voices were occasionally punctuated by the higher chime and warble of a female elder. Disruption. Chaos. Insanity. Heavy emotions were roiling below the sound, and above it all a quick chatter of telepathic communication clicked along unimpeded, evidence that a handful of Uplanders were observing and commenting among themselves.

Serendipity took in a sharp, frightened breath. 'What *is* happening?' she said to herself. She went to the stairs on the left and ran lightly up, two steps at a time, to face the turmoil.

CHAPTER SIX

The anger and tension in the Hall were directed outwards, not inwards. The Consul's peremptory deportation of a valued colleague (and a female one at that, which made her twice-valued) was but one of several indignities that had been piling up for months. The Government of New Sadira restricted mobility, pressured certain young families (with daughters? with purer heritage?) to emigrate to New Sadira and made many fruitless attempts to police what they saw as 'cultural deviations' on the Sadiri settlement.

Then there was the taSadiri contingent, mainly represented by semi-adopted female Sadiri elders and a few young women, most of them new brides from Tirtha. The community of telepaths was now actively seeking full integration with Sadira-on-Cygnus with the option of a special relationship that would connect all taSadiri communities (subject to terms to be agreed on by the Cygnian government, of course).

Finally there were the pilots. They had no formal Council representation, and yet, somehow, at some stage months earlier it had become necessary to include them in the plans to develop Grand

115

Bay. Then there were consultations on the effective oversight of the airspace over the settlement, and then it was a natural step to allow for a few 'special representatives' from the pilot community who could attend meetings, hold Council privileges and cast their vote.

It was messy and exhausting, especially for those who remembered the early days of settlement, when the Council was not much more than a few old men half-heartedly arguing procedure and trying not to fall apart, break down or otherwise go to pieces in front of the youngsters.

The majority opinion was clear. Sadira-on-Cygnus could not continue as the off-planet annexe of New Sadira. What new status it should have was a matter of debate. Several Sadiri Councillors were happy to become entirely Cygnian, with no conflicting loyalties. Most of the taSadiri Councillors were less eager to settle for the Cygnian citizenship they already possessed, and those from Tirtha were entirely sceptical, pointing to institutions like the Lyceum as proof that Cygnus Beta was still not ready to accept psi-based societies. The pilots, of course, were looking far beyond the planet and talking about maintaining old galactic networks and creating new ones – trade and science and transport from Zhinu to Punartam to Ntshune and farther yet. Grand Bay could become a new terminal, benefiting Cygnian and Sadiri alike.

The permanent presence of Sadiri mindships in Cygnian oceans was an open secret. The Sadiri knew, and they hoped with the strength of prayer that both human and mindship populations would flourish. The Cygnians said nothing, but they granted the settlement both autonomy and assistance with an abundance and generosity that only made sense if they were expecting some future dividend, perhaps in the form of a collaboration that would see Cygnus Beta finally get its own interstellar fleet.

Some of the Sadiri Councillors, still traumatised by their fall from the pinnacle of galactic society, were giddy at any potential opportunity for leverage and influence, and it made them misbehave a little during the formal debates. Eventually, Chief Councillor Edrasde recognised that they were feeding off each other's high emotions in a vicious and dangerous loop. The meeting was adjourned until the following morning. When the inner doors were unsealed and opened, the grumbling, seething assembly rose up and walked out, carrying the bad mood with them like a trailing miasma.

The observers in the public gallery were also leaving. Serendipity joined them, going quickly down the stairs and into the busy foyer. She kept to the edges, careful not to bump into anyone, and dashed through the outer doors the moment there was a sliver of space to do so. She was so intent on not being noticed that she did not see when Dllenahkh turned aside from the general flow of the crowd and went up the opposite staircase to the place she had just left.

The public gallery was empty; the Hall below was empty. Dllenahkh sat on a front bench, seized the railing before him with both hands and tried to take the emptiness into his mind. Such a turbulent atmosphere – it drained him of strength and disturbed his equilibrium. He craved cool, deep breaths of quietness: either the chill, humid air of the forest uplands monastery, or the dry nip of the wind at the monastery in Montserrat. Both reminded him of early-morning meditation.

There was too little time, always, even for a breath. Slow

steps approached – only slow, not hesitant. The emptiness was filled with a growing sense of presence. Not ominous, but implacable ... yes ... even stubborn. He would not escape this talk though he had tried for many months to preserve his innocence. The bench rocked slightly under added weight as the presence settled in beside him and waited patiently. Dllenahkh exhaled and relaxed his grip, letting his hands fall palms-upwards into his lap in resignation.

'You've changed,' he muttered to his hands. 'The younger you appear, the more familiar your face becomes to me, the more I realise that you are very far from the pilot I knew in the days before.'

'Too much has happened,' Naraldi said softly. 'We are both changed, but my friend – those worlds, those lives! You have not seen what I have seen, the best and the worst of what could be!'

'Do you think you can direct fate?'

Naraldi laughed, a bitter, indignant huff of air. 'Please, Dllenahkh. Directing fate *is* a pilot's vocation – or, if you prefer, directing our path around fate's immovables. It's the same thing. You must start thinking like a pilot; you're almost one of us already.'

He stretched out a hand and matched it to Dllenahkh's, curving his fingers around the hollow of his friend's hand as if keeping space for a sphere therein. 'See? Together we preserve Sadira, together we hold and protect our world—'

Dllenahkh cut off his poetry with bluntness. 'You want me to lead a rebellion.'

'I want you to be the foundation and centre from which others will lead.' Naraldi collapsed the empty sphere with a quick clasp of Dllenahkh's hand, then withdrew and quickly changed the subject. 'The pilots have petitioned for title to the lands around Grand Bay. The Cygnian Government is in agreement. I believe they have chosen to focus on the benefits to the settlement rather than scrutinise our motives.'

'How unusually pragmatic of them,' said Dllenahkh. The words suggested sarcasm, but he sounded tired and heavy.

Naraldi was taken aback by his tone. 'Old friend, do not tell me you are disappointed in me.'

Dllenahkh struck his fist on the railing. 'I am disappointed in all of us! Tell the truth, Naraldi. We are not preserving Sadira – we are breaking it apart.'

'It broke apart some time ago, Dllenahkh. Help me to preserve the best of it.' He spoke with a deep, sincere sadness that was harder to bear than a simple plea.

'I have to think it over,' Dllenahkh said finally.

'Think, then, but not for too long. Events are moving on without us and there is no time.'

The bench shifted again as Naraldi stood and left. Dllenahkh stayed a while longer, trying to fully restore his equilibrium, but the sight of the Hall brought him no peace. He could still see ghostly imprints of debating representatives moving in the space below and their voices clattered in his memory with an echo that was almost audible. Eventually, he gave up and went to find his wife.

When Serendipity emerged from the crush of people exiting, Ntenman asked Delarua for a ride back to the homestead and explained why.

'You parked an *entire* aerolight in our workshop?' she said, shaking her head. She was not feeling hospitable, not today.

119

'Pardon me, but I have called my cousin and I must go with her,' Serendipity said. Perhaps it was a courteous withdrawal in response to Delarua's stressed tone, but her eyes were turned away, seeking out others from Tirtha.

Delarua noticed and made a mental note to follow up later, but for the moment she merely replied to Serendipity's polite good-bye and focused on Ntenman once more. 'I still don't understand why you've been tracking down Rafi so diligently. Is the Lyceum sending students out as spies now?'

Ntenman answered absently, watching Serendipity leave. 'Oh, the Lyceum doesn't know he's missing yet – and if anyone should call and ask, tell them that Rafi is recovering nicely but will be contagious for a while longer.'

Delarua questioned him with a stare.

'Chickenpox,' Ntenman clarified.

'Well, thank you, I think. So you'll fly back tomorrow, then?' She was pushing him to be gone. Dllenahkh was approaching, there was a lot to decide and do, and she did not want this strange boy and his murky motives hanging around.

He gave her a reproachful look. 'Rafi's my friend, and I don't have many friends. I know that cap wasn't doing him any good. And if I were a spy, it would not be for the Lyceum.'

She said nothing, waiting for him to explain further. His expression was serious, but she kept her face and her feelings guarded.

'If Rafi comes back from Stage One, the Lyceum will be the least of his problems. He needs to be somewhere else, somewhere off-planet. I know people on Punartam.'

'Thank you for your suggestion,' she said with only a touch of sarcasm. 'I know people on Punartam, too. The problem is how to get him there. First-flight quarantine is expensive and lengthy, and that ticket he has won't take him much further. And we can't help. We can risk our homestead credit for local travel, but beyond orbit is another thing.'

'I can take care of that.'

She laughed. 'You have galactic credit?'

'Yes. I do. I owe Rafi, and someone owes me. It's enough to get us both to Punartam.'

At last she remembered. Ntenman was the boy who went with Rafi for a vacation in the forest uplands, paid for with *her* credit, no less. Murky motives or no, the boy had a very Ntshune sense of obligation.

Dllenahkh came into view. His face was unreadable but Delarua could feel what was beneath the surface – he was exhausted. All at once she despaired. How could she find time to worry about Rafi and fret over Nasiha when she also had to hold her husband together so that he could hold the settlement together? She reined herself in quickly before her bleakness could touch him. One thing at a time.

'Let's go home,' she told him.

Ntenman stood awkwardly in place as she took Dllenahkh's arm and they began to walk away. She looked back at the boy, surprised at his sudden shyness. 'You, too.'

Ntenman ended up staying for more than one day. Delarua was fascinated at how quickly he became part of the homestead. He remembered everyone's name and face after a single meeting, and they remembered him, for he charmed, flattered and flirted his way through the homestead's small population.

'He's a baby con-man,' Delarua said to Dllenahkh with a mixture of disdain and admiration. 'He's like Ioan without the nasty mind-coercion.'

She was making small talk for the sake of distraction. They were in the office she had shared with Nasiha, cleaning it out thoroughly – files, specimens, souvenirs and personal effects. Should the Consul send anyone to search for clues to Nasiha's location, they would find only bare walls, scant furniture and empty cabinets.

'He reminds me of you,' her husband said, and was startled when she swiftly smacked his arm. 'But Grace, he does. He likes people and he likes to be liked. He's nowhere near Ioan's level.'

'You're being duped already,' Delarua warned him. 'Can't you see how he's building networks and notching up credit? In a little while, he could get away with anything, and if you tried to get one of the homesteaders to go against him they'd protest that *he's such a great guy* and *there must be some mistake*.'

'Yes, I do understand,' Dllenahkh said. 'That's how I feel about you.'

'That's not a compliment,' Delarua protested.

'Neither is it an insult. It is simply the way you do things. Do you distrust this boy?'

There was a good question. 'I don't know. I need someone to look out for Rafi, and right now that can't be me . . . not with everything that's happening.'

'Maria . . . ?' he asked delicately.

She simply shook her head.

'Freyda?'

'Ah . . . if Freyda ends up on Punartam, I don't want to be involved. Not with how Lanuri's taking things.'

Lanuri had become unusually possessive, convinced that if Freyda left the homestead, she would be kidnapped, coerced or otherwise taken by the megalomaniacs who were running New Sadira.

'Where *is* Nasiha?' Delarua fretted aloud.

'That is something I do not think we are meant to know, but I do believe she is safe – or at least safer than she would be on New Sadira.'

Delarua said nothing. Tarik, always quiet but now almost silent, had remained in Tlaxce City for a few days to 'put certain things in order'. She did not press, allowing him secrecy and space for grieving, but she felt useless and helpless.

'I believe that we cannot make any impact at the individual level unless we create systemic change,' Dllenahkh said forcefully.

Delarua sighed. There was more behind the words, as usual. She knew he was angry and tired, facing a task he knew had to be done but wishing someone else would do it.

'But how,' he continued, 'can we control change amid chaos? The Zhinuvians charge more and more for transportation and communication, the Ntshune have taken over the galactic institutions but do only the bare minimum, and on Punartam, studies and research proliferate in the Academes, but no answers are forthcoming.'

She let him talk. It was not a time for solutions, but for venting and comforting.

'I have a meeting this evening,' he grumbled. 'They expect me to say yes. Edrasde will remain as Chief Councillor, and the new title may be Governor . . . or Guardian . . . but I think we will start with Governor.'

Delarua felt her pulse beat thickly in her throat. Governor

meant provincial ambitions. Guardian was a planetary title, suitable for a second-tier bioformed planet needing a few more generations to fully mature.

He sensed her anxiety. 'Do not be concerned. There are many involved, all with enough expertise for me to be merely a figurehead if I wish. But I do worry. I worry that history will associate my name with the greatest mistake of our era.'

'Well,' Delarua said at last, her voice squeaking a bit from tension, 'ask Naraldi. With all the other timelines he's seen, he probably knows about that, too.'

He stared, then relaxed and smiled. 'An excellent suggestion. I could do much worse than to listen to Naraldi's advice.'

Serendipity did not expect to both envy and pity Ivaliheni, but she did. At first, even in the midst of the community's turmoil and the anxiety of Rafi's absence, she found bliss in the flow of straight mindtalk, like guzzling from a goblet of heady wine after months of being forced to sip water from a faulty straw. It made pausing for verbal speech even harder to take, and Ivali *would* pause and talk to her husband, Thalen. A sweetly smiling young Sadiri, he mostly kept his head down and concentrated on what he could sense of their silent conversation, like a man keen to absorb a foreign language but still too shy to risk the embarrassment of speaking up and exposing the flaws in his communication. Ivali was not so shy; when she spoke to him, half her words were in Cygnian Standard and half in halting Sadiri.

Ivaliheni, telepath of Tirtha, was happy, comfortable and completely at home, even in a place where she was forced to limit herself in order for others to communicate with her. Serendipity buried her incredulity beneath several layers of courtesy. Ivali gave her a glance and a blink that said the effort was discernible, but adequate.

One thing Serendipity still shared with Ivaliheni was mixed feelings about the profoundly communal life of Tirtha, where familiarity could bring both comfort and contempt. Ivali showed off the small dwelling that was hers and Thalen's, and her pride in their privacy and possession was evident. Serendipity showed but a touch of jealousy, enough to compliment Ivali for her choices, and hid her resentment at her own poor choices even further below the incredulity. It was ironic, given all her efforts at dissembling, that Thalen was the one to suggest that the two take a drive out to Grand Bay so they could spend some time with each other. But perhaps not ironic – Serendipity sensed the edge of the swift, subtle flash of gratitude Ivali sent to her husband and felt slightly ashamed that in her quickness to judge Thalen's telepathy, she had underestimated his intuition.

'This place suits you,' she admitted aloud as they started off in Ivali's car.

Ivali looked at her. 'I take it that the Lyceum did not suit you?'

A neat mental bundle of exasperation, disgust, disappointment and mild horror was all Serendipity needed to communicate her judgement on the Lyceum.

And the boy? Ivali wanted to know.

Blankness was no refuge from insight. Silence did not preserve secrets. It was Serendipity's turn to be the object of pity and she did not like it, especially when that pity was so encompassing and general and concerned about her failings rather than the specific situation she was facing.

The old car hitched and sighed, adjusting itself as the road began the descent to sea level. The burden of Ivali's pity lifted as they gladly allowed themselves to be distracted by what lay ahead. Serendipity had heard about the pilots and their ships and the place they had made their own, but descriptions and holos could not do justice to her first view of Grand Bay. A sprinkling of solar roofs speckled the landscape's dusty browns and greens like bright confetti. The white sand of the coastline was a silver ribbon holding back the ocean. Long piers segmented the water and connected shallow to deep, and small craft of all kinds clustered along the piers and dotted the spaces in-between. The darker, more distant blues of the sea were quiet and empty.

'You won't see much more than a glimpse of them during the day,' Ivali warned, smiling at her friend's awe and anticipation.

Them being the mindships, obviously. Serendipity did not hide her disappointment.

'We can go to a quieter part of the bay where there's a better chance of seeing them,' Ivali offered in consolation.

The main road for Grand Bay ran parallel to the coastline. Serendipity was struck by how much more a capital Grand Bay appeared to be than Newbridge. Newbridge was for the bureaucrats and their necessary interactions with Cygnian Central Government. Grand Bay was the cultural and commercial heart of the Sadiri settlement. Pilots brought news and cargo; needed information, supplies and shelter – and Grand Bay took what they had to offer and provided them with what they wanted. The layout was neat in a typically thoughtful Sadiri way, but the tents, prefab structures and half-finished buildings revealed how quickly and organically development had surged, outstripping mere bureaucratic planning with the urgency of immediate necessity. One popular style was the dome, and when they passed one under construction, it was easy to see why. A mould was set on a prepared base, inflated to the required size and sprayed with quick-set permarock. The mould could be dismantled after twenty-four hours, leaving a dome ready for use. Left unpainted and unplastered, like raw limestone, the permarock might later be enhanced with geometric patterns of solar sheeting and weatherproofed with clear spackle to match the other domes of Grand Bay.

When Serendipity complimented the dome design, Ivali only laughed and said, 'Wait. You will soon see.'

The beach changed from sand to rock and from level to sharply sloping, and finally cliffs marked the end of the curve of the bay. A set of domes clung to that last curl of coastline, some on land, some on solid piles in the water, all connected by covered walkways. Ivali parked the car in a field on the landward side of the road and they crossed over to a stone pathway that led down to the complex. Serendipity sensed and recognised the peaceful hum of a contemplative community, very like Tirtha, and yet not quite like. The ordinary might have noted no difference, but to a telepath, this was a very quiet place. Conversations were few, and what communication she could detect was more at the level of polite greeting than intense discussion.

Ivali skirted the main buildings and led her down a long walkway towards the farthest sea-based dome. She almost ran, tugging Serendipity's hand and pulling her through the doorway, across a floor made of thick, smoky glass in a mosaic of blues and up to the wide-open windows on the far side. She spoke aloud in her excitement. 'It's the perfect lookout point!'

Serendipity tried to glance at the gorgeous colours of the floor as she was hustled past but was soon captivated by the promised view, even more stunning than their first sight of Grand Bay from the hilltop. She did not have long to enjoy it.

'It is also a perfect place to meditate – *usually*.'

Ivali and Serendipity turned with the swiftness of fear and forgotten dignity. The voice was familiar. The aged face of the black-robed woman seated on the floor near the entrance was familiar. She had never been known to insist on any other form of address than her own simple name, and yet somehow when people spoke it, they felt an irresistible urge to add a bow, a lowering of the eyes or at the very least a respectful lean.

'Zhera,' the two young women said, their voices hushed and their heads bowed.

The Sadiri elder stood slowly and advanced on them with graceful yet menacing power in her step. 'Ivaliheni. You were not at the Council Hall for the latest debates.'

Ivaliheni flinched resentfully, appearing seconds from saying, *Neither were you*, then clearly thought better of it. 'No, Zhera,' she said politely. 'But I have heard from those who were. I know what is happening.'

'Do you?' Zhera enquired enigmatically. She turned her hard gaze on Serendipity. 'Child – I remember you. Have you now decided to settle for a Sadiri husband? Or are you ready to return to a life of monastic discipline?'

Serendipity was too confused and mortified to answer.

Zhera made a noise that might have been amusement or disdain or both. She turned her back on them and returned to her position near the door. Folding her legs under her, she sat back on her ankles and stared grimly at the glass floor.

Serendipity and Ivali exchanged a glance and began to walk quietly to the door. They might have escaped, except Serendipity's downcast eyes saw a strange shadow shifting below the semi-opaque glass. She halted, unsure of her vision, but other senses took over and she saw more clearly. There was a mindship below the dome. A fan of tendrils extended from the main mass of the creature into the waters below them. Each tendril traced a line of subtle electricity that cut golden through the blues of water and glass. She found herself yearning for a touch of that electricity.

Zhera raised her eyes and gave Serendipity a considering look. 'What do you see, child? Look closely.'

Unfazed by Ivali's bewilderment, Serendipity knelt and pressed her face to a pale blue segment of the glass mosaic. The sea below moved sluggishly, as if thickly matted with weed and moss, but she realised it was not weed but a multitude of the mindship's fine, strong tendrils. More startling was the human shape that drifted in the midst of those tendrils. Serendipity stared closely. It was a pilot. Long dark hair streamed in the water, so tangled with the mindship's net that they moved as one in the tide. The pilot's silvery suit was so badly torn that patches and strips fluttered in the current. It was possible to see, even through the thick glass, that the pilot was a woman.

'Who is she?' Serendipity whispered against the cool glass. 'What happened to her?'

She did not ask if the pilot was dead. She could tell that she was not, even though she could not explain how she knew.

'We know who she is. Her name is Yhala and she was last stationed on New Sadira. As for what happened, that we do not know. We hope she will be able to answer for herself some day. For now, we can only wait and hope that her ship is up to the task of healing her. It is a risk, a matter of legend, for a mindship to take over and restore the body of a pilot. But I believe you have witnessed a precedent for this in your own community?'

Of course. The elders of Tirtha had shown Councillor Dllenahkh how to extend the boundaries of self and heal the woman who would become his wife. Serendipity straightened slowly, sat back and thought.

Zhera began to speak, the habitual command in her voice tempered by sadness. 'I remember what it was like on New Sadira. We tried so many things to move past the point of crisis. Desperate planning. Strong structures. The illusion of certainty. Kind lies. But eventually we became ruthless and ranked people by their usefulness and their degree of compliance. These are not helpful criteria for an old woman like myself, so I chose to take my chances with the new settlement on Cygnus Beta. I did wonder what would happen to the ones whose lack of compliance outweighed their usefulness. We have heard some tales from the second wave of refugees now on Punartam. This, however, is an example come directly home to chasten us for our inaction.'

She stood wearily. 'Ivaliheni, try to attend the Council meetings, especially during these strange, changing times. Listen to the contemplatives as well as the goodwives. Inaction will cost us dearly, and ignorance even more so. Serendipity . . .' She trailed off for a moment, puzzled, pondering. 'Think about your place in this community, either here or at Tirtha. I will be in both places from time to time, and I can advise if you will listen.'

Serendipity stood beside Ivali and watched the venerable elder depart. A random realisation came to her. She had not given any thought to Rafi for over an hour. She looked down at her feet, still seeing and sensing the floating pilot, tangled in the nerves of a mindship, perhaps temporarily, perhaps for ever. She wondered what it felt like.

*   *   *

Three days gone, and I knew it was time to go. Three fruitful days – enough time to share a laugh and a drink, to help lift or move something, to fetch and to carry. To listen, chat a little about next to nothing and listen again. Do you think that spy-talk was a joke? Well, maybe it was, but I know how to get information.

I found out about Tarik and learned that his child was rarely taken outdoors. Excessive caution from a man who had just lost his wife, literally lost, no euphemism for death or bond-breaking? Or something more? No time to find out, so I filed it away.

I learned, from Serendipity of all people, much more about the pilots in Grand Bay, their ships spawning in deep ocean and the taSadiri who would try their luck, to see if they had the right smell or spark or sizzle to capture the attention of a mindship beyond the span of a single lick. She said she was going to stay and try to find out more about them, maybe swim with a mindship one day and see what could happen. Restless Serendipity, constantly seeking a new attachment. At least I knew I would never have been enough for her; scarcely a minute's worth of novelty, me.

I heard about the petition for provincial status and how it affected Dllenahkh. It was all very thrilling, but I felt a twinge of guilt at my enjoyment when I looked at Grace Delarua and saw how she was torn between galactic and personal affairs. She stayed suspicious and talked trivia like a pro whenever I was around, but I could tell she was thinking hard, trying to measure my character.

On the day that I pushed my aerolight out onto the road and got ready to trundle it to a stretch with less forest and more open sky, she made a decision. She gave me a small bag.

'What's that?' I asked her pleasantly.

'Why, only lunch,' she replied sweetly, and while she was

holding my eyes with a not-quite-innocent smile, she put two fingers into her comm's wristband, drew out a datachip, and dropped it deliberately into the lunch bag.

'I don't know if you can get to Punartam,' she said, 'and I don't know if you can get Rafi to Punartam, but if you do, give that to him, and it will get him to where he needs to go.'

Lunch and a datachip. Many an apocalypse has been started by less, my friends. I took my leave, blessed the pilots for their favour in permitting me the freedom of their airspace and started to wing myself home. I was done with the Lyceum. I was ready to make some decisions. Ready to stand up to my padr. Ready to return to Punartam.

Stage One personnel always said that quarantine was like birth, a rite of passage best shrouded in amnesia. They also said it was easier to handle at a young age, and perhaps it was for the body, but for an unprepared mind it was a horrible shock, especially if you were one of that tiny percentage who *did* remember the initial regimen of blood-scrubbing, lung-flushing and skin-irradiation. Even for the majority, it felt like emerging from a long session of nightmarish drowning to float for a while, weak but peaceful, on the surface of life.

Everyone remembered the food: bland, mushy and designed to do terrible things to the digestion. The staff did show some remorse for that. Something about the nanotechnology no longer being readily available, requiring a return to earlier techniques of regulating alimentary flora. It became tradition to curse Zhinuvian transport price mark-up at mealtimes.

Rafi got through it because he knew it would come to an end, and he would only have to do it once.

Some architect, steeped in aesthetics but unburdened by a knowledge of human psychology, had designed the quarantine area so that the dining and recreation room looked onto a similar room for the seasoned travellers via a transparent wall. A few were heartless enough to wave cheerfully at the sick, glum faces of the first-timers. For a second trip taken within ten years you needed just a quick and painless booster procedure . . . but only if you had the nanotech. Rafi panicked at first when he heard that an essential part of the process was missing, but the medics reassured him that a brief session with the quarantine specialists at his destination would put him on the same level as the most widely travelled soldier in Galactic Patrol.

'For a small fee, in galactic credit,' they added in more muted tones as a disclaimer.

One of the medics teased him. 'You weren't so keen on getting the procedure when you first got here.'

'What?' Rafi asked. 'What do you mean?'

'You kept saying there was a mistake and you wanted to go back. Cold feet. It's normal . . . nothing to be ashamed of.'

Rafi frowned hard and tried to think through the drug fog. Why would he want to go back?

'But don't worry. Your friend completed his booster a few days ago and he's waiting for you on the other side so you can travel on to Punartam together.'

Rafi's sense of self-preservation, honed by years living with his father and his shorter but still educational time at the Lyceum, told him to say nothing until he had a better idea of what was going on.

Once he got to the recovery stage when there were fewer drugs and less malaise, he began to discover the awe in the experience.

The medical rooms and surgeries were cold-white and precisely arranged; the medics in their hooded overalls, masks and goggles looked like ghosts, or maybe alien angel midwives to some pristine afterlife. The quarantined travellers, the patients, wore loose, sterile shifts that were frequently changed and discarded as Cygnus Beta was peeled away from them, squeezed out of them, extracted and excreted.

He slept on a windowless ward where active privacy screens blurred each personal space, and it made him long for something distant to stretch his vision and colours to stimulate his brain. On the other side of the wall, where decontaminated travellers waited for their onward transport, greenery flourished in odd but beautiful configurations caused by the low gravity. It made him jealous. He asked the information manual in his ward if there was an observation gallery and was directed to the common room's massive, full-wall monitor which tracked different views: the surface of Cygnus Beta, an oblique and carefully filtered glimpse sunwards and the cool black and bright glitter of space. It was beautiful, but . . .

'Is that it?' he asked in disappointment.

The common room manual responded automatically with a gentle but firm lecture on the cost of viewports and the hazards of agoraphobia and large-scale panic in hallucination-prone patients on medication. Rafi wandered away after about three minutes.

He returned to counting the days. There had been almost a week of semi-coma, a few days of slow recovery and then an intense three days of rebuild therapy. When he emerged from that, shaky but feeling human again, he was hit by an unexpected allergic reaction to something on the post-build menu which caused him to spend about a day and a half unable to keep anything down. The medics were a little worried about that one, worried enough that Rafi wondered if someone had made a mistake. They monitored him for a few more days before releasing him to the Other Side. He was assigned a tiny sleep compartment in a massive grid of infinite bunk-beds, and there too was his small allotment of luggage, newly decontaminated, in the attached foot locker. He went immediately for Nasiha's comm – his comm now – and turned it on. A deluge of messages flashed across the screen and he smiled at the names with a mixture of fondness, guilt and worry. Aunt Grace was there of course, several times. Serendipity once or twice – strange, but pleasant. Nothing from Nasiha, which made him frown because she had been the one to fit the fresh chip into the comm for his use and set it to his ID. There was a message from his mother which made his heart beat with a sick heaviness. He promised himself he would open it last. Then, at the very top, there was the last name he expected to see. He opened it and listened.

'My dear Moo, this is to wish you an early happy birthday. Meet me at the observation gallery as soon as you get out of quarantine. We'll celebrate!'

'What?' Rafi went hunting through the earlier messages for enlightenment. The messages from Aunt Grace made little sense at first. They were cheerful. They were filled with advice and encouragement for his first space trip. Not once did she chastise him for dashing off without warning or order him to return to Cygnus Beta as soon as possible. A familiar and unwelcome feeling came over him. This was the language of their correspondence in the days when his father might overhear. It was the kind of message that belonged to unlocked datachips, public forums, megaphones and sky-high billboards. Someone was listening in.

He switched off the comm and lay for a while in a shivering

cold sweat. After a few minutes, he calmed down, stripped off his patient shift and dressed himself in his own clothes. He put the comm on his wrist and his belongings back in the footlocker, and off he went to find the observation gallery.

He was glad to be seeing a familiar face and doubly glad it was Ntenman. In spite of the fact that he would be legally an adult in a few days, he was weary enough to let someone else take charge of his confusing, messy and dangerous life for at least a little while.

PART TWO

Punartam

CHAPTER SEVEN

The nights of Punartam are unique and the days are intense. The seasons, regardless of latitude, are bizarre, extreme and predictable only by highly specialised climatologists using complex models. As a result, the flora is simple, tenacious, short-lived and frighteningly fecund, and the fauna is cautious and canny, omnivorous and expert at hiding. Some people claim that if you spend enough time on Punartam, you will acquire the characteristics of one of those two groups in an attempt to cope with the most variable and stressful environment that ever tested a circadian rhythm.

The culture of Punartam is . . . complicated. At the level of greatest simplicity, it is no more than a colony of Ntshune born out of war and necessity. This bare, uncomplicated fact is a remnant of the untidy truth. Ntshune and Punartam have their own Dark Ages in which the causes and consequences of the Great Galactic War were buried by mutual will and shame as well as by circumstance.

Punartam's younger generation is strongly influenced by Ntshune culture, which may seem counterintuitive unless you consider how many Ntshune choose Punartam for their last year of childhood. There is a tradition that challenge, sacrifice and symbolic death are required to attain to adult status, but that is not the only reason. Punartam still offers the best

*pool of raw Wallrunning talent in the galaxy, and many a matriarch
sends her daughter-successor to Punartam in the hope of gaining fresh
blood for her string of teams, or even the lesser ranks of her dynasty.*

*Older Punarthai of the ruling class fall into one of two categories. There
is an anti-Ntshune, pro-Zhinuvian faction which runs a rogue InterPlanetary Wallrunning League in defiance of the standard Ntshune-based
Galactic League. The leagues' teams never compete, except for a few opti-
mistically labelled 'friendlies' on special occasions, but the battle for
sponsorship, audience share, media attention and pure, raw, ugly celebrity
is brutal, bloody and unceasing.*

*The other pole of power is centred on the Academes. Ecumenical in out-
reach, they represent the intelligentsia of every planet, who comport
themselves as if they are above the petty pride and crass commercialism of
the Wallrunning leagues (though it does no harm to enjoy a match or two,
purely as entertainment, of course). Their focus is knowledge, their currency is communication and the Sadiri pilots and their mindships do very
well as the swiftest conduits of weightless, intangible, priceless information. Each Academe has its own spire to the Equatorial Ring, stretching
their topless towers beyond the very atmosphere. Each also connects to a
system of linked underground reservoirs. These are less visible but equally
essential and large enough to accommodate a brace of mindships coming
in and going out. Matter and mind, material and memory, up the spaceline to scant air and naked vacuum, or down to drown in the hidden
waters of cool, damp caves.*

Rafi ripped the audioplug from his ear and tossed it onto the
table; it went further than he expected and almost landed in a
nearby cactus. 'This idiot's going off again.'

'What's that?' asked Ntenman vaguely, distracted by his own

morning's media, a curious little lens that rode his eyebrow like a half-monocle and projected images directly to his retina.

'This Punartam guide. It's always wandering from the point.'

'If you don't like it, choose a guide from another Academe. There are plenty.'

Rafi grimaced and admitted, 'This one's the easiest. There aren't many in Standard Cygnian.'

'Um,' Ntenman muttered, an utterance of sympathy as profound as it was lengthy.

They were in a bubble, quite literally, shielded from the full Punartam experience within the transition biodome for visitors from Cygnus Beta. The structure was a temporary extension within the recreational Terran biodome in the heart of the metropolitan range. The location was unusual – most quarantine areas were orbital or rural, carefully distant from high urban density – but it had become a necessary measure after Cygnian quarantine standards dipped below galactic requirements. So claimed, and declaimed, the Punartam guide.

It was a scenic prison. Beyond the spare, clean dormitories, which resembled a rack of morgue shelves even more than the facilities on Stage One, there was room to wander and enjoy an eclectic mix of Terran habitats. The semi-arid desert habitat had been purposely expanded as the closest match to the climate of the surrounding boroughs of the Metropolis, and the view from the open-air lounge showed palms, succulents and prickly things with tiny, vivid blossoms.

Ntenman didn't have to be there, but he was and Rafi was grateful for it because he was incredibly bored. The most interesting new thing was the reduced gravity. He found himself walking with a bounce. Ntenman gave him a look that begged him to remember dignity, but he didn't care. The lightness even took the slight slouch out of Ntenman's back so he looked less like a floppy joker and more like an elegant, heroic moko jumbie. Rafi felt so buoyed by the change that he immediately asked if there were any places nearby where they could do a couple of Wallruns, just for practice, but Ntenman shut that down brutally by telling him he had no right running anything until he learned to walk properly again.

It was as if the old Tinman had been replaced with an elder version, more sober, more critical and much less inclined to tolerate nonsense, far less instigate it. Now, in the light of the biodome's artificial morning, he looked tired and preoccupied. Rafi examined his features and noted the small crease of worry between his eyebrows.

'Why are you so miserable?' Rafi complained.

Ntenman looked at him, glared at him in fact, and said nothing for a while, but eventually he snapped, 'What are you going to do while you're here? How long do you plan to stay on Punartam?'

At first Rafi began to laugh because those were the two questions he had heard on Stage One as Ntenman organised their passage on a mindship. He heard them again when the ship docked with the Equatorial Ring and they were awakened with the rest of the human cargo to face a thorough examination by the Punartam Planetary Guard. Down the spaceline and into a second quarantine, and again the staff asked the same two questions – politely, almost conversationally, but they asked. He thought Ntenman was making sport, but no – he was dead serious. Rafi felt his scalp prickle and his hands go cold.

'I don't know.'

He truly did not, and it frightened him to acknowledge how much he had been ignoring reality. Unopened messages still sat in his comm's memory, messages that he could not answer until he breached the Cygnian atmosphere once more. He had a data-charm (still locked) and a datachip (not yet accessed) and an audioplug provided by the biodome staff which had all but drowned him in information, much of it not immediately useful. So much stuff – he had no idea where to start. It had been easier to let Ntenman do the steering and tell him what to do, where to go, what to expect.

'Good. As long as you realise that. As long as you realise you don't have room to be . . . *frivolous* about all this.'

Rafi gaped for a moment then burst out laughing as Ntenman's anxiety suddenly made sense. 'That's not me you're talking about. You're scared. *You're* scared. Why?'

Ntenman slid the media lens carefully from his brow and rested it gently on the table. Suspicious of such studied calmness, Rafi eased out of range, but he received nothing more than another sharp glare. 'We need to build some credit,' Ntenman stated. 'Too long at too low a level and they'll ship you back to Cygnus Beta.'

'You know where we can find work?'

'Work?' Ntenman said, bemused and scornful. 'We want credit, not pay.'

'Well, how will we eat if we don't have pay?' Rafi asked, irritated.

'Moo, do us both a favour and put back in the audioplug. Learn to love the voice of the Academes because I will not be explaining everything to you at every step. Pay is for survival; credit is for living. I'm here, and I want to live.'

'You've been here before?' Rafi said, curiosity and accusation making it a question.

'Yes.' His reply sounded hesitant. 'Yes,' he said again, more firmly. 'I've survived here. I even gained some credit. It was almost a year before my padr got them to send me back.'

Rafi noticed a slight difference in the timbre of his voice that suggested Ntenman was not referring to the usual authorities. 'Them?'

'My other parentals . . . or they would be if they acknowledged me. "Mother" and "stepfathers" are not quite correct, but they're titles you'll understand until you can recite that Punartam guide in your sleep.'

Rafi's heart skipped painfully. Many of the Lyceum's students were half-orphaned or abandoned outright, but Ntenman spoke so often of his padr and was so obviously spoiled by the same that it had never crossed Rafi's mind to ask about a mother. 'Your mother . . . doesn't call you her son?'

'She tried,' Ntenman said, his face pinched with discomfort. 'Now is not the time, Moo. Listen to the wise voices from our towers of knowledge. After that you may be ready to hear my sordid family history.'

'Well, at least tell me what your plan is so I know what topics to look up,' Rafi said.

Ntenman picked up his media lens and smiled enigmatically, but Rafi knew he was being baited and merely sat patiently. 'So, you want to go Wallrunning?' Ntenman said casually. 'There's a lot of that where I'm planning to take you.'

My first attempt at a Punartam Year went foolishly wrong. I was young, so young! I was the kind of fourteen that Rafi's never been. I got as far as Stage One on bluff and bribery before they shipped me back.

My second attempt came soon after and it brought a kind of success. I made a deal with one of my padr's competitors to travel with his next batch of cargo. I didn't even get off the homestead before my padr found out. He was proud at the cargo idea but vexed that I had embarrassed him by going to an outsider, so he compromised by giving me reward and punishment bundled together. He let me go to Punartam on a 'family visit'. Getting there was indeed a gift; meeting my relatives was the punishment. It was supposed to be for three weeks, but I disappeared after two and it took my so-called family months before they deigned to involve themselves in a proper search-and-seize. In that time I learned many things, such things that the Academes would never teach an off-worlder. But it wasn't a Year.

My padr was hard to read. His feelings were definitely mixed. He voiced some pride at my commitment and a significant amount of exasperation at my stubbornness. I tried to point out to him that they were the same thing and that went badly. He sent me to the Lyceum 'to catch up on my Cygnian certification'. Liar. What good was I to the Lyceum, and what good were they to me? He wanted me watched. I behaved until I could be sure he trusted me again, then I behaved for a little while longer. I met Rafi, and then Serendipity, and I dragged out my classes and delayed my departure, playing the idiot to my advantage. I knew the opportunity would come, though for a while I thought Serendipity would be the first to wing her way out of the Cygnian gravity well and taste the air of another world. But Rafi – ha! Long periods of quietness then sudden explosive action. *Decisive* action, nothing like Serendipity's directionless yearning.

I faced my padr like a man. I was honest. 'Look,' I said, 'I have an obligation to help this boy, but I won't lie – if it takes me a year on

Punartam to do it, that suits me, too. Let me have your blessing this time.'

Years of good behaviour meant maturity in my padr's mind, and that swayed him to give consent – with conditions. He entreated me with all formal, fervid zeal not to bring any shame to my family on Punartam or Cygnus Beta. He insisted that I return after a year, or whenever Rafi could fend for himself. And then, because he is a practical and canny businessman, he gave me a list of tasks and contacts that would smooth the way to improved credit and increased trade for his company. I agreed, especially to the last condition. I didn't want to take over my padr's business, but I did want to see him succeed because no one needs a Zhinuvian trade monopoly, not now, not ever.

I had my padr's blessing. I had experience of living on Punartam. I knew people, and I was known. No one could say that I had no idea what I was doing. My actions, given the information at the time, made perfect sense, but somewhere between the commitment of an adult and the recklessness of a child, I found a new thing – fear of failure. Rafi saw it, and if he could see it, so would everyone else. That wasn't good. The usual cheery mask wouldn't do, either; any hint of artificiality would brand me forever a foreigner. I had to get back into the game with seriousness, focus and intent. Fear comes before a fall, and they don't bother with body-catchers in the Punartam pro leagues.

At last it was time to leave the biodome. Five Terran days had passed, each one hours shorter than a Cygnian day and minutes shorter than a Standard day, but all five days together could not match the shortest Punartam day when both suns set at the same time.

'You are now on a twelve-siesta planet; have a nice day,' said a member of the biodome staff after he finished processing the details of their departure into his tiny microphone, a silvery etching that curved along his jaw and punctuated his lower lip with a highly decorative bracket. He sounded sincere, but there was something about his absent-mindedness that hinted this was his standard farewell, a joke he had repeated so often that it no longer registered in his brain.

Rafi bounced nervously. His clothes felt strange. Punartam fashion started with the familiar beige tunic, but after that it got complicated. Ntenman had trussed him up with two thin sashes and a broad belt with a pouch, clasped a metal band over the looped lanyard on his arm that carried his datacharm, and tied up his hair with a hasp-and-pin contraption made of some material that was as smooth as copper but as warm as wood.

Ntenman's tunic was covered with a simple brown tabard – no strings, bands or belts for him. Rafi eyed him with suspicion, but he forgot to feel silly when they crossed the biodome's threshold and he gasped at his first few lungfuls of thin, cool Punartam air.

'Yes, let's see you bounce now,' Ntenman said, laughing at his struggle. 'I still say Punartam has the edge for Wallrunning training. Gravity may vary from Wall to Wall and world to world, but a good, efficient oxygen intake is a gift for all occasions.'

Rafi touched the oxygen breather at his belt but let his hand fall away. Ntenman shook his head. 'It takes you without warning. Better sneak a few nips here and there than wait for a full collapse.'

'How far are we . . . going?' Rafi snatched a quick breath mid-sentence.

'Thought you'd like to see the sights,' came the indirect response.

Rafi let it pass because he was indeed caught up in seeing the sights. In Tlaxce City, as in so many Terran megacities and most Zhinuvian warrens and domains, the sky would be almost blocked out by several centuries' and storeys' worth of architecture. Punartam's Metropolis was an inversion; the architecture was deep below the surface, hidden from the sun. Above-ground was open sky save for the towering Academes which locals called the Range, all the more majestic for having no competition, but slender, delicate, as if the spiky vertebrae of a saildragon had been stripped of meat and left to dry under the two suns.

The rest of the landscape consisted of parks and single-storey buildings with rooftop gardens. They gave the Metropolis its dominant colours – dark green, hazy purple and faint silver. Some of the gardens were under domes and those showed a wider variety of plants. Rafi thought he saw heliconias, their vivid orange and red striking him with a pang of homesickness, but they were too far away for him to be sure. There were no trains or cars, at least none visible, only a few small aerolights gliding from tower to tower. People stood and sat and walked in the parks, gardens and pathways, but there were not enough people, never enough people for such an important city. He knew why.

'Roughly one-third,' said Ntenman. 'Two-thirds below, working or sleeping. It's a maze down there. You're better off staying topside until you learn not to get lost.'

Rafi held up a hand in a silent plea, leaned over for several seconds, then reluctantly straightened. He dragged a few deep breaths through the oxygen breather and tucked it back into his belt. 'Ready,' he said.

He thought he could see where they were going, and it looked *far*. The base of the Academe was set within the concentric ripples of a terraced garden, a pretty effect that made the tower resemble a spear rising up from the depths of a green lake.

'Isn't there a pedestrian path nearby? One that . . . moves?' he asked.

'There's that soft Terran constitution coming through. Try to hide it better, Moo. You don't *look* overly alien. Use that to your advantage. And put in your audioplug. I'll point out what's interesting as we walk.'

After fifteen minutes and another stop to breathe, Rafi gave in and strapped the breather to his face. It cleared his head and his vision sufficiently that he was able to take interest once more in what was going on around him. Excitement slowly built, fizzing in his blood like a fast-acting stimulant and almost sending him from the thrill of newness to the thrill of fear. He was no novice to alien life. Cygnus Beta collected every aspect of the galaxy, Tlaxce was a proper galactic-class metropolis, and even if he had managed to stay blinkered and cloistered with only Terran influences, there was plenty in both homestead and Lyceum education to ensure that he had no reason to gawk. But, but, but . . . the *difference*, the sheer unsettling *difference* of the place was overwhelming to the point that he could not figure out whether to be gleeful or petrified.

Two people walked side by side behind the low wall of a nearby terrace, half-obscured by the fall of green vines and purple flowers that pushed over the wall and down the steep slant of the buttressing earth. There was nothing familiar by which Rafi could measure size, but one of the figures was twice the height of the other, and their arms swung with a jerky arc that hinted at unusual jointedness. A man (at least, he *looked* like a man) passed them on the path with a creature at his heel. The animal (*at least*, thought Rafi, beginning to panic, *it* looked *like an animal*) was covered with something too mobile to be fur and too fuzzy to be feathers, and it moved with a hopping, bipedal gait that bounced its narrow, bird-like head between elbow and shoulder height. Rafi searched for a reference, could not determine what it was and settled for thinking of it as a miniature ostrich, though without the long neck and the round body. The odd pair were in a hurry, too distracted for even a brief greeting-gesture, but when Rafi's heart skipped at the nearness of the unknown, the man gave him a blinked side-look and a tiny wry smile as if he had heard the muffled thump from within Rafi's chest.

Ntenman missed the exchange. 'It used to be a lot busier aboveground. Some of the old vids and holos we get on Cygnus Beta still give the wrong impression, but Punartam culture goes through these phases. Once it was the Academes that influenced everything. You had working and residential communities pooled like ink around the base of the towers, and you could tell just by looking at the landscape who the biggies were. Now it's all subtle and discreet and below the surface. You see neat little gardens around the towers and—'

'And the Walls?' asked Rafi eagerly.

Ntenman looked at him. 'Yes. The commercial leagues play and practise below now, but there are still amateur leagues that play friendly games on the tower-side walls.'

'What?' said Rafi, confused at the look.

Ntenman looked away again. 'I know it's new and exciting, but don't get too excited and don't act too new. Now, put these in your listening queue: Five Trees Escape. Central Fastline Station. Sundome Mezzanine Slowline. The Board of Credit Assessors (that's the only non-Academe tower, by the way). The Credit Exchange

Bureau is the low bump next to it; we're going there after our next sleep. And Academe Surinastraya – that's where we're headed – which specialises in Energy.'

Ntenman's chatter got them halfway to the tower, but by then Rafi's dizzied exhaustion had become a stagger. Ntenman complained under his breath, but he led Rafi along a fork in the path, under a metal archway set in a stone wall and into a capsule of the Sundome Slowline. It looked innocent, paused and poised on an antigrav pad in a small chamber with an open sky, but then it lurched off at speed, a single pearl zipping along the Slowline, half-sunk in a trench with sky and a sliver of horizon as the only view options. Rafi tumbled at the start and only saved himself by clutching the lower edge of the high window-ceiling. Ntenman sighed tolerantly and waited, leaning safely and comfortably, until the motion had steadied, then came over to show him where to park his centre of gravity.

'I keep forgetting what a booby I was when I first got here,' he admitted, unpeeling a seat from its wall recess. He remained standing, nonchalant in his ability to anticipate changes in the capsule's direction and speed – not very different from the changing gravity of a Wall, in fact.

The journey was short, but Rafi, to his embarrassment, fell asleep halfway, going from avidly listening to the topics Ntenman had suggested straight to sudden unconsciousness with ridiculous speed. Ntenman shook him awake and pulled him up with a smile of amused sympathy. Rafi surreptitiously wiped a line of drool from the left corner of his mouth and trailed behind him to exit the capsule. Their single pearl had joined a chain of five others. Shadowy passengers moved within their translucent walls; some were coming, some going, dancing up or down their capsule's little gangway which connected to the upper pavement and open air above the Slowline track. They moved with the speed of ease and familiarity, but Rafi stepped like an elderly traveller, sober and cautious, until he stood on the broad, flat lawn at the base of the Academe. He gazed around, then up and up, feeling that curious thrill of reverse-vertigo created by an edifice being too tall and too close. Its needle was an imperfect sundial with two shadows, each of a slightly different hue, but true dark at the overlap.

'Here we are,' said Ntenman. 'And look – they're expecting us.'

Rafi uncraned his neck and refocused his vision on a nearer point. *They* were two figures, one tall and roundly heavy, dressed in the common galactic suit of tunic and trousers and a light, short robe of office that indicated an administrative rather than academic function; the other taller and trimmer, in what looked like Galactic Patrol urban kit, but unarmed except for a ceremonial knife at the waist. They walked down the wide stone ramp of the Academe's main entrance, and as they drew nearer, Rafi noted a touch of tension, if not outright haste, in their movements.

'Long years time I haven't seen you, Ntenman, and now look. You. Here without so much as warning, far less invitation. Here with child in hand like an elder but still a child yourself. Here like Punartam belongs to you. Can you be bothered to learn shame, if not manners?'

The harshness of the words became a lie with the broadness of the smile, and yet that smile still carried the hint of an edge – Rafi could not tell how or why. In contrast, Ntenman's smile was painfully, obviously brave.

'Revered Haviranthiya,' was all he said as he submitted to the administrator's hard embrace.

Ordinarily Rafi would be waiting attentively for an introduction, but the identity of the second figure had become clear to him at last. The uniform was the first clue, then the face familiar enough from a single brief meeting on the Sadiri settlement, but it was the expression of annoyance and reproach that triggered his guilt reflex and jogged his memory. 'Corporal Lian?'

First a calm correction. 'Second Lieutenant Lian, newest officer of the Galactic Gendarmerie.' Then a stern glare. 'Your aunt is worried sick. Why haven't you been in touch?'

Conversation continued at Rafi's side while he stammered out apologies. 'So tall,' Haviranthiya was saying, slapping a wincing Ntenman with cheerful yet painful force about the shoulders. 'So broad. And still a child.'

Rafi fought his way out of the fog of contrition. 'Wait. How do you expect me to be in touch? There's about a month's message delay for ordinary mail.'

A tired look and a sad shaking of the head were the only reply. Guilt prompted Rafi's brain a little further and he felt his face go hot as he recalled the still-unread data chip. He spasmed, grabbing the pouch at his waist as if seized with sudden incontinence, and said pathetically, 'Things have been so busy.'

'Your friend Ntenman contacted the Revered, who then contacted us Cygnians. I had a separate communication that gave me some more information on the situation . . . so I got a few days' leave and came here.'

'Came here from where?'

Lian gestured vaguely east. 'Academe Bhumniastraya. Terran Studies. Doctor Daniyel is there.'

Rafi shook his head. He had heard of her but never met her. With another pang of guilt he remembered the datacharm and the many, many papers he had saved there. He was holding his information everywhere but inside his head.

'The Academe asked her to come. She's very good, so good in fact that they wanted her to plan *and* lead the fieldwork.'

'Wasn't she sick?' Rafi asked, somewhat amazed by this small talk but happy for the illusion of ordinariness. At his side, Ntenman was being subjected to a resonant, top-volume and frighteningly happy interrogation sprinkled with reminders of his lack of status and common sense. Rafi was desperate to keep out of it.

'She was, but they asked her to reconsider taking a full cure, and so she did. Exigencies of the Service and so on. Physically, she's doing very well, but she says they give her so much to do that she's still as chronically fatigued as ever.'

The uncomfortable, one-sided conversation ongoing nearby overcame their polite attempts to ignore it and drew them in. 'And this is your friend! Does he know he is dressed like a child? So strange, when you are not and should be! Ntenman, you cannot be responsible for a child if I am to be responsible for you. Perhaps our esteemed Second Lieutenant will take charge of him for us?'

'There's no need, Revered Haviranthiya,' said Lian with a cautious smile. 'Rafi has reached partial majority under Cygnian law. He's not a full adult, but he's not a child. He can go where he chooses . . . for now.'

Rafi kept his mouth shut at those last ominous words. It had just occurred to him in a blood-chilling, bone-numbing instant that although Lian was a friend of his aunt's, a posting in the Galactic Gendarmerie meant a shift in location, not role. Strictly speaking, Lian was a representative of the military police and had the authority to send him back to Cygnus Beta.

Haviranthiya's smile had not once faded, but there was a

detectable shift from sarcastic irritation to unshakeable intent. 'Then let him choose to stay here a while with his friend. I can educate them both on what it is to be a man on Punartam.'

Lian's smile also did not falter though it did quirk questioningly, conveying more warning than uncertainty. At least it appeared to be friendly warning, as between equals. 'Do keep me updated,' was all Lian said. 'I will organise for his credit—'

Haviranthiya cut the sentence in half with an imperious chop of his broad right hand. 'Not at all necessary. It would be an honour and a pleasure to arrange for his introductions, his keys, his essentials and his accoutrements.'

Rafi wondered if it was possible to pass out from the sheer pressure of mounting bewilderment. Lian gave him a quick, amused glance.

'In fact,' Lian added, with a lilt that suggested suppressed laughter, 'after you've given the boys an initial briefing, perhaps Rafi could join me later for some pre-sleep refreshment and recreation. I think we need to talk.'

CHAPTER EIGHT

'The Ntshune, who are the alleged emotional centre of humanity, have elaborate, calculated forms of retaliation. The Sadiri, for all their mental capacity and apparent coolness, are blunt, direct and passionate in revenge. These are crude generalisations, but they are so attractively paradoxical, so charmingly mythic, that they have acquired a kind of truth as both Sadiri and Ntshune try to live up to their respective reputations.'

Ntenman roused slightly from his slouch on the daybed and glared at Rafi, obviously still tender from the prolonged flaying of his ego. 'Listen and learn all you like, but there's no need to share.'

Rafi took the audioplug from his ear and glared back. 'Well, it explains your ingenious ways of torturing me. Dressing me like a fool. Dragging me around until I collapse and then letting me embarrass myself at the Academe. How much Ntshune *are* you, Tinman? More than most Cygnians, surely?'

'I've dressed you like a child because that's what you are in this place. No one told you to take off the oxygen filter and run yourself ragged. Again, no one told you to hold on to that datachip as if you had for ever to read it. Your aunt's friend is a *policeman*? You should have prepared me for that, at least. Thank day and night I got us here legally.'

'And you haven't answered my question.'

Ntenman looked embarrassed. 'Mostly Ntshune. Three-quarters, in fact. My padr's half-Terran.'

'You sound so ashamed! Most Cygnians would be stupidly proud of that.'

He huffed resentfully. 'You really haven't guessed by now? I'm . . . incapable of functioning in Ntshune society. Insufficient psi ability. Easier to be Cygnian.' His sentences became more and more staccato as he tried and failed to speak lightly about what was clearly a source of deep, long-term hurt.

'I didn't know,' Rafi said in quiet apology.

He went to the window and looked out to give Ntenman a bit of space. The smooth, opaque exterior of the tower was a hollow tube set like a translucent bell over a skyscraper, hiding myriad wide windows to offices, living quarters, lecture halls and rooms upon rooms. About fifty metres of broad-bladed green and purple grass covered the ground between the outer and inner walls, and the inner walls also ran verdant with hanging vegetation. Inside their room, the harsh light of the suns filtered through as cool aqua and the dry air was gentled by the moist exhalation of many plants clustered together.

This window was on the quiet side of the tower, the side for resting, meditating and, with the window's screening turned to full opacity, sleeping. Haviranthiya had explained that to him; the Academe dealt with the long days by making time into place. There was also a work section and a recreation section, and people moved to where they needed to be as the hours turned. The basic accommodation in the Academe was called a 'three-roomer', with none of the rooms adjacent. As non-academics, Rafi and Ntenman had something less than basic, two rooms only, one very private for sleep and quiet, the other more open and public for eating, entertainment and being gregarious. He had not seen that room yet, but he knew already that it would have a good view of the several game Walls poised over the inside of the tower's outer casing. He was eager to watch a game, but Haviranthiya, anticipating the fatigue of the newly arrived, had taken them to sleeping quarters and ordered him to rest for an hour.

When Rafi turned back, he found Ntenman was propped up on his elbows, frowning at him, diverted from his brief moment of weakness by a lingering mystery. 'How can you not know, Moo? You can't hide what you are. Serendipity saw it the moment she met you.'

'What do you mean?' Rafi asked. His voice was calm, his face was calm, but his eyes were wide and hurt.

'You're like a lighthouse. Most times you're barely noticeable, and then there's this great sweep of . . .' Ntenman lay back and combed his hands vigorously through the air in an attempt at description. 'Of *something*,' he said weakly. 'Anyone can feel it. *I've* felt it.'

Rafi blinked and turned away. 'So I can shout. Doesn't mean I can speak,' he muttered.

'Maybe you should have let the Lyceum help you— Wait, what am I saying? They can barely help themselves. But Moo, *someone* has to help you, and this may be the best place for it. What are you afraid of, exactly?'

'I don't know. I . . . I . . .' He tried to find more words, but his throat tightened and would not release them. His aunt's explanation, that they had mutually influenced each other into silence, was a comforting one, but there was an undertow of fear and shame that felt both foreign and familiar. He pushed his hands at the invisible barrier. 'I don't know!' he cried out. 'I don't know what I'm afraid of. I'm just afraid.'

'Don't yell,' Ntenman said quietly. 'Not in this section. It's important to be good neighbours in the Metropolis. It matters a lot.'

Rafi murmured an apology.

'As I was saying, you could get help here. Be a child, learn from scratch. The Academe is a galactic environment. It caters to Sadiri and Cygnians and Zhinuvians all the time, but there are some communities below-ground that have the full Punarthai experience. You could go there and learn what you are and what to do with it.'

'I don't want to be a child again. I am an adult.' It was an embarrassing thing to have to say, so he said it with as much quiet dignity as he could manage.

'By homestead standards, Moo!' Ntenman made his tone just as quiet and twice as intense. 'If you want to be an adult here you have to prove you can do more than herd goats, chop wood and breed.'

'If I want to be here at all, I can't give Lian any legal excuse to ship me back,' Rafi explained.

Ntenman began to speak, then paused, pondering. 'Oh,' was all he said. 'But—' He paused again. 'But there are other ways, if you're willing to try them.'

Rafi gave him a look of tired suspicion.

'But perhaps you should first hear what Lian has to tell you when you go and eat,' Ntenman continued. The sentence ended in a yawn which he tried to smother with both hands.

Rafi felt worried again. 'I should look at that datachip.' He winced, expecting a few sarcastic words from Ntenman along the lines of, 'I told you so,' but surprisingly, there was silence and then, less surprisingly, a series of soft, almost musical snores.

Rafi could not sleep. First he went to the dressing area of their quarters. There he had a quiet chat with the garment fabricator, dumped the post-quarantine outfit into its recycler and received a standard galactic suit in return. Moving slowly so as not to get dizzy, he tested the facilities. The shower-like cubicle extruded nozzles which puffed hot, abrasive air at him, covered him in a sticky glitter which quickly dissolved, then surrounded him with cool mist. He thought he was finished but the door refused to open, gently advising him to use the special chamois provided to tend to his crevices. Tentatively, he did so and disposed of it in the designated niche. As he exited, the door rewarded him with a frighteningly brisk gust that took the last of the mist droplets from his hair.

By the time he was fully dressed and watching himself turn as a mirrored holo, he felt ridiculously proud of what he had managed. He saw before him a sober figure, perhaps too slender still for a grown man but too tall for a child. Lian might yet take him seriously – which brought him to his second task.

He set the datachip next to the sensor in the dressing room. His slowly spinning holo vanished and several lines of font spilled down the wall. He scanned, searched and sorted. His aunt had given him introductory guides to Punartam, specialised tours and maps of the Metropolis above- and below-ground. Some of them looked similar to what he had received in quarantine, but they were likely outdated editions. Others were completely new to him, and those he carefully put aside to be examined later. Then there were names and titles and locations of colleagues and friends, people she knew from her research. She had flagged certain names for specific help such as obtaining introductions and credit, and others to contact in case of dire emergency.

Haviranthiya's name did not appear, which was no surprise as most of the names were attached to Academe Bhumniastraya and a few to Academe Maenevastraya. Dr Qeturah Daniyel's name appeared unflagged.

Lian's name did not appear at all.

Later, Rafi left the living quarters (and Ntenman, who was still sleeping) to follow the directions Lian had sent to his audioplug channel. He carried Commander Nasiha's comm with him but it had no value beyond the nostalgic in the Metropolis. People on Punartam did not have comms per se; they had channels. They did not call. They joined ongoing public discussions, reserved bands for private topics, sent messages, maps and other information about how to access the next gathering of voices or persons. Everything important was oral and aural. He was amazed at their ability to pay attention to two and three conversations at once without faltering. They could have an Academe lecture whispering in their ear while they passionately debated the merits of a new player on their favourite Wallrunning team and never miss a detail of either topic.

Rafi knew all of that, and still the level of chatter in the dining hall was a shock to his ears and confusion to his brain. He lost track of what the directions were saying and hovered, lost for a moment, but then he saw Lian waving to him from a table near the centre of the room. He quickly went over and they spent the first few minutes in casual talk as they selected dishes from a mini-carousel in the middle of the table. By the time Rafi took the first mouthful, he was feeling sufficiently relaxed to mention, not without reproach, the absence of Lian's name on Delarua's list of contacts.

Lian merely smiled. 'Your aunt is a good secret-keeper. She has a way of telling you everything except for what might get you into trouble. She didn't want to put me in an awkward position, so I was left off the list.'

'And yet, as far as awkward positions go, here you are,' Rafi noted cautiously.

Lian sipped at a cup of some lightly fizzing beverage, inhaled at the wrong moment and was momentarily caught up in an attempt not to sneeze. 'Yes, here I am. Nothing stays secret in the Metropolis. Ntenman told Haviranthiya he was on his way. Haviranthiya spoke to some of his circle in Academe Maenevastraya, who in turn brought the news to Academe Bhumniastraya. Doctor Daniyel isn't contactable at the moment, so they spoke to me instead. Of course, by then I already knew. In fact, I wouldn't be surprised if those at Academe Maenevastraya knew before me *and* Haviranthiya.' Lian paused to fix him with a meaningful look. 'Academe Maenevastraya specialises in Interstellar Communications and Transport. Drink your drink. It's good for the digestion.'

Rafi tried the pale, warm, bubbling liquid. It tasted of chlorophyll and sting, flavours that rather suited the atmosphere of the dining hall. The windows were large and open and carried partial shutters that appeared to temper the wind's gusts but otherwise let in most of the air and a lot of light. The light was needed; the vertical verdure outside had been encouraged to push past the edges of the windows and spread over the room's walls. Rafi recognised a recurring theme. The dry, over-bright Metropolis had oases tucked into every nook and niche. He did wonder, though, where they had got the wood for the tables and stools, or if indeed the wood was from actual trees and not some fabricated facsimile, or a complete fake with knots and grain painted on.

Unlike the living quarters, there appeared to be no noise restriction whatsoever in this dining hall. People moved from table to table, talking and laughing loudly, sometimes stopping long enough that it became necessary to bring over another stool, or put two tables together. Rafi began to understand why the plates and bowls were so easily carried and the utensils few and simple in design. People set bowls down to eat and converse with one group, then were waved over by another group to hear some news or piece of wit. They would return eventually to the first table, but overall it was a pool of Brownian motion, with laughter and information bouncing like a benign contagion from table to table.

He drank again and coughed. 'Does everything here run on gossip?'

'Gossip, information, intelligence. Whatever it is, it's the fuel and the glue and the lifeblood of anything touched by the Ntshune.'

'So, if you didn't hear about me from Academe Maenevastraya, who told you?' asked Rafi. He had been paying attention and thinking carefully.

With another smile and a shake of the head, Lian backed away from the question. 'Like your aunt, I prefer not to tell people things that might get them in trouble. You really should drink more of that. Your stomach will thank you.'

'Why, what are we eating?' Rafi asked, frowning at the selection of bowls and platters. Most of the contents looked familiar. He had eaten in enough restaurants in Tlaxce to recognise authentic Punartam fare.

'Oh, protein, carbohydrates, the usual. We're all human, after all. But our interior ecosystems are a little different, and this drink helps the Terran digestion. Lots of enzymes and . . . er . . . other stuff.' The final words were muffled as Lian bit into a bread-like ball.

'Drink it or a fungus will grow out of your throat so fast you'll think the follicles of your beard have reversed. Hello, Lian.'

Rafi jumped. The new voice belonged to a middle-aged, cheerful face and a large, heavy hand that smacked him on the shoulder in a friendly fashion. The smack came with a similarly heavy surge of complex sensory impressions. Rafi was shocked. Was it mere introduction or gross liberty? Had he seen the galactic garb and assumed Rafi would feel nothing, or had he already picked up something from Rafi and offered a standard greeting?

The newcomer pulled up a stool and joined them, oblivious to Rafi's turmoil. 'So this is the nephew?'

'Yes, Tshalo, this is my friend's nephew. Rafiabowen— But no, you made some changes when you became an adult, didn't you? Rafidelarua, Hanekitshalo.'

'Ah, Terran, of course.'

'Cygnian,' Rafi answered, but a dismissive hand was already being waved before he completed the final syllable.

'It is all the same,' said Tshalo. 'And yet— No, don't offer me anything. I have eaten.' He gently pushed away the platter Lian had shoved under his nose.

Lian eyed him blandly and kept chewing. 'So you are here because . . . ?'

'Mistrustful child! If you wished to speak privately, you would not be in the public rooms, correct? But I am not here for information. I came for an introduction, and I have accomplished that.'

Lian stopped eating and sat back. 'You unregistered, unclaimed superfluous spawn of a renegade mother. You're taking advantage of my Terran courtesy to play Academe politics. Rafi, don't say another word. This specimen is from Academe Maenevastraya and he's trying to cut in front of Haviranthiya. Rude and unnecessary.'

'Such words, Lian! Please have some patience. We are not so terrible as that.'

'We? Who is "we", now?'

'We who would be on very good terms with Cygnus Beta, and with Sadira-on-Cygnus,' Tshalo replied, all hint of teasing gone. 'And there are a lot of us. Are you understanding me yet?'

Lian glared at him for a moment, then relaxed enough to pick up a large slice of vegetable, bite it in half and resume chewing. 'I am beginning to, for all that I am a slow, untalented Terran-type.'

'Terran-types are very much in fashion during these times of great uncertainty and change,' Tshalo said cryptically. 'Remember me, Rafidelarua. I am sure we will meet again soon.'

He stood, snagged a leaf from the platter under Lian's right hand, rolled it and scooped it full of mashed tuber. Saluting them with a slight upward raise of the treat, he walked off, munching.

Lian sat momentarily paralysed at the audacity, then began to speak slowly. 'I'll try to tell you what just happened, but don't feel bad if you make no more sense of it than I can.'

'Is he someone important at his Academe?'

'His mother is. Very, *very* important. Whether or not he is actually speaking for the Haneki family is debatable. He is as I called him – unregistered and unclaimed. But he has the gene tags to prove his origins and he uses them for leverage whenever he can.'

'What leverage could I give him?' Rafi wondered.

Lian gave him a quizzical look. 'Don't you follow the news?'

Rafi thought for a brief, painful moment of the datacharm brimming with information from the Sadira-on-Cygnus network, the datachip from his aunt, the audioplug and other information from the transit and quarantine staff, and the latest manuals on Academe living kindly provided by Haviranthiya. 'No,' he said in a small voice.

'Your uncle is now Governor of Sadira-on-Cygnus. They say it's likely he'll be made Guardian next. New Sadira is *not* taking it well. Ntshune and Punartam have made no formal comment, but there have been some private congratulations.'

Rafi remembered something distracting. 'You said my aunt was worried about me. How do you know that?'

Lian looked down briefly, as if struggling with an impulse to lie. 'The same way I knew your arrival date. Let's leave it at that. Now, tell me, what are you doing here? No, stop it, I don't mean here at this table, or here in this Academe. I mean why Punartam?'

Rafi quickly erased the daft and confused expression that had so irritated Lian and tried to look resolute. 'I'm here to get help for my condition.'

Raised eyebrows, blank eyes, sarcastic flutter of the eyelashes – Lian was still not impressed. 'Your condition? You have a condition?'

'Yes,' Rafi continued boldly. 'One that the Lyceum failed to diagnose and treat. I learned that the best research on psionic behaviours is happening here on Punartam.'

Cynicism and suspicion gave way to grudging interest and respect. 'This sounds almost believable. Keep going.'

'And since I knew a friend who had been to Punartam,' he said, the words coming with ease and eloquence, 'I seized the opportunity and—'

'Bravo!' Lian clapped softly. 'You're very good at that – reinventing the past. A little mental push with that and you'd be set. Don't do it. Don't try that with me, and don't try it with anyone else. If you do, I will have you restrained and shipped back to Cygnus Beta before you can blink.'

Rafi gaped. The menace of the words and the cheerfulness of Lian's voice clashed with a kind of surreal horror that rivalled any ordinary threat. 'I won't,' he said indignantly.

'Good. I can file a nice, straightforward report at my next waketime.'

An awkward silence grew, only mildly alleviated by the ongoing background gaiety, the clash of busy forks and dedicated mastication.

'So, who should I go to for psionic research at Academe Bhumniastraya?' Rafi asked meekly, avoiding the question of where the report would be filed.

'I have no idea, but I will try to find out for you,' Lian promised. 'I think it would be a good idea to work on whatever talent you have. Cygnian authorities don't mind properly socialised talent. It's the wild cards that make them jittery, and for good reason, *very* good reason.'

'When is your leave over?' Rafi asked, desperate to find and keep to an innocuous topic.

Lian began to answer but paused in confusion, distracted by a sudden surging roar outdoors. The people inside the dining hall cheered in reply and nearly half of them got up and rushed to the wall-side windows, adding the scraping and screeching of furniture on floor to the cacophony. Lian's look of bafflement eased into resigned comprehension. 'Oh, the Wallrunners are warming up.'

'Wallrunners?' Rafi leapt up and almost knocked over his stool in his haste to get to the windows.

Lian followed him at a slower pace, taking along a bowl and continuing to eat unhurriedly. Beyond the window, a small, dark figure went sideways in a diving arc along the curve of the wall. Several similar figures followed, mimicking their leader's trajectory with flair and spin. Faint howls and chants began to echo between the tower and the outer wall, but they were immediately drowned out by the ululations within the dining hall. Rafi instinctively joined in and had to stop, panting, after only a few seconds. Lian kindly passed him a square of some unidentifiable compressed fruit. It was so sweet that when he bit into it his ears tingled and his mouth overwatered almost painfully, but it steadied his shaky pulse and cleared his head. The crowd began to quieten and thin out, ready for more food and gossip at their tables now that the brief show was over, and Lian drifted back with them. Rafi sighed but did not yet follow, wanting to savour the moment. He wondered if he could find some visual record of the dive.

'Who were they?' he asked the person on his left, another lingerer leaning on the windowsill.

'The Academe's second line, practising for the demonstration next twilight.' The voice was familiar. The fading fall of the words as they turned to him in surprise suggested that this feeling of familiarity was mutual. He looked up and, as the figure straightened fully, up again. That height was unforgettable. He recalled another brief instance of Wallrunning, the taste of perrenuts making his mouth water for reasons other than sweetness, and a tall, dark stranger whose name he had never learned.

She looked down at him, blinking in shock, silently processing a number of things that came out as a single conclusion. 'You're Rafidelarua.'

'Who are you?' he demanded.

She glanced guiltily around the room to check the location of Lian's still-turned back, then answered. 'I am Ixiaralhaneki. I will find you later.'

With that, she moved quickly away from the windows and left the dining hall, no more remarkable than the rest who had stopped to watch the Wallrunners and were now slowly returning to meals, conversations and work. Rafi reluctantly went back to Lian, who immediately misunderstood his disgruntled expression.

'Cheer up. There'll be plenty of Wallrunning to see and do around the Academes.'

'Yes,' Rafi agreed absently. 'Lian, what's so important about the Haneki family?'

Lian's expression became guarded, and Rafi knew that whatever he was about to hear would be carefully censored. 'It is said,' Lian spoke with careful emphasis, 'that the Hanekis and the . . . Mwenils are trying to find a new form of interstellar transportation, or possibly rediscover an old one.' The verbal stumble was caused by an unfamiliar consonant. Rafi was amused at the musical sip and click of the 'mw'. It looked like the second lieutenant was blowing him kisses.

'Are they your source of off-planet information?' he asked with a cheeky grin.

Lian smirked at him. 'No, no, I am not helping you go through any process of elimination to find the answer. Punartam is filled with possibilities. Did you know that this was the place where the Great Galactic War ended?'

Rafi admitted aloud that if it had not been for the ramblings of that irritating Punartam guide audioplug, he would not even have known there had been a Great Galactic War.

'It's not a big thing on Cygnus Beta because it barely touched us and it happened a long time before we had Galactic Standard anything. Still, to get the full details you need to look at the research of the data archaeologists from Academe Nkhaleëngomi. They restore all kinds of obsolete tech – especially information storage devices that are supposed to be locked or destroyed. But between you and me, I'm not sure the galaxy is ready for what they might uncover.'

Lian contemplated the remains of their meal, sighed and stacked the empty dishes on the carousel. The contraption retracted itself into the table, perhaps in obedience to Lian's sharp tap on its base, perhaps not. 'So, you were asking about my leave. I go back two days from now. Do you want to meet for lunch next day-cycle? Bring your friend. I'll bring one, too.'

Rafi nodded, struck by Lian's sudden collapse into weariness of tone and posture. He wondered if, on a world like Punartam where networks were everything, a member of the Galactic Patrol could ever be anything but an outsider. He had seen something like this at the Lyceum – two of the students were imports from distant Kir'tahsg. They were from the same social class and yet they detested each other. In spite of that, they drew together in the face of the strangeness around them, clinging to their shared norms, talking and working together, and somehow still hating each other. Lyceum Masters called it the isolationist syndrome: introverts forced to be selectively and excessively gregarious due to the loneliness of immersion in a highly alien environment.

'We can eat in a private dining room next time,' he promised, not knowing how to arrange such a thing but determined to do so.

'That would be nice,' Lian murmured. 'These crowds make my head hurt.'

CHAPTER NINE

Two Standard weeks later, when the nosebleeds stopped and the shortness of breath was easing, Ntenman declared Rafi ready to meet some of his old Wallrunning friends. Ntenman had spent the days going out and about, reviving old connections and doing what he briefly and bluntly called 'my padr's business'. Rafi did not press him. He was still in the phase of gratitude that made him meek and obedient – which was why he also did not object to Ntenman's proposal for descending from their high-rise quarters to the base of the tower.

'Every tower has emergency chutes,' Ntenman explained. 'It makes sense to learn to use them when you're not having an emergency. Plus it's good practice for Wallrunning.'

Rafi leaned cautiously against the doorway, peered up and glanced down. From the outside, doors closed, it appeared to be a standard elevator. On the inside, the shaft was empty and it looked like pure, certain death.

'It's an overflow evacuation route for when the normal elevators are overcrowded. It's perfectly safe. Power failure is never a problem at this Academe, and if anything goes wrong, the safety lines will kick in.'

'Good,' said Rafi faintly. 'And how do we get down?'

'We jump. The microgravity will slow us a bit and there's a body-catcher at the bottom. There are safety belts and lines for complete novices, but I didn't request any because we're beyond that.'

'Am I? Oh. Well. After you.'

Ntenman grinned, seized his arm and jumped.

The first few seconds were teeth-gritting terror, but then there was a gradual slowing of pace. Rafi could easily imagine he was Alice, falling gently down the rabbit hole to Wonderland. The body-catcher caught him by surprise; it extended higher than he was used to from Wallrunning and stopped them centimetres above the floor before cutting out suddenly and dropping them on their heels. At the same time, a wide door opened into a half-circle of hazy golden light. Artificial light, Rafi would have called it, or lamplight, but on Punartam that term was reserved for indoor lighting during the day. Outside lighting was *recycled sunlight* whenever it was used to illuminate the long night. Ntenman stepped out into the cool air, shivered and tucked his hands into his tunic sleeves. Rafi simply stayed close to the tower; heat radiated gently from it and the upper baffles offered some protection from the breeze.

It was odd. During the daytime, the tower's inner ring was little used, but the long night gave excuse for a semi-carnival of activity which the Academe encouraged by leaving its gates open to the public. Families and friends walked slowly around the tower and everything was on offer: confectionery, savouries, tumblers and contortionists, songsters, comedians and players of curious instruments. There was light everywhere, not only mundane light to make the entertainment and food visible, but artistic, enchanting, fun expressions of light. Children carried bright, rainbow-tinted bubbles that burst with damp, harmless sparks. Scarves and shawls were tipped in glow that streaked across the retina when the wearer flipped the ends with flair. Footsteps gleamed with delayed phosphorescence that left trails from previous passers-by for newcomers to follow. Rafi's vision was dazzled and his spirit delighted.

'I didn't know it would be like this at night,' he said happily to Ntenman. 'I would have gone out sooner.'

'You've been busy, very busy.' Ntenman managed to wrap envy, admiration, irritation and sheer disbelief into one dry sentence.

'What have I done?' Rafi said anxiously. His fear was well justified. He had been cramming Punartam culture and etiquette and discovered several unexpected pitfalls which had, so far, only caused amusement, embarrassment and confusion. Still, he never discounted the potential for delayed disaster.

'Your introductions?' Ntenman said with even deeper sarcasm.

'Oh. I didn't know about all that.'

The introductions – now *that* had been disturbing. Haviranthiya told him very soberly that it appeared Academe Maenevastraya had registered a prior claim on his acquaintance and he could no longer provide Rafi with an Academe Surinastraya recommendation as a starting nexus for future Punartam interactions. Rafi had tried to demur and was met with an appalled look, as if he had suggested they ignore the wetness of water and the brightness of sunlight in favour of some other delusion.

'And your essentials,' Ntenman continued.

'There's nothing wrong with them. You should approve of that.'

Essentials were harder to understand, but after Lian dumped a message and a quantity of voice-access credit into his channel, things became clearer. The credit was 'a loan, not a gift', and the fact that Lian had extended it made Lian one of his primary essentials. 'Stay neutral,' Lian's message warned. 'Do not accept credit from non-Cygnians.' Fortunately, Ntenman still qualified as Cygnian. Rafi was already leaning on him for funds and was likely to continue doing so, and thus Ntenman was considered another primary essential.

'Your keys are your peers,' Lian's message explained further. 'I've introduced you to a couple of mine and I'll introduce you to more in time. I know your family and I shared food and drink with you in public, so I'm one of your first-tier keys. Keys you meet through me will be your second-tier keys. You will have to acquire more keys by your own efforts.'

Poor Lian. It was not the loneliness of a foreign culture that imposed sociability on the solitary; it was the very nature of the culture itself. He understood a little better that old Ntshune insult – *one who eats alone.*

Accoutrements still baffled him. Lian's message shed no light on the matter, but only provided more dire warnings. 'Do not wear *anything* that anyone gives you – not a pin, not a ribbon, not a shoelace. Stick to either urban-Cygnian or galactic, which is almost the same thing.' Of course, that advice came a bit late considering that Ntenman had dressed him and paraded him along the pathways of the Metropolis. That now felt less of a joke and more of a strategy, or at least an attempt at one. Whether Ntenman had meant to use him or to protect him, he could not tell, and that made him nervous.

There was still a lot to learn. He quickly discovered that for every variant of the credit system, there were several academic interpretations and models on how they should work. 'Economic credit is mere financial engineering,' sneered his Academe guide. 'Social credit is art.' At that point he did what Ntenman had advised him to do long before and ditched the guide in favour of a Bhumniastraya edition that drew a clearer line between the factual and the fanciful.

'So, financial credit is what gets me food and shelter?' Rafi asked. He had discovered that teaching him the basics appeared to put Ntenman in a better mood, as if doing so re-established the correct order of things.

'Yes, that's survival. But social credit determines what you will eat, and where, and with whom.'

'And I get financial credit from my essentials but social credit from my keys.'

'More or less. That depends on where your nexus is located and the allegiance of your keys. Sometimes it's worthwhile to have a broad representation, but sometimes a nexus will refuse to acknowledge certain keys or networks, or will itself be shunned by other networks.' Ntenman exhaled sharply, already frustrated. 'It's a complex formula. The size, density and degree of overlap of your networks is measured, your net worth is calculated with reference to recommendations from your keys, and only a fully qualified Credit Assessor can work out the result.'

'But good social credit makes my financial credit more valuable, is that right?'

'More or less. You're in a higher consumer bracket for some things.'

'So this is good! I have a nexus and I'm making a start on my social credit. I'll be able to pay you back.'

'Don't be rude,' said Ntenman, only half-joking, and Rafi

belatedly remembered that on Punartam, it was bad manners for anyone, be they creditor, debtor or completely uninvolved, to harp on an unpaid debt. Still, Ntenman sounded almost worried at the idea that Rafi might one day need no essentials.

The outer wall suddenly flashed with a line of falling stars and all talk of money stopped. 'They're starting. We're late,' said Ntenman, and he began to run. Rafi followed, ducking and dodging through the crowd until they came to a space where the tower's base curved inwards and up in terraced balconies, like an amphitheatre. The balconies were filled with spectators and their focus was the opposite wall, which sparkled like a constellation of dancing stars. The Wallrunners moved like divers, like acrobats, with lights strapped to their waists, wrists and ankles. This was not a game. This was pure artistry, but unlike that glimpse of the last demonstration Rafi had witnessed, it was modelled on traditional Wallrunning, with the falls and climbs vertical and the neutral translations horizontal.

Ntenman did not join the crowd sitting in front of the first terrace. Instead he unexpectedly dashed behind the backscreen, where the coaches, reserves and suspended players would sit. Rafi hesitated, but when Ntenman re-emerged and beckoned impatiently, he glanced around guiltily and went in.

'Sit,' said a deep voice.

Rafi peered around in the darkness and scant, intermittent light, saw a line of cross-legged figures against the wall with Ntenman at the end and joined them. The voice was not loud or harsh, but it demanded obedience without questions. Then he tilted back his head and watched the reverse side of play, etched in light at a sharp slant above them. It was mesmerising – visual light and screen-light trails combined into a display of cold, ever-changing fire.

There was murmuring in the dark. He pretended not to hear but suspected he was meant to.

'This boy?'

'Yes.' The volume dropped, the words muddled and then a phrase rose out of the mess clearly. ' . . . Terran trial, and it didn't work well . . .'

'Greed-induced incompetence with a supporting wingline of complacency . . .' came the mumbled response, and harsh, loud laughter burst out all round, making Rafi jump.

'No sense discussing them. Our aims are different.' That was the deep voice. It had not joined the laughter and appeared unable to whisper. It sent vibrations down to the marrow of the bone even when speaking quietly. 'Let him try.'

Ntenman's hand came down heavy on Rafi's shoulder and he whispered in his ear, 'When the demo is over, they open the Wall to anyone who wants to play. You get in there and do what I taught you.' He paused, and his grip tightened as he pondered. 'On second thought, don't do what I taught you. Just have fun.'

'What?' Sheer terror closed Rafi's throat, compressing his voice to a squeak.

Ntenman poked him in the ribs. 'Relax, Moo. It's just playing. You won't gain or lose any credit.'

The crowd howled its approval of another team manoeuvre and, strangely enough, Rafi found the sound comforting. There was no competition. Everything in the long night was for fun and entertainment. He had seen it in the faces they had passed on the way, but more importantly he could feel it, not with any special talent, but with the purely Cygnian sensing of the mood of the crowd.

Rafi took off his tunic, folded it carefully and tied the arms around his waist, and rolled up his trousers snugly to the knee. He took a deep breath and said in a more normal tone, 'Okay.'

Rafi Abowen . . . well, now Rafidelarua. Rafi fall-on-his-feet-accidentally-popular-I-swear-I-don't-know-what-I'm-doing Delarua. I've met his family. We've shared food more times than I can count. I'm one of his first-tier keys *and* an essential, and I can't believe he's gone so far so fast. Rafidelarua! At least I can still call him *Moo*. It reminds him – and them – that I knew him back when.

He's catching up to what's happening around him, and yes, he had to start from square one, which I never did. But he still doesn't understand what it means to have a nexus in Academe Maenev-astraya. He hasn't tried to find out *who* the nexus is. He can declare he's an adult till the suns set for ever but he's acting like a child, a typical Terran child. He thinks if he doesn't see it, if he doesn't know about it, it can't exist and he doesn't have to worry about it. I'm not going to help him with that. I've got my own circles and networks and credit to consider, and I'm not going to waste time on his.

Besides, I was right. He's got it. Bitter, bitter irony. The greatest booby in the history of the game projects the warmest, strongest binding ever seen in a non-Ntshune Wallrunner. Then there's me – all the skills, none of the spark. Splice the two of us together and we'd make one outstanding player. You see – even more irony – another name for *booby* is *nexus*. That's where the term originally came from, from old-style Wallrunning. The nexus links with everyone, keeps them aware of each other, and the team moves as a single body with the nexus as the core. Sometimes the nexus is a good Wallrunner; sometimes they have to be thrown and caught and carried like baggage. It's a balancing act to decide which is more important: having a skilled nexus to lead the running and call strategy for the team, or having a skilled team with a strong nexus who knows just enough to stay out of the bodycatcher.

Rafi didn't know what he was doing, as usual. He was nervous at first when he got on the Wall, but when he started to slip and loosen up and laugh you could see everyone on the Wall . . . *buzz*. They all woke up and turned to him and looked at him and at each other as if it was the first time they'd noticed there were other people around. Then they began to move like sentient ribbons of fire – weaving, connecting, dispersing. And this was not the team! There were a handful of players and the rest were Wallrunning amateurs out of the crowd, glad for the chance to play around on a half-decent Wall. Most of the crowd didn't know what they were seeing but they knew they liked it. They started to cheer for them almost as loudly as they did for the team. Baranngaithe realised immediately. He was standing behind the screen watching, and I was watching him. Slowly he sat down; slowly he lay back. I came closer. He was squinting, as if trying to blur out the individuals and see the motion as coming from one entity. What he saw pleased him because he began to grin and then to chuckle.

'Oh, Ntenman,' he said to me. 'Well done. Very well done!'

And that warmed me. You see, Baranngaithe used to be a nexus, in every sense of the word. He began as a Wallrunner, naturally, but then he got into the managing aspect of the game and used his flair for binding to build and lead one of the most efficient corporations in the third tier of the Galactic League.

This was pure scandal. Some men own individual teams. A smaller number have a few minor strings of teams to their credit. But Baranngaithe was the first man to have a full eight-string corporation in the Galactic League.

Of course, it couldn't last. In my opinion, the Punarthai matriarchs and Patronae were secretly proud of him, but the Ntshune dynasties tore the bottom out of the bag with ruthless dispatch. I do not exaggerate. Blood was shed. Baranngaithe survived it somehow and ended up in his third life as an academic, studying the history of the game and its associated traditions. His so-called fieldwork soon outpaced his research and writings. He revived the old Brotherhoods and trained teams for form, skill and beauty rather than competition.

He used to mock his life and say that he would spend his final years as a solitary to try to remember who he was away from all the push and pull of other people. But he never left. He was as he had been on my last Punartam almost-Year: wandering the Academe green coaching his teams and overseeing their demonstrations with a delight that was personal as well as professional. If only demonstration teams counted for anything, we could have bragged that he had the equivalent of two and a half corporations, but at least no one would be trying to kill him for these.

'I am minded,' he said, 'to go back to my research. Here is a worthy subject. I could spend some time on this. I think I will postpone my retirement a little longer. This is very much to your credit, Ntenman. I had not thought my teachings would stick with you, and here you have found me something remarkable from a world away!'

I could not stop smiling. Ignition was always slow for Baranngaithe, but when he caught fire he was irresistible.

'But his Wallrunning technique is atrocious,' Baranngaithe continued. 'We shall have to work on that. He must carry himself, at least. We will have no dead weight here.'

I regretfully decided it was time to make sure he knew everything. 'Revered Baranngaithe, you know his nexus lies with Academe Maenevastraya?'

He tensed immediately but quickly came to terms with the less-than-perfect world. 'I had heard. Nothing wrong with that. I have some esteemed colleagues in Maenevastraya. They might even be interested in a little collaboration, but I must have him remain here to facilitate training.'

'You also have competitors in Academe Maenevastraya,' I noted mildly.

'I saw him first; they must respect that.' He sat up and frowned at me. 'I told you this was to your credit, Ntenman. I do not speak idly. Remember your allegiances from times past and do not play for the highest bidder like a Zhinuvian trader.'

I did not have to pretend to be offended. 'Rafi is my friend. I only want what's best for him. He has had a hard time.'

Baranngaithe searched my face and sniffed the edges of my spirit for any hint of insincerity and found, if not truth, at least sufficient self-interest to satisfy him that I would not dabble in that messy combination of Wallrunning and Academe politics.

'Well,' he said at last, 'let it be. Bring him for training before you sleep and after you wake. Make him always take the emergency chutes. Draw on my credit and get him proper kit. Outfit yourself as well. Nothing fabricated. There's a craftsman who does some good bespoke work. You can find him on the green most long nights, but his workshop is below, closest to Five Trees Escape. Do you need a guide, or can you find your way below-ground?'

'It has been some time, Revered. I should take a guide,' I said honestly.

'I will send a guide to your channel. You should go after the next sunrise. We have no time to waste.'

'Revered,' I acknowledged, in full obedience, just as in times past.

So Rafi found us when he came down from Wallrunning at last, worn out and happy. I was standing near the edge of the screen and stepped out to greet him, but Baranngaithe stayed sitting in the shadows and only answered Rafi's curious look with a nod.

'When can we come back, Tinman? This Wall is incredible. I might actually learn something on a Wall like this.' He was excited and I couldn't blame him. The Lyceum had been his first and only Wall – serviceable, but not at all inspiring.

'Soon,' Baranngaithe replied from the shadows like a night-shrouded oracle.

I saw Rafi react to the timbre of his voice, a string struck invisibly by resonance – that buzz, that sudden tension and added wakefulness. For a moment, a brief moment, my jealousy returned and I wondered what could have been if I'd had a fraction of that sensitivity. I consoled myself. I would never be a nexus, but at least I was learning how to move in their inner circles. It was less than a month and my social credit was already going up. I could work with what I had. This would be my Year.

The walk back took time, partly because Rafi had pushed himself hard and now could only stumble weakly, bouncing from various shoulders and sides as the growing crowd moved around him with that particularly Punarthai lack of concern about personal space. Ntenman took the slower pace as an opportunity to dawdle and talk to friends and acquaintances, some of whom he introduced to Rafi and some he did not, leaving Rafi to stand awkwardly nearby and pretend to look interested in some other distraction.

He was hoping to see her. He was expecting to see her. He had looked for her among the spectators at the Wall; he had half-convinced himself that if he went behind the screen she would be there, just like the first time. He leaned against the tower and let his gaze linger on every tall person in the crowd – and on Punartam, there were plenty.

When the moment finally came, it did not disappoint. A small box rattled near his ear. He looked at it, watched it tip and automatically placed his hand underneath. Five perrenuts were shaken out onto his palm. He carefully selected three and put the remaining two back in the box, feeling very smug as a low laugh approved his actions.

'Ixiaralhaneki,' he said. She was wearing a long tunic and a broad scarf that draped around her head and shoulders. Separate sleeves and leggings wrapped her limbs in scrunched, wrinkled material. Thanks to his daily lessons with the guides, he was noticing things and understanding them better – for example, the bands and badges on her sleeves told the tale of her family line, her credit level and her work. Two things were absolutely clear to him and neither was news: she was a Haneki, and well-off.

He glanced quickly behind him. Ntenman was a good way down the green, fully engaged in conversation and half-hidden in the crowd. As he turned back, he wondered to himself why he was glad of that.

She smiled down at him as she put her snack away into a side pocket. 'You may call me Ixiaral,' she told him, sliding down the wall from a lean to a half-sit to bring herself closer to his line of sight.

'And I'm just Rafi.' He paused, wracked his brain for some courteous nothings to say and found it empty. 'Are you from Academe Maenevastraya? Are you my nexus?'

'I'm sorry I came too late to see you run the Wall,' she replied obliquely, unfazed by his outburst. 'Did you enjoy yourself?'

'Very much,' said Rafi. 'But how did you know—'

'I heard,' was all she said, but immediately Rafi pictured it – a single person speaking into a comm or sending a message, but a few whispered words, repeating from mouth to ear, mouth to ear, sweeping along the green and perhaps even out through the gates to wherever Ixiaral had been previously. 'We should talk indeed. I'm not formally associated with the Academe but I do some work for them on occasion.'

'You're a scout,' Rafi guessed. 'A talent recruiter.'

'Yes. I go around the Academes and see if there are any amateurs with the will and the skill for the commercial leagues. I negotiate with the teams over who they will take and what the credit exchange will be.'

'And you go beyond the Academes as well. Beyond Punartam.'

Her face creased up with disapproval. 'That is not one of the things we are going to talk about.'

'Understood,' Rafi said, outwardly obliging but inwardly curious.

She looked as if she was trying not to laugh at him, but in a kindly way. 'Come. Lose your friend for a little while and follow me.' She took off her scarf and whipped it around him before he could protest, keeping one end in her fist. 'Come on!'

He did not look back. He crammed a perrenut in his mouth,

eager for the rush of energy and bliss, and followed her long strides further across the green. It was impossible to get lost on a circular path, impossible to come to harm with so many witnesses, and he was bored and restless after several Cygnian days without sun. She turned off the path and into a doorway that opened for her without challenge. Before he could take time to wonder at her ease of access to the Academe, she pulled him onto a small elevator, spinning him teasingly until the scarf wound around his eyes and nose. By the time he untangled himself, the elevator was moving at speed – down. Not up, to all the places he had mapped and researched and walked through, but below-ground, which he had not yet seen and knew nothing about.

'Wait,' he began, finally worried. 'Where are we going?'

'You wanted to know about your nexus?' she queried, watching his panic with a lazy curiosity. 'You should have presented yourself – but you are Terran and you don't know how things are done here, not yet.'

'Let me go back for Ntenman,' Rafi said as calmly and firmly as he could manage.

Ixiaral turned to the elevator doors. 'But we're already here.'

The doors opened. The first thing that Rafi noticed was the heat, and the second was the smell. Above-ground was dry and any scent in the air was generally due to whatever plants were nearby. Here it was a mixture of machinery, movement and humanity into an imperfectly filtered, moist and slightly metallic urban bouquet. There was light, a shy and muted light that radiated from large, long sconces above, but it was contained in pools within the larger ocean of primal dark.

Ixiaral dropped the end of the scarf and looked back over her shoulder. 'Are you coming?'

Rafi hesitated a moment, listening. Beyond the doors of the elevator, and around the corner of the passageway that led from it, he could hear people talking, laughing, moving about. It did not sound like a trap. He nodded warily and ate a second perrenut to fortify himself.

Ixiaral turned and walked quickly away, leaving him to gather his wits and scramble after her. As he rounded the corner, he almost ran into her heels. She had stopped and was staring out at the panorama. He stopped and stared with her. One of the guides had told him that the underground city went by a number of names: Belowground commonly, the Twilight Metropolis poetically and Sub-Metropolis officially. He privately approved most of Twilight Metropolis. Viewed from a distance, the city showed that light and darkness had found balance and truce. People walked briskly in the darker areas and congregated cheerfully in the oases of light near doorways and crossings at intersections. There was an occasional glimmer from above, almost as if the brightest stars were beginning to take over the sky, but he dismissed it as a trick of light on minerals partially exposed in the cut rock.

'It may appear dim, but full darkness and full light are private things kept within walls for sleep and for work and play,' Ixiaral explained. 'We are going to the sun rooms.'

As she spoke, a small transit bubble drew up beside them, startling Rafi badly with its silent, sudden appearance. Ixiaral bundled him inside the small space and they sat peacefully for a short while until the bubble took to the air without warning. Rafi almost vomited in fear on the transparent floor of their fairy-tale carriage, but eventually he started to orientate himself and realised that the glimmers of interior starlight he had seen earlier were not reflective minerals but the rising and setting of the bubbles that formed the Sub-Metropolis transportation system.

Ixiaral watched his reactions with mild confusion and pity. 'I thought the walk would have been too much for you,' she said in apology. 'Have you never been below-ground before?'

'No,' said Rafi, keeping his voice steady – his last hope for a show of dignity. 'I have not been here for very long at all.'

She kept a solicitous eye on him for the remainder of the journey and on arrival she lifted him out of the bubble as if he were a fragile bit of cargo. Rafi felt a little embarrassed, but also a little safer. He doubted she would take so much trouble with him if she intended harm.

'What is this place?' he asked, looking up at the huge entrance before him and the great curving wings of a vast building that appeared to stretch up indefinitely.

'These are the sun rooms in the base levels of Academe Maenevastraya. Are you feeling better? Are you ready?'

Rafi ate the last perrenut, more as a symbolic action than for any hope that it could revive his flagging spirits. He was drained, anxious and bewildered, and not at all in a position to show any of those weaknesses. He considered his tunic, still tied around his waist after all the excitement on and off the Wall. The knotted arms had pulled so tight that he suspected it would take a lot of time and calm to undo it. He wrapped up in Ixiaral's scarf instead and straightened his back.

'Lead on,' he said.

CHAPTER TEN

A little recycled sunlight looked far more impressive in an enclosed area. Rafi winced, his eyes watering at the brightness, the mirrors and the glass. He blinked, and then wished he had kept his vision clouded. Ixiaral held him lightly before her, her hands on his shoulders in a grip that might be meant to comfort, but could also be to ensure that he did not bolt. She spoke over his head to the door attendant.

'The Controller, the Patrona and the Dean are expecting us,' she told her.

The attendant stared at Rafi as she gave Ixiaral directions, more curious than disapproving. He tried not to stare back, conscious not merely of her bare torso, but of the massive scar that carved vertically over her ribs where her left breast had been. Ixiaral nodded in thanks and went on, keeping a hand on Rafi's shoulder.

'Some soldiers consider it an honour to keep their battle scars and will do so even after retirement,' she said into his ear as softly and confidentially as any audioplug. 'But you already know about this – Wallrunners think the same way, don't they?'

191

'I thought the players had no choice after the enhancement scandals,' Rafi whispered back.

'True, but to keep the memory and limitations of injuries long after a sports career has ended speaks of philosophy, not necessity. Now, here we are. Don't be *too* nervous.'

He was about to deny that he was nervous, an automatic verbal reflex from the Cygnian habit of wearing brave, courteous masks, but it was useless to lie.

'But be a *little* nervous,' Ixiaral continued. 'They like it when new boys are nervous. Smile!' She trilled the last word, clapped him once on the shoulder and pushed him through a doorway into an even brighter room.

Four pairs of eyes turned in his direction. A fifth pair belonged to a young man dressed in a remarkably stripped-down version of Wallrunning gear, and he kept them dutifully trained on the platter of fruit he was offering around before quietly withdrawing from the room. The remaining occupants, all women, lounged or sat on large cushions around a small central pool with Punarthai water lilies afloat on the surface. They were elegant, with dark Ntshune curls close-cut to frame and flatter their cheekbones and jawlines to full aesthetic advantage. He could tell from their eyes that they were not young, but their skin was smooth and radiant, earth-hues deepening in the ubiquitous sunlight. Even in relaxation there was something in the way they held their tall, strong bodies that gave the air of grace and power combined. He could see how in a few years Ixiaral would follow this template by adding solidity to her height and a certain carelessness to her posture. Not that Ixiaral lacked poise, but compared to these women who exuded effortlessness, Ixiaral had clearly not completed her formation.

They accepted Ixiaral's greeting with infinitesimal attention – a nod, a half-hearted wave, a brief mumble – but they examined Rafi with terrifying closeness. The little confidence he had managed to preserve shrank to nothing under the regard of those alien eyes which were judging him by standards he could not guess at and was sure he did not meet. He tried not to look uncomfortable, failed and stared at his feet instead, awkward and bitterly chagrined at his failure.

The group of women silently sunned themselves and watched him get flustered. After a slight pause, one of them said with devastating kindness, 'But he is still young.'

Ixiaral gently loosened Rafi's grip on her scarf and took it away from him, which made him feel both embarrassed *and* naked. 'Revered Dean Suyanahaneki of Academe Maenevastraya, Revered Controller Devunalhaneki of the Credit Exchange Bureau, and my respected superior and Patrona whose name I am not yet allowed to speak. I present to you Rafidelarua of Cygnus Beta. Forgive his appearance. I may have kidnapped him somewhat.'

The women laughed. They did not sound malicious, but neither did they sound as if they were taking him seriously. Rafi noted that Ixiaral had not introduced that same one who had commented on his age, and he further noted with tired cynicism that she was the youngest out of all of them, Ixiaral included. Something made him look a little more closely, and he began to see that, unlike her named and titled colleagues, her leisure was studied. She glanced frequently at the other three women to match her reactions and pose to theirs. They did not return her glances, but the Dean and the Controller looked occasionally to the Patrona. The Patrona kept a quiet, steady gaze on him.

'What was he doing?' the Controller asked.

'Wallrunning on one of the Academe's Walls,' Ixiaral replied.

'Is he any good?' enquired the Dean.

'No, ma'am, not really,' Rafi answered, raising his chin and looking at her with a small smile.

Her face changed from coolly amused to mildly impressed, and then, with a speed that made him blink, to flirtatious mischief. The curve of her mouth never changed. It was all in and around her eyes, from smoothly supercilious through to laugh-lined warmth and a hint of an eyelash flutter. She looked old enough to be his grandmother, and she was probably older than that, but in that moment he was mesmerised by her eyes.

The Patrona spoke at last. 'Do you know why you are here?'

'Because you have prior claim over Academe Surinastraya? Is this because I spoke to Tshalo?'

He flinched as they laughed again in earnest. Ixiaral tried to suppress a smile.

'My son, but not of my line. A youthful indiscretion,' explained the Dean, and her eyes no longer looked alluring but narrow, tired and disappointed. 'No, it has nothing to do with him.'

'You met Ixiaral twice by chance on two worlds. It would be a missed opportunity not to make something of it.' The Patrona was cautious at first, but then she spoke more directly. 'According to tradition, you took food from her hand and spoke together. There was no one to witness it, but her word is good and I will confirm it if needs be. But of course there are other reasons. You saw Ixiaral on Cygnus Beta at a time when she was known to be on Punartam. If you know our secrets, we may have to make you one of us.'

'Who is "us"?' Ixiaral asked sweetly. 'I see three overlapping interests represented here.'

The Dean crossed her hands before her protectively. 'Not me. He already has shelter in one Academe, a nexus in another and protectors in a third. Let us broaden his horizons. What do you think, Dev?'

The Controller glanced at the youngest woman, who had neither spoken nor been spoken to since that first comment, and shook her head. 'I must wait and see for a little longer.'

The Patrona mused, 'I believe I will do the same. I can see there could be mutual advantages, but it also cannot hurt to take time to assess the situation thoroughly.'

'Are there many Sadiri pilots at Academe Maenevastraya?' Rafi asked abruptly.

There was a sudden, tense silence. The Patrona was the first to recover. 'There are several Sadiri at Maenevastraya. Some of them are pilots. Perhaps you should pose that question to your fellow-Cygnian Lian.'

Rafi decided to be honest. 'There's something about you that reminds me of the Sadiri.'

The Patrona's stern face relaxed into an almost-smile. 'Some of my dearest keys are Sadiri. I may introduce you some day if our networks grow together.'

'Patrona—' He was not sure if that was the correct address but somehow 'ma'am' felt insufficient. 'Patrona, tell me, who is my nexus?'

That started them laughing again, except for Ixiaral, who looked very embarrassed.

'Well,' said the Patrona, quickly sobering, 'that is partly what this meeting is about. You have presented yourself . . . after a fashion. You are young, but you have potential. Ixiaral is your nexus, of course. I will confirm it. Don't disappoint her.'

She turned her gaze to Ixiaral and her voice hardened. 'Be sure that he learns his duties and appreciates his benefits. He may wear any minor variation on the Maenevastraya theme, but keep him clear of accoutrements for now. We will wait and observe. Train him well.'

At last she spoke to the quiet woman who had not been introduced. 'Hanekivaryai, walk with our friends as they leave.'

A flash of anger passed briefly over the young woman's face, but she quickly suppressed it and went calmly and politely to escort Ixiaral and Rafi to the entrance foyer. Rafi kept expecting her to reveal something important, but she was there for courtesy, not information, and she did her duty and left them to sit for a while and adjust to the dimmer light before venturing out once more into the Twilight Metropolis. Rafi did not dare speak openly until they were alone in a transit bubble.

'Why didn't you introduce me to that other woman?' he asked.

Ixiaral looked sorrowful. 'I avoided saying her name out of kindness. I wish the Patrona could have done the same.'

'I don't understand,' Rafi admitted. He was beginning to feel sleepy and wondered how many hours he had been awake. It was still too easy to lose track of Standard hours on Punartam.

Ixiaral began to say something, then looked at his nodding head and unfocused eyes. 'Another time,' she said softly.

He fell asleep before they reached the elevator to Academe Surinastraya.

When he woke up, back in his own bed at the Academe's living quarters, he had a hazy memory of stumbling around the green, fatigue-drunk and disorientated, in a vain attempt to find Ntenman. He sat up slowly, feeling the aches and agonies of too much vigorous exercise after long idleness, and was hit in the face with a vambrace.

'Come on, get ready. I have to take you to Wallrunning training in less than an hour.'

Rafi grabbed the vambrace, primed to swear at Ntenman or perhaps throw it back, but then he realised what he was holding. 'This is a proper vambrace!'

'Yes! None of those little wristy bands the amateurs use on Cygnus Beta. *And* I got you handguard extensions because novices like you tend to lose your little fingers in the micrograv fluctuations of a pro-level Wall.'

'Where did—?'

'I got them for you. You owe me. Don't worry, we'll sort it out later.'

'I haven't eaten. I have to freshen up—'

'You do that too often. It's not like a bath, you know. You have to let it go for a few days, give the algae time to establish itself for full effect.'

Rafi gave Ntenman a look of tired disbelief but privately made a note to get more detailed information on the scour-and-steam process just in case it was no joke.

'If you must eat before going on the Wall, eat this.' Ntenman gave Rafi a coiled ribbon of some compressed organic matter which smelled sweet and salty and looked rich with fat. 'But not too much. You don't want to unsettle your stomach.'

There were only two Standard days left until the full light of sunrise, but Rafi found himself almost irrationally resentful at the combination of natural darkness and artificial light. It galled him even more to know that when the long day finally began he would likely spend two Standard days outside rejoicing in the light, three Standard days acting as normal and the rest indoors as much as possible, complaining about the world being too bright. When he told Ntenman as much just before they took the fall down the emergency chute, Ntenman let out a great hoot of laughter that echoed eerily up the hard walls of the empty shaft, and Rafi could not help laughing in turn.

'Give it a couple of months,' Ntenman told him after they bounced out of the bodycatcher and strolled onto the green. 'By the time you get back to Cygnus Beta you'll be complaining about the speed of the sun and the tyranny of the twenty-four-hour clock.'

To Rafi's newly cynical eyes, the festival on the green had a slightly jaded atmosphere. People moved with less energy and cheerfulness than the previous day, as if they too had done all they could to endure the long night and were more than ready for sunrise. Or perhaps it was simply the character of the new shift and the truly festive were now in their work mode, tucked away in offices below-ground or in the tower, waiting for the hours to turn so they could go and reclaim the green from their sluggish colleagues and kin.

When they got to the Wall, there were a few players and would-be players milling about in front of the screen. Rafi was pleased to see some bleary eyes and wide yawns in spite of the bright light that overhung the area, brighter than the last time when the players were lit up and on show.

He raised his hand in a non-committal greeting and tried not to let the awkwardness he was feeling show on the surface. Everyone there looked as if they were meant to be there. There were thick-bodied, heavyset boys who would be perfect as pivots or tippers; extra-tall, lanky types who could be ladders, slingers or hookers; small, wiry boys as quick-moving snakes; and one truly massive individual who could only be the team anchor. And then there was Rafi, a common if there ever was one – too short to be a ladder, too tall to be a snake, too skinny to tip, pivot or anchor and too weak to sling. Maybe, if someone else held him securely, he could hook, but he could barely run all the levels without tripping, and he still lost all sense of up and down when the Wall began to tip. He imagined that people were looking at him curiously, perhaps wondering if he was there to watch.

'Rafidelarua.'

Rafi spun around instantly, recognising the voice behind the screen, the voice in the dark that commanded with timbre and tone rather than volume. Now he had the chance to see the face of the person who had chosen to remain in the shadows.

'I am Baranngaithe.' He was a small one, probably a retired snake, and his voice was all out of proportion to his body, but when he gazed up at Rafi with an expression that was as assured as his voice, Rafi bowed his head, raised his greeting hand and mumbled something he had never tried before – the traditional Wallrunning phrase from junior to elder. 'I am your child, Revered Baranngaithe.'

Baranngaithe chuckled. 'Not yet, but soon. In the first light of next sunrise we shall bind you to our blood, but till then you may still run with us. Do you know who I am?'

Rafi did not. He was still unable to do that double-tasking most Punarthai did, listening to their channel and having a conversation simultaneously. 'You were Ntenman's coach?'

'Yes. I am the coach for four teams of Academe Surinastraya and a consultant coach at other Academes. I am also a nexus. You can train with my team, learn to run the Wall and carry yourself creditably, but as for the rest, there are few things worse than one nexus teaching another. When two come together, one must be the centre and the other the satellite. This can only be avoided by giving each their own sphere, and that is what I shall do. You will learn from a colleague of mine at Academe Maenevastraya. She is Syanrimwenil, and she has been involved in the logistics arm of the Galactic League for some time.'

'But . . . she is not a nexus?' Rafi spoke calmly but he felt an inner pang of excitement. The name was familiar. He was certain he had seen it on his aunt's list when he scanned it for Hanekis and Mwenils after his talk with Lian.

'She is . . . inactive. Don't worry. She understands the nexus mentality and philosophy better than anyone.'

'This is . . . I owe you much credit, Revered Baranngaithe. How may I serve you and pay my debt?'

Baranngaithe smiled. 'Work hard. Fulfil your potential. We will talk of service after you have been trained.'

Rafi learned two things during training. First, he had not yet fully adjusted to the Punartam atmosphere; second, a weaker planetary gravity made no difference to the gravity settings on a Wall. Baranngaithe liked to run high gravity during training runs. Rafi understood the warning about losing little fingers – the dreaded shear was a real danger during a fast tip and higher gravity speeded up both tips and falls. And yet, because the focus was on form and not scoring, it was in some ways easier than running with the Lyceum team – not physically easier, not at all, but more structured, more predictable and thus easier for the mind to control the body. He noticed some older women and a few men watching them train with a keenness that went beyond mere spectating, and Ntenman explained to him that they were likely game strategists, come to see whether a Wallrunner with excellent form could be enticed away to a commercial team, even for a short stint.

Rafi doubted he could interest them, especially after he fell into the bodycatcher and vomited up the small breakfast Ntenman had allowed him.

He returned to quarters, cleaned up and collapsed in bed for a nap, and naturally woke up ravenous. He was scheduled to have a meal with Ixiaral at Academe Maenevastraya, but first he was going to use the directions Baranngaithe had sent to his channel, directions that would lead him to the retired nexus. He told Ntenman where he was going, but offhandedly and last-minute so that he could override Ntenman's protests that he needed to come along and make sure Rafi did not get lost.

'At least take the below-ground route,' Ntenman advised. 'There's too much nonsense going on during the long night outside of the Academe walls.'

Rafi did not query further. There could never be enough 'recycled sunlight' to cover the entire Metropolis, and after almost nine Standard days of night he was feeling spooked at the mere idea of going beyond the safe, well-lit places. He followed his directions carefully and arrived at the work section of Academe Maenevastraya, a place that looked nothing like the government offices and university lecture halls of Cygnus Beta. It looked slightly like a Zen garden, but greener and twisty with soundproof nooks, paths for walking and thinking, and large tables at intervals for group meetings. People listened to their audioplugs or spoke messages destined for their colleagues' channels. Rafi wondered for a moment why there was no such thing as a slate or handheld to be found, but then he realised that even the research was being dictated, the exquisite verbal control of the Punarthai ensuring that any transcription would be as clean and coherent as anything typed by a Cygnian. That made him think of Dr Daniyel and how she was doing, and whether she still needed to lean on a comm and handheld to get her work done.

He was feeling thoroughly homesick by the time he found the niche where Revered Syanrimwenil was waiting, an emotion that would prove to be extremely unhelpful as their conversation unfolded.

She was elderly; her dark hair was greying throughout, tied back but shorter than the usual masculine style. Her body was soft in a way that told of years spent sitting in quiet niches rather than walking and thinking, and yet there was something to her that reminded him more of Ntenman's mercurial energy than Ixiaral's gravitas. She barely glanced at him as she waved him to sit on a mat opposite her. He puzzled at her distraction for a moment, then realised she was listening to her audioplug channel. It appeared to contain more information on him than was comfortable.

'Hmm. Your father. A man who wants a peaceful life, a loving family. No fretful babies or troublesome toddlers allowed. But I wonder what it was like when he started to feel you push back. Did you fight? Was it a tug of war, and if so, was it your mother or your sister who served as the rope? Or perhaps you crashed antlers together until one day you won?'

Rafi was speechless. He sat down and tried to steady the sudden shaking in his hands, placing his palms flat on the floor so that he would not hit an old woman.

'You protected your sister but you didn't know how to protect yourself,' Syanrimwenil continued ruthlessly, still not looking at him. 'And now you've left your sister and your mother. It must have become tiring, looking out for them constantly.'

Rafi blinked and inhaled sharply, now both angry and upset.

'But you were their nexus. There were genuine bonds between you, however snarled and tainted they were. Strange that your therapists did not realise that. Instead of treating your sister and your mother solely for your father's abuse, they should also have been weaning them from dependency on you—'

'Stop it!' Rafi shouted.

The background buzz in the sector dipped for a moment as heads turned and people stared at his breach of etiquette, but Syanrimwenil waved a hand gently to dismiss their concern.

'I am done,' she said, with no regret in her voice. 'Now, as I have looked at your soul stripped bare, it is only fair that I offer a little of myself in turn. You did not ask, not by eyes or voice or attitude, and that makes you one of the most courteous Terrans I have met. But yes, I am a woman who was once a boy. Furthermore, I am that special oddity, a boy who was never a Wallrunning nexus but became a corporate nexus straight away. Naturally the two facts are related. Did you know that men were once barred from acting as corporate nexus?'

Rafi shook his head and said nothing, recognising the dig at his 'courtesy' but also aware that she would tell him everything more quickly if he refrained from interrupting with questions. He simply accessed his audioplug channel to get clarification on those terms and phrases he did not understand.

'They were, and so I was forced to disguise myself to achieve my goal. You would think that impossible in this world, in this era, but my mother abetted me. I was Mwenilsyanri then, just another unclaimed brat running the Academe Walls and taking whatever work I could find below-ground for credit. She saw my potential, and she knew that my name would no longer hinder me if they took me to be a woman, so she claimed me and named me her daughter. I suppose it helped that she only produced sons after me, and she was very Ntshune – an unregistered daughter was more valuable than a legitimate son.

'I didn't need her help for very long. I am a strong nexus, and the logistics team I assembled and led became legendary in the Galactic League.'

Rafi hesitated, not wanting to lose that early compliment on his courteousness, but he was still Cygnian and he had to ask. 'Did you mind, being a woman for so long?'

The corner of Syanri's mouth quirked briefly downward, then she gave a slight grimace that was not so much disappointed as resigned. 'I am not quite like your Lian, who cares nothing at all for such things. Perhaps I minded a little. But I tell you, Rafi, for any true nexus, there is nothing more important than the chance to be what they are, whatever the personal cost. I did not do this for my own comfort, or to embarrass and outsmart the matriarchs. I did this because I couldn't imagine not being a nexus and there seemed no other way to achieve my desire.

'I moved on and up through the hierarchy, and by the time they knew I had been born a boy I held too much influence and power, so they let me keep my place for a while. A girl who becomes a man is on an accepted path – the most he can do is run the Walls. But a boy who becomes a woman shows arrogant folly, especially when she dares aspire to run the Game. There is the difference. The matriarchs may have admired my talent and ambition, but they still felt I had overleapt my natural place in society. The ousting was slow but it was relentless, and now I cling to the fringes by the grace of the few friends who have not forgotten me and who have forgiven me for my necessary deception.'

She spread her hands wide and smiled with a tinge of bitterness. 'And that is how I came to be a semi-retired corporate nexus. Be careful, Rafidelarua. My friends are indeed few. There is no fury like that of an abandoned network. You may be blameless, powerless, of pure intent, but their betrayal will not be rational.'

'Then why be a nexus at all?' Rafi retorted.

She looked at him finally. 'Wrong question. You cannot help being a nexus. You *can* learn not to abandon your networks. You can learn to leave them strong and self-sufficient.'

'Very well,' Rafi said, his words short with irritation. 'Teach me that, Revered Syanrimwenil.'

She laughed. 'Very good! Very good! But you must call me Syanri. You are neither my student nor a test subject.'

Rafi felt it then. Perhaps she had been holding herself back previously, but now he could sense a light vibration, a tremor that buzzed along his nerves and raised the hair on his arms. He glanced around, almost expecting to see some kind of sway or shudder in the furniture and plants near them, but the physical world remained undisturbed. She watched him, her slight smile amused at his reaction and her half-lidded eyes assessing him.

'What we do,' she said, 'is either so strange or so primal to our being that our senses do not interpret the stimuli in the usual way. Sight, hearing, touch, taste and smell may be blended or confused. For example, my dear colleague Baran tells me that he registers my presence as a cooling of the air, a pale tint to his vision and a sharp tingle on the tip of his tongue. I hear him and

I wonder if he thinks of me as ice and unconsciously influences his own brain so that the input can be adjusted accordingly. Your aunt, Gracedelarua, perceives you as sunlight, warm and golden. What do you perceive, Rafidelarua?'

'Vibration,' said Rafi, surprising himself with his certainty. 'Resonance. A tickle or a . . . Once I felt it like a thunderclap through my bones.'

She opened her eyes wide. 'Who was that?'

'Dllenahkh, my uncle. He stopped my father, and I felt it. It shook me.'

'Hm, interesting. I believe you perceive me?'

'Yes. Like the beginning of an earthquake, but very gentle.'

She slapped the edge of her seat and laughed. 'I would call that flattery, but I will accept it. Let me tell you what a nexus is. We are artists and our medium is people. We weave and knot, we contrast and complement, we make a whole that is so much more than the sum of its parts. You, Rafi, will use your perception and skill to fashion a body of humanity with mind, strength and heart surpassing what any individual could accomplish.'

'I don't want to do what my father did!' The words choked out of him under pressure, under force. Pure nerves set him trembling again.

Syanri was shocked. 'Your father? Your father tried to tie everyone to himself – a selfish, foolish, cruel use of his talents. That is not the work of a nexus. You create a team by binding each to each, acting as glue, not as god. But you raise an important point. You have not been educated in good habits. How have you misused your skill?'

Rafi tried to calm down, but this request was worse than anything else she had said. He could not remember; he did not know everything he had done that he was not supposed to do. He thought quickly over the last few months and found his sharpest guilt. 'I fooled a schoolmaster into thinking I had permission to leave for the weekend.'

It would have been better if she had looked disappointed, but she only folded her mouth briefly, bit her lip and nodded. 'That was not right and should not be repeated. Continue.'

'And I . . . I tickled my little sister. No hands, just . . . a kind of mental push.'

Again she bit her lip, but this time it served to suppress a giggle. 'That is . . . not precisely common, but you had no malicious intent and the effects were positive. Leave that one off your conscience.'

Rafi thought for a moment of his mother's reaction and wished his conscience could be cleared so easily, but that was too long and complicated to explain to Syanri. He tried to think of some other infractions and could only recall times when he had challenged his father, sometimes unsuccessfully, in order to be left alone. His mind blanked and he stared at her anxiously.

She stared back implacably. 'Guilt. The stale taste of it is still there. There was a girl?'

In a rush, Rafi remembered adolescent dreams that bled into cap-induced nightmares, where he became every monstrous thing his father had been and could have been. *Serendipity*. He tried to speak and coughed instead, his mouth suddenly dry.

'This is interesting,' Syanrimwenil said with almost obscene delight, too caught up in fascination to be distressed by distress as she dug ruthlessly through the thoughts he did not speak. 'It makes sense that you would fixate on someone possessing a level of talent similar to your own, but why did you keep yourself from her?'

Rafi had no words to answer, but in a moment of clarity that was new and unusual, he understood his past indecision. Serendipity possessed a different song and sound, and that had attracted him, but he could also hear behind that song the hollow echo of an insatiable hunger that had not yet learned what to do to satisfy itself.

Syanri laughed and laughed until Rafi could not be sure he was not being mocked.

'Such wisdom!' she cried. 'A thousand poets would never have died and a thousand poems would never have been written if more young men had your caution and restraint. Well, you are quite the walled garden. It will take much to scale you, that is certain.'

Rafi bit his lip, trying to control his shaking, knowing she was testing him, and yet wondering what would happen to him if he struck a nexus.

'That will do for now,' Syanri said placatingly, pulling back abruptly to a less intense mode. 'More may come to mind as we begin training.'

She stood and began to walk out of the niche, glancing back at him as he continued to sit, uncertain if the interview was over or if he was meant to follow. She paused in answer and he walked warily to her side.

'Let me show you the Academe,' she said.

After ten minutes of walking and passing introductions, Rafi realised that her aim was not to show him the Academe but to show him off. His aunt's name was well known, a fact that was no longer a surprise since he had taken to sifting through and organising the papers and articles from Sadira-on-Cygnus. What had initially been a snarl of names piled together was gradually resolving into discrete circles. Research on Cygnian-Sadiri culture was the preserve of Academe Bhumniastraya, but there was a connection due to the many Sadiri pilots engaged in study and research at Academe Maenevastraya, especially those concerned with the adaptation of mindships to Cygnian and Terran ocean environments. To his surprise, nexus-related studies were also a minor speciality at Academe Maenevastraya.

'The connection between pilot and mindship has been compared to that of a nexus and network,' Syanri explained. 'The comparison is even more apt when you consider that mindships are not a single organism, but a colony. Mindships may travel by themselves, but a pilot needs a mindship. There is something about the collective binding that enables the preservation of identity and consciousness post-transit.'

'Um,' Rafi answered, out of his depth.

She was not impressed by his ignorance. 'How did you get here, Rafidelarua?'

'On a mindship. A personnel transport. But I don't remember any of it. They put you in a coma.'

'Not a coma,' she corrected. 'A carefully monitored state of physical paralysis and mental alertness similar to dreaming. Few people remember it, and for good reason. It's claustrophobic torture, and they condition and treat you to forget it. Why do you think you need to be mentally alert during transit?'

'So the mindship can carry you over,' he answered. 'So it can make you part of its colony.'

She stopped and stared at him. 'Good. Very, very good.'

They continued walking in silence for a while, passing through a large hall or hangar with a half-constructed skeleton or scaffolding in the centre. 'Rebuilding ancient technologies,' Syanri said, nodding to the structure. 'A collaboration with Academe Nkhaleëngomi. They say it might be an early interplanetary transport.'

Rafi frowned as he gazed at it. 'But how can humans travel through space without ships? A nexus can't be the only thing, can it?'

'Oh, Rafi, are you imagining we would splashdown like mindships into the ocean in nothing but our bare skin? We used to travel from surface to surface. Why else do you think the Great Galactic War was so devastating? Both sides agreed to de-weaponise, and the greatest weapon of all was the portals. One of the main conditions for peace was the closure of the entire system of portals. They brought people and cargo, but they also opened the door to toxins and disease.'

'Is that how Sadira—'

Syanri cut him off with a look. 'Maybe. If that were the case, if portal technology has been reinvented or rediscovered, then what sense would it make for any of us to hold on to the requirements of obsolete treaties? If we want to avoid Sadira's fate, we must be prepared.'

He had no answer so he avoided the question. 'What do you do here? You said you're semi-retired.'

Syanri accepted the swerve in topic with grace. 'I no longer work in the Galactic League Logistics Division, but my former apprentices and colleagues still ask for my advice. At the moment, we are at an impasse with the Zhinuvian cartels. So few mindships now travel to Ntshune that the Zhinuvian trading fleets can name their price – and do. We need other options, or our Walls and equipment will deteriorate for lack of maintenance and parts, and travel for interplanetary fixtures will become impossible.'

Rafi thought somewhat bitterly about his additional days in quarantine due to the Cygnian government being unable to afford overpriced nanotech, and he uttered words that he never thought he would ever say. 'But it's just a game.'

'Just a game, Rafi? The third greatest source of social and financial credit on Punartam after trade and academia? Legends and traditions that go back generations, even millennia? We would not survive losing the Game. Ntshune would, but then they would not survive losing us. The Zhinuvian cartels are doing their best to fracture and consume what remains of our galactic core and they are doing it by attacking the glue, by making it difficult for us to communicate with each other and be in each other's presence.'

'Do you think they were involved in the downfall of the Sadiri?' Rafi asked. It was a common conspiracy theory, in spite of Ain's confession and disappearance from contact.

Syanri shook her head sadly. 'No. I believe the blame lies with the Sadiri and the Ainya alone. I think the cartels are run by opportunists who will help along anything that helps them. If we do not adopt the same mentality, and quickly, they will win.'

Rafi wondered how the conversation had come to this point. They had started with personal examination and ended at galactic collapse. He was sure that if he dared asked her what one had to do with the other, she would tell him 'the glue'.

She glared at him, obviously frustrated at his bafflement. 'You think more with your body than your brain. Very well. Come with me.'

Rafi followed her and soon found himself a large hall in the recreational section of Academe Maenevastraya. His eyes were immediately drawn to a small training Wall. The players were unusual. Older men, some of whom he recognised as coaches and others who possessed the casual skill and confidence of retired players, were trying a few nostalgic runs. If there was scoring going on, it was to no rulebook that he knew. Younger players, including one or two women, stayed close to the edges of the Wall and appeared to be having more fun falling between levels than doing any actual running. There was a familiarity about their motion, and suddenly Rafi remembered Sadiri pilots using Dllenahkh's training hall for certain obscure exercises that they claimed were for three-dimensional awareness, but which had looked a lot to Rafi like mere play.

Syanrimwenil put her hands on his shoulders and guided him to stand in front of the Wall at a distance where he could see every part of it without straining when he focused on the centre. 'Pay attention,' she told him. 'What have we been discussing? Look at the players, feel the motion, then close your eyes and concentrate.'

It still made no sense, but Rafi decided to at least pretend to try. He looked at the Wall until the separate movements of individuals coalesced into the stretch and flex and contraction of a flock or shoal. He let his eyes close.

A hum tingled through his body, bringing vague discomfort and a sharp memory – the waters of Grand Bay and a silent, curious behemoth testing him and finding him not to its taste. That same buzz covered the Wall before him in a sixth sense he could not describe or define. He could sense the pilots tumbling their straight relays at the sides, and in the centre the complex plays moved like a single weight tugging several threads. But the weight moved, the centre of the game moved from person to person, body to body, and in that moment Rafi realised that he was watching a group of nexuses, a collection of boobies, playing the game at a level that could never be seen by the average spectator. The pilots drew from that buzz of motion and connection like flitting dragon-flies sipping at the edge of a pond. The intoxication reached him as well; he felt the world shifting, the borders and boundaries of reality falling away to vastness. Not space, for it was not empty, but filled with tangible, never-ending harmonies and a light whose scintillations pricked at every nerve in his being. He swayed, shook free of the vision and gasped for air.

Syanrimwenil's hands stayed on his shoulders, steadying him and feeling his epiphany. She laughed. 'Baran contributed much to research on Wallrunning history and traditions. He distilled a little fact from a wealth of myth about Wallrunners re-enacting a warrior's journey through a portal. Now do you understand a little better what I am trying to tell you?'

Only one thing was important to Rafi. 'Will you teach me that?' he asked, his eyes half-closed and voice slightly hushed.

She laughed. 'Of course.' She turned him around, away from the Wall. 'Now it's time for your next appointment, isn't it? Let me walk you to the main dining hall. The view is remarkable. Some people are put off by the transparent wall and floor, but I find it aesthetically strong and daring. We stand on nothing in the midst of space. This is true. This has always been true.'

Rafi enjoyed a friendly and relaxed meal and discussion with Ixiaral during which he openly and sincerely admired the astound-ing view through glass wall and floor. Later, he had a hard training session with Ntenman and another team coached by Revered

Baranngaithe where he managed to reduce his number of accidental falls. Yet, in spite of all that, when sleeptime came and his overtired brain rebelled, the nightmare it chose was one of deep, starry space and Syanri's voice echoing mournfully, 'We stand on nothing,' while he tried and failed to keep his team of Wallrunners from falling into a distant sun.

CHAPTER ELEVEN

The suns had risen five Standard days ago. We were lounging around waiting for the rain to stop and training to begin. Rain in the Metropolis was welcome, even when it came scant and fine, more like an ambitious mist. Instead of having our usual huddle behind the screen, we were sitting in a row of the empty auditorium. Mostly we watched in appreciation as the water droplets spun and swerved along the Wall, here compressed, there rarefied, revealing the invisible steps and grav-changes in faint grey shading. Often we argued.

'Trade, profit, harnessing the engine of human desire! Name one thing that isn't based on commerce.' I kept my voice level enough to sound courteous, but still condescending to a sensitive soul. Baranngaithe was there, silently observing us, and I wouldn't be accused of instigating.

'There speaks a Zhinuvian tradeboy,' sneered Tavna. He was one of the semi-pro players who still hung around the amateurs for a taste of Baranngaithe's coaching. I hated semi-pros. They thought they were purists. 'One thing? Art! Art never makes money. People like you try to commodify it, but you can't put a price on—'

215

'Is Wallrunning art?' I interrupted, pressing my argument with jabbing hand and jutting chin. 'Does it make money?'

'Yes, it makes money! No, it isn't art!' That was Feidris, another semi-pro. He was usually a quiet one, so his raised voice shocked us all into an attentive silence. He took a quick breath and found control enough to add in a quieter voice, 'It's war.'

Feidris took up his vambraces and exited with passion and drama. I couldn't help it. I began to laugh, and a few others joined me.

Baranngaithe was not laughing and neither was Rafi. 'Ignore them,' the coach told him. 'It's both. For art, you master yourself. For war, you master another. It's both.'

Baranngaithe's voice was too resonant to ever not be heard, but he could still manage, with a trick of tone and the tilt of his head, to convey the impression that he was talking to you and no one else. Rafi glanced at him but said nothing.

It felt like a good time to break the tension with idle chat about idle thoughts. I had decided Rafi should learn to fly, and I told him so.

'It would be good practice,' I said. 'Helps you get a sense of three dimensions.'

'No,' Rafi said. 'I've already got Wallrunning and nexus training filling up my time. Definitely no.'

By Standard reckoning, three and a half months had passed since our arrival. We had settled into a routine. I found time for training, having meetings with my padr's networks and infiltrating the aerolight cliques. Rafi *thought* he was busy. He could be doing more. The boy lacked ambition. Or maybe . . . maybe I was being too harsh. Rafi had gone through the blood-binding ceremony. I could have sponsored him on Cygnus Beta, but not on

Punartam where my status as an adult was in question. It would have been better for him if I had, because Revered Baranngaithe stepped up as sponsor instead and eyes opened wide everywhere. I saw Rafi fidget as he felt the changed atmosphere just as clearly as I heard the whispers of 'fresh meat'. He learned the basic greetings and responses, shared blood with a few of the team members and for a while it looked as if he would make friends and gain some keys of his own. But then Baranngaithe kept shifting him from team to team for training instead of placing him with one group after the usual trial period. He spoke to Rafi differently, more like a friend than a coach, and the whispers and dirty looks only got worse when everyone saw how little skill Rafi had for Wallrunning.

Rafi got mad. He didn't even want to be seen standing next to Baranngaithe for more than ten seconds. He dragged me around like a buffer – or a witness – to all their interactions. Finally, he told off Baranngaithe, wanting to know how he could learn to become a proper nexus when Baranngaithe was doing everything possible to feed the rumours that he was just the coach's pet plaything. 'The others despise me,' he complained.

Baranngaithe's reply shocked me. 'Of course they do. *I'm* their nexus, not you, and I'm keeping it that way.'

To my continuing surprise, it did not shock Rafi. He stared at Baranngaithe for a moment, his face suddenly calm and controlled, and an intense look in his eyes that made me wonder what memories were seething beneath. He nodded, a courteous gesture of perfect understanding, and after that all he did was turn up to train, push himself to the point of exhaustion and leave. He hardly spoke and never tried to make friends again, and for that I felt angry at Baranngaithe. I knew Rafi had other social outlets. He dined regularly with the Second Lieutenant – a friend-ship fuelled more by homesickness than sense, in my opinion. He got on well with Syanrimwenil, and through her became friendly with a fair few Maenevastraya academics. Then there was his own nexus, Ixiaral, and her keys and circles. I didn't begrudge him that, but it worried me that he looked so much more comfortable with people who were not men. The Wallrunning brotherhood would have been perfect if Baranngaithe hadn't tainted it for him on purpose.

That's why I kept pushing. I raised it again after training when we were back in our quarters.

'What about your free time with Ixiaral and that unregistered cousin of hers?' I teased him. 'She decided yet if you're worth a temporary contract?'

My needling had an effect, but not the one I would have pre-dicted. First he looked embarrassed, in that half-sly, half-stupid way he used to get when he couldn't figure out if he liked Seren-dipity enough to do something about it. Then he got shifty, like I was asking about something he'd done wrong and I was corner-ing him into a confession, but the last and longest look was one of pure bafflement.

'I have *no* idea what you are talking about,' he said.

I believed him. 'Check your channel, Moo,' I told him smugly. 'Talk to me when you're done.'

I didn't expect he'd learn about kin contracts from his nexus training. Everything I've seen and heard about nexus romance tells me they're as bad as Sadiri pilots. They don't do for-mal, exclusive bonds with other humans. There's a set, especially in and around Academe Maenevastraya, who have variations and combinations of privacy and liberality, from those who keep their liaisons or lack thereof well hidden, to those who make it clear that one night or nothing is all you or anyone will ever get. And let me tell you, when the senior party is someone high-up in the Galactic League administration and the junior she's got her eye on is an amateur Wallrunner, the junior will happily make that one night as memorable as he can if it means he'll get noticed for his game skills on another occasion.

I've had a few 'memorable' nights. Waste of time. Not that it can't be fun, but I was too young, and Rafi – for all his 'I am an adult' posturing – is too young. When men fall into that hole of trying to be noticed, trying to create an emotional bond that will lead to higher credit or better opportunities, it's hard to crawl out. It's hard to stop saying 'this one's the last', to say that and mean it. I've seen the old amateurs, men past their prime but not yet past hope, flexing muscles and trying to look fresh and young for the crowd, just in case someone important might be looking in their direction. They do a lot of their Wallrunning during the long night, when the light is merciful to them. Sometimes they snag a catch. Often they don't.

I wasn't sure what these women wanted with Rafi, but I felt . . . I *suspected* they wanted him to feel loyal to the Hanekis. Perhaps they want that bond in reserve, in case Dllenahkh becomes more than Governor and a tangible link to Sadira-on-Cygnus suddenly gains value. Perhaps they're intrigued by a boy-nexus, a Terran at that, and think he'll be useful some day. Perhaps, perhaps – I don't know. I don't plot. But I know that cousin with the unclaimed name, that Hanekivaryai, she is not high credit, not top tier. She does not matter. She can be thrown away on an impressionable Terran boy.

Rafi listened to the information I had dumped in his channel. He laughed harshly. 'Be serious. You think Ixiaral wants a short-term marriage with me?'

Utter incredulity stretched my face in various directions, then I laughed and laughed. So many things wrong with his statement, but I only had time to pick on the most outrageous one. '*Ixiaral-haneki*? Rafi, I apologise. You *are* ambitious after all. Stupid, but ambitious. It's natural to feel some attachment to one's nexus. It's *expected*. But find a new way to admire her because she is nowhere near your level.'

Rafi was giving me a flat stare of pure fury. 'Thank you,' he choked out. 'Such marvellous, unbiased and above all knowledge-able advice. I'll be sure to take it.'

I backed off, spreading my hands before me in a gesture of peace. 'I will say nothing more. Ixiaralhaneki is known to be a woman of discretion and I trust her not to take advantage of you. Hanekivaryai, on the other hand, has every reason to do whatever it takes to gain a respected name.'

'What's *your* name, Ntenman?' Rafi asked with more than a hint of malice.

I grinned. 'Score zero, Rafi. I do not take, nor have I ever taken, the name of my mother's family. My padr and the Cygnian desig-nation are enough for me, and so I am Ntenman Perreira o-Raenledd and presently i-Metropolis Punarthai. I will play their games only so far. I want credit, not contracts. I will never be a nexus, but I want to have *some* influence on networks and doings and affairs. I will be as Punarthai as I need to be and as Cygnian as is convenient.'

Rafi's anger burned off a little. 'Well said,' he murmured.

'Good, because there's no reason for us to argue with each other. Now, about flying . . .'

Life was stable. Credit was available and cleanly earned. Everything was going rather well. And yet . . . Punartam had changed. There were more Sadiri pilots in residence, for example, most of them women, and I heard rumours of them taking permanent refuge. I then learned of the absence of a New Sadira representative on Punartam and realised that although we had not yet come to open conflict, sides were quietly being chosen. Worst of all, the Zhinuvian cartels were getting brazen. They had their bosses and captains mingling with the Metropolis circles, pretending to understand social credit and trying to ingratiate themselves with the established Punarthai networks. People kept them at a pre-occupied, bemused-but-polite arm's length, waiting to see what game they were playing. Meanwhile, the prices of off-world commodities went up and up and all any Zhinuvian had to offer in response was a sad shrug and the excuse that 'times are hard for us all'.

My padr has a unique line of trade. He specialises in cargo that can be duplicated. Duplication is not as straightforward as it sounds. Sometimes we still have to ship in a rare metal or compound or mould in order to get the composition and structure just right, but at least it's far cheaper than shipping in the entire original cargo. His networks in the Metropolis are partly commercial, partly Academe. Research is very important to getting good results from duplication, and so is sourcing high-quality commodities and well-crafted manufacture. We have an edge over our competitors who only bring in cargo, and in some ways the increasing Zhinuvian chokehold on commerce is to our benefit. But we're not shortsighted. We want healthy competition, the kind where you curse your neighbour on accounting day but dance at his festivals and wish him joy. The cartels are just greedy. If they ever took over Punartam, they'd dismantle it and sell off the pieces for scrap. They *might* keep the tower Range as a trophy, like a necklace of drawn teeth.

Healthy competition aside, there are plenty of opportunities to be found on the black market, and thanks to the rise in prices, the black market was flourishing. Small, essential parts that cannot be made or duplicated on-planet have become very, very valuable. Once people smuggled small quantities of rare and precious substances in their gut; now they disguise and implant all manner of mechanical, electronic and quantal devices. We all hate the poxy Zhinuvian cartels, but there's also the individual Zhinuvian out to gain credit like anyone else. I have no problem with them, especially now that they're the best source for black-market items. They smuggle small parts and rare substances on and in their bodies whenever they take advantage of their special 'citizen's fare' on Zhinuvian interstellar ships, and no one begrudges them their cut. It's a risky thing. Getting caught means a loss of social capital, impossible for a Punarthai to contemplate, but thinkable – barely – for an off-worlder who can leave and try again on another planet.

The Metropolis Below had become *the* location for finding such enterprising Zhinuvians. They carried out their business in quiet corners within the work sections, keeping close to Academe base levels where the mindships and surface-to-orbit craft were regularly stationed. The best ones were never greedy. They worked diligently but cautiously, never allowing their activities to become noticeably threatening to the cartels. I got a little introduction via a third-tier key, made a few small transactions to show I was reliable, and there I was, getting as comfortable with the shadow-business community as with the usual networks. It helped, I think, that one of the brokers liked me at first glance and liked me even more after he heard about my padr's company. Someone whispered my mother's name to him, the name I would not take, and oh, he was my friend for life. I couldn't decide whether I wanted to be flattered or offended. It's nice to be liked for your own sweet self, but there's another little thrill when people find you attractively well connected. I decided to be charmed yet also peeved so that he would feel motivated to make it up to me.

A few days after my conversation with Rafi, I sought out my admirer in his usual haunt, a shop that supplied fuel and lubricants for both bionic and organic needs. He was reclining in the service area, sipping something fermented and semi-toxic while a technician operated on his knee with microprobes burrowed neatly under the artificial skin and a scanscreen to illuminate the workings below. I wondered if the drink was medicinal or recreational.

'Damal,' I said (for that's the name he went by), 'Maintenance only, I hope? I need you to do something for me.'

He smiled happily at this chance to gain a little credit over me. 'Routine maintenance, my esteemed Ntenman. In a minute or two I will be entirely at your service. What do you need?'

I gave the tech a brief, worried glance, but she was Zhinuvian and looked like she didn't much care what Punarthai clients blabbed about. Still, I told Damal I would wait for him to finish, went to a private niche and had drinks ordered and delivered by the time he showed up. He walked with an exaggerated skip, as if enjoying the smoothness of his newly serviced knee, and slid into the seat opposite me.

'For me?' he said, reaching for the bowl before him. 'What new delicacy is this? More plant matter?'

'It's a Cygnian drink, a regional speciality. Fermented sucrose flavoured with aged dark wood. Be careful, it's strong.'

He drank, squeezed his eyes shut, pushed his lips out and shook his head vigorously. 'Ahh,' he exhaled, smacking his lips. 'No chlorophyll flavour. I'll try this again. Yes, my friend, what do you need?'

'Information. I know you've been involved in setting up some kin contracts lately, especially between off-worlders and—'

'And those of twisted name, yes. It is becoming a very popular pairing of mutual benefit to both parties. I'm surprised you haven't considered it. Unless . . . there is someone waiting for you on Cygnus Beta?'

A memory flashed briefly – Serendipity's face on a rare occasion when she was at peace with me rather than irritated by me – and left no greater pang than wistfulness. My expression must have showed enough of my mind, for Damal's face was highly amused.

'Ah, perhaps and perhaps! But there's more to the tale, I gather?'

'She didn't want me,' I said brusquely and tried to turn the topic back to business.

'You did not persuade her?' he pressed on, with a tone of half-mocking surprise. 'You accepted the rejection placidly? So civilised, so extremely Ntshune of you to bow to the woman's whim! I can think of a kin contract that would suit you very well.'

I was too dumbfounded to be insulted. 'Why? *My* name isn't

twisted. I'm Cygnian, Damal, don't get confused. My padr has not disowned me, nor is my birth irregular. But for those outside the family fold, yes, I can see how kin contracts with Zhinuvian entrepreneurs might be a useful strategy. Have you had any unregistered Hanekis pass through?'

Damal inhaled the fumes from his hand-warmed bowl and chuckled. 'Tshalo, of course. He is the most persistent, but he has no head for business and some consider him to be on the wrong side of sixty Standard years.'

'What about Hanekivaryai? Is the name known to you?'

Damal stopped cuddling his bowl and straightened up. 'Oh. Oh yes, well known, but not for kin contracts. She's a shifter – she takes contraband and converts it to Punarthai credit.'

'Social or financial?' I asked.

'Both! She has a powerful backer in the family and connections to the Academes. Imagine: the cartels have raised the price one too many times on some product essential for an ongoing experiment, or worse, ceased importation entirely due to lack of demand. Does the dedicated researcher end project, shut down channel, pack up apparatus and call it a day? She does not. She finds something from the black market that will do as well. The Academe records may never know that such a replacement occurred, but a little Galactic credit and a lot of gratitude flow our way. Financial and social credit gained, and the Board of Credit Assessors none the wiser.' Damal grinned, his tone almost loving – clever swindles always excited him. But I was less thrilled. I couldn't see how Rafi factored into this scenario.

'Is that all she does?' I insisted.

He began to speak, stopped his words with a little 'aha' breath and exhaled in brief contemplative silence. 'That is an interesting question,' he said at last. 'You're the second person today to ask me that.'

'Well, what did you tell the first person?'

He hid his face with a long sip from his bowl. 'I didn't tell them anything, but I did start asking elsewhere. Let me ask for a few more days.'

I left it there and almost forgot about it until one day at a Wall-running session, I went behind the screen and noticed Rafi all confidential and close with Feidris, that sober-minded semi-pro player who felt so passionately about the Game. At first I blinked and backed up a step, afraid I had disturbed Rafi in a rare moment of intimacy, but before my eyes averted fully my brain made sense of what I was seeing and I swung back inside, furious.

'Give me that,' I snarled, gripping Rafi's wrist to make him open his hand.

If it hadn't been for my time with the shadow networks I wouldn't have recognised it, but when I prised apart his fingers far enough to get a good look, it was unmistakable. Feidris dithered between flight and fight, but as soon as I got my glimpse I backed off, momentarily nonplussed. Rafi quickly flicked the diamond case to Feidris, who caught it and glared at me threateningly for a moment. Then two other Wallrunners came behind the screen and we all quickly assumed relaxed expressions and postures. They weren't fooled; they noticed the strange tension immediately, but Rafi's reputation had been set and their curious looks at the three of us quickly became smirks. I guessed the day's gossip would be about the stunted Ntshune trying to control his gifted but fast

Terran friend. Which, in a manner of speaking, was an accurate assessment of the actual situation.

I dragged him away from practice early and took him the only place I knew we would not be overheard, up in an aerolight over the Metropolis. It was a double pleasure to discover that flying made Rafi uncomfortable.

'You see, this proves you should be working on your three-dimensional sense,' I said, happily taking a sharp bank around an Academe tower. At the edge of my vision, I saw him go taupe with fear and nausea, and I levelled off quickly so that any gastric ejecta would fall on his side of the aerolight, preferably in his lap and not on the windscreen.

'Do you know what you gave to Feidris?' I asked him when I was sure he could safely open his mouth.

He grimaced. He didn't want to talk but he knew he would have to or never walk the ground again. 'Payment.'

I froze. I didn't expect that. 'What?'

'Payment. Feidris did three full runs in a turn.'

I hit him across the head. 'That was an etched fullerite diamond! That's not bonus pay for a pretty bit of Wallrunning, that's speculation pay. Betting. *Illegal*. Who gave it to you? Who are you running for?'

Rafi winced, but there was no space to cringe away in the tiny cockpit. 'It goes to his coach and the whole team. Not just Feidris.'

'That's *still* not bonus-level pay. Answer me!'

He folded his mouth and I lost my temper. I let the aerolight stall, fall and spin, recovered with ease and waited patiently for him to stop screaming.

'You're going to kill us both over something like this?' he managed finally, his voice still in the upper register.

'The Galactic League doesn't like speculation, Moo.'

'The Galactic League is *running* the speculation, Tinman! How are you so stupid?'

I went silent and sullen for a couple of minutes, then my curiosity overruled my irritation. 'Keep talking.'

He explained it all. I could not believe I had been wasting my time feeling sorry for this boy. He was using the Wallrunning training and his connection to Syanrimwenil to let rival coaches (by which I mean coaches other than Baranngaithe) know who to check out, who could consistently deliver fast, full runs, eye-catching acrobatics and spectacular falls. They recruited accordingly, even drafting up short-term contracts, and came up with bet scenarios. Rafi took the information back to Ixiaral, who let Varyai spread the word to her shadow network. When the speculators got the result they wanted, they paid a cut of their winnings to Varyai, and thus to Ixiaral, to Rafi, the coaches, the players and everyone involved in the whole mess. I suspected that Ixiaral got the largest portion and I told Rafi so with great cynicism.

'Yes, because she needs it,' Rafi said. 'They all need it. And before you ask me what it's needed for, you speak to Ixiaral. And you're no better than us, with your below-ground shadow-market dealing, so don't pretend to lecture me on what's illegal.'

After indulging in a quick roll to take the edge off his insolence, I relented and flew us home, giving him a gentle landing in semi-apology. He was right, after all. I had my own back-door doings, and although I wasn't hurting anyone, it could look suspicious if certain facts were presented in a particular way to the authorities. We held the power of disclosure over each other; it made no sense to quarrel. Even my leverage over Rafi as his essential could be weakening if Ixiaral was paying him under the blanket for little errands run and other favours. I had to be careful. I could already feel a shift in the balance of credit between us, and that shift was not in my favour.

Rafi told Ntenman, swearing on his word and his credit, that he would take him to see Ixiaral within two Standard days, then made himself scarce for several hours, privately furious at his friend's aerial antics. He sent a message to Second Lieutenant Lian, who kept to roughly the same sleep-wake cycle as he did, and the reply made him smile and relax slightly. A quick journey on the Slowline and he was in the courtyard of Academe Bhumni-astraya. There, the staff relied on the indigenous succulents, scrub and rock-based fungus to decorate their exterior gardens. The inner pathways were crafted in patterns of rock, sand and firm-packed earth, and the walls of the tower were the same material as the outer shell – grey and fully opaque at first glance, layered like shingles or armour on closer inspection.

He went through unchallenged; he was known and he knew where to go. The Academe had felt familiar from his first visit, entirely Cygnian/Terran in design. Their work section was divided into communal spaces and closed-room offices with actual desks, shelves and cabinets, plus screens that hung from the ceiling and displayed flat images on their surfaces or holos in the space between two screens. There were fewer chairs than he expected – desk height varied to suit those who would stand and those who preferred to sit on the floor. Lian was a floor-sitter and had a dedicated spot in Dr Daniyel's office. Rafi stood before the office door and lingered for a while reading the notices and news on its screen, some of them referencing Cygnus Beta.

Lian put a stop to it by opening the door. 'Why didn't you speak to the door so it would let you in?'

'Sorry, I got distracted,' Rafi said, crossing the threshold and unconsciously looking around for something else to read as Lian got resettled behind the desk.

'I've offered to lend you a handheld,' Lian reminded him, sliding one across the desk.

Rafi sat down and took up the handheld, considered for a moment, but finally shook his head. With so many screens and surfaces available to plug into, he had grown accustomed to travelling light. His datacharm now held everything from Cygnus Beta, his audioplug channel gave him access to all he needed for Punartam and the still-useless comm on his wrist remained for purely sentimental reasons.

'Well, before you leave, write something to your aunt,' Lian said sternly.

Rafi composed his message and Lian returned to work. Several minutes passed quietly.

'Finished,' Rafi said. 'How soon can you get it to her?'

Lian took the handheld from him and tapped the screen with a stylus, both avoiding Rafi's eyes and failing to suppress a smirk of secret knowledge. 'I can't say exactly. It depends on the route. She's probably got your first and third messages by now. Not the second, not yet.'

Rafi pretended to be unconcerned. 'I'm not going to beg you to tell me.' He had a fair idea; Lian's connections with Academe Maenevastraya pilots meant unorthodox ways to send messages but also unreliable timing. He had a vague idea that some of them were involved in the same kind of experimental travel that Naraldi had pioneered, in which case he could only hope that his messages were reaching the Aunt Grace who actually shared a timeline with him.

He changed the subject slightly, looking for an opportunity to put Lian on the defensive. 'What do you do exactly when Doctor Daniyel is away?'

Lian gave a strangled laugh and cast a weary eye over the several text displays attached to the desk and a handful of planetary holos hovering in mobile suspension between the desk and the ceiling. 'Organise her messy notes. Prepare background briefs so she'll know what she's doing. It keeps me busy enough to get Maenevastraya off my back.'

Rafi forgot he was pretending not to care. 'The pilots at Maenevastraya want you to travel with them?'

Lian looked startled, as if the idea had never come up, then thoughtful, as if unexpectedly interested by the possibility. 'No, they want my help with some of the New Sadiri refugees. I used to be a trained medic and war trauma counsellor back on Cygnus Beta. Not the highest level – I didn't have Galactic Patrol experience then . . .' The words trailed off as Lian's face grew even more thoughtful.

'But now you do, so . . . ?' Rafi prompted.

Lian grimaced. 'I said *used* to be. I'm not one now and I'll never be one again, Maenevastraya pressure or no.'

'I'm sure you have your reasons,' Rafi murmured placatingly. Once more he found himself revising his opinion of Lian. The symptoms were the same: forced sociability, secrets half-hinted, abrupt lapses into silence and long periods of no contact counterposed by sessions of almost desperate amiability. Now, however, instead of blaming introversion and mild xenophobia, or clumsy Punarthai networking, Rafi wondered if the answer was the pure, simple, chronic stress of keeping too many secrets for and from too many people.

He changed the subject, relating a carefully edited version of his falling-out with Ntenman, not wanting to burden Lian with more secrets but so vexed that he needed to tell *someone*. Lian watched him speak with a quizzical frown.

'Your friend is angry at you because you have friends that aren't his friends?'

'More or less,' Rafi hedged, squirming slightly at the missing facts.

Lian did not press further but the frown became sceptical. 'Include him if he's feeling left out. Do you need more credit? Have you quarrelled to the point where you have to pay him back?'

It was a practical question, but it only made Rafi feel more ashamed, as if he were slandering Ntenman with his half-truths, and uneasy, because he was not in a position to discuss certain other sources of income. 'I'm fine.'

The two stared at each other, almost friends, far from confidants.

'I'll let you get back to work,' Rafi mumbled.

'I'll get the message to your aunt,' Lian promised.

A combination of Ntenman's insistence and Rafi's own cowardice meant that it was only one Standard day later when the two went, with no prior warning, to visit Rafi's nexus. Ixiaral was in one of the sun rooms below Academe Maenevastraya. Rafi had asked her once why she chose to visit the sun rooms during the long day when everyone preferred to go to the parks and woods aboveground. Her reply had been simple: less of a crowd, more staff attention and marvellous peace and quiet. She looked the embodiment of those three factors as she sat on a padded bench, eyes half-closed and hands upturned and empty on her knees, with two male servers standing quietly nearby, awaiting her signal for food, drink, a cold cloth . . . anything.

With eyesight now more attuned to Punarthai ways, Rafi looked at her and was able to identify the concentration of a person who was listening to their channel – or, in Ixiaral's case, three or more channels at the same time. The complexity of her tracings indicated as much, and he smiled at the memory of a time not so long ago, yet ages away in experience, when he had innocently admired the pretty art on her skin with only a vague thought that it might have utility. He sat beside her and waited to be noticed.

She exhaled a long breath but did not move. 'What is it, Rafi?'

'Ntenman has questions about what I'm doing. He wants to talk to you.'

Her eyes opened wide and she turned to him, irritation tensing her jaw and creasing her forehead. 'You thought he wouldn't notice you.'

Rafi shrugged. 'It was luck that he did at all. He's waiting outside now. Do you want to speak to him?'

Ixiaral's posture sagged, now wearied instead of relaxed. 'Yes,' she said, but her hand swept out to stop him when he tried to get to his feet. 'I'll have him sent in.' She beckoned to the nearest server with a tilt of her head. 'Ytsani, take him up to the gardens.'

Rafi questioned her with a look, but she turned away and half-closed her eyes again in dismissal. Ytsani approached and stood politely but implacably before him until he unwillingly got to his feet and allowed himself to be ushered out of the door and past a confused Ntenman who had been hovering close to try to eavesdrop. He gave Ntenman a semi-encouraging smile as he went by. The other server came to the entrance and escorted Ntenman in. Rafi slowed his steps and strained his ears to hear the opening greetings between them.

'Esteemed Ixiaralhaneki . . .' Ntenman began.

Ixiaral spoke briskly over his words. 'There is more at stake here than your good opinion and even if it were not so, I would not be inclined to explain myself to you. Let us instead discuss a more sensible topic – the price of your silence.'

Ytsani's hand rested on Rafi's shoulder, steering him away from the door, his expression and attitude so obviously disdainful of Terran discourtesy that no Ntshune sensitivity was needed to discern it. Rafi shook him off with irritation. 'I know how to get to the gardens from here.'

CHAPTER TWELVE

I know how to bargain. I'm no off-kilter booby. I can hold my ground. When Ixiaralhaneki did her little bluster and bluff about the price of my silence I told her direct – knowledge is worth more than credit. Knowledge can create unlimited credit whereas credit can only buy limited knowledge. She gave me a hard stare for that, but I stayed smiling until I saw the smallest bit of a considering expression on her face, as if perhaps I *might* be worth dealing with.

She began by undercutting me. 'I see that your father uses the Haneki–Mwenil transit on occasion.'

'He does, and I hope he may continue to do so,' I replied, reproachful at the whiff of blackmail. 'Your rates are high enough; there's no need to put more obstacles in his way.'

'That wasn't my intent,' Ixiaralhaneki said. I had misjudged her – something I was far too apt to do in Punarthai society – and that little flicker of sympathy she'd shown for me was extinguished. 'I was merely stating that we know what your father does and how he manages to do it. We are a private entity and we are under no obligation to offer services to someone who is acting against our interests.'

'Fair enough,' I said, and went on the attack. 'Then tell me how illegal speculation on semi-pro Wallrunning game results is acting in your best interests.'

She did not flinch. 'The results are sacred. We do not permit anyone to speculate on wins and losses. We only entertain bets on individual skills and stylings. You should be pleased. Our main customer base is Zhinuvian. What we give up in transit and communication fees, we later collect in the name of entertainment. That's balance and symmetry, don't you agree?'

'That depends on who's drinking up the majority of the credit – galactic credit at that. Is it you, Ixiaralhaneki?' I did not have to pretend to sound disgusted.

'Not me, not personally. I really cannot tell you more, Ntenman. What will you do next? Denounce me to the Credit Exchange Bureau? Then you should really denounce yourself.'

'I, at least, have the excuse of being an off-worlder with too much Terran in my line, and a juvenile as well,' I snapped. Her coolness, her utter arrogance was waking up some old, untapped vein of idealism in my soul. She didn't care about the Game, she didn't respect our galaxy's oldest and most reliable monetary system and she was still talking down to me as if I was complaining about shoddy umpiring at a junior league scramble.

She lowered her eyes discreetly and said with effort, 'If you're looking for a cut—'

'No!' my voice shouted. *Maybe*, my mind whispered. 'I'm looking for you to tell me that you haven't involved my friend in something that could lead to his being wanted by the law on three planets instead of one. He's running out of galaxy to run to, you know.'

'Witnesses will attest that Rafidelarua merely runs personal errands for us, carrying our tokens of appreciation and esteem to prospective additions to our networks.'

I sneered reflexively. She was not impressed. The situation was going down a bad road. I tried to salvage some pride for both of us. 'Esteemed Ixiaralhaneki, look at me. Yes, I am a mere Cygnian, but I am bound by ties of love and heritage to both the world that birthed you and the world that provides you with credit, attachments and good business. Grant me a little credit in this! I have made promises to Rafi's family; I have made promises to my padr. Help me keep my word!'

The bare walls of the sun room rang with my last words and left behind a silence that was no less loud. The attendants, who were supposed to be invisible and unobtrusive, vibrated with the tension of pretending to have neither ears nor eyes in the midst of such excellent theatre. Ixiaral was the only one of us who looked at peace, her hands in the hollow of her lap, her eyes half-closed and her breathing steady, steady as counting.

'Come with me.'

When the words came, I was bracing so hard to hear 'no' that I could barely understand them.

She spoke again, gently. 'Come with me. I have things to show you and discuss with you.'

As soon as she heard my kitten-squeak of *yes* we made our way by fast chute from the depths of Academe Maenevastraya to its heights, only a few levels below the start of the orbital spire. I was deferent, quiet and obedient – in the right context, that can be a part of hard bargaining, too. I was also very, very excited and trying my best not to project that excitement like an incontinent child. There had been rumours (there are always rumours) about secret research at the Academes; not the ordinary, everyday secret research, but projects specifically geared to address the hole the Sadiri had left in galactic operations. Minor projects are easily funded with private credit from an individual or a small group, but that kind of undertaking would be massive. If such large-scale research did exist, it meant that Punartam – and possibly also Ntshune – was trying to make a move to tilt the field in their favour.

To my surprise, Ixiaralhaneki did not take me to the work section but to a place in the recreation centre that I knew well, what we Cygnians might call a museum or showroom of transportation. It held everything from aerolights to orbital shuttles to interplanetary probes and exploratory skiffs. The largest display hall held a replica of a Sadiri passenger module – *sans* mindship of course – with its nautilus array of coffin-like dream chambers. Beauty, utility and awe-inspiring complexity ... I wanted to spend a moment to admire it, but she hustled me through it to a door on the opposite side.

The door opened before we reached it, revealing a sour-faced Syanrimwenil. He (can you really call a discredited nexus *she*?) glared at me. We had never met, strangely enough, but I figured he had heard plenty about me via his channel from Ixiaralhaneki and he'd very likely filled in the gaps with bits and pieces about my failed Year. My mother's father's brother was linked by kin contract to a Mwenil; they were close enough to my line to have too much information on me, distant enough to owe me no favours.

'In and close the door,' he said abruptly, without greeting or welcome.

The bad temper was for Ixiaralhaneki as well, not only me, so I kept my courteous, accommodating mask in place, walked in and was immediately lost in curiosity. The hall beyond rivalled the previous one for size, but it was filled with more than one exhibit in mid-assembly, or disassembly – I didn't know which. They looked like variations on a template, and from the shape of them, the tiers of shallow recesses like strings of half-pearls, I guessed it was another kind of passenger module, but for what manner of ship I could not tell. What fascinated me was that unlike the replica on the other side of the door, this one, like a real mindship module, was being *grown*. Curators and caretakers tended to vats of nutrient liquid and recycling filters set on scaffolding surrounding the specimens. I thought it resembled the apparatus that kept our tower wall flora verdant and captive.

'You don't know what you're looking at,' Syanrimwenil scoffed at my interest. 'But you'll remember this day because in the future these will be as familiar as aerolights.'

'This is where the majority of the credit goes, Ntenman,' said Ixiaral. 'This and improved duplication technology. Soon you will be able to tell your Zhinuvian tradesmen that you no longer have any need for their commodities.'

'I look forward to that!' I said, surprising even myself with my intensity.

'Then perhaps you would like to help?' Syanrimwenil suggested with a hint, just a hint, of slyness.

I opened my mouth to say yes, but then I froze, frowned and pondered. 'My padr would have to approve. I have duties to him, as you know.'

It was the correct thing to say. Syanrimwenil looked less dyspeptic and Ixiaralhaneki appeared almost relieved.

'Prepare a message for him,' Ixiaral said. 'I can have it delivered as soon as possible, and we can hope for his reply before the next long night.'

'I do have a question,' I said, still taking in the sight of the module and trying to discern its workings. 'How do you send a live person via the Haneki–Mwenil transit?'

Syanrimwenil laughed in disbelief. 'I assumed you knew. Did you not try to bribe your way through some years ago?'

'I know it can be done, but I want to know *how*. Transit isn't kind to the human brain.'

Ixiaralhaneki and Syanrimwenil looked at each other, a significant look. 'It is not easy. Someone has to take you,' Ixiaral said, still looking at Syanrimwenil. The expression on her face ... there was a bad memory underneath that, and Syanrimwenil replied with a gaze full of very mixed emotions: sympathy, regret and a little defensiveness.

'Prepare your message,' Ixiaralhaneki repeated, shaking off the shade of the past. 'Ask your father whether he is willing to work with us.'

'We need allies and backers,' Syanrimwenil added. 'We are stretched beyond our resources.'

The admission scared me, and it brought me to the question which, for all my speculating, I had not wanted to ask. 'Who is all this for? Is it the Academes, or something greater?'

Another look passed between them.

'Let us hear from your father first,' said Ixiaralhaneki.

I nodded, accepting that the conversation was over, and went back to my quarters at my own Academe to figure out how to explain this to my padr.

* * *

240

Rafi fell slowly.

He was falling along the Wall in the recreational section of Academe Maenevastraya. The old Wallrunners and coaches kept shifting the levels, never satisfied with the standard gravitational topography of a League Wall, and the constant unfamiliarity made boobies of even the most seasoned players. At least the pilots kept the edges standardised as a safety net. But Rafi liked it. It was play by instinct rather than rote, and even if he did not learn the standard runs in this way, he did learn how to adapt and react quickly. He often wished he could run that Wall always and drop the harsh and increasingly unfriendly training under Baranngaithe, but he knew that was impossible.

Old players tended to think like coaches, coordinating team plays rather than indulging in personal gimmickry. Pilots, interestingly enough, were similarly collective, moving in mutual awareness and mimicry like birds, or fish, or a fleet of ships in silent communication. That was why, even though he was falling, and even though this small and not-very-perilous wall had no body-catcher, he did not feel worried.

'There you go!' A strong grip caught him by the ankle and swung him out of the light grav-field to crash into a ledge with four times the pull.

'Thanks, Oestengeryok,' Rafi croaked.

The stringy, bald man, once a slinger in his pro-running days, waved cheerily as he leapt past. On *this* Wall, falls were never at dangerous speeds, and there was always someone willing to catch you.

Teruyai, a Sadiri pilot, stopped for a moment on the ledge. 'You're getting shaky, Rafidelarua. When last did you eat?' she teased him. 'Come, Oesten! Gather up your team and let us go to the dining hall before the boy faints.'

Rafi smiled at her. Beyond the covered hair and hands typical of pilots, she looked just a little bit like Freyda, enough to make him pleasantly homesick, and she always had a joke and a kind word for him. He remembered asking her once whether she had been to Cygnus Beta. Her answer had been instant and strongly in the negative.

'I preferred the Ntshune–Punartam routes,' she replied. 'That's what saved my life back then, and that's what saves my sanity now.'

She looked nothing like Commander Nasiha, but when she said that, her face set and her eyes grew cold in a way that reminded him of the Commander's implacable determination in situations that would have made most people surrender. According to Second Lieutenant Lian, she was one of the pilots who helped women escape from New Sadira, but Rafi never dared to ask her if she could confirm the rumours of abuse and captivity.

She stepped through and out of the varying grav-fields until she reached the edge of the Wall, beckoning to Rafi to follow. 'Let's go eat.'

The panorama from the dining hall was especially fine. One sun had dipped halfway below the horizon and the other lingered so close by that the molten gold of the rim appeared to feather-kiss the edge of the world. Thin streaks of cloud painted the dimming sky with twilight hues, and all of it was beautifully fractured and distorted through the honeycomb, near-transparent outer shell of the tower, a collaboration in stained glass between nature and architecture. Teruyai rushed to choose a seat in a far corner where all was glass – two walls, floor and ceiling. Oesten laughed at her, but he took in the view with an appreciative eye as he settled himself. Everyone sat facing the sunset and backing the rest of the dining hall. Everyone saw what happened.

Afterwards, people claimed to have felt a little shudder run through the tower, like a minor tremor from an ancient fault-line. If so, it was so slight that no one moved or took particular notice. Seconds later, a bright ribbon blazed and faded across the sky, too sharp to be an illuminated cloud and the wrong shape for a comet or a meteor trail. That was noticed. By then the first warnings and reports had begun to arrive via channel and people started to look thoughtful, perturbed, then alarmed.

Finally, there was a loud crack like lightning and a massive chunk of some burning matter smashed into the overhang of the dining hall. All Ntshune born and bred reacted immediately, running for the exits and projecting urgency for any who could sense it to do the same. The Sadiri were a split second behind them, but the Cygnians and Zhinuvians paused in confusion and shock as reinforced glass gave way under the heat and pressure of what appeared to be the tailpiece of an orbital shuttle. Oesten seized Rafi's arm and hauled him to a safer spot near the centre of the hall beside a main structural beam. As they moved, Rafi saw the hanging remnants of the glass gallery buckle, break upwards into shards and pieces and fall back, down and down the side of the tower to join the rest of the debris.

'The orbital spire is gone,' Oesten said. 'Cut. Sabotaged.' A cold, dry wind was howling through the gap in the tower wall and it muted his words and stole his breath.

'We must get below,' Teruyai shouted.

They ran to the emergency chutes. Rafi plunged down without hesitation, his only thought to get to Ntenman and find the safest part of Academe Surinastraya to cower in until whatever was chopping down orbital spires went away. He bounced out of the bodycatcher and found his feet with practised ease, but when he made for the main exit, Oesten held him back. 'No. Further down. We're needed on the lower levels.'

Teruyai and Rafi followed him without question as he spoke open another door and led them down another emergency chute.

'Who would dare?' Oesten said angrily, talking as much to his channel as to his companions. 'Who would dare!'

'Definitely not an accident, then?' Teruyai said with bitter, unbelieving hope.

Oesten listened for a while to the other voices in his head. 'Zhinuvians. They're almost sure.'

'This is an Academe of Punartam, not a low-tech town on a backwater colony planet! What are they thinking?'

'They're thinking they can get away with it,' Oesten replied, 'and I'm thinking we've been too slow to realise what's possible without the Sadiri to keep us all peaceful and polite.'

Amid his panic, Rafi found a moment to wonder what was further down than the sun rooms of the Academe. He tried to remember, made a fumbling attempt to access his guides and his channel, but with Oesten and Teruyai shouting over his head it was a disaster in mental coordination, like trying to run, hold a handheld and read an article at the same time.

'The tower is structurally safe,' Oesten reassured him. 'The dining hall was probably the most vulnerable area, and they're sealing it off now.'

'Then where are we going?' Rafi demanded. 'Why are we running?'

'The tower is safe but the Academe is not,' Teruyai said.

'Is it an attack? Are we at war?' Rafi asked, voice high-pitched with nerves.

Teruyai gave him a shocked look. 'War? Why imagine such a primitive—?'

'Hard to tell,' Oesten interrupted, and Teruyai turned to him. They communicated with a single, swift look. His expression was sober; hers went from blank disbelief to a frown of deep thought. 'If it's really the cartels doing this,' Oesten continued, 'then it's mere negotiation, but with a heavier hand than we expected.'

If that was meant as an explanation, it only left Rafi more confused. He shut his mouth and focused on extricating himself from the last bodycatcher. Beyond the door there was deep, cold darkness and deeper silence.

'What is it?' he whispered.

A faint glow outlined the border of . . . something, something that surged and retreated with little sucking, slapping sounds. Water. They were standing on the edge of a reservoir. Rafi heard a rustling noise to his right and realised that Teruyai was taking off her clothes.

'I can take both of you,' she said. 'Hurry.'

Rafi felt suddenly sick. He heard Oesten stripping on the other side of him, but his attention was caught by the sight of the brightening glow resolving into the flexible lines of filaments unfolding and extending. 'My data,' he said, struggling weakly for an excuse.

'Bare as much of your skin's surface as you can manage. Little things don't matter.' Teruyai dived in smoothly with a soft splash.

Oesten went next, feet first, and bobbed for a while, a dark form surrounded by a halo of pale golden light. 'Hurry, Rafi!'

Rafi quickly undressed, touched his audioplug and datacharm

twice with a quick, almost superstitious gesture and tumbled into the water before he could overthink it.

I knew immediately it was one of those things that, years and years later, would be a pivot point in history. You would be able to start up a good conversation by asking, 'Do you remember where you were when you first heard that the Zhinuvian cartels had severed the Academe Maenevastraya orbital spire?' Well, I was below-ground. I caught the warnings on my channel and rushed to the surface, but I was too late to catch the descending whip of fire that was the lower portion of the spire burning through the atmosphere. I did see the damage done by the lowest of the shuttles on the line as they crashed through the outer shell. Bad design, that honeycomb structure. I had always wondered how it would stand up to serious impact, and the answer was clear.

The first thing I did, even as I gawked with the rest of the crowd in the Academe's gardens, was to send a *Where in all the plaguelands are you?* message to Rafi's channel. Then I picked up an unexpected warning from Damal, advising me that I might want to clear out of Academe property for a while and come and stay with him. I looked at the sad, frayed tuft that had once been the Maenevastraya spire and felt immense gratitude at the suggestion.

Next my channel blew up. I took messages from Baranngaithe (training cancelled, how surprising), from Haviranthiya (official reminders of the evacuation protocols for Academe Surinastraya and personal exhortations to stay safe), Lian (where is Rafi?), a general appeal for calm from Hanekitshalo (that poxy panjandrum – who put him in charge?) and an announcement from the Aerolight Airspace Authority (all flights along the Metropolitan Range cancelled, all access and permissions withdrawn, updates to follow). When the message from Ixiaralhaneki came through I dropped all the rest, stepped out of the crowd and found a quiet spot on the edge of the gardens.

It was as I guessed. My padr had responded by asking for a face-to-face meeting at the Haneki–Mwenil transit point. To that, Ixiaral had appended a note telling me to come to the Academe Surinastraya sun rooms immediately because 'the situation was volatile'. I rolled my eyes; of course it was. I went to my quarters, packed up my small amount of necessaries and descended to our sun rooms. They were bigger and busier than the Maenevastraya rooms both day and night due to their very innovative light displays and therapeutic treatments. I knew a lot of semi-pro Wallrunners who worked there as attendants – another way to catch the eye of a team owner. But not today, not with a damaged spire and a cracked tower wall on display aboveground. Today was fewer people and more chatter, with staff and clients talking anxiously about what it all meant.

When I found Ixiaralhaneki, she was huddling – yes, *huddling* – in a small private room, hunched over a desk screen and gabbling messages or memos. I was unkindly pleased to see her usual self-possession completely shattered. She blinked rapidly at me and started speaking immediately, her occasional abrupt pauses proving that she was still half-listening to her channel.

'How soon can we see your father?' she asked.

I raised my hands, entreating her to slow down. 'How soon? Were you thinking about going through the transit? Because I'm not sure I'd like that option based on what I've heard from you.'

'Our options are becoming increasingly limited,' she said. 'Can you go now?'

'I need to find Rafi first—'

She cut me off. 'Rafi is already on his way to Cygnus Beta.'

I gaped at her.

'Don't you understand? This is the start of an evacuation. Don't your Zhinuvian friends below-ground tell you anything?'

Damal and his invitation . . . I shook my head. 'Let me hear it from you.'

'The cartels are taking over. They need to control the transportation technology or they'll lose their monopoly.'

I felt my own composure cracking. 'I have to go see someone.'

'When can we leave to meet with your father?' she insisted.

I tallied silently before answering. 'Five hours. Where should I meet you?'

'Academe Bhumniastraya, upper levels. Let us use the spires while we can.'

I fled and grabbed the nearest transit bubble, sending out message after urgent message to Damal. He was at a warehouse by the lower levels of Academe Nkhaleëngomi, far from his usual haunts. It was an odd relief to find him looking worried as he shouted orders to minions, scribbled on a handheld and skated up and down the aisles of inventory on a cheap grav-board.

'Damal, what's going on?'

He beckoned to me to keep up. 'Changes, my friend. Will you ride this one out, or will you go back home? You've got enough cred with us shadow-marketers, and the cartels will tolerate us for a while if all we're doing is strict mini-cargo.'

'Damal, there's a shattered tower above and my friends are disappearing! I need to know what's going on!'

He stopped dead. 'Your friends are disappearing?'

My big mouth. My uncontrollable tongue. My slow, stupid brain.

'What an interesting thing,' he mused. 'Is this the big one? I have to assess the risk carefully, consult with some colleagues. But I think I can guess what will happen. No one will claim responsibility. The cartels will step in and offer credit and protection in exchange for control over and profit from Academe research. The Academes may hesitate, but after a while, with a little encouragement, they will say yes. Don't look so upset, Ntenman. My offer still stands. You can do business in other places besides Punartam and Cygnus Beta, you know. Come with us. We can find niches where the cartels will never notice us.'

In other circumstances that would have been tempting, but for now I could only say weakly, 'I have to speak to my padr.'

He looked at me fondly, and I was embarrassed. Perhaps I had said it more like a child than a business partner. 'How long should I wait?'

I estimated frantically, throwing in extra time for all kinds of contingencies that hours earlier would have been unthinkable, floundered, dithered and finally picked a common number at random. 'Thirty Standard days.'

'Very well, but in case your fate is such that we do not meet again – take this.'

He dipped into his sash and pulled out a token. I recognised what it was: a datachip of Zhinuvian currency. It represented a symbolic modicum of financial credit, but, more importantly, it would include Damal's personal endorsement of me as a business colleague. I was touched but flustered. I had nothing to give in return. He saw my discomfort and laughed ruefully as he put the token into my hand and gently folded my fingers over it.

'My dear Ntenman, true friendships have no balance sheets. And they say we Zhinuvians are mercenary! You're a very likeable person when you're not fretting about status and credit. Remember that.'

The second time waking up after the coma of mindship sting was even more disorientating than the first. Rafi came to his senses in mid-step. He stopped walking and thought about who he was and what he was doing. He was clutching a damp sheet around his body and his hair was dripping into his eyes. He was outdoors, standing barefoot on paving stones that led to a group of buildings a short distance away. The sun was shining; it was probably around ten o'clock in the morning. The air was a little cool but rich in oxygen and his feet pressed hard on the stone.

'Cygnus Beta?' he mumbled.

'Good, you are with us at last,' Teruyai said, rubbing his arm reassuringly. 'I think you are a little bit allergic to mindship secretions. Be careful with that. We're in Vaya Province.'

Rafi looked at her. She was damp, but clothed. He turned his head slowly and noticed Oesten on his left in similar condition but with a worried expression. They appeared ready to catch him if he stumbled or fainted. Rafi started walking again and let another slow thought percolate. 'Is the Commander here?'

Teruyai hesitated, flashing a quick, concerned look over his head at Oesten. 'I don't know of any commanders.'

'She disappeared,' Rafi murmured. 'Have we disappeared, too?'

By the time they reached the buildings, he was sufficiently himself to ask accusingly, 'Where did you get clothes?'

The Masuf Lagoon stretched several miles inland and underground from the same ocean that washed the shores of Grand Bay. The semi-arid desert above was slightly reminiscent of the indigenous climate of the Punartam Metropolis, but the extra gravity dragged at Rafi's steps and the rich air made him slightly giddy. It vexed him that after such a short time on Punartam he was able to feel alien on Cygnus Beta.

The people of the region mostly lived in or near the capital Piedra, a rock-cut city carved into the side of a butte. They were nominally taSadiri but thoroughly Cygnian in outlook and culture. They welcomed the pilot community with hospitality and courtesy but, unlike Sadira-on-Cygnus, there was little integration. The pilots themselves lived like transients and used their hostel to sleep, eat and rest before journeying on.

'The Lagoon is part of their territory, and we pay them in goods and information for its use,' Teruyai explained to Oestengeryok as they took breakfast together in a single-storey dining hall where the window views were less spectacular but much more comforting than those of the Punartam Academes.

Rafi tugged at the sleeves of his robe, a loan from the communal clothes bank, and felt the fabric strain over the datacharm on his upper arm. He was glad that his data had survived, but his comm and audioplug were being repaired; they too had been incompatible with the mindship's secretions. It did not matter. Teruyai refused to allow him to contact his family directly. After an initial rush of anger, he saw her point. They had arrived secretly and the aim was to stay hidden. The Masuf rest station used other means to communicate. Unusual activity within the global comm networks would only attract attention and force the Cygnian Central Government to become officially aware of their presence.

'The arrangement with Piedra has worked well this far and it could become permanent,' she continued. 'Let's not push our luck.'

Rafi quietly wondered if the Cygnian government was informally aware of the details of this arrangement. He figured somewhat cynically that the government was likely to be even *less* efficient at detecting and stopping contraband than before and, given the cartels' stranglehold on the galactic market, perhaps mindfully so.

Oesten, for all his quick recovery from mindship travel, looked aged by worry. 'I could see the Academes moving to Cygnus Beta. Not all of them. A few. Definitely those of particular interest to the Zhinuvian cartels.'

Teruyai looked at Rafi as she answered Oesten. 'Academe Bhumniastraya would always do well on Cygnus Beta, but I believe Academe Maenevastraya should go to Sadira-on-Cygnus. Do you agree, Rafi?'

'I don't know,' he answered honestly. Most conversations between Teruyai and Oesten went over his head in more ways than one. 'Won't the cartels put a stop to that?'

'They can try,' Oesten said grimly, 'but I think Cygnus Beta in alliance with Sadira-on-Cygnus will be stronger than they realise. What are we waiting for?'

Teruyai drank some of her broth, licked her lips and exhaled deliberately. 'The slowest evacuation in the history of galactic conquest.'

'Our resources are not what they once were,' Oesten noted. 'And the cartels have been so diplomatically coy about the nature of their "assistance" to Maenevastraya that some still believe there has been no conquest.'

'They'll believe it when the Bhumniastraya spire is the next to be cut,' she predicted.

'They'll take their time,' said Oesten. 'Knock them off one by one.'

'Fear and anticipation work in their favour. No one likes to operate in an environment of vague threat. Can you blame the remaining Academes for trying to negotiate?'

'But why doesn't Galactic Patrol do something?' Rafi said aloud. The other two gave him such an astounded look that he decided henceforth to keep his mouth shut when they discussed galactic affairs.

'Galactic Patrol hasn't worked properly since Sadira fell,' Teruyai told him, speaking as gently as a doctor breaking bad news to a terminal patient.

'No money, no transportation, no authorising body,' Oesten listed. 'What you see of their operations is the twitching of a headless corpse.'

Rafi spared a thought for Lian and Dr Daniyel, and for the first time he understood enough to feel afraid. It was one thing to have no judges, but to have no police – anyone could do anything with impunity.

'We've been here almost a week doing nothing but waiting,' he said despondently. 'I might as well go back home to Tlaxce or Sadira-on-Cygnus.' It was a selfish thing to say to two people who had lost everything they had known, but he was young, oblivious and desperate for something useful to do.

Teruyai answered him with more politeness than he deserved. 'Be patient, Rafi. Certain transits take time.'

Confused, Rafi looked to Oesten for clarification. Oesten obliged. 'It has been too long since the last Galactic Consortium Meeting. The rulers of Ntshune are sending representatives to Cygnus Beta.'

'I should really try to get home,' Rafi fretted. 'You stay here if you like, but as soon as my stuff is fixed, I'm going home.'

'How?' Oesten asked him gently. 'Will you walk to Piedra and borrow a desert scooter? Find a port or a track after about a week's travel? Or are you hoping a private shuttle will pass by and give you a ride?'

Rafi considered. He tried to remember where the sub-Consulate in Vaya was located, but all he knew was that it was nowhere near Piedra. He tried to think about other ways to send a message to his family, ways that the Cygnian government would not detect, and found his mind blank.

'Does this place at least have a Wall?' he asked, resigned.

PART THREE

Vanguard

CHAPTER THIRTEEN

'This is days old,' Delarua noted calmly, tapping the chip with a steady finger. It held the latest personal dispatches from Grand Bay, and it was projecting to her handheld one particular message, origin Punartam.

Dllenahkh stood beside her chair and looked over her shoulder to scan the message. 'Yes.'

'Dated a little before the Zhinuvian cartels began their takeover of the Academes,' she continued.

A tear spilled over her eyelid and swept quickly down her cheek. Dllenahkh raised his hand, his initial impulse to wipe away the tear, but another, deeper instinct made him lower his hand, gently clasp his wrist and exhale deeply, quietly, until Delarua's breaths matched his. Only then did he speak.

'We have some information. There is little new, and nothing confirmed, but it is very likely that Rafi, Lian and Qeturah are no longer on Punartam . . . and are safe.'

The speculation was comforting. Dllenahkh did not have it in him to idly reassure. Delarua took a deep breath and set the handheld aside. 'Well, Governor, what now? Has Central Government said anything official?'

He found another chair, pulled it close and sat tiredly. 'Most of our trade comes via Punartam, which means everything is at a halt. The settlements and homesteads are fairly self-sufficient but the urban areas will suffer.'

'And that's what makes Grand Bay valuable,' she concluded.

'Of course. Central Government has hinted at this arrangement before. Their terms are generous. It many ways, it is a natural step in our settlement's development.'

'And what do the pilots say?' Delarua asked, hearing the unspoken 'but'.

Dllenahkh sighed. 'Some of them no longer wish to owe allegiance to any planet. We may have to negotiate separately. We do not hold any authority over them.'

'But Naraldi—'

'—is an icon, a legend, a symbol. Not a leader. He refuses to get involved. He says things like "interesting" or "I remember this". Once I heard him mutter "that's different", but when I pressed him he only shook his head and smiled. At times I truly dislike him.'

Delarua laughed lightly, sympathetic to his irritation. 'Perhaps he's right. Knowing what *could* happen is never the same as knowing what *should* happen.'

'Anything that could give us an advantage would be welcome at this point. I find him so strange now. He's less engaged. Perhaps that's to be expected, if he's seen several versions of us live and die, but I hope that does not mean he will sit happily on the sidelines to observe whether or not we'll bring about our own destruction.'

'No, he wouldn't. Not Naraldi. Not where you're concerned.' She gladly took her turn to reassure, knowing how desperately he needed it. Some figurehead. The Council was expecting him to produce miracles and it was exhausting him. For all her kind words about Naraldi, there were times when she truly disliked him as well for encouraging her quiet, introspective husband to take up such a stressful post.

He tried to smile and rested his head on the desk, near enough to her hand to be a subtle invitation. She sighed and took up her handheld again, but in mere seconds her free hand was moving lightly over his hair and curling around the tender skin behind his ear. The quiet moment did not last long. Freyda came in and slammed the door, complaining bitterly and loudly.

'*Just* when I was getting ready to go to Punartam the Zhinuvians have to pull something like this. It's almost like Lanuri planned it— Oh! Sorry. I didn't mean to interrupt.'

Delarua withdrew her hand from her husband with almost guilty speed. Dllenahkh sat up straight. Both of them looked elsewhere to avoid noticing the tears of frustration in Freyda's eyes.

'I'm sorry,' she said again, thoroughly mortified. 'I—'

Irritated at her behaviour, Delarua said, 'I'm in my office, I'm working, stay!'

Dllenahkh glanced from one to the other, stood up without haste and left the room.

'I just wanted to say,' Freyda mumbled, 'that another Academe's orbital spire has been sabotaged. The entire Terra project has shifted to Cygnus Beta temporarily.'

'That's good— I mean, it's bad for the Academes, but that's good for you, right? You can still work with them? Where are they located?'

Freyda shrugged miserably. 'For now, at Tlaxce City.'

Delarua stared at her in confusion, then gradually worked it out. 'Oh. Still too close to Lanuri.'

Freyda nodded, ashamed. 'I wanted to get away, *really* get away.'

Delarua squeezed her eyes tightly shut for a moment. 'Freyda, there's a lot happening in the galaxy right now. Focus on what you *need* to do. If you're lucky, we'll all get kidnapped by a Zhinu-vian cartel and you won't have to worry about how to avoid Lanuri.'

'That's unkind,' Freyda said, both hurt and angry. 'Isn't it ironic that you can focus on "what we need to do" while you're so comfortable in your perfect marriage.'

Please, thought Delarua, briefly closing her eyes again, *I want you to shut up now so we can still be friends.*

Freyda groaned and covered her face with one hand. 'I'm sorry,' she said again. 'You know my problem. I'm restless. I need to move on again, do something different. I should never have got married, especially not to a Sadiri.'

There was an uncomfortable cough at the door. Dllenahkh stood there, visibly embarrassed at his poor timing, with a completely blank-faced Lanuri beside him. 'An emergency meeting of the Galactic Consortium has been scheduled to take place four weeks from now in Tlaxce City. I must go to represent Sadiri-on-Cygnus.'

'And Naraldi has designated me as the spokesperson for the pilots of Grand Bay,' Lanuri said, his voice grave and level, as if he could never experience or even understand what boredom and anger felt like. 'However, we are making plans to leave earlier in order to have our own discussions with the Consul of New Sadira and other representatives from the heritage communities. You are welcome to join us.'

He tried to say something more, managed only a hesitant parting of the lips, then turned abruptly and left. Dllenahkh gave Freyda an apologetic look and followed his friend.

Freyda laughed unhappily. 'What does *he* have to be sorry about?'

Delarua rubbed her arms, trying to remove the chilly tension that was the backwash of Dllenahkh's emotions. 'Well, he *did* introduce you to Lanuri. I think he feels responsible.'

Rafi set himself to walk every day and occasionally climbed the small mesas dotted around the Masuf Hostel. Returning to Punartam seemed both reckless and impossible with no way to get to the Tlaxce spaceport and none of the mindships of Cygnus Beta available for non-essential travel. The best thing he could do, besides practise on the little Wall maintained at the hostel, was to build back his muscles and stamina to accept Cygnian gravity. His legs shrieked pain at him but his lungs felt better than ever. He thought to himself that he might measure his height and weight again. He felt stronger in some ways, less awkward, as if his brain's idea of his body was finally matching the reality.

He saw a figure coming along the main path at a run. It turned in mid-stride, recognising him, and bounced to an untidy halt. It was Oestengeryok. 'I was right,' he shouted, excited but far from pleased. 'I was right. Academe Surinastraya's spire was destroyed days after we left. Now Bhumniastraya's is gone, and Academe Nkhaleëngomi has declared unconditional surrender to the cartels.'

'What? How do you know that?' Rafi yelled, picking up his pace to join Oesten on the path.

'New arrivals,' Oesten told him, hopping in place as if eager to be gone again. 'At least ten new mindships. The cartels are not at all popular!'

He spun and hastened away to the main entrance, off to warn people to make preparations for the newcomers.

After a few more days, the sight of new refugees arriving from Punartam was no longer remarkable. The hostel's resources became strained. Rafi was put to work with other semi-permanent residents to erect quick-build shelters of rock and textile, and some of the pilots began to take the unusual step of regular sub-light travel by sea, to bring in supplies with greater frequency and speed than could be managed via overground routes. The population in and around the Masuf Lagoon and Hostel, human and mindship, increased sharply and yet without incident. There was no challenge from the authorities. The Cygnian government appeared to be continuing its policy of turning a blind eye to mindship movements as long as they could gain benefit in the long term.

Rafi's abused tech had been successfully repaired, but instead of rushing to use his comm to call his aunt, he put a cautious and non-revealing message of reassurance onto a fresh datacharm and asked one of the pilots bound for Grand Bay to deliver it to the Dllenahkh homestead.

He still went walking when he had time. It was a good excuse to be nearby when new people came up from the lagoon to take the path to the hostel's main reception. He looked for familiar faces and found a few – old coaches and semi-pro players he had met at training or during a clandestine exchange of credit; research assistants, curators and technicians reluctantly and sorrowfully deserting their exhibits and projects; and several unaccompanied children sent by nervous parents to a safer environment.

It made him nervous as well. He had been caught up in Teruyai's sudden flight, following without questioning, and only afterwards, when the mindship toxins had worn off, did he question whether it had been worth it. Now, looking at the faces of those who had waited to leave, he felt a strange chill. Perhaps, as a pilot and one already made rootless, Teruyai found it easy to cut losses and run; perhaps her experience with refugees from New Sadira had warned her how insidiously bonds could be tightened while a hopeful population waited to ride out a temporary crisis. Perhaps it was both, because when he asked her, she said, 'Coming back is easy. Getting out is hard. Always do the hard thing as quickly as possible.'

There was nothing, however, to match the pang that struck him when weeks later he saw an unusually large group of pilots, senior coaches and academics escorting a familiar figure along the broadened path to the hostel.

'Revered Patrona!' he cried out.

She looked around immediately. Her face was tired, but she could not suppress a smile at the incorrect but sincerely meant address. 'Rafidelarua, have you come to welcome me to your planet?'

'Welcome, Patrona. I'm glad you're safe. Who else is with you?'

'Ixiaral and the Dean of Maenevastraya accompanied me. The Controller and Hanekivaryai have chosen to remain on Punartam to do what they can. Credit must not fail and commerce continues always! But I fear the Dean may return to try to mitigate Hanekitshalo's nonsense.'

The Patrona moved on, pulled aside by one of the senior pilots for a conversation. Rafi remained where he was, momentarily bewildered by her final words. Oesten appeared at his side.

'Didn't you know?' he said quietly to Rafi. 'Tshalo's in deep with the cartels. Anything for recognition and credit. He calls it "adjusting to the new realities of our galactic structures". I could call it something shorter. I could call *him* something shorter, but how do you dishonour a name that never had much honour to begin with?'

Rafi listened and nodded, but then he saw a very distracting sight on the lower path. 'Ixiaral! And Ntenman!'

Ntenman laughed and took a couple of running steps past Ixiaral. He slung a heavy bag over Rafi's half-unwilling shoulder. '*And* Ntenman. I like your order of importance. *And* Ntenman indeed. Do you even care to let your friends know you're still alive? Lazy, lazy Moo. Always waiting for the world to come to you. Well, here we are.'

'Who is "we"?' Rafi said, grimacing under the weight of the bag. 'Welcome, Ixiaral!'

'Thank you, Rafi. Come, walk along with us.' She looked more than distracted; her gaze often flitted to the Patrona and her forehead was creased in a semi-permanent frown.

Rafi staggered along and looked meaningfully at Ntenman to get his explanations. 'When did you get here? I was in the dining hall; I saw when it fell. Teruyai and Oestengeryok were with me and we got out immediately.'

Ntenman lowered his voice. 'Then we left a Standard day after you did. I think Ixiaral wanted to leave earlier, but Syanrimwenil needed a bit of extra time to prepare for taking the Patrona and the Dean through transit.' His expression grew sombre. 'I had no idea. Is that the kind of training you go through?'

'What are you talking about?'

'He— *She* carried all four of us. She's resting now at my padr's estate. It was very hard on her.'

Rafi opened and shut his mouth, briefly speechless with worry. He tried to explain. 'I've never done it. I've learned to be part of collective movement, like with a team on a Wall, but that's with others who have some ability to either be a nexus or respond to a nexus. I can't imagine doing it with people who don't have that.'

A flash of self-loathing crossed Ntenman's face. 'I thought as much. *I* was the dead weight. Well, that's yet another person I owe.'

Rafi frowned, recalling Syanri's insights about his mother and his sister. 'I don't think it's that simple.'

'It isn't,' Ixiaral confirmed, focusing on them at last as they entered the main building. 'It rests on the level of knowledge the nexus has of the passengers, and that made you no more dead weight than the Patrona.'

'Thanks,' Ntenman muttered, relieved but still sarcastic.

'That was the purpose of the research at Maenevastraya, to simplify that knowledge for the nexus, or remove the need for it. Mindships carry most of the passenger information so that the pilots are free to navigate.' Ixiaral looked around the crowded entrance hallway. 'I did not realise there were so many people here.'

Rafi let the bag drop to the ground. 'More and more every day. Are you all staying, or returning to Ntenman's place?'

'We're going to Tlaxce City,' Ntenman declared. 'That's where all the key players are assembling, Rafi. You should come with us.'

Rafi would willingly have gone anywhere, but – Tlaxce City? He badly wanted to see his mother and Gracie again, but going near the headquarters of the government that had caused him so much grief felt stupidly risky.

'Or will you stay *here*,' Ntenman asked, giving a slightly contemptuous stress to the final word.

'I'll come with you,' Rafi decided.

Ixiaral's frown vanished in one quick, magical second and she grinned at him. 'Good. We have plans, and you can be part of them.'

The following day there was an open-air rally. The Patrona and the Dean had arrived with a purpose, and the Patrona gave detailed, passionate, eloquent speeches to a gathering that grew as the day wore on. The Transit Project – backers, consultants, researchers and guinea pigs – was set to regroup and relocate.

Rafi was quite sure the crowd included taSadiri from the neighbouring areas, some of whom were transmitting the Patrona's words via their comms to other unseen audiences. Within a day or two, it would probably be included in the local network's filtered content to the rest of Cygnus Beta. At the end of four hours, Rafi was exhausted and there was a definite ebb-and-flow of focus-challenged Cygnians at the fringes, but the Punarthai refugees and Sadiri pilots kept keen attention on the discussion, constantly asking questions and querying the answers given down to the smallest details of schedule and logistics.

The Patrona was cagey about one thing – the new location.

'That remains to be seen,' was all she would say even while requiring pledges of absolute loyalty and commitment from all who would participate. Yet no one pressed her. She was a powerful nexus and she had the charisma to draw in even the doubters with nothing more than a 'perhaps'. Rafi watched her in fascination. He was no stranger to detecting compulsion, but this was something more refined. She seduced using blunt invitation and inspired with unpalatable facts. So much honesty should have gained her no followers, but by the end she had converted almost the entire hostel, turning refugees into volunteers.

'If their guardians will allow, let the children come as well,' she said unexpectedly. 'We will need young, flexible minds for early training in these new modes of operation.'

At sundown, the Patrona and many other Punarthai appeared startled by the sudden onset of twilight, but it was decided to take it as a good time to stop talking and start preparing. Rafi went to the dormitories to pack up the few things he had acquired – clothes, utensils, a basic datareader – not to take with him, but to return to the communal pool of belongings. He could borrow something simple to wear from Ntenman, but everything else was non-essential. Teruyai came up to him as he was putting together a neat, small pile on his cot.

'You are not coming with us?' she asked, sitting down and making the thin pallet slope towards her, disturbing the structure of his pile.

'I think I am,' Rafi said, grabbing a mug that was trying to roll off the cot. 'Just not the same route.'

She looked at him for a while as if hoping he had some inside information to share, but he remained focused on centring the pile on the cot's thin blanket and tying the corners together into a rough bundle. When that was done, he met her gaze with a rueful expression.

'I don't know what's happening,' he confessed. 'I've realised that I don't plan my life very well. I dodge things and end up on a different path. I hop on passing cars. I follow my friends until I make other friends and follow them instead.' He recognised it was starting to sound like an apology and stopped talking.

Teruyai took his admission of weakness in stride, probably expecting no less of a Cygnian. 'Make good choices, Rafi, even if – *especially* if they are last-minute. We thought Sadira would always be there to come home to. We thought we had found a place on Punartam. Things happen, but if you still have friends to follow, that is a good thing.'

He should have thanked her then for dragging him out of that dining room and across several light-years of galaxy to safety, but there were too many things to do and too much to think about, and Ntenman had just appeared in the doorway waving his hands frantically. He excused himself quickly and ran to his friend.

'The shuttle's ready,' Ntenman said. 'If we leave now, we can get the next sub-orbital flight to Tlaxce City.'

We had returned! Not a Year – barely eight months of actually being on Punartam and almost three months' thumb-twiddling in quarantine or comatose in transit. Speaking of which, interstellar transportation with proper passenger modules could not compare to small-group jaunts by naked mindship or remarkably gifted nexus for speed and sheer terror. I have so, so much respect for Revered Syanrimwenil. I should never have listened to those who labelled her a failed nexus. Punartam's society had hardly been kind to me, so I should have had more sympathy.

She told me that in theory a perfect transit should be instant-aneous, something which I cannot understand, far less explain, but it has something to do with living, conscious matter being able to access certain dimensions and bypass certain others in a way that purely inanimate matter cannot. Of course, it's not as straightforward as that. A single person can't stroll through a transit. There's something about having a critical mass of sen-tience, which is how the mindships and their pilots do as well as they do. And the Wallrunning Brotherhoods, they were armies, trained to go through transits awake and alert by becoming a kind of temporary collective organism, and then carrying that shared consciousness into battle. They couldn't bring much beyond themselves, but what weaponry they did bear was disrup-tive enough to cause galactic war and shut down all the transits for good . . . almost all . . . except for a few, rediscovered and used secretly by those of us who knew enough to coax through a few grams of rare cargo.

Bringing the four of us through the Haneki–Mwenil transit alive, intact and sane was a feat. I bow to Revered Syanrimwenil. I gushed about her to my padr before I left and made sure she was treated like the queen she is. She was tired – more than tired, slightly unanchored from this world, perhaps, sleeping often, dreaming with eyes open and slowly regaining control over her own body instead of, for example, trying to flex my fingers, turn Ixiaral's head, blink the Patrona's eyelids and twiddle the Dean's toes.

Not that it was easy for us. We spent a day or two out of it ourselves, but at least when we were ready and able to stand unaided, the rest of the cargo had come in and the duplications were proceeding perfectly. I was impressed. The Academes had prepared for the worst, and that meant a swift transit of everything important in the only way that mattered – as information. We received duplication templates for several experimental transit systems, datachips galore, seeds and other things I could not recognise and they refused to identify. Ixiaral guided me in packing a bag with particular templates and datachips and then made me carry it as the junior of the group.

It took a lot of resources. We called in favours, made some unexpected alliances and became ridiculously busy at a time when all other galactic commerce to Cygnus Beta was grinding to a halt. My padr was torn between debilitating anxiety and equally paralysing pride when he realised that his cooperation would mean an immense drain on his financial credit but a skyrocketing of his social credit. But old habits remained and I heard him chuckle and mutter something about getting ahead of my mother and her present husbands ... ahead by Punarthai reckoning, of course. I sighed and let him gloat. I had no ground to stand on. Wasn't I the one who not too long ago had been desperate for a successful Year and recognition as an adult?

In another matter, he managed to have the last word over me, pointing out that for a son who had complained and resisted taking over the family business, I had somehow managed to turn my act of independence in going to Punartam into an accidental display of complete filial obedience and loyalty. I wasn't sure whether to be horrified or amused at myself, but then he formally named me a full partner and I really didn't care how many laughs he had at my expense. He gave me a platinum pin with a green diamond as an accoutrement to mark the occasion. I wore it on a thin band like a Wallrunner, because whether I made my next transit naked in a mindship or stripped-down in a passenger module, I was never taking it off. Never.

But I digress. We had returned! We were once more in Tlaxce City. Once an insignificant lowlister in the annals of galactic cities; now, by process of elimination and a fortunate history of blended heritage, the host of its first Galactic Consortium Meeting, albeit one that was hastily done up and ragged around the edges. Tlaxce's Halls of Parliament had been reserved for the purpose and the spectator galleries of the Primary House were massive. We plebeians of Punartam found ourselves a comfortable corner and settled in to hear the deliberations of our rulers and betters. Rafi was nowhere to be found. He had muttered something earlier about keeping a low profile and I hadn't seen him since. I decided I would wait until the end of the day before sending out the search parties.

Ixiaral gave me a few details and I was curious enough to look up the rest. The only full delegates were those who had come from Punartam and Ntshune. There was, surprisingly enough, a delegate from the planet Zhinu A – well, not entirely a surprise considering they're the only one of the Zhinuvian home planets and associated colonies to have anything approaching a planetary government, but they usually sent their local Consul or Ambassador to attend the proceedings in whatever city the Meeting was held. To spend money and time on a ship from Zhinu was within their means, but they had never demonstrated such interest before.

The rest of Zhinu was loosely represented, if you can call it that, by a group of Tlaxce-based Consuls who insisted quite happily that they were only there to observe. Sadira-on-Cygnus was there, of course; the pilots appeared to have formed some kind of space nomad free state, whatever that meant; and the New Sadira Consul spent a long hour blathering out his complaint concerning the unseemly haste with which the Meeting had been convened, such haste having prevented him from either bringing in a full delegate or obtaining accreditation from his government to be their delegate. The sidelong looks and narrow-eyed glares he got from both pilots and Cygnian-Sadiri were a joy to behold.

The real excitement came not from a delegate but an observer. Revered Bezhtan of Academe Nkhaleëngomi had lived several years on Punartam but was originally from Ain. The murmur that ran through the crowd of delegates, observers and spectators was thrilling. Bezhtan was registered as academic rather than governmental representation so there was no reason to bar her, but you could feel the air go prickly with unresolved emotions as the Sadiri eyed her uneasily. Bezhtan sat and calmly bore the stares of curiosity and hatred with an expression that looked more like resignation than contrition.

That was only the morning session, everyone having their own little introductory piece to say, but it was already exciting. Ixiaral had to attend to the Patrona so I went to find Rafi, desperate to talk about the possibilities from this Meeting. Before I saw him, I noticed another familiar face, one that made me forget any memory of embarrassment or awkwardness when I saw how it lit up at my presence. Serendipity! We all but ran to each other and gripped arms in a cheerful mockery of the old Lyceum greeting.

'Ntenman, so good to see you!' she cried.

I laughed and only said, 'Serendipity!' but with enough fondness that she could decipher the rest.

Were we finally old enough to forget about pettiness? I can't tell you what changed, whether I had finally found my place in the galaxy or she had become more settled and secure, but we were simply glad to see each other alive and well in an unpredictable time.

'I was looking for Rafi,' I told her.

Her expression changed to wry amusement. 'Don't. He's with Delarua and she hasn't finished with him yet. Why didn't you let us know you were here?'

I stammered out my truthful but somehow inadequate-sounding explanation that we'd arrived separately and we'd both been very busy. 'Regardless,' I concluded, 'please keep me away from Grace Delarua. I'm convinced she dislikes me, and if she thinks I kept Rafi from her, she won't like me any better.'

We went to get a snack and sat outside in a small park nearby. I told her briefly and incompletely what wonders we had seen and perpetrated on Punartam, and she told me about her time in Grand Bay, swimming with baby mindships.

'What?' I demanded in shock. 'Does this mean you're a pilot now?'

'No.' She laughed, but there was a little wistfulness in it. 'I'm only a passenger. I'm a pretty good one because I do have a connection with them, but becoming a pilot takes years of training and a certain kind of biology that Cygnians don't have.'

She sounded a little in love with them. I knew enough not to scoff. Communication and intimacy but also privacy – that was all Serendipity had ever wanted. I smiled and showed her I was happy for her but felt at the same time slightly guilty that my crush had subsided enough that I could do this with complete sincerity.

'Come sit with us for the next session.' My invitation was offered with impure motives. Of course I desired the pleasure of her company, but another thing I greatly desired was the opportunity to watch her reaction to the coming revelations. Rafi would have done as well, but it sounded as if he was going to be busy for some time. To be honest, I wasn't exactly in the know myself. I was aware that certain options were being explored. I had my own guesses as to which way the decision would swing. It could have been fun to make a bet on it, but I preferred to say nothing of my speculations and instead enjoy to the fullest Serendipity's amazement when the time came.

The afternoon session went directly to the reason for the Meeting being convened. I knew that some spectators thought it would be about the cartels taking over the Academes, or the pilots' general shift in allegiance from New Sadira to their own sweet selves, but it was a mundane, almost banal request. Ntshune was requesting permission to implement a galactic transportation system. I glanced at Serendipity out of the corner of my eye, just in case she'd had any hints from pilots and might be less shocked than I hoped, but she was leaning forward and frowning, almost biting her nails.

Cygnus Beta had no objections. Sadira-on-Cygnus had no objections. New Sadira grudgingly offered no objections pending later authorisation by their government. The pilots applauded the move and pledged their support and assistance. After that, Zhinu A promptly offered no objections but the other Zhinuvian observers looked a little nervous, as if they were not sure what it all meant.

Then the Ntshune delegate explained the basis for the transit system and the huge hall rang with voices of alarm. I exhaled slowly, trying to control the urge to giggle. Serendipity's face was a picture of bewilderment. I sighed. I wanted shock but she was clearly out of her depth.

'Don't you remember that the airspace over Sadira-on-Cygnus is restricted?' I hinted. 'Why is that, do you think?'

'Because surface-to-surface transit isn't permit— Ohhh.'

'Exactly. Since the Great Galactic War, we've only allowed space-ships to come as close as orbit. We screen and process everyone before bringing them to the surface using our own transporta-tion. The Ntshune want to resurrect the old surface transits.'

Finally some order was returned to the cacophony. One of the Zhinuvian observers had passed from mere nervousness to out-right panic, seizing the floor to inform everyone what an incredibly dangerous and terrible idea it was. I smiled and watched him rant, and was more than satisfied when the Punarthai dele-gate, our own dear Patrona, took the floor next to inform the gathering that the technology and data the Zhinuvian cartels had taken by force from the Academes would inevitably allow said car-tels to construct their own surface transits, with predictably bad results for everyone else's commerce and security. Everyone looked at the Zhinuvians suspiciously, and the delegate for Zhinu A took the opportunity to calmly state that their position had not changed. Zhinu A would not offer any objections and, like the pilots, was willing to offer support and assistance. Splendid con-fusion amid the Zhinuvian observers! Smug insouciance from the Zhinu A delegate! I caught myself rubbing my hands together in glee, like a villain in an *opera rustica*. Serendipity gaped at me as if I was going mad, but it was pure entertainment!

The Ntshune delegate then spoke again, accepting the concerns raised and stating that to mitigate those concerns, they wished to make the new transit system a truly galactic project with input and oversight from every planetary government. To that end, they were inviting Punarthai academics, Sadiri pilots and the transportation specialists of Zhinu A to come to Ntshune and establish a base there which would be neutral territory, a true galactic port.

The Primary House buzzed again, less loudly than before but with a telling intensity as one by one delegates spoke their agreement and acceptance with such speed and equanimity that it was obvious pre-Meeting negotiations had taken place. The Consul of New Sadira and the Zhinuvian observers were helpless to intervene as they lacked any authorisation. I think they had assumed the Meeting would be all about the cartels. Ntshune was light-years ahead of them.

Serendipity laughed behind her hand, finally catching the adrenalin of the moment. 'Has no one realised that the Ntshune delegate just got near-unanimous approval to create a galactic capital?'

I gave her a wide-eyed stare. I had not realised, and she had shocked me, not the other way around. We leaned against each other, giggling ridiculously as if the entire caper was some Lyceum prank we had cooked up ourselves. Giddy with our new camaraderie, I wondered whether I could persuade her to come with us to the new centre of the galaxy, to Ntshune.

Delarua raised her hand to touch the door, paused and let it drop. 'Are you sure you want to do this?'

Rafi folded his arms and nodded firmly. 'Yes, I'm sure.'

She examined his face for a long moment and sighed. 'Very well.'

She pressed her hand to the door. Maria had disposed of the welcome mat – Delarua wasn't sure why – and programmed the door to announce a very narrow range of visitors. She hoped she was still on the list.

Maria herself opened the door, already looking at her sister with a tired expression, but her eyes widened in shock as she noticed Rafi. For a moment she simply froze and stared at him as her eyes grew shiny with unshed tears.

'You've grown so tall,' she whispered at last.

'Please—' He stopped, swallowed. 'Will you let me in?'

He had come back to say I love you and goodbye. Delarua understood that. It had taken her a while to forgive him for not using the comm to contact her, and for timing his message so badly and addressing it so vaguely that it had arrived days after they left for Tlaxce City and was probably still sitting at the Grand Bay clearing house in a general pile for 'the Dllenahkh homestead'. But when she calmed down enough to seriously consider what kind of future he would have on Cygnus Beta, she understood that he could not and would not stay.

Delarua watched Maria gazing at Rafi as he played a game with Gracie and swiftly, painfully realised that Maria did not understand.

She spoke a little louder than usual, to catch everyone's attention. 'When will you be leaving for Ntshune, Rafi?'

He was startled. 'Ntshune?'

Delarua softened her voice. 'Yes. Didn't you know? Or . . . will you be staying here?'

He bowed his head. Maria looked bewildered, then distressed. Gracie glanced fearfully from face to face, understanding nothing.

'If that's where my friends are going, then yes,' he said. Before Maria had time to react, he said to her, 'You could come with me, both of you. Please?'

Delarua saw the moment when Maria's yearning towards her son met her antipathy against all psionically gifted societies. The opposing desires struggled briefly, then the antipathy won with a visible recoil. 'It's not a place for people like us,' she said stiffly.

Rafi's face fell.

Delarua felt a pang and knew it was partly guilt for raising the topic, standing aside and seeing what would result. She rushed to tell the rest of the story. 'Don't worry, Maria. He'll be travelling a lot in his job, and I'm sure we can expect to see him occasionally.'

'Of course,' Rafi agreed hastily, looking at her worriedly. *What travel in what job?* his eyes asked her frantically.

If you paid attention to things you would know, her exasperated expression replied. She had seen him sitting near the Patrona and the Dean for a short while during the morning session, which had led to her finding him minutes later in the corridor and taking him by the scruff of the neck, to the amusement and bemusement of various onlookers. She had been present for part of the earlier negotiations with Ntshune delegates, Punarthai academics and the pilots of Grand Bay. He had enough time to tell her about his training as a nexus and how that related to transits. For a young man with direct access to a lot of information, he was incredibly bad at connecting the pieces.

'*I'd* like to visit Ntshune,' Gracie said suddenly.

Rafi laughed, his face brightening with relief. 'You will, Gracie. Sooner than you realise. Soon everyone will be able to go anywhere they want to, faster than any Zhinuvian transport.'

'Don't get carried away,' Delarua muttered, but she could not help smiling.

CHAPTER FOURTEEN

'The modern ice age on Ntshune has been of such intensity and duration as to rival anything that the worlds of the civilised galaxy, crafted or bioformed, has seen. Ice covers the entirety of our planet's land mass. Even at the equator the ocean remains oozy with slush and crowded with icebergs. Nevertheless, Janojya, our capital city, stays warm and lively within the shelter of a massive biodome. We are located several metres under ice at the base of a tamed shield volcano. A steady outflow of water is heated by the city's excess energy and poured into the nearest sea where it keeps a channel ice-free for mindships and orbital shuttles to splashdown.

'This has been an era of change. Improvements in bioforming technology, emigration to Punartam, even the Great Galactic War – it all came from this ice age. The Ntshune know what it means for a civilisation to lose what we most take for granted: a stable and favourable planetary atmosphere.'

It was fine diplomatic language, but Rafi was only paying partial attention to their guide. He had arrived mere weeks earlier, the city was busy and there was a lot to see. Janojya boasted a more homogeneous population with the expected traits: curly hair, dark long-lashed eyes and average frames. There were no broad-boned Sadiri, and none of the long-limbed giants Punartam sometimes produced, although he did catch a glimpse of something that could have been a distant cousin of the ostrich-like creature he had seen once on his first day in the Metropolis and never again. He wondered if they were bioengineered, and if they were pets, companions or more.

The architecture was interesting, but logical considering the protection of the dome. Most buildings were U-shaped, cradling small gardens within their curves. There were no roofs, and walls and floors were often translucent and sometimes transparent. People moved like tiny shadow-puppets within their lit honeycombs, and each glowing cell added to the ambient brightness.

Ixiaral abruptly veered from the path, apologising hastily to their guide as she grabbed Rafi's arm. 'You must see this,' she said, almost childlike in her eagerness.

This was a huge grassy mount almost at the centre of the city's dome, whether natural or artificial, Rafi could not tell. It took time to ascend the steps cut spiral around its sides, but Rafi saw no other option and Ixiaral did not offer any. When they reached the top, she tumbled onto her back and raised an arm to point at the apex of the biodome.

'Do you see that? Where the ice is transparent?'

He lay down beside her and squinted along her pointing finger. The biodome surface was faintly purple and the ice showed mainly blue, but there was a faint pattern like water rings pushing out from the lightest patch of blue.

'That's the thinnest point of ice,' she said as proudly as if she had made it herself. 'It appeared twenty Standard years ago. The ice is melting.'

His gaze flashed from the pale blue window to her excited face. 'How many more years?'

'Less than five hundred. We could make it sooner, I suppose. Most biotechs don't like to tamper too much with crafted worlds. They'd rather experiment somewhere else, just in case.'

Rafi looked again at the translucent spot. Serendipity had said something about Ntshune positioning itself for a rise in galactic importance. Five hundred years sounded like a good stretch of time to plan and carry out a long-term domination so gentle and gradual that it would be nearly undetectable, and thus unstoppable. He could imagine the expansion and strengthening when Ntshune finally regained their land surface. And yet ... they were so quiet. Their way of living was unusually simple, with all major technology saved for the maintenance of the city and for research. Essential needs were taken care of, but there were no open expressions of personal luxury or extravagance.

He sat up and glanced down at the city. Their guide, temporarily abandoned at the foot of the mount, walked back and forth and looked up occasionally, but he was waiting, patiently and courteously, until they returned and needed his services once more, or until they gave him a proper farewell. He could have been an ordinary citizen whose most significant work was to flip the switches on the sewage treatment plant, or a retired scientist of great renown who felt like strolling through the city and decided to take along some newcomers as a gesture of kindness. It was difficult to tell. In some respects, the concept of hierarchy was so absent in the society that it was considered rude to introduce yourself with the accomplishments of your line and your name. In other ways, hierarchy was part of everything, unconscious and automatic. The social credit was there, but it was never discussed, like any gross but necessary function of human existence not to be mentioned in polite company. Rafi wondered if the Ntshune were secretly ashamed of not having yet achieved a fully egalitarian and currency-free civilisation.

Farther out, the view told more tales about the society. Buildings encircled gardens, but clusters of buildings were themselves encircled by parks, thin stretches of wilderness where the Ntshune fought to preserve the original flora of pre-ice days. Each cluster was a domain dedicated to a particular dynastic or industry, and sometimes both. Their own cluster, the new site for the survivors of Sadira's mindship fleet and Punartam's seized Academes, stood far from the centre, but still auspiciously placed as a matter of courtesy and an expression of hope for the success of the Transit Project.

Ixiaral shot up suddenly, her face serious. 'The Patrona needs us. Let's go.'

Rafi regarded her jealously. Punartam audioplugs were as useless here as Cygnian comms, but Ixiaral still had some kind of connection via the tracing on her skin. They hastened down the mount and took time to thank their guide and bid him farewell before rushing to the nearest canal transport. Janojya was compact enough to travel by foot, but going cluster to cluster was easiest via the waterways in the wilds.

The Patrona had chosen a huge workroom with clear walls and floor. It was too large to feel like a glass cage, but it did give most people a sense of vertigo, something Rafi suspected the Patrona secretly liked and used to her advantage. At the moment, she was sitting on the large, thick mat of the central dais, surrounded by hanging screens and a chatter of disembodied voices speaking schedules and logistics into the air. She looked far calmer than he would have expected.

'Rafi, Ixiaral, take a seat,' she said, waving at the floor.

He looked around, grabbed a large cushion and sat on a smaller dais in front of her. Ixiaral found a small mat and sat cross-legged beside her mentor and boss.

'I am completing the list of Punarthai for the Recorder of the Ntshune dynasties. Are you from Punartam, or are you from Cygnus Beta?'

Rafi could not hide his confusion. 'I am originally from Cygnus Beta, as you know, Esteemed Patrona.'

'Yes, Rafi, we do know, but you must choose a single place of origin while you are here,' Ixiaral explained.

Rafi sat and pondered. On Cygnus Beta he had the benefit of adult status, but on Punartam he had the benefit of not being on the government's wanted list. 'Punartam,' he said firmly. 'That makes sense. Ixiaral's still my nexus, isn't she?'

'Things are different here,' Ixiaral said. 'I no longer have my old networks, and I need to see where they will place me in the new structure.'

'In other words,' the Patrona said, 'Ixiaral's speciality is spotting opportunities to make money off the Game to fund our research, and that skill isn't needed now. The dynasty has work for her in another area, if she is prepared to take it up.'

Ixiaral tensed, as if bracing for either good news or bad. The Patrona simply smiled at her, a small but proud smile, and Ixiaral glowed, apparently understanding the unspoken message and finding it very much to her liking.

'But you, Rafi, have a skill that makes you a valuable part of the Transit Project research team,' the Patrona continued. 'It is to our credit to claim you as ours.'

'Claim me. Would that entail a kin contract?'

The Patrona looked a little amused and a little surprised. Ixiaral laughed and said, 'What do you know about kin contracts?'

'Not much,' Rafi admitted. 'I had some very basic guides and a not very helpful friend explain them to me, and I thought at first they were the same as marriages. But I've done more research since then and I realise they can be adoptions, or business partnerships, or diplomatic allegiance.'

The Patrona nodded cautiously. 'And to whom do you wish to be contracted?'

'Well, you, I suppose. Is that all right?'

Ixiaral cast down her eyes and folded her lips, whether in contemplation or suppressed laughter, he could not tell. The Patrona merely stared at him for a while before picking up a stylus and tapping something into a screen.

'Let us put you down as "under consideration for full kin contract to the Haneki dynasty, on limited kin contract for five years". You still have a lot to learn, Rafi. When you have learned it, you may begin the process of application to the Haneki dynasty.'

Of *course* I had to tease Rafi about his new status . . . after I stopped gaping and choking and flailing about in disbelief. I was relieved to discover that he now knew enough about kin contracts not to embarrass himself, but completely discombobulated when he told me he'd offered himself to be contracted to the Patrona. '*You?*' I said, then thrashed about on the floor of his studio in an extended seizure of near-death dramatics. He picked up a cushion and hit me a few times, but half-heartedly.

'For how long? Five minutes? For what purpose? To tidy her workroom?' I laughed loudly until he thumped me with more vigour.

I tried to get hold of myself. 'But seriously, Moo, the Hanekis are big on Punartam because they're big on Ntshune. Don't be the callow Terran homesteader about this. You've been useful to them in the past and if you can be useful to them now – well, good. Make sure it's all to your credit, but be sensible and don't over-reach yourself.'

He gave me a sceptical frown. 'You're one to talk. Why do they want you to go to Zhinu A?'

I smiled proudly. 'I, too, can be useful, my dear Moo. All my below-ground shadow-market shenanigans are bearing fruit with the Zhinuvians – who, by the way, are less keen about doing business in the shadow of cartel-occupied Academes. Some of my old colleagues have relocated to Zhinu A, and so our little galactic enterprise continues to expand.'

I saw he looked uninterested, so I made it clearer. 'Trade, Moo. There are always commercial aspects to transits, especially when speed matters far more than quantity. You might say my padr and his rivals pioneered what could become the standard for micro-merchandise logistics. The Patrona is going to negotiate some kind of agreement with the planetary authority while I and my colleagues will be allowed to feel out the microtech magnates.'

We did a little mutual congratulatory chest-slapping and arm-clasping: he patted my new partnership pin that symbolised my padr's faith in me, and I gripped the skin-filigree vambraces that were his accoutrements for his new status.

'You'll be back soon?' he asked abruptly.

He looked a little lost, and I recalled that we had been together on three planets for almost three Standard years. It *would* be strange to be going somewhere without him. 'I hope so,' I said slowly. 'It depends. I'll probably be travelling a lot. In and out and about.'

He nodded. I tried to cheer him up.

'Don't worry, Moo. I'll hand over to Serendipity. If she's not too busy with the mindships, I'm sure she'll keep an eye on you.'

He tried a half-smile. 'And vice versa.'

I said farewell soon after, leaving him to his quarters in the Transit Project domain. Although I saw him frequently as one or the other of us passed through Ntshune or Cygnus Beta, it would be several years before we were once more settled in the same place at the same time, years in which we would have plenty of opportunities to build up our accoutrements, our credit and our reputations.

Their first morning of real work was a preliminary briefing in the large central hall of the project's domain. The project coordinator, who was younger than Rafi had expected, was a Punarthai academic called Isahenalaatye. He looked at the mixed group of Wallrunners, coaches and nexuses representing various degrees of the telepathic, the empathic and the academic. He smiled at them all bravely and unfurled his map into the space above their heads. They gazed upwards in wonderment, watching the sparkle and spin of a new view of their corner of the galaxy.

'These are the old transit points. Some are known to be operational. Others may be a risk.'

Heads turned, stern stares regarded him.

'Not to worry,' he said cheerfully. 'We're going on established

288

runs first. Sadira. Ain. Zhinu A hasn't authorised the reopening of their surface transit just yet. In the meantime, we're working on creating new transits using one of their moons. That's a challenge. We've practised biodome set-up on Sadira, but that's easy because their transit's old and very stable. Setting up biodomes with a fresh new transit – that's a risk.'

'If I hear this word *risk* one more time,' Oestengeryok murmured to Rafi.

'He said Ain. Are we really going to Ain? Isn't Ain cut off?' Rafi whispered back, distracted from worry by excitement.

'Why does that holo look so strange,' Serendipity asked, tilting her head from side to side as she tried to assess the angles.

'It's a three-dimensional projection of a four-dimensional space,' Oesten said, also tilting his head. 'Pay no attention to the topography. The only thing that concerns us is the network of lines that connect transit to transit. And yes, Rafi, we can go to Ain. We're not approaching their orbit; we'll be arriving on the surface. The navigational issues won't affect us.'

'If I could have your full attention?' Isahenalaatye entreated. 'Continuing the established runs – Cygnus Beta, Terra, Punartam . . .'

Rafi leaned in to Oesten. 'Did he say Terra?' The quiet question was both drowned and echoed in a murmur that filled the room.

Someone near the back spoke up at last. 'Who authorised Terra?' she asked directly.

Isahena smiled a sunny little smile which deepened slightly at the corners with sarcasm. 'Everyone. Almost everyone. Zhinu A abstained.'

'But why? Why break the embargo now?'

Nervous laughter swept through the room, but Isahena's face sobered. 'The Terran embargo is a myth, I'm afraid. Research from the Punarthai Academes has been confirmed by our colleagues from Zhinu A. A group of minor Zhinuvian cartels have been operating on Terra for over two centuries.'

Dead silence. Everyone assumed Zhinuvian interference in Terran affairs; no one had guessed it was of such long duration. Isahena lowered his gaze slightly. 'In fact, to be truthful, none of us can claim to have been entirely innocent of breaking the embargo. However, it has become clear that these Zhinuvians have crossed the boundary and interfered to a degree that cannot be overlooked. We must have an open transit on Terra or consider it ceded to Zhinu.'

Rafi exchanged a significant look with Serendipity. If Ntshune did have a five-hundred-year plan for galactic dominance, it was perhaps two hundred years too late.

'Terra will be our last run. We have to consult with a group of specialists. Sadira will be our first; that's the best-known location. Whenever possible, a mindship crew will travel ahead before each transit and remain until the transit is successfully completed, both arrival and departure. No one will be stranded.'

Teruyai stood up. 'I would like to go with the team that's transiting to Sadira.'

Isahena paused before answering. 'We will not be able to have a mindship backup contingent for that run. The oceans are not yet able to support life.'

'I'm a pilot – don't you think I know that? I want to walk on my planet's surface again, just for a while.'

Isahena lowered his eyes pensively while the room erupted with sound and motion as other pilots jumped to their feet and shouted their demands. Finally he raised his head and looked soberly at Teruyai. 'I will allow it,' he said loudly, beating down the other voices. 'I will allow it, but only one or two additions to the selected team, and only those pilots who have practised with Wallrunners.'

'Did you want to go?' Rafi asked Serendipity when the briefing ended and they slowly made their way out of the room.

She shook her head. 'Sadira may be where my ancestors came from but it's not that special to me. Besides, I won't be travelling much. I'm assigned to the land crews at the port.'

'You're not staying in the city?' he asked in dismay.

'It's only for work, Rafi. I'll be here otherwise.'

'Oh, good.'

She regarded him with a touch of ruefulness, and it felt like when Ntenman told him he was going – the bitter-sweet knowledge that he was loved, he had friends, and yet they were not dependent on him. They were moving on with their lives and leaving him behind.

'Do you want to get something to eat and go over some project information?' she suggested, sounding sincere and not at all as if she was offering a consolation prize.

'I would, but I have to go to a ceremony for Ixiaralhaneki, my former boss. The dynasties are elevating her to an important post in their hierarchy as a reward for doing well during her time on Punartam. She's going to help rule the Haneki domain. I really owe it to her to turn up.'

She nodded understandingly. 'Another time, then. Goodbye, Rafi.'

He stood still in the corridor and watched for a moment as she walked away. Then he turned and went about his own business.

Watching the Patrona negotiate was an education.

I could have left the rest of the delegation and gone straight to my own work. Part of me had wished that by some stroke of luck I would find Damal on Zhinu A, but no, he was still butting about on Punartam enjoying the risk and annoying the cartels. Nevertheless, he had some fairly solid connections and the token of his endorsement was already paying off in prospective introductions and expressions of interest. And yet, I wanted to be careful. I understood that there was more to this game than making money, and I needed to see what tone the Patrona was going to set and adjust my actions accordingly.

And, like I said, it was an education.

They didn't hold back. They gave our delegation full honour with the best of comforts and a full roster of meetings with the most influential magnates on the planet. But the best, the most interesting meeting was that between the Patrona and the Chief Archivist. Don't ask me what exactly his title meant. The Patrona had already had a short, respectful and meaningless chat with the Head of the Planetary Authority. I was getting the impression that whatever titles and appearances might be, the Chief Archivist was the person who actually ran the place.

The Patrona knew it immediately. She looked around his workplace, appraised his appearance, assessed his minions and took a completely different tone.

'Let me speak frankly. I am less concerned about what Zhinu A might gain from this agreement and more interested in what it can bring.'

He learned forward with a smile. 'Well, if you're bargaining—'

The Patrona held up a hand in a request for silence. 'Don't misunderstand. I am talking about stakes. If you have no investment in this, if you pretend or even intend to cooperate out of goodwill, you shall lose interest as soon as a better deal comes along. I want to know what you are risking to become part of this project.'

He spread his hands in a gesture that looked as if he was trying to convince himself. 'The cartels are not pleased with our actions . . .'

She merely shook her head at him.

'We have heavy trade losses. Every commercial run our ships skip because they will be helping you—'

She cut him off. 'Even now we make minimal use of your ships and the majority of the Sadiri pilots are already with us,' she replied, her expression becoming distant.

He recognised that she was about to dismiss him and launched into his best entreaty. 'Respected and highly esteemed Patrona, be fair! Even neutrality is a choice in this situation, and we are giving you much more than neutrality. Can you blame us for wanting to see how this venture pays before we sink resources into it? We will not obstruct, we *will* assist, and we do so knowing that we run counter to the cartels. As an additional gesture of goodwill, we will open to you the transit on the surface of Zhinu A. Surely this is sufficient for now.'

'For now,' she said, backing down for the moment. 'But should you decide you want to become a full partner in this venture, you know how to reach us.'

And that was that. When I went to my own meetings, I made sure to keep things as light and introductory as I could, promising nothing and simply making conversation. However, I did enjoy occasionally dropping one broad hint, that I was anticipating a 'deeper cooperation between Ntshune and Zhinu A which would bring benefit to all concerned'. I varied the phrasing each time and noted with great interest the few split-second reactions that slipped out: startled, pensive, calculating. The Patrona went back to Ntshune and I went back to Cygnus Beta to report to my father, and it was months before those conversations bore fruit in a highly unexpected way.

One advantage, if it could be called that, of the decimation of the mindship fleet was that the smaller ships which would have once been unsuitable for passenger travel were now the popular choice to carry tiny passenger modules that could withstand the rigours of splashdown. Serendipity had travelled both by naked mindship and by small-scale module, and she had helped those who travelled. Disorientation was usually the greatest danger, as both methods relied on the use of the mindship's own toxins to alter the consciousness of both pilot and passengers. Pilots shook off the effects almost instantly. Some passengers needed more time. In those cases it was best to detach the passenger module, crack it open to the atmosphere and allow the occupants a half-hour or so to recline and return to full awareness. If they remained groggy after that, they were usually taken to another area for monitoring.

Even without the flight schedules and information, she was able to recognise the mindship that dived through the entrance and settled into one of the port's several berths. Most of the berths were claimed by ships from Punartam and Grand Bay, and they tended to pick a favourite and return to it. The other side of the port, where amphibious Zhinuvian shuttles parked for unloading and maintenance, looked deserted in comparison.

Serendipity walked along the pier with the disembarkation crew, all five of them dressed warmly in hoods, gloves and boots. She stood aside as they opened the module's large side hatch. She came forward and connected her handheld to the module's systems to view the passengers' vital signs. To her surprise, one of them was already on the verge of awakening. She quickly reached in and detached the upper casing from their pod. The face that greeted her was very striking even as it reacted in shock to the sudden influx of cold air with wide eyes, gasping and coughing.

'I'm sorry, I'm sorry.' Serendipity pulled down her hood. 'I'm Serendipity. Welcome to Ntshune. Just lie still for a little while. You're the first to wake up.'

The reply emerged hoarsely from a dry, chilled throat. 'Familiar accent . . . hmm . . . you're Cygnian. I'm Second Lieutenant Lian. I'm one of the Terra specialists you requested.'

'Glad you could join us, Lieutenant,' Serendipity said. 'I was sure you would be staying on Cygnus Beta after the Academes fell. But where is Doctor Daniyel? I thought she was the leader of your research team?'

Lian's brave attempt at a smile looked more like a grimace. 'That's partly why I'm here. When the cartels attacked . . .' After a pause and a sigh, Lian got straight to the point. 'We were unable to extract Doctor Daniyel from the field. She is still on Terra, and we hope you can help us to get her back.'

CHAPTER FIFTEEN

The transit was housed in its own small dome close to Janojya. If anything exploded, if any unwanted thing as small as a pathogen or as large as an army came through the transit, it could be contained. The Wall for transit was nothing like Serendipity expected. 'It looks like a vertical garden crashed into a Zhinuvian space raft,' she said sceptically as she craned her neck up to scan it from floor to top. The strange construction hung between two sets of scaffolding like the façade of a green building, and members of the ground crew moved up and down the scaffolding and around the floor, carefully making their last adjustments and carrying out final tests.

Rafi tried to explain. 'Think of it as a kind of organic passenger module. A single nexus can take a few people through a transit, but for a larger group we need to have a kind of ecosphere. You should know – it's like the mindships. We're creating a collective consciousness, a temporary colony organism. That makes it easier to hold everything together when travelling.'

'I understand the concept,' she said truthfully. She had been about to ask how plants could be sentient, but then she remembered the unusual additions that appeared to be of Zhinuvian manufacture and said nothing more.

Rafi grinned. 'Anyone who allows themselves to be stung and swallowed by a two-thousand-tonne beast is in no position to judge. The point is, it works.'

She pointed up and waved a finger around uncertainly. 'Which bit is the actual transit?'

'It's underneath.' Rafi said.

Serendipity took a step back and stared at the ground beside the Wall. The bottom of the Wall appeared to be suspended about ten centimetres from the floor. 'I can't see anything.'

'It's mostly power inputs. There's a slight shimmer, nothing more.' He gently touched her arm and directed her to another part of the dome to point out the Wall from the other side. From this angle, the passenger aspect of the Wall was clearly visible. Half-sunken cocoons, slightly reminiscent of the pods in a mindship module, were arranged in a neat central grid. Surrounding the grid was a series of what looked like steps or ledges.

'Do you run on this Wall? Is that what the ledges are for?' she asked.

'No!' Rafi laughed at the picture. 'We stand. The game Wall is stationary and we move, but the transit Wall moves and we are stationary.'

She walked another slow half-circle around the back of the Wall. 'What does it feel like?'

He tilted his head and smiled at her. 'What does travelling with a mindship feel like? I'm usually unconscious for that.'

She tried to find words. 'Transcendent,' she whispered. 'It's a powerful experience, but they're in complete control. You feel what they're feeling and sense what they sense. You dissolve and become a part of them, but you feel more like yourself than when you're alone. They're beautiful.'

He smiled with more politeness than understanding. 'That sounds very calm. Transits with one or two people are hard. You feel like you're being dragged back when you just want to dive in and get where you're going. But a Wall transit . . . it's dynamic. There's vertigo and you feel like you're falling and rising and your adrenalin— it's a rush! You forget yourself, you don't think, you become pure motion. And everything's balanced with a Wall, so you don't feel like you're being pulled in all the wrong directions. We don't have to pilot anything – it's a straight road – but we have to stay on that road. I've only been on a few practice runs to nowhere and back, but . . . that's what it feels like.'

'Sadira will be your first major run,' she said, looking at him proudly.

He glowed with happiness. 'Yes. It's frightening, and we all know the risk, but I can't wait.'

She laughed with him and hugged him, stroking the textured material of his pilot-like transit suit as she stepped away. 'Be careful, Rafi. Always come back.'

Later that night, Rafi tried not to shiver as the ground crew secured him to his assigned position on the Wall. The full Vanguard suit was in many ways like a more flexible version of a single passenger pod, but without a doubt it was less heavily protected and less secure as they had to sacrifice safety to mobility. For a moment he envied those in the pods, but when he glanced around and saw them in their half-open capsules, they looked uncomfortable and slightly claustrophobic, not to mention tense with anticipation of the moment when the crew would close the top half of the pod and leave them in relative isolation. Rafi's excitement completely dampened when he saw Teruyai's face – bleak, cold, resolute. He took a moment to call to her.

'Teruyai!'

She blinked, mildly startled.

'Stay with us,' he mouthed.

She stared at him, but the words gradually sank in until her expression softened and she gave him a half-nod of understanding as they closed down her pod.

The crew vacated the area. Rafi breathed deeply, trying to slow the thundering pace of his heart. It began as a single vibration, purely physical, in his bones. The Wall was pulsing as the power increased. Then a familiar tingle washed over him, building to a buzz that galvanised his blood and brain. He closed his eyes, already starting to feel the doubling, tripling sensation of other minds and other bodies fretting, fidgeting, all caught in the buzzing net like insects secured to a single web. Both vibrations grew to the point of irritation . . .

. . . and suddenly vanished.

This was a real transit. The vertigo was intense, like the difference between looking over a two-storey balcony and staring up (or down) an orbital spire. Rafi reached towards the centre and anchor of the Wall and kept his focus there as the frequency soared into higher chimes and cooler hues, rising and falling in volume and brightness as the Wall tumbled (or was it the universe that spun?) endlessly down and then, with a tug, flew effortlessly up until the colours grew warmer, the sounds hummed lower and once more everything returned to a gentle buzz.

Days later, meditating on the experience, Rafi would wonder what that lowest point signified. He wondered what they would see if they stopped the Wall there, and if indeed either stopping or seeing was possible in that place.

He shook his head and started to unfasten himself from the Wall. Unlike mindship travel, the transits energised him. He wanted to leap past all the ledges and jump down to the surface of this new place he had never seen, but he made himself move soberly and show respect for Sadira, the largest graveyard of humanity the galaxy had ever known. He also remembered to unlatch the pods nearest to him before he finally touched ground – and immediately stumbled over his own feet, tricked by slight increase in gravity.

Teruyai jumped down beside him, staring around her. 'Look at this,' she said. 'Look.'

The new biodome on Sadira was small and rudimentary but strong, set to the maximum possible specifications for hostile atmosphere and temperatures beyond the border, and showing a slight shimmer at its apex. Most of its floor was shielded from ground contamination, which meant that the edge of the dome rode high on its own artificial plateau. The centre was a hollow with bare ground visible, and it was there that showed signs of life and work: a few low shelters scattered around the transit platform and several installations that resembled greenhouses, one of which appeared to burrow into the ground like a huge glass well.

What could be seen of the land past the boundary looked burned and naked of debris.

A small ground crew approached them, most of them familiar faces from Punartam. Rafi noted with interest that the majority were Ainya academics and technicians. They did a quick medical assessment of the Vanguard runners and passengers, then allowed them to roam the area while the engineers performed checks of the Wall and the transit. Rafi walked along the circumference, looking at the scorched landscape, his emotions swinging from exhilaration to terror as he thought of how far they had come, the thin protection of the biodome and the emptiness of the world beyond.

'If I could, I would make every person who had any kind of desire to serve or rule the galaxy come to this point to stand here and look.'

The bitterness in Teruyai's voice pulled Rafi's attention back to her. She, too, had been roaming the circumference of the dome and looking out restlessly as if hoping to see something, anything that appeared remotely recognisable.

He looked at her anxiously. 'Let's go back,' he said.

'No, wait. There's something I want to do.'

She went to the centre of the dome, avoiding the path to the grounded transit, and knelt to touch the small area of safe, treated ground. It was unevenly graded, gravel and small rocks and stone dust all mixed together. She surreptitiously picked up three small stones, closed her fist around them and sighed. Then she stepped close to Rafi, took one and gave it to him.

'There,' she said. 'It's precious. Don't tell or—' She stopped to laugh weakly. 'Or everyone will want one.'

Rafi touched her hand gently. 'Don't worry, Teruyai. When we come back, there'll be more.'

She put an arm about his waist and they walked back to the transit platform, leaning against each other for comfort.

The port was sited several kilometres away from Janojya, beside the channel that carried the city's warm current of treated waste water. The building was ancient, relying on old, common forms of insulation and protection rather than a full biodome, but the temperatures at the coast were sufficiently mild and stable that no more was required. A reinforced, insulated, transparent wall shielded the observation deck from the outside air and offered a clear view of the gently surging water in the protected bay. Swirls of colour heightened the wave patterns where warm water met cold and traces of algae bloomed.

Second Lieutenant Lian stood and watched the water, waiting.

After a while, Serendipity got up from her seat and joined Lian. 'There's still a little time before the scouting mission returns from Terra,' she noted timidly.

'I know,' said Lian, not at all rudely, and yet without invitation for further conversation.

Serendipity stayed for a while, shifting her feet awkwardly, then turned to go back to her seat.

'I notice that all the test runs are being coordinated from here, and I've also heard that the transit from Punartam to Cygnus Beta no longer works. Does this mean that Ntshune will be the hub for all galactic transits?' Lian enquired.

'Well, yes, but only initially, while we're still doing test runs and other experiments. We don't want to lose anyone by rushing things, and it's very important that we develop the necessary training for the transit operators. I don't know why that transit doesn't work any more. Perhaps they shut it down so the cartels couldn't use it?'

'Perhaps,' Lian admitted.

That was almost friendly, and certainly less preoccupied. Serendipity felt a little bolder. 'Was that why you came here by mind-ship instead of transit?' she asked. 'Were you afraid it might malfunction?'

'Honestly, a little,' said Lian, still gazing out at the mesmeris-ing, iridescent ripple of the current. 'But I don't adapt well to galactic travel at the best of times. They tried to take me through the transits but I had some issues.'

Curiosity won over politeness. 'Issues?' Serendipity asked timidly.

'Hallucinations, or perhaps they were nightmares. Maybe I can't handle the level of consciousness needed for a transit. I appreciate that the advantage of a well-done transit is being able to walk around seconds after arriving, but I don't mind being knocked out. I don't want to know I'm travelling— What—? What *is* that? By the Destroyer, do you see that?'

Serendipity looked away from Lian's suddenly panicked face. The current, which should have been gentled with the weight of slush and the snarl of algae, had become a surge. They both stum-bled back, uselessly slow and with no higher floor to escape to, as the water rushed up and hit the lower half-metre of the massive viewport window with a booming slap. Mercifully, whatever glass, gem or metal had gone into the making of the walls and windows, they did not crack or shatter. The water receded just as quickly, but now there was something more than algae-pink ice and slush to be seen, something which made Serendipity's heart race. Two mindships thrashed dangerously close to the port build-ing, struggling to free themselves from each other. Serendipity saw the problem: the passenger module of one ship was snagged in a shredded and thoroughly tangled mesh that half-covered the other ship.

Port crews were already running to their hovercrafts. Seren-dipity shouted at them to stop, but only a few figures turned and glanced at her before hastening on. In that moment, out of instinct and terror, she did something she had never done before.

'*Stop!*' she cried, putting the full force of her mind behind the command.

Everyone faltered or staggered. She had their attention.

'You can't go out there. There's nothing we can do. Wait. The rest are coming.'

The crew leader began to walk towards her. 'How can you—?'

There was a loud crack. The module had shattered, releasing its pods into the icy water and scoring the mindships so deeply that the slush and water turned a deeper hue than the tint of algae. Serendipity almost wept, feeling the anguish and pain from the two ships. High waves surged out from the writhing ships again, making the crew leader pause and reassess.

'Get the pods if you can,' she said. 'But leave the mindships alone! They're too massive for us to handle.'

She turned to say something to Lian and was stunned to see the second lieutenant sitting on the floor, dazed, head in hands.

'I'm sorry,' she said, dropping to her knees and putting a hand cautiously on Lian's shoulder. 'I had to be loud. They weren't listening.'

'Uh.' Lian's head slowly came up. Serendipity placed a gentle, supporting hand under Lian's ear, trying to ease some of the concussion.

While Serendipity was focused on Lian, Lian's eyes drifted to the outside view again. 'Here they are. How did you know?'

Serendipity glanced up and saw several mindships skilfully and carefully breaching the water's surface. They barely paused. They immediately furled themselves around the bleeding mass of the broken ships, forming a restraining, healing embrace.

'That's what they do,' she said. 'They know how to take care of each other.'

Lian slowly got up with Serendipity's help. They went to the ground floor and waited at the berths with the medical crews. When the hovercrafts returned, five pods were offloaded and laid out carefully on the dock. One of them, broken and oozing far too much red matter, was respectfully hidden beneath a dark cover. A medic came and looked under the fabric, but lowered it again within seconds.

Technicians and medics carefully opened the other four. Serendipity felt Lian tense, as if bracing for the worst. They came closer, close enough to see the faces without obstructing the medics. As they walked beside the pods, Lian exhaled a slow breath, relaxing more and more with each face recognised.

'Revered Waneshianeso, field specialist of Academe Bhumni-astraya. Mission Captain Dan Fergus o-Muir i-Tlaxce, survivalist and security expert. Doctor Daniyel . . .' Lian lost almost all breath with relief. 'Good, good, excellent. And Mission Corporal Zariah Fa o-Vayanir i-Tlaxce, administrator and technologist.' Lian's head bowed briefly. 'I should see who is in the broken pod. It is probably Asirianeso, assistant to Revered Waneshianeso.'

'Take your time,' Serendipity said faintly. 'Let us step back and give the medics a chance to do their work.'

The glass cells of the medical centre were programmed to adjust to the patient's comfort. Dr Daniyel had chosen a muted, warm illumination like shaded sunlight and kept one of the cells transparent to the view of the park outside. She was more than alive; she was alert, grieving, determined. The crash had caused internal injuries which would take time to heal, but she insisted on a debriefing for the Terra transit.

A small group clustered around her reclining bed: Lian,

standing attentively nearby, watching her for signs of pain or weakness; Fergus, brooding and uncomfortable on a motorised chair with his leg encased in a support that braced the bones and fed nutrients and painkillers to his blood supply; Isahenalaatye, subdued and clearly in the grip of that high-level, eerily calm panic which can result when unusual crises push a man far, far beyond his job description; and Serendipity, wide-eyed and worried, still traumatised by the incident at the port.

'I was told,' Dr Daniyel said, speaking slowly and softly, 'that there were two or more transit sites on Terra. Is that correct?'

Isahena cleared his throat and answered. 'The practice was for every planet to have at least two transits to allow for maintenance or accidents, but there could be more depending on available locations and population density.'

'We went through one, from Punartam. The cartels seized that one from us at the same time as they attacked the Academes. We were guarding the Punartam side, of course, and we did not expect an ambush from the Terra side.'

'So that is what happened?' Isahena asked, resigned. 'The cartels are that well entrenched on Terra?'

Dr Daniyel nodded slowly. Lian instinctively offered her water from a bottle at her bedside. She accepted it with a smile and took a few cautious sips before handing it back.

'We went to find the second transit. We had visited it before but it was not functioning, so we left it alone for the time being. We went carefully, expecting it to be guarded by Zhinuvians.'

'It was guarded by Sadiri,' Fergus said grimly.

'And we thought, "Hooray, we're saved!".' Dr Daniyel's mocking tone ended in an unhappy chuckle.

'First they questioned us about breaking embargo. We could

have asked them the same thing, but we only pleaded extenuating circumstances and asked to send a message to Punartam or even Ntshune, as it was closer. That was how we managed to contact you at first.'

'That message was very carefully phrased,' Lian commented.

'It had to be. Then we heard nothing.'

Lian scoffed. 'We replied. We sent the proofs about what happened with the Academes, the nature of your research, the permissions you had been given. Then *we* heard nothing. That's why we sent the scouting mission.'

'And one of them found us and got us out of there, but after that I don't know what happened.'

Serendipity spoke up. 'They sent another mindship to stop you. We questioned the pilot, and his ship is recovering.'

'But why did it attack us? I never thought they would attack each other.'

Serendipity tried to explain. 'It was a collision, not an attack. The mindship was covered in some kind of interference mesh. I suppose it works against Terran sonar. The mindships were too close as they were coming in and they got tangled.'

Dr Daniyel nodded. 'That's a small relief. I couldn't bear to think of mindships fighting. Bad enough that New Sadira is on Terra.'

'We're the ones late to the game,' Isahena said ruefully. 'New Sadira is closest to Terra, and they could argue that they know about the Zhinuvians and are trying to enforce the embargo with limited resources. I don't know any more. All I know is that New Sadira is not communicating or cooperating with us, and we still don't have a working transit on Terra. We'll have to work with the Zhinu A specialists to make a new one.'

'We must go back to Terra.' Dr Daniyel sounded weaker and Lian looked at her with concern. 'I was tasked to design an encounter programme to end the embargo gradually, without disruption and exploitation. It's all useless now. There's been too much interference. I don't know how we're going to salvage this.'

A quiet voice interjected, 'We will manage things from here, Doctor Daniyel. Rest, recover and do not lose hope. We have resources and allies. We will find a way.'

Heads turned. The Patrona was standing in the doorway. 'Isahenalaatye, Serendipity, come with me. I have a meeting to attend, and I will need you both to be present.'

The Patrona's workroom glowed almost blue, filled with several holos in rich, deep-space indigo studded with brightly coloured points that represented orbital stations, satellites, moons, planets and stars in various degrees of scale and angles of perspective. They hung low, suspended from the ceiling, but bounced up or glided aside obligingly to accommodate passing heads and shoulders. The Patrona spun one with her finger as she walked past it on her way to the room's central dais. Trailing behind her were Isahenalaatye, Serendipity and two of the top-ranking Zhinuvians on Ntshune: Raizven, one of the senior engineers on the Transit Project and leader of the team tasked to create new transits; and Hydlor, coordinator of the trade and communications rosters, who balanced urgency, importance and availability of credit, and assigned each cargo and message its appropriate place in the schedule.

Settling herself on the dais, the Patrona banished all but two of the holos with one hand and motioned with the other to her guests, inviting them to make themselves comfortable. As they did so, she activated floor-screens in a semicircle around her and beckoned the holos closer.

'Two of you do not know why you are here,' she stated. 'Isahena-laatye and Serendipity, could you please brief our Zhinuvian colleagues on the port incident and what it means for our plans for Terra?'

Serendipity told them what she had witnessed and Isahena added Dr Daniyel's account concerning the Sadiri on Terra. The Zhinuvians looked at each other, nonplussed, and leaned closer to take in every word. The Patrona watched them intently until Isahena and Serendipity completed their report.

'You did not know that New Sadira were operating in Terran oceans?' she asked.

Serendipity felt a shiver in the atmosphere. The meeting had gone beyond mere courtesy. The Patrona was actively assessing their emotions and compelling truth, demonstrating not only her innate abilities as an Ntshune but also her powers as nexus.

The Zhinuvians reacted to the strong-arm tactic with fear. 'We did not!' Hydlor insisted. 'There has been no information on that, not a rumour, not a hint. This is as much of a shock to us as it is to you.'

Raizven agreed fervently. 'Remember, we were the ones who told you that the cartels have been infiltrating Terra for decades. Why would we undercut our own people and give the Sadiri a free run?'

The Patrona glanced down at one of the floor-screens. The shift of her attention was like a sudden easing of pressure. 'Why indeed? I can think of a few reasons why, including the possibility that you are trying to stay friends with every potential player in the game, but that is something you might not know. My next question is this: how will you help us in this new situation? Your technical assistance, even your non-interference in Cygnian and Ntshune trade, have been a boon, but I must reiterate what I said before to your superiors on Zhinu A. The stakes are not high enough for you. I do not sense that you are fully committed to this project. How can you reassure me?'

Raizven looked quickly at Hydlor and raised his hands helplessly. 'We could work on creating a new transit for Ntshune to Terra.'

'Is that what you are offering?' the Patrona said sharply, her eyes on them once more while her fingers remained poised on the screen by her right knee. 'Is that the best, the most effective course of action?'

The two Zhinuvians only stared back in terror, frozen like insects caught in amber. She gentled her voice a little. 'We do not have much time. If there is a decision to be made, you must make it quickly.'

Hydlor got to his feet hastily. 'Five days, Esteemed Patrona. You will have your answer in five days, I promise.'

Dissatisfied, but resigned, she nodded. 'Five days or earlier, Hydlor. There is too much happening and we are falling farther and farther behind.'

She dismissed them both and looked tiredly towards Isahena and Serendipity. 'Did I do too much?'

Isahenalaatye swallowed, unsure how to take this invitation to criticise. 'That depends on the results, Esteemed Patrona.'

She smiled. 'Well put, Isahena. That is true; it does indeed.'

CHAPTER SIXTEEN

It was a pleasure to sit on Rafi's head to wake him up, just like the old days back at the Lyceum. He thrashed and kicked and threw me off, no longer the short and scrawny boy I could subdue in minutes. I landed on my backside on the floor, cursed him and laughed. I'd missed him.

'Why are you waking me up in the middle of the night?' he grumbled.

'We're going on an adventure, Moo! Your lovely Patrona sent me to collect you. Serendipity is already up. It's the three of us once more! Will you please get up and cover your body with some garments appropriate to this quest? Or, to put it more directly, where is your flight suit and can you be wearing it within one minute?'

Rafi moaned and complained, but he gradually attained a vertical position, slowly went from slack-faced somnolence to a determined expression and muttered, 'Yes, yes,' nodding to himself. I thought he was a little unhinged until I noticed the new spidery tracing behind his ear, blue-black on dark-amber, still small and reasonably discreet.

He got dressed. 'I assume you have been briefed?' he said to me.

Pompous *moujin*. I answered in kind. 'I have my itinerary and task list. It may not be the same as yours.'

'Then let's compare. We're off to Zhinu A first, correct?'

'Yes,' I confirmed, pushing him through the door with my palm flat between his shoulder blades. 'And that will be my first and last stop for a while. Given recent events, I plan to have some follow-up discussions with various magnates.'

'Ah, well, it's good to see you, however briefly. Because, if I understand correctly, I'm then off to Terra?'

'You most certainly are!'

'Zhinu A has a Terran transit?'

'Kept secret for millennia! They *are* impressive, aren't they!'

He shook his head, not in disagreement but as if he was trying to get too many facts to settle in his skull. 'And I will meet Serendipity there. She is travelling with a backup mindship crew.'

'Correct. Now hurry and let's get to the transit dome.'

I love it when a judicious bluff pays off. Zhinu A was going all in, gifting their transit and base on Terra to the Transit Project to use as they saw fit to the benefit of the entire galaxy. Not for free, however, and I could not blame them. I was there to help start trade negotiations and talk them down from a giddy high of a sudden influx credit, but I could be realistic about it. They wanted concessions, they deserved concessions. The transit was fast, but we still needed Zhinuvian transport for larger cargo and passenger movement. None of us was saying it yet, but now we had better control over transport and communications, I was sure that the near-moribund Galactic Patrol would be next up for reorganisation and revival. I heard about what's been happening on Terra, and we're going to need some form of military reinforcement.

That's someone else's job, though. I'm happily occupied where I am.

The transit to Zhinu A had barely enough personnel for a Wall to be needed. Rafi and Oestengeryok were the only Vanguard runners. The remainder were their passengers – the Patrona, Raizven, Ntenman, Lian, Waneshianeso and Zariah Fa, the latter two now fully recovered from the mindship accident. On arrival, Ntenman promptly disappeared to 'get a start on his task list'. The Patrona surprised Rafi when she said that she would be staying on as witness and facilitator to what Raizven was about to do, which was to allow them to go through the transit to Terra and then close it.

'This transit on Zhinu A will now be linked permanently to Ntshune, and that is how I shall return,' she said. 'You will return to Ntshune via the Terra transit. If there are any difficulties, any at all, use the mindship backup.'

Oesten also remained with the Patrona, leaving Rafi the sole runner to transport Lian, Waneshianeso and Zariah Fa to Terra. 'Easy run,' he reassured Rafi. 'The Wall keeps everything stable, so stay focused and you'll be fine.'

Rafi nodded, trying to look unworried, especially in front of his passengers. 'Of course, Oesten. Safe run to you.'

After the buzz faded, Rafi's first impression was of dimly lit fog. The atmosphere was thick with mist and pools of water collected in every dip and crevice in the stone floor. He inhaled and coughed. There was enough oxygen, but there was something not quite right about the air. He detached himself, swung around to unlatch the passenger pods, then carefully made his way down the steps, which were already damp with condensation. The gravity felt weaker than on Cygnus Beta or Ntshune but stronger than Punartam. He did not try to test it with any bouncing.

Waneshianeso and Zariah Fa immediately put the geosensors on their wrists to work. 'High levels of carbon dioxide,' Zariah said. 'Put your breathers on.'

Rafi obeyed immediately. He looked up and saw only more rock, uneven and stained in the dim light. He began to search for the source of the light.

'This isn't very exciting,' Lian muttered. 'Where are we?'

'Give us a minute,' Waneshi said, a slight edge to her tone. She went over to Zariah and they began to talk in hushed tones.

'There you are! I thought I heard something.' The familiar voice bounced happily off the rock, an incongruous intrusion into their moment of anxiety.

'Naraldi!' Rafi shouted, and added cheekily, 'I thought you were keeping to the sidelines?'

'I am not yet so jaded that I cannot appreciate a historic moment,' Naraldi replied, walking with slow caution along a downward-sloping path. 'Why are you lurking in the basement? Come up! It's much better on the upper levels.'

Rafi smiled fondly to himself as they followed Naraldi up the path, understanding at last that this was the Patrona's gift to him: his name on the records as the runner for the first modern transit between Terra and Ntshune. The light grew brighter and brighter until they came up into a vast empty space of cooler, drier air and pale blue light.

Naraldi stopped and looked around with great satisfaction. 'This must be where the Ntshune perfected their ice-construction techniques. Very impressive.'

Rafi looked up at the ceiling of blue ice, slightly blurred by the familiar haze of a biodome's boundary. He grinned. 'It's like Janojya!'

Zariah did not look any happier than before. 'I appreciate their dedication to maintaining the transit and the dome but we're near the South Pole. How much can we do from here? This is the harshest climate on Terra.'

Waneshi interrupted. 'You're bringing a Cygnian mentality to the problem. Remember Ntshune? Centuries of survival in an ice age? I don't think they will see this place the same way you do.'

'And this could be an advantage in terms of security,' Lian pointed out. 'We don't have to worry about anyone stumbling over us accidentally.'

'Where's Serendipity?' Rafi asked suddenly.

'She's waiting with my ship at the reservoirs,' Naraldi said. 'Speaking of which, do you have space to take her back with you? Since I'm here, I thought I might look around a little.'

'Spy, you mean,' said Rafi. 'Do you really think that's wise?'

'Please, no more clashes with New Sadira,' Waneshi added.

'Can we go back now?' Serendipity's voice called out.

They looked around, baffled, until they saw her head ascending from another path leading to the lower levels. She looked reasonably alert, but tired and a little stressed.

Rafi smiled as she approached and took the opportunity to savour the moment. He was standing on the Earth of his ancestors, he had now seen five planets including all four of the crafted worlds, his childhood crush was about to join him in a transcendent experience which he would control using the talent he had once feared and hated ... and it was simply part of a day's work. It was thrilling that his dreams come true could be made so mundane, so beautifully ordinary, so ridiculously normal.

Quietly laughing at the cosmic joke, he looked at Serendipity and said, 'Let's go.'

A new hall had been constructed in a patch of wilds between the Haneki domain and the Transit Project domain. It was a veritable glass palace with trees, shrubs and creeping plants pressing greenly against the walls as if peering in at the spectacle. Globes of sun-like light floated high above the room, roofless as was the custom, and it felt open and airy in spite of the number of delegates, observers, recorders and spectators crammed into the space.

The Galactic Consortium Meeting was in session, the second extraordinary meeting of the post-Galactic War era.

Serendipity marvelled at the ability of the Ntshune recorders to transcribe overlapping voices with ease. She was trying to learn to listen but she knew she was cheating, using light touches of telepathy when her ears became overwhelmed. She was keeping records for the Union of Pilots, which had recognised her commitment to the mindships and accepted her as an auxiliary member. There was so much of importance to report.

Given the advances in the new transit system, Ntshune was the natural choice for the Meeting. The results were mixed. Cygnus Beta, Ntshune, Sadira-on-Cygnus with the Union of Pilots and Zhinu A formed a comfortable bloc of shared interests and approaches. Punartam was trying to re-enter the game as a newly formed Zhinuvian–Punarthai alliance, an entity which most delegates did not take very seriously. The cartels, thwarted by the closure of the only known working transit and stymied by local sabotage in their efforts to reopen it, were scrabbling to legitimise themselves in some other way. Regardless, Punartam was experiencing a steady haemorrhage of academics and personnel by means unknown (or at least unreported), to the enrichment of research centres on Ntshune and Cygnus Beta. To add insult to injury, Ntshune had opened another transit well beyond the reach and influence of the Metropolis in the small city of Saro, now listed as the fastest growing urban development in the galaxy.

The delegation from Zhinu A, which consisted of both governmental and commercial representatives, was known to be holding private negotiations with observers from other Zhinuvian planets and colonies. The Patrona predicted that within the year, the galaxy would see either a new Zhinuvian conglomerate to rival the cartels, or a multi-planetary authority with Zhinu A at the head, or both.

The Union of Pilots did not have much to say, preferring to rely on Dllenahkh and Lanuri for representation. However, the invitation to the pilots of New Sadira to join the Union raised some eyebrows – and some hackles. Primed by the sting of the perceived insult, the accredited delegate for New Sadira spoke heatedly about 'the incident on Terra', demanding explanations for the Union pilots' failure to honour the embargo. The documentation permitting Dr Daniyel and her colleagues to travel to Terra to conduct small-scale research was produced again and argued over vigorously. When the question was eventually turned back to New Sadira, they dismissed their presence on Terra as 'a small team of pilots and scientists, exploring the feasibility of stabling mindships on Terra given recent problems maintaining mindship population in the hostile marine environment of New Sadira'. After that and a range of other excuses of varying credibility from the Zhinuvian observers, the meeting went rapidly downhill with no resolution to what was now being called 'The Terran Problem'.

Finally, New Sadira withdrew in protest and departed with their non-union pilots. The Meeting was brought to a formal though unsatisfactory conclusion, and transit staff began the chore of ferrying the delegates home.

Serendipity emerged at last from the fog of intense focus, checked her messages and regretfully declined an invitation from Rafi to share a meal with him and his uncle. There was still so much to do and she was needed at the port to assist with those travelling by mindship or taking a hop to a larger transport via orbital shuttle. She'd make it up to him later.

Dllenahkh could see that Rafi was very proud of his new apartment in the Haneki domain. He was also proud of his flight suit, the decorative traceries on his forearms, the functional tracery behind his ear and his new name. He explained about the kin contracts and begged Dllenahkh to make Grace understand it was not a rejection of his home and heritage.

'It will actually make it easier for me to come to Cygnus Beta. As far as Central Government is concerned, I'm no longer their problem. I'm Ntshune, and there are plenty of people stronger than me to keep me in line.'

Dllenahkh acknowledged this fact and promised soberly to convey the message to Grace. 'And your work here satisfies you?'

'Absolutely! I know I fell into it, but I couldn't have chosen anything better if I tried.'

'Good, very good. Perhaps I could pay my respects to your employer, the Patrona?'

Rafi eyed Dllenahkh warily. There was something a little too bland, a little too innocent in his responses to Rafi's news. 'Haven't you negotiated together before or something?'

'Well, yes, but I am talking about meeting her as Rafi's uncle, not the Governor of Sadira-on-Cygnus. I am sure you can appreciate the difference.'

'Very well,' Rafi replied, still wary. 'Let me take you to her workroom.'

'No need,' said Dllenahkh blithely. 'I know where it is. Send word ahead that I am on my way and meet me outside the workroom in a half-hour.'

Rafi stared sternly at Dllenahkh. Dllenahkh looked back, immoveable.

'I will not lie to my wife when she asks me how you are,' he said.

Rafi sighed and sent the message.

The first half of the meeting with the Patrona was spent discussing the recently concluded Meeting, commenting on the progress made with the Transit Project and admiring the architecture and design of the Haneki domain. From that final topic, Dllenahkh stretched and took a stepping stone to what he really wanted to say.

'I could not help but admire the accoutrements my nephew is now wearing, especially the particularly fine filigree vambraces. The last time I saw such work, it was on the favoured husband of an Ntshune matriarch.'

'Such patterns have become very popular recently now that Wallrunning is seen as more than a game. I thought, with his background, it was appropriate.'

Dllenahkh absorbed the deflection and the slightly teasing tone and tried again. 'Rafi mentioned kin contracts. I have only a little knowledge of the practice. Have you been involved in any . . . serious contracts?'

The Patrona laughed at the hint in his voice and gave an answer as oblique as the question. 'I have had three spousal contracts. Lovely individuals, but they couldn't keep up.'

Dllenahkh smiled at the Patrona's dry humour and slipped in an edged statement amid the lightheartedness. 'Do you think Rafi can keep up?'

The Patrona gave him a sober look, a look between equals. 'He has potential but he is still young.'

'He is,' Dllenahkh agreed diplomatically.

'And how many more years will you have with your Cygnian wife, Dllenahkh?' It was more than edge; the Patrona had mastered the art of the verbal stiletto.

Dllenahkh bowed his head very slightly and raised a hand in surrender. 'Esteemed Patrona, I would always have peace between your domain and my homestead.'

'That is also my wish,' she replied with sweet sincerity.

'In that case, may I know your name?'

She looked a little surprised, as if she had expected him to ask something else. 'My name is Ixiaral. It comes from the word "believe" in one of our many dead languages . . . that is to say, one who has the power to make others believe. Several of the daughters of the Haneki dynasty, including my own, bear that name or some variation of it. When my own Mother retires, and if I am found worthy, I will be the new Matriarch of the dynasty, and the few who are still permitted to call me Ixiaral will do so no more.'

'How sad,' Dllenahkh murmured. 'There should always be someone who will call you by your name.'

'To be called Mother is not such a bad replacement. The important thing is that both are said with love.' She smiled. 'I have heard

Rafi call you by your name, but he also calls you uncle. I can see why.'

Disarmed, Dllenahkh bowed again. 'I know we are allies, Esteemed Patrona, but I believe we will also be friends.'

'We are,' she said, rising from her dais to help him to his feet. She held his arms in a comrade's clasp for a moment. 'Call me Ixiaral while you still can.'

Rafi sat outside the Patrona's office and nervously flexed his fingers. At last Dllenahkh emerged. Rafi searched his face and he appeared genuinely relaxed and calm. He sighed and let some of his own tension flow away. He knew better than to ask for details of a conversation from which he had been dismissed. Instead he approached his uncle and reached into the pouch at his waist.

'I have something for you.' He held out the small rock from Sadira.

Dllenahkh frowned in curiosity but extended an open palm. Rafi placed it carefully in his hand and explained. 'I was part of the test run to Sadira.'

Dllenahkh's expression did not change. His eyelids fluttered briefly, not blinking away tears but perhaps trying to dispel a moment of dizziness. He curved his hand a little more to hold the rock securely and examined it.

'A pilot who was with me gave it to me,' Rafi clarified, not wanting to appear blasé about carrying away what would be a highly precious stone to any Sadiri. 'It's safe – it came from the reclaimed area.'

Dllenahkh stopped examining the stone and raised his eyes to Rafi. 'Reclaimed area?'

Rafi froze with his mouth open as his breath caught in panic. *Don't tell*, Teruyai had said. Was it meant to be a secret? He thought the pilots would tell every single Sadiri they met. A calmer inner voice said it was more likely that they were waiting to see whether the Ainya scientists were capable of expanding their efforts to something more significant than a hundred-metre circle of decontaminated rubble.

'Is the transit to Sadira restricted?'

'I don't understand—'

'Can anyone go?' Dllenahkh rephrased, his voice still patient but with a growing edge.

Rafi blinked nervously. 'I'll ask.'

Rafi spoke to the Patrona, who spoke to Revered Bezhtan. What the academic thought of the request was never said, though her frightened face spoke volumes, but she agreed quickly enough and insisted on accompanying Dllenahkh through the transit and into Sadira. They descended from the Wall with the now-traditional silence that was expected of a Sadira transit, and Dllenahkh, not at all fazed by the journey, began a slow walk around the dome, unknowingly mirroring what most new Sadiri visitors did – test the gravity with a stamp, scan the landscape for any sign of familiarity.

'So, how did this happen?' he asked. His voice was too level. He pre-emptively kept his hands away from each other, knowing their tendency to unconsciously react to stress even when the rest of his body forgot what to do. He paid attention to her words, in spite of realising within minutes that she was answering him as if he had asked *why* not *how*.

'The conclusion of an old grudge, I'm afraid. The weapon

was sent by our ancestors long before the Galactic War. There were legends about it, but no one believed it could have survived and remained on target for millennia. When the disaster happened and the Academes proved it with their research, we took responsibility.'

She paused and spoke more directly. 'As for how *we* got here, that was the other part of our research. There was a one-way transit from Sadira to Ain, used to banish criminals. We still say "dumping down the well" to refer to getting rid of trash or someone undesirable. We found a way not only to reopen old transits but also to restore two-way function. A lot of Ainya were stranded when Ain was cut off, but a few of us knew there was another option. We worked with Academe contacts in Ntshune to establish a biodome on Sadira around the transit site, and then we reopened the transit to Ain.'

Dllenahkh nodded, listening patiently. 'And how did you manage to secure Ain?'

'A trick of perception which confuses navigation, nothing more. That's why the transits still work. We expected full retaliation but there was another fear.' She paused and breathed heavily. 'Two of my colleagues were kidnapped and killed. They were tortured to give up information on how to make a weapon that could sterilise the biosphere. No one has that information, so of course they died. They weren't the only ones. Our planetary authority decided it was better to withdraw from the galaxy completely.'

'I can see the wisdom in that,' he replied noncommittally.

She looked at him out of the corner of her eye, disconcerted by his extreme self-control, then said hesitantly, 'Let me show you something.'

She brought him to a fenced area in the biodome. He looked at the uncovered ground and saw a modest monument, a granite block laid flat and low like a giant's tombstone. The words were in Galactic Standard, Ainya script and contemporary Sadiri type. It was the motto of the planet Ain, a motto for those seeking new lives, repurposed for a world being pulled back from the brink of death.

THERE WAS AN END. HERE IS A BEGINNING.

Dllenahkh tried to calm his initial reaction, which was pure rage. He could sense that Revered Bezhtan meant well, he believed that the stone and the inscription had been chosen with all kindness and sincerity and care, but to see the motto of Ain stamped on the dead soil of Sadira looked like conquest rather than apology.

Solicitous but unperceptive, Bezhtan waited for him to collect himself, no doubt assuming grief was the cause of his sudden tension.

'The restoration of Sadira is the first and foremost project Ain approved when it was discovered that the transit not only worked but worked more swiftly than other methods of transportation,' she explained softly. 'We shall continue this work quietly, but of course we welcome the input of the Interplanetary Science Council—'

'How long will it take?'

Her mouth stayed open, stopped before she could utter another of the platitudes on her list. 'Hundreds of years rather than thousands but . . . not in your lifetime or mine.'

'Ah.' It was an acknowledgement, an exhalation. It sounded like sorrow and letting go. Dllenahkh took the stone Rafi had given him and examined it for a brief moment, then laid it carefully on the ground below the monument. 'I should go,' he said, with both wistfulness and warning. *I should go, before I do something I will regret, see something that will haunt me further, speak the wrong words at the wrong time.*

'As you wish,' she said, her voice betraying that she was almost in tears.

She had not asked for forgiveness. She had merely asked him to bear witness that restitution had begun. He pushed his fury down and away from his lips and tongue and said, 'We will discuss this in the next Council meeting. Assistance with this new beginning would be beneficial to all involved.'

She nodded. He turned away and walked back to the transit point. Thus concluded the first informal yet significant rapprochement between Sadiri and Ainya.

Months later, when he had finished meditating on the feelings stirred up by his brief return to Sadira, he took the occasion of a long walk on the beach to confide in Delarua, telling her everything the Ainya academic had revealed.

'She kept some information from me, I believe,' he concluded. 'There is only one thing that could make a biohazard weapon so swift and so potent, and it is the same thing that would allow a mere navigational trick to confuse modern ships. I think you can guess . . .'

It took her only a few minutes. 'Time,' she said. 'Time is what turns a technique for gradual bioforming into an explosive, extreme and irreversible change or a long detour into a sudden, inexplicable jump. You're saying the Ainya have learned to manipulate time?'

Before he answered, he looked around at the sky, the sea and the land's horizon to reassure himself of their emptiness. Cygnians had become very accustomed to constant surveillance of one kind or another, but when Sadira-on-Cygnus was granted control of its own airspace, he began to study how to seek out private, unwatched areas. Until Tirtha-level telepathy was achieved throughout the settlement, such spaces would always be needed.

'Learned, or rediscovered. I cannot be sure of it, but I know she did not dare tell me all that she knew.'

Delarua gave a soft, cynical laugh. 'Remember when I convinced you that it was the Caretakers? Now there is nothing I have seen in this galaxy that cannot match what we once thought only the Caretakers could do.'

'And yet,' Dllenahkh said soothingly, 'we have met a Caretaker, or something like them. A failure of attribution does not always mean a failure of existence.'

'I wish we were less powerful and more wise,' Delarua said sorrowfully. 'That is the real reason for the Caretaker myth, isn't it? Hoping someone will step in and stop us when we get out of hand.'

Dllenahkh thought of the wastelands of Sadira. 'I understand that hope.'

There were now three ways to get to Cygnus Beta. The usual way was by mindship or Zhinuvian transport to the orbital station, then shuttle to the surface. For Sadira-on-Cygnus, it was more common to use the port at Grand Bay, but the passenger modules and mindships were smaller and the numbers permitted to travel this route were few. Finally, there was the transit located on the fringes of Tlaxce Province near the boundary of the Fa-Ne Provinces. It was still experimental but certified as stable. A few courageous people spent the extra credits to travel more quickly for urgent business, but otherwise it was mainly used by seasoned couriers carrying communications and other forms of microcargo.

As much as he liked his job, Rafi thought of the transit as too much like work, and Grand Bay was closest to his second home, so he took the extra time and a long sleep to travel via mindship.

After the usual family visits at the Dllenahkh homestead, Tlaxce City and Tlaxce Lake, he went to visit Ntenman at his father's estate. Ntenman was out again, but Syanrimwenil was there and happy to see him. At first Rafi was worried that she had not fully recovered from that rushed transit escaping Punartam, but she assured him that was not the case.

'I am enjoying full retirement, Rafi,' she declared.

Rafi looked at her, looked around and could not disagree. They were sitting on the patio of her cottage at the corner of the estate, surrounded by well-kept gardens and blessed with a beautiful view beyond. Ntenman's father had made sure of her comforts. Rafi asked her if she missed Punartam at all and she gave him a vigorous negative.

'Cygnus Beta is a fascinating world. So much to see! Everyone and everything from all over the galaxy is here! Besides, you Cygnians have surprised us. Cygnus Beta may have been primarily a refuge for Terrans, but for the rest of us it was . . . what is that expression . . . "in the country of the blind, the one-eyed man is king"? Many one-eyed Ntshune came to Cygnus Beta because it was better than staying home to be pitied or overlooked. And now their descendants come to us to show us a new way of seeing. It is very fitting.'

'What do you mean? Being a nexus isn't new. I've been trained by people who are much better at it than I am.'

'Oh, Rafihaneki, I was not referring to you!' Syanri said, smiling broadly at his coyly casual compliment. 'Have you not heard of the marvellous things happening in Oleha Province? You should know – your friend Serendipity hails from there. There is a team, a sister and brother, who have discovered how to transit from one place to another on the same planet. That has never been done, not even in the era before the Galactic War. They are the offspring of a Sadiri pilot and a Cygnian teacher. They appeared one day out of thin air, floating on the pool at the Tirtha monastery. It is difficult to startle the monks, but they managed it!'

'Floating?' asked Rafi, trying to picture it.

'Their ship is a wooden floor. They say the woman never leaves it, but her brother is devoted to her and makes sure she has everything she needs. She is the brains of the team, by all accounts. It will take years of research to understand how she is able to pilot transitless with only two simple human minds in tandem.'

Rafi frowned, trying to unearth a memory.

'Perhaps you know them. The brother's name is Silvan? Silyan? Oh, ignore me. Here I am, acting as if you should know everyone on Cygnus Beta.'

'Actually,' Rafi said, his voice a little strained, 'I do know him. And so do you. I told you about him, how I . . . influenced him once.'

Syanri became very serious. 'Rafi, you must meet with him and apologise. Let him know you have had better guidance since then.'

'Perhaps I will,' Rafi replied neutrally, thinking of the cap and the nightmares and the strictures of the Lyceum.

'Now – tell me more about Terra.'

He laughed and told her what he could. Several Cygnians specialising in biotech, including Dr Freyda Mar, had swelled the ranks of Dr Daniyel's small team, taking up residence with Zhinuvians, Sadiri pilots and Ntshune in the dome below the ice of Antarctica.

As he spoke, he remembered how philosophical Lanuri had been about Freyda's absence. 'She has the spirit of a pilot,' he said. 'I must let her go for a while.' At first he thought it was meant poetically, but then his aunt explained that genetic research had in fact traced Freyda's taSadiri roots to a pilot lineage. He was not sure how seriously he was meant to take that.

'Whatever happened to the Interplanetary Science Council?' Syanri enquired.

'Fragmented,' Rafi replied, a diplomatic term for so many of the defections from New Sadira. 'Most of it is on New Sadira, but those who were at the Academes are now on Ntshune, focusing their attention on the restoration of Sadira.'

'Ah, how sad, and yet how fitting. Did you not have a friend who—?'

Rafi cut her off, the pain of Nasiha's memory still poignant. 'Yes, Tarik. He has relocated to Masuf Lagoon, as far away from the New Sadira Consulate as possible.' Rafi did not mention his suspicion that Tarik asked each pilot who passed through the lagoon about his wife's whereabouts. He hoped Tarik would hear something about her, someday.

EPILOGUE

'Did he?' Rafi asked softly.

The traveller known as Narua stirred from his contemplative daze as the workroom lights gradually brightened. He nodded slowly. 'What little we know of her, we know because of him.'

'I have not seen Tarik in years,' Rafi said regretfully. 'There is always something happening, and being able to travel freely doesn't always mean having time or justification to do so.'

'I know,' Narua said, accepting the small apology. He unfastened his bracelet and began to slowly finger his way along the charms, pressing each one gently as if in ritual. 'No one blames you, Patron. Let me show you something.'

Rafi smiled and leaned forward in curiosity when Narua lingered over a particular charm and then, at last, unhooked it from the rest. 'I wondered about that one. It's Lyceum make. Master Silyan's work?'

Narua confirmed it with a brief nod. 'Made for me when I was still called Kiratsiha, but there's nothing here I would keep from you. Look at the last entry. I think he would want you to see it.'

What does it feel like?

Falling or flying, it was all the same. The only change was the tilt of the Wall, and the Wall was nothing but a frame for the human mind to hold the universe. Master Silyan was a practical man who believed no more in destiny and determinism than in Caretakers and Lady Luck, but he acknowledged the jubilant song in his spirit, his heart and his blood, and counted it proof that his pilot genes were happy to be flitting through space and time. And Galia, his anchor as always, said nothing, but her mind was a hum of satisfaction, her feet stood firm and steady on the floor she had crafted, and where her body would rarely twitch a finger, her expanded self devised greater and more complicated falls and flights, skimming and skipping the surface of their world like a flat stone tossed with playful skill. Her favourite stops were Masuf Lagoon and Tirtha, where she was revered by pilots and monastics and given quiet but ungrudging admiration by Sadiri elders, many themselves former monastics and almost-pilots.

The freedom of their new life was so intoxicating that it was weeks before Silyan thought to contact the Lyceum and tender his resignation. He was shocked to discover that Galia was continuing to record classes and assess students, but after brief reflection he realised that she had never interacted with students in person and so nothing had changed.

He was also surprised and worried that there was no reaction to their disappearance, but Zhera, chief among the Sadiri elders at Tirtha, scoffed at his concern. 'Why should the Cygnian government involve itself in affairs it cannot understand, far less control? Tirtha and Sadira-on-Cygnus have their own laws and social order. They know that we neither produce nor accept psi-renegades here and they do not challenge us.'

Silyan imagined a future where the Lyceum and its dubious approach could become obsolete, swept under the rug of history as the aberration of a primitive culture unable to comprehend and nurture the abilities of truly civilised humans. The thought was bitter-sweet, especially when he considered Rafi and others who had not been helped by the Lyceum's crude methods and his own participation in that process. He told no one, but his work was driven by a deep-seated desire for atonement.

Galia, of course, knew his thoughts but she did not share his sensitive conscience. As always, her sole motivation was the beauty and mystery of the mathematics that made and moved the universe. Silyan came to realise that she saw *him* as the anchor, the one who was connected to quotidian life while she stayed immersed, wholly or in part, in the invisible existence that held more of truth and reality than the illusions of the senses. Ironically, that was precisely his reason for thinking of her as anchor. He had lost trust in the importance of the everyday long ago.

How do you do it?

And there was another common question. What was that 'it'? The rare transit from place to place on a single planet? The unique bond between brother and sister that gave them the critical mass of consciousness the universe required for access to its back roads and secret ways? Perhaps they were the same thing, but he was at a loss to explain either.

One day he met a man who asked that old question in a way

that demanded an answer – if not immediately, then at least as soon as he was capable. He was a Sadiri, but not a pilot, and a semi-recluse whose origins were carefully protected by the pilots at the Masuf Hostel. Silyan found himself as intrigued by Tarik as Tarik was by him and Galia. Brief exchanges over food in the dining hall became longer discussions during walks, and then one day some threshold of trust or risk was reached and Tarik invited Silyan to see where he lived. Galia, as usual, remained with her familiar floor and did not come with them.

Tarik lived in an old stone watchtower, an offshoot of Piedra sited partway between that ancient city and the Masuf Lagoon. His small hovercar made quick work of the varieties of ground along the way, from soft sand to hard gravel, and also provided the final step of elevating them to the second-storey entrance of the tower. Silyan immediately felt that he was entering a stronghold for some great treasure, and when two young monastics of Tirtha welcomed them in, like acolytes to a temple, the impression was only strengthened.

'I always ask for two,' Tarik said as they went inside. 'Girls or boys, it doesn't matter, but there must be two, and they must be able to speak to the mind as easily as to the ear.' He paused and looked momentarily anguished, then said by way of explanation and apology, 'It is a necessary experiment.'

Silyan followed him into the main living room, let himself be seated comfortably amid rugs and cushions and given refreshments, and prepared himself for the revelation. When it came, it was in the form of two toddlers each holding tight to the hand of their carer. At first glance he knew them to be Tarik's children. A second glance convinced him they were identical twins, but a

336

longer look made him less sure. They were quietly shy and he smiled at them reassuringly.

'What is your name, little one?' he asked, holding out a hand to one of the children.

Tarik answered. 'The name registered with the authorities is Kiratsiha. This one, my daughter, is sometimes called Siha and this one, my son, is sometimes called Kirat.'

Siha lowered her head and drew away from Silyan's now-frozen hand. Kirat, though farther away, mimicked her motion precisely. Silyan let his hand fall, silenced by a terrible thought that he did not wish to believe.

Tarik began to speak more swiftly and volubly than Silyan had ever heard him do in all their days of acquaintance. 'As I said before . . . a necessary experiment. New Sadira does not want our sons, and we do not wish to give them our daughters. Sadira-on-Cygnus is a far better place to be than New Sadira, and still – do you know there were young men approaching us before Siha was even born? Some wanted to be her husbands, and some wanted her to bear their children or raise them, according whatever terms were agreeable to us. A pureblooded Sadiri female is a precious thing in our society, and they were bidding for whatever genetic and psionic influence she could bring to their line. Nasiha, my wife, demanded that we find a way to protect them from being used, whether for good or ill.'

'How is it that they look so alike?' Silyan wondered.

'There are medical treatments that encourage the blending of phenotype. We began such treatments in utero and they will continue for the rest of their lives, or until Siha and Kirat no longer need them or want them.'

Silyan met the eyes of the carers. 'And Tirtha is encouraging the development of their telepathy from a very early stage.'

'It strengthens communication between them,' Tarik said. 'The isolation is also an important part of the process.'

'Each will be able to impersonate the other,' Silyan noted.

Tarik nodded. 'New Sadira's influence is fading, but if required, Siha can present herself as my son.'

'And Kirat as your daughter?' Silyan guessed.

'Yes.' Tarik smiled, immersed in memory. 'My wife insisted. She wanted them to be able to go anywhere in the galaxy on their own terms. She appreciated Punarthai culture but she did not want them to trade one set of restrictions for another.'

Kirat began to fuss slightly, bored at all the talk. Tarik raised a hand and the two young novices took the children out of the room. Silyan brought his hands to his face and dragged them slowly over his eyes. 'This is . . . ambitious.'

'But it could save both their lives,' Tarik replied quietly. 'Once we hoped it would be enough to keep our family together.'

Silyan knew what was coming. He had sensed it even from those early days of polite greetings and casual conversation. He knew that Tarik wanted something from him.

'Can you teach Kirat and Siha to have what you have with Galia?'

'I don't know!' he cried out. Why did people ask him such things, as if it had not been enough to produce that one miracle of transit? 'Can such things be taught? We were abandoned, untutored, unsocialised. No one taught us how to *be*.'

'Can you try? You and Galia may be the first, but you must not be the last. I am asking you and Galia to raise Kiratsiha as best you can. Another experiment, another necessity.' His expression became suddenly, tragically agonised. 'My wife is still missing. I have searched this entire planet for her, and now I must search elsewhere. I have heard of a mindship whose pilot was so badly injured that it was forced to absorb the physical body to keep the human consciousness alive and intact. If that rumour is true, it means there remains one pilot from Cygnus Beta whom I have not yet asked about my wife.'

'Where is this mindship now?' Silyan asked.

Tarik exhaled slowly. 'I have been told to try the old Sadiri monasteries and retreat colonies,' he mumbled. 'That will be my first step.'

Silyan tried to warn Tarik about the utter lunacy of seeking a single human in the vastness of the inhabited galaxy, but he could not find the words and he could not keep the pity from his eyes.

Rather than be offended by that pity, Tarik chose to use it. 'If Kiratsiha stays with me, New Sadira may discover his secret and Siha will be taken away from us. Siha and Kirat can live with you as orphans from the Lyceum or acolytes from Tirtha. Whatever tale you care to tell, it will be accepted.'

Silyan's secret guilt pricked him and he hesitated, suspended between the cruelty of no and the folly of yes. At last he spoke, faltering but honest. 'I think I will say yes – I know I will. Perhaps I owe this to the universe for all my sins and all my gifts, but . . . when I say yes, I fear your children may never see you again.'

Tears filled Tarik's eyes, but he stayed resolutely focused on Silyan. 'That may be the case. I would rather them safe and distant than close and in peril.'

Silyan bowed his head in respect for Tarik's hard choice. 'I need a moment alone.'

Tarik got up and opened a small door at the side of the room. 'These steps lead to the top of the tower. No one will disturb you there.'

The curving staircase went up and up and ended at another small door secured with a crude bolt on the inside. Silyan unfastened it, took a few more steps up and found himself space and solitude in the form of a circle bordered with low battlements, low enough for him to see the distant lights of Piedra and Masuf glimmering in the twilight. That same twilight greyed the surrounding semi-desert to emptiness, a void in which the twin cities floated with the watchtower as midpoint, fulcrum, nexus and anchor. What did Galia think of all this, of bringing two strangers into their self-contained circle? He questioned her mind within his and felt her unique response: she was intrigued; she wondered about the balance; she would try the experiment for the sake of the possible findings. Silyan laughed to himself. She would leave the guilt and the pity for Tarik to him; her mind was and always had been on another plane. There was no one like her, and he doubted either part of Kiratsiha could compare, but he did miss his students a little and here were two for the asking.

And yet Tarik's pain spoke to him – the pain of losing his wife, giving up his children and leaving his community. He had been part of that kind of pain through his work with the Lyceum. Something was owed.

The battlements were ancient and crumbling, with decaying mortar and weathered rubble. He took time to gather a talisman for a promise. Descending to the living room, he gave Tarik three stones and said, 'You will lend us your children for a while and we will do our best. But the stones of this watchtower will draw you to return. Say it.'

Tarik's eyes were still wet but his face was peaceful and his voice was steady as he held the dusty stones in his hand and promised, 'By the stones of the watchtower, I will return.'

ACKNOWLEDGEMENTS

Continued thanks and appreciation go to my father and my sister; to Robert Edison Sandiford, Esther Phillips and so many others in the Barbadian literary community who inspire me to improve and persevere; to the staff of the Cooke Agency, especially Sally Harding and Ron Eckel, for outstanding professional support; to Betsy Mitchell, Dvorah Simon, Karen Burnham and Cheryl Morgan for help both great and small on the first draft; to the editors and publicists at Del Rey and Jo Fletcher Books, especially Tricia Narwani, Greg Kubie, Alexandra Coumbis, Jo Fletcher and Nicola Budd; and to the readers . . . because as much as I enjoy writing these stories for myself, I get even more pleasure from the knowledge that someone else is enjoying them too.

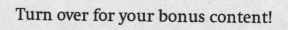

Turn over for your bonus content!

ASTRONOMY LESSON

There is a boy on the highest level of the water tower. Do not be concerned. He will not jump. He has thought of suicide before, but tonight those thoughts are diverted. He has been distracted by a catastrophe big enough and distant enough to provide an indulgent rush of excitement and angst with no depressing requirement for action on his part. Sometimes it is easier to grieve, however uselessly, for someone else's tragedy.

In daylight, standing on the tower gave him enough vertigo to make the view hardly worth it. His family's homestead became a flattened map: the main house and the scattered outbuildings, the dark green shadow of the orchards (sometimes brightened with the faint haze of tiny blossoms), the pale green and gold of the field grass, and the tracks – narrow ones etched by foot and hoof, broader ones for wheels and micrograv treads – tracing through it all.

At night there was a different view and a more thrilling vertigo when he lay on his back and skimmed the articles on his mother's hardly-used handheld while looking up at the stars. The standard astronomy syllabus taught only the basics, but hobbyist astronomy, especially on Cygnus Beta, was another thing entirely. Loyalty to a new planet did not diminish love for the old world. As a result, pockets of enthusiasts from settlements all over had created a large collection of multicultural trivia about star systems: legends, old names, still-unfulfilled prophecies, and beautifully complex conspiracy theories of past events and potential fates.

He stargazed and he browsed. Crafted worlds found seeded with life – Ntshune, Sadira, Zhinu and Terra – were given precedence as the First Four. Then there were the colonies, bioformed planets shaped and settled by emigrants from the First Four – Punartam, Ain, Tolimán and more – some of them mere planetoids visited only by scientists, adventurers and ascetics.

Terra was closest to the Cygnian heart, but there was nothing new from that distant quarter, only memories and nostalgia several generations removed. The Punartam system was a better place to start, closest to home in travel time and galactic rank. Its sole habitable planet was an ancient colony that was now almost as prominent as the First Four. It was reputed to be the first fully bioformed planet, but they still argued about that in the academes. Was Cygnus Beta a crafted world that failed and had been restored by human or non-human effort, or a bioforming experiment from an obscured patch in human history? Punartam could prove its origins, Cygnus Beta couldn't, and so the debate was at an end . . . for now.

Cygnian name: Punartam (from a Terran language, like so many Cygnian names). Terran stellar nomenclature: ß Geminorum. Galactic Standard name: a collection of syllables that told the full story of the star's location, age, luminosity, and life-bearing potential. The name they used for themselves was in Simplified Ntshune and it meant the same thing as in Galactic Standard – behold! we are here, we have been here long, see how brightly we shine, we are we.

The founders of Punartam traced their beginnings to the system called the Mother of humanity. Alleged by many to be eldest of the First Four, it was a crafted world and former galactic leader. It existed in a kind of comfortable dotage with most of its voice and verve delegated to Punartam. Cygnian name: Ntshune, also from a Terran language, easier to pronounce than the alternative. Terran name: – Piscis Austrini. True name . . . the boy sang it hesitantly and off-key in Traditional Ntshune.

Next nearest system. Cygnian name: Zhinu. Terran name: – Lyrae. What did the Zhinuvians call it? He didn't know. They didn't have anything close to a planetary government, far less a standard language. Most used the Galactic Standard name or an abbreviation of it. In spite of several layers of tech and some extreme bioforming, it was a crafted world and thus one of the First Four. Top rank, and yet the Zhinuvians had a poor reputation. Not their fault, with their early development complicated by outside forces pushing first one direction, then another.

Then, of course, there was Terra, Old Earth. Source of most of the settlers on Cygnus Beta (Terran stellar nomenclature, the unmelodious 16 Cygni B). Youngest of the First Four and most in need of protection from both good and evil influence. The two elder siblings of the Four had pledged not to repeat their mistake and adopted a hands-off policy. Zhinu, delinquent sibling still reeling from their well-intentioned meddling, had nothing to say about that, but untamed elements from their merchant fleets periodically nipped at the edges of the Terran embargo and were smacked for their impertinence.

The last of the Four was Sadira. Terran name: ε Eridani. Sadiri name: something unreadable and unpronounceable (the Sadiri language, even in the simplified, standard form, was too hard for most Cygnians, though the characters and symbols were quite popular as decoration). Leader of the galaxy . . . or at least policeman and judge and occasional executioner. Not much liked, though rarely hated. Cygnians were more comfortable with Ntshune ways, but that was not the only reason. The superior attitude of the Sadiri provoked reflexive disdain.

He watched and listened to the flash and murmur of the handheld. The news updated by the minute, the provincial aether was buzzing, and the crackpots were as vocal as the pros. Of all the planets, the name they spoke most was Sadira. They had been speaking that name for more than a week and they would likely be speaking it for generations to come in that same chilling tone of fear and awe and profound sorrow.

Cygnians were accustomed to being days or even weeks behind on galactic affairs, but the attack on Sadira was a special case. Although the sober details arrived much later, within less than a day of the attack, all Cygnians had heard some version of the unimaginable tale. A small Sadiri mindship had come tumbling out thin air, quenched its speed in the vast and forgiving Cygnian oceans, then ferried its pilot to shore so he could share the dreadful news. By means yet unknown, every living being on Sadira had been wiped out. All communication with the surface had ceased instantly, and nothing and no-one emerged from the atmosphere. Incoming mindships attempted rescue and paid with their lives and their pilots lives. A few Sadiri remained, scattered throughout the galaxy, but they had no Punartam to fall back to. Their largest settlement was the distant prison colony called Ain, and if the rumours were true−

'Rafi?' That was his father's voice below in the darkness.

'Yes?' he answered, and coughed to give an excuse for his tear-choked voice.

'Don't fall asleep up there.'

'Five more minutes,' Rafi said.

The boy gazes into starlight with tear-fractured vision, crying for a place he has never seen and people he has never met. That is a good reason to cry; there are few things worse than having your entire world destroyed. There are also things that make him prefer to be up on the water tower and out of his father's reach. He is not sure that such things deserve his tears, but he wonders if maybe, someday, in a distant tomorrow, a stranger will hear of his story and cry on his behalf.

Karen Lord has been a physics teacher, a diplomat, a part-time soldier and an academic at various times and in various countries. She is now a writer and research consultant in Barbados. Her debut novel, *Redemption in Indigo* won the 2008 Frank Collymore Literary Award, the 2011 William L. Crawford Award, the 2012 Kitschies Golden Tentacle Award for Best Debut Novel and the Mythopoeic Award, and was shortlisted for the World Fantasy Award. *Redemption in Indigo* and *The Best of All Possible Worlds*, the prequel to *The Galaxy Game*, are published by Jo Fletcher Books.

Author photo © Russell Watson of R Studio

REDEMPTION IN INDIGO
Karen Lord

Paama's husband is a fool and a glutton. Bad enough that he followed her to her parents' home in the village of Makendha, now he's disgraced himself by murdering livestock and stealing corn. When Paama leaves him for good, she attracts the attention of the undying ones - the djombi - who present her with a gift: the Chaos Stick, which allows her to manipulate the subtle forces of the world. Unfortunately, not all the djombi are happy about this gift: the indigo lord believes this power should be his and his alone, and he sets about trying to persuade Paama to return the Chaos Stick. Chaos is about to reign supreme . . .

Jo Fletcher
BOOKS

THE BEST OF ALL POSSIBLE WORLDS

Karen Lord

This is a story of hope. Grace Delarua, a civil servant with the government of Cygnus Beta, remembers when the Sadiri arrived on their planet, a galactic hinterland for pioneers and refugees.

This is a story of survival. Dllenahkh, leader of the small group of Sadiri settlers on Cygnus Beta, remembers the cool strong blues and gentle sunlight of his home world. He also remembers the moment he was told his planet was destroyed.

This is a story of love. Now they must work together to rebuild his decimated population by searching for the last surviving members of his race.

This is a story about finding the best of all possible worlds.

Jo Fletcher
BOOKS